TILUS WAS NOT EXPECTING THE POUNCE. For a time during his charge he might have been wary of a counterattack, but after a while all fights tend to settle into a rhythm. It is the primary weakness of inexperience, the true cost of youthful ignorance, though, that leads young fighters into embracing the pattern. For Tilus, paths like this would have always been in his favor, his superior strength and skill allowing him to lead the dance until he won.

When the dance is forcibly changed, though, such men are often left reeling.

The boy had just brought his blade up for another crossward blow when Raz was suddenly moving *at* him rather than away from him. To his credit he didn't hesitate in his strike, bringing it down just as he'd intended, aiming for Raz's left shoulder. Raz, though, closed the gap between them faster than any steel could fall. He was already beside Tilus by the time the blow would have reached him, and the sword—driven downward with all the hopes of a killing strike—dug into the snow and earth, sticking there. Before the boy had the chance to pull it out, Raz's foot collided with the back of his weight-bearing leg, bringing him to his knees. He still clung one-handed to the blade, his grasp at an awkward angle with the sword lodged in the ground. Without hesitating, Raz punched down with a mailed fist, crushing the boy's right shoulder. As Tilus screamed in pain, his hand dropping loosely from the bastard sword's handle, Raz reached out and pulled the blade free.

Then, in a single motion, he swung the blade around and dragged its razor edge across Brek Tilus' throat.

If one has never seen the force with which arterial blood can spray, it is a terrifying thing. A gush of red, misting in the icy air, erupted across the snowy ground and stained the stone of the angled wall beside them. Tilus didn't even have time to choke on his own blood. Raz had cut so quick and so deep that he was gone in seconds, allowing for only one bubbling rasp from his severed windpipe before he was still.

Putting a foot to his back, Raz shoved the boy so that he fell facedown into the slush and mud.

"Fool," he said sadly, watching the red creep into the brown and white of the snow.

THE WARRING SON
Book Two of *The Wings of War* series
Bryce O'Connor

ISBN: 0-9988106-2-2
ISBN-13: 978-0-9988106-2-1
Edited by Marcus Trower
Map by Bryce O'Connor

Cover art by Andreas Zafiratos
Cover design by Bryce O'Connor and Andreas Zafiratos

THE WARRING SON

BRYCE O'CONNOR

BOOKS BY BRYCE O'CONNOR

The Wings of War Series

Child of the Daystar

The Warring Son

Winter's King

For my Bonne Maman,
without whom my childhood,
for which I credit all things,
would have been truly lacking.

ACKNOWLEDGMENTS

It is incredible to me that I once again find myself at that point in which it is time for me to look back and reflect on all the amazing people and personalities that have lent themselves to my arrival at the publishing of *The Warring Son.* Again, I would need a whole tome to really be able to dedicate the magnitude of the gratitude I owe and feel to so many people around the world, and am saddened that I must limited my desire to give thanks to only a few short paragraphs. If you don't find yourself within these lines, know that your work is not unnoticed, and that I could never have completed the second work in *The Wings of War* series without you.

As always, I must firstly thank my family for all their support and encouragement. My father Vince, for his undending support, my mother Isaure for her enthusiasm (and continuous requests to translate the book for me), and my sister Sabine, for her feedback and encouragement.

Once again to Professor Katharyn Howd Machan, who I realize as I am writing this is very likely to have my head because I never actually TOLD her she was in the acknowledgements of these books…

To Dan, for helping me think outside the box when I'm stuck within its walls, and to Bev for her excitement on my behalf.

To Gary, for teaching me that I can learn to deal with losing, and to Barb, for teaching me that I can learn to deal with Gary.

Always to Kate, for granting me a friendship that will outlast the Sun, the Moon, and All Her Stars put together.

Once more to my absolutely amazing cover artist, Andreas Zafiratos, for continuing to craft such incredible renditions of Raz and his world. See more of his work at www.facebook.com/artofalbinoz

Again to the numerous musical prodigies that comprise Two Steps From Hell. You continue to provide the score that backlights the realms of the North and South and every land under, above, and around them.

To the countless multitude of authors and writers who have affected and inspired me to be all that I can be as a creator. For crafting worlds with words that that I can pick and poke at, turning over leaves and stones and mountains to find the things for my stories that my own imagination falls short on.

And finally, for the first time, but far from the last, to you readers. As of this moment, *Child of the Daystar* has been downloaded tens of thousands of time, with millions of pages read. I cannot express to you, by any means known to man, beast, or god, how much your enthusiasm and appreciation of my work ignites my life. I can only continue to create, continue to push other writers to do the same, and continue to walk Raz down his path, one bloody step at a time. I love you all. Thank you.

ACKNOWLEDGMENTS 2.0

It is incredible to me that I once again find myself at that point in which it is time for me to look back and reflect on all the amazing people and personalities that have lent themselves to my arrival at the publishing of *The Warring Son.* Again, I would need a whole tome to really be able to dedicate the magnitude of the gratitude I owe and feel to so many people around the world, and am saddened that I must limited my desire to give thanks to only a few short paragraphs. If you don't find yourself within these lines, know that your work is not unnoticed, and that I could never have completed the second work in *The Wings of War* series without you.

As always, I must firstly thank

Visit *patreon.com/ bryceoconnor*

and become a PATRON

to recieve:

EARLY ACCESS TO CHAPTERS OF THE NEXT BOOK!

ALTERNATE COVERS!

YOUR NAME IN THE BOOKS!

UNIQUE PRINT EDITIONS!

AMAZING ART!

AND MUCH MORE!

Become my patron on patreon

THE WARRING SON

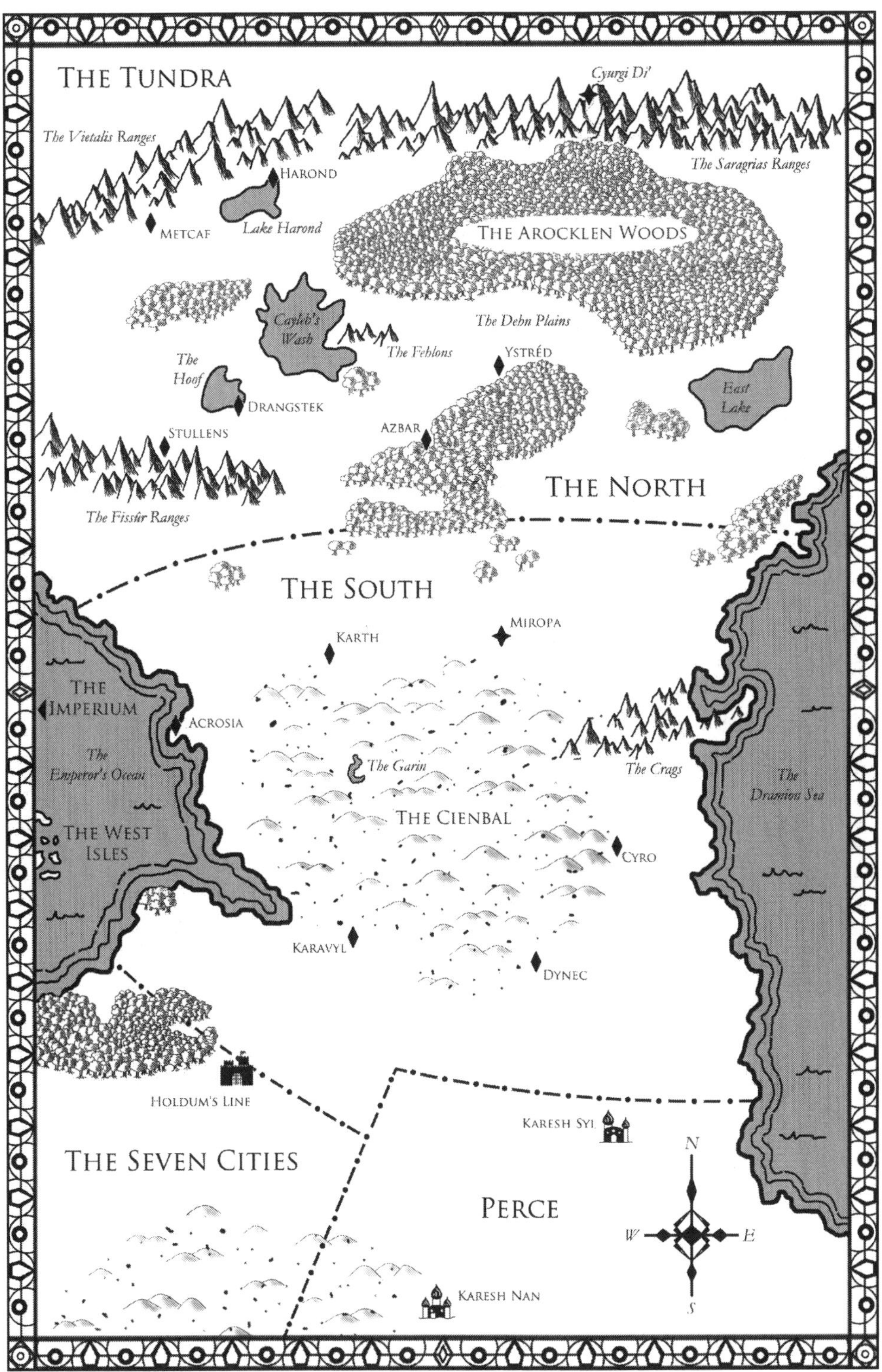
The Tundra
Cyurgi Di'
The Vietalis Ranges
The Saragrias Ranges
Harond
Metcaf
Lake Harond
The Arocklen Woods
Cayleb's Wash
The Fehlons
The Dehn Plains
Ystréd
The Hoof
Drangstek
East Lake
Azbar
Stullens
The North
The Fissúr Ranges
The South
Karth
Miropa
The Imperium
Acrosia
The Emperor's Ocean
The Garin
The Crags
The Dramion Sea
The West Isles
The Cienbal
Cyro
Karavyl
Dynec
Holdum's Line
Karesh Syl
The Seven Cities
N
Perce
W
E
S
Karesh Nan

861 v.S.

PROLOGUE

"The mountain men of the Northern Ranges are, like any people, a diverse sort. While most hold their ways and traditions in generally high regard, there are always outliers, extreme opinions on either side of a political spectrum not unlike our own. On one hand, those of an emerging school of thought, one that drifts away from ritual in favor of peace, prosperity, and the development of civil exchange between the tribes and the scattered valley towns below. On the other, though, the battered side of the same coin. Those harder men of the tribes who hold tight to the old ways, refusing to bend even the slightest towards what they deem to be a weakening of their people, a conscious sacrifice of culture and will. It is these men we must fear. It is these men who will bloody every snowy hill of the North before they see the fall of their Stone Gods to the warmer embrace of the Lifegiver and all his mercy."

—*Studying the Lifegiver*, by Carro al'Dor

Gûlraht Baoill stood tall upon the precipice of Crone's Hook, toeing the edge of the narrow cliff even as the wind buffeted his heavy frame in all directions. Dark blue eyes took in the first light of dawn as the sun crested the snowy caps of the Vietalis Ranges, washing the mountainsides in yellows and golds. The colors were harsh against the gray and black of stone and early-morning shadows, but Gûlraht knew the edge of that contrast would fade as the day grew older. He knew many things, in fact, about these cliffs. As vast as they were, as endless and angry as the mountains seemed to many, to Gûlraht they spoke only of the warmth of home, the strength of honor.

And the power of ritual, tradition, and death.

Taking a final moment to absorb the morning glow, Gûlraht reached down for the haft of the double-headed great-ax he'd been resting both palms on. The weapon, a massive thing of dark wood, decorative leather thongs, and honed steel, felt comfortingly heavy in his hand as he turned his back on the morning, making his way down the Hook towards the group waiting for him below. His fur-lined boots, thick leather layered with darkened wolf pelts, kept good footing despite the several inches of snow that hid the treacherous ground from sight. The wind refused to let up as well, kicking flakes of white into Gûlraht's thick brown hair and beard, already heavy with bone beads and iron rings. It ruffled the tufts of matted fur that comprised the rest of his armor: gauntlets, bracers, and iron-studded breastplate. Only the upper halves of his arms were bare to the elements, as was tradition, the skin there dark and hardened to near leather itself, stretching harshly against the mass of muscle and sinew beneath as Gûlraht picked his way carefully down the ice and uneven earth.

Reaching flat ground at last, he looked down on the four men standing there in wait, each at least two heads shorter than he.

"Speak."

To his right, Erek Rathst started up at once.

"The hounds tracked down the last of the Amreht runaways early this morning. They await your judgment in the center of camp, as per your instruction. Once we've dealt with them, I expect the rest of the tribe to abandon these tedious mutinies for good."

Gûlraht nodded once, then turned to the man to Erek's right.

"And of the Kregoan?" he asked. "What news?"

"More came in the night to join our ranks," Kareth Grahst, Gûlraht's cousin, responded as the wind whipped between them all, throwing beaded hair about. "With the fall of the Amreht, and our march on the Goatmen of Gähs, they seem to think it prudent to enter the fold willingly, without bloodshed."

"Wise of them." Gûlraht nodded again, watching the twitching of their shadows against the snow as the sun continued to rise behind them. "Not to mention fortunate. Between the battle and these rebellions, we've lost half the numbers the Amreht might have provided us with."

"You are cruel with them, my Kayle," one of the other men, an older figure who stood furthest to Gûlraht's left, said testily. "This sort of cancer festers under the weight of a boot, but not in the palm of an extended hand. Emhret would never have condoned such—"

"Do not presume to voice the late Kayle's opinion in my presence, Rako," Gûlraht growled, staring down the older man. "You may be my uncle by marriage, but Emhret Grahst was so by blood. It didn't stop me from taking his head when I saw fit. He grew weak, seduced by the White Witch, and you should know well I do not abide weakness in my people."

To his right, Kareth twitched involuntarily.

Gûlraht frowned. "Do my words trouble you, Cousin?" he asked pointedly, looking down upon the smaller man.

Kareth shook his head at once.

"My father bent knee to the towns, to the Witch, and to their soft god," he spat with every ounce as much venom as was painted across his weathered face. "He claimed necessity due to the freeze, but we are men of the mountains. We face the storms and endure. We do not turn our backs to the wind and cringe our way through the winter."

"Well enough said," the last man, Agor Vareks, agreed with a nod before looking to Rako. "There may be a time for mercy, old friend, but that time is not now. This cancer may have festered beneath the weight of a boot, as you say, but it is that boot which will crush it."

He turned back to Gûlraht.

"The same boot, I dare presume, that will eventually stomp out the larger sickness plaguing these lands of ours."

In response, Gûlraht looked over his shoulder, down the cliff edge this time. There, tucked between the mountainside and the evergreen sweeps of the glen below, stood the valley town. Like a scar on the world, its great circular stone wall cut a swath around thousands of buildings and homes, grayish smoke furling from twice as many chimneys as day broke for the city-folk, too. Like the ants they were they crawled from the timber houses, milling about and over each other, a wash of vermin all packed together, feeling safe behind their wall.

Metcaf, the town was called by its inhabitants. They gave a name to each such place, attempting in vain to distinguish them from one another.

The mountain men had a single name for all of them in the language of the tribes, but no word of equal vulgarity existed in the Common tongue.

"We will continue to leave the tamed men to their comforts for the time being," Gûlraht said, his eyes not leaving the walls of Metcaf. "The treaties Emhret established give them a sense of security. There will be a day we can use that to our advantage."

"And when will that day be, exactly?"

It was Agor who asked. The man was not as aged as Rako, but he was old enough to be forgiven some limited patience.

Unlike Rako, though, he bore no weak sympathies.

Gûlraht turned again, but looked beyond his advisors now to the camp behind them. In scattered rows of cloth and pelt tents, twenty thousand tribesmen awaited his command. They spotted the flattened mountaintop to its edge and beyond, claiming whatever patch of snowless earth they'd been able to find. Muddy trenches cut paths at random every which way, churned to muck by booted feet and the hooves of the long-haired oxen the tribes had used as beasts of burden for as long as anyone could recall. With the new day came the rousing of the slumbering beast that was the army, and even as he listened Gûlraht could make out the growing roar of awakening as men and their camp slaves started to stir, shouting to one another and prepping to move.

A word was all it would take. A single command, and Gûlraht could swarm the cliffs with the army at his back, descending like some great dark bird of prey on Metcaf far below.

For a moment, the temptation was there.

But no. Now was not the time.

"Soon, Agor," Gûlraht finally responded. "The townsmen will have their turn, I swear it to you all, but the Goatmen come first. They are seven thousand we could use."

Hefting the great-ax in one hand, Gûlraht pushed between the men, making for camp.

"Take me to the runaways, Uncle," he commanded Rako over his shoulder. "It's time this cruel boot of mine crushed your 'Amreht cancer' once and for all."

I

"There were once no marked borders separating the North and South. For the better part of the near-thousand v.S years, in fact, there lacked any distinct boundaries between the two realms. Instead, a width of fifty or so miles above the sandy plains of the South and just below the thick evergreen groves of the North was recognized as neutral territory, a sort of buffer land. In the years of 734 and 737, however, disputes involving taxation and ownership rights broke out amongst a number of small settlements along this narrow strip. To avoid an inter-border incident, it was agreed that distinct markers would be placed along every major road and trade route, designating the exact spot in which a traveler crossed from one land into the next."

—*The Development of Trade of the 700's*, by Vâl Shrune

Raz watched the cart pull away, heading south once more, back in the direction they'd come. For a long time he stood at the edge of the woodland road, waiting until the old man and his horse were long gone, disappearing around a bend in the trees.

Then he turned northward, looking around with shameless awe.

It was like nothing he'd ever seen.

Everything was so *green.* For the last two days of their weeklong journey, Raz had seen hints of things his father had described to him years before. Patches of long, thick grass mixing with the sandy Southern soil. Scattered examples of monolithic trees that dwarfed the palms he remembered from the summer months his family had spent along the banks of the Garin. He'd seen the signs, known that the world was changing around him, shifting into something magnificent. The land was coming alive, reshaping itself into something so far come from the arid dryness of the Cienbal.

And yet, despite all those warnings, nothing could have prepared him for what he saw now.

Behind and before him, lining the road for as far as the eye could see, a forest seemed to have sprouted overnight. Trees like nothing he could have ever dreamed of, their sharp, needlelike leaves ranging in color from dark green to twilight blue, towered upwards to hang staggered overhead. The ground around Raz's clawed feet was a kaleidoscope of shadows and tumbling patches of light. The wind here was still dry, but it didn't drain the body with oppressive heat. Instead it bit playfully, a cool, crisp whisper that snuck into the folds of his clothes.

Apart from the grass and twin dirt wheel-paths of the cleared road, the ground was covered in a webbed foliage of earthy moss. Overlaying this was a thin blanket of spiny leaves, a rust-colored coat that seemed to have fallen right from the trees. Every few feet were odd, almost-oval objects, smooth and scaly in appearance, some old and dry, others green and heavy. Stepping off the path, Raz stooped to pick one up, rolling it in his hand.

Pine cone, he remembered, and he looked up at the great expanse of woods around him. *Pine trees.*

His father had told him stories of the North, and with every second Raz's eyes took in the sights around him he could recall more and more of what the man had said.

"I fall asleep for a few hours, and this is where I wake up," he chuckled, pulling the hood of his patchwork fur cloak over his head. The old man who'd smuggled him out of the Miropa had prepared the skins for him, mostly small rodents and the like, and Raz had spent the week putting old merchant skills to use. He'd fashioned himself a decent set of warm clothes, complete with a—if poorly done—fur-lined mantel and long britches. Winter was coming, and while Raz didn't know exactly what to expect, he did know that he didn't do well in the cold. He doubted the hasty work would do much when the freeze took full hold, but he hoped it would be enough to last until he could find somewhere to weather the next few months, or at least procure more suitable apparel.

The fact that winter, a strange idea in and of itself to him, was nearing didn't much bother Raz. On the contrary, he felt strangely elated, glancing over his shoulder southward. He was leaving behind everything, cutting all ties he might have had. On one hand, he really had little choice. By now runners would have been sent out to every fringe city by some of the Mahsadën's lesser officers, pleading for help. If he'd given it a week, Miropa would have been overrun by assassins and sarydâ out for blood. Within the month a new Mahsadën might already be in place, probably just as powerful as the previous one, and the šef would stop at nothing until Raz's head was on a spear strung atop the Cages.

It was another reason the change in season was less inconvenience than advantage. Even before Raz had managed to escape the city, dispatch riders were thundering constantly through Miropa's gates, gathering information from every direction. It was only a matter of time before someone realized he'd fled the fringe cities altogether, and from there he had only three options: catch sea passage to the West Imperial Isles from the ports of Acrosia, make his way south for Perce or the Seven Cities, or flee northward. Trouble was, the first two options generally involved crossing the Cienbal, an impossible feat on one's own, even for Raz. In the end, the reality was that he'd been left with only one option:

The North.

The coming winter would hopefully buy him enough time to find shelter as he figured out what his next step would be. In a few weeks or so the roads would hopefully become too icy and snowed-in to travel by, and for the next eight to nine months the North and South would be almost entirely cut off from each other.

For a time, Raz might be safe.

"At least somewhat, huh, Ahna?" He smirked, shifting the dviassegai so that she sat more comfortably over his shoulder. A heavy traveling bag, containing his armor, some spare clothes, flint, and enough food and water for a week, hung from the top of her haft. Her twin blades, wicked things not to be kept in the open in unfamiliar land, were covered by the same old leather pouch Raz had been using since the day Allihmad Jerr forged him the weapon. He felt a pang as he thought of the old blacksmith, but pushed it aside.

The few friends he'd had would be better off without him.

Taking a deep breath, Raz began walking, marveling at the sights and sounds around him as he followed the road. Songbirds chirped from the hidden nooks in the trees, sometimes flitting above the road in flashes of red and blue wings. More than once Raz's sharp eyes caught slim, four-legged creatures with small white tails and horselike ears leaping away through the forest, frightened off by his appearance. High above, through the spaces in the entwined branches, a clear sky smattered with clouds hung like a tent over the world. Every so often one passed over the Sun, and the pattern of light that swept the ground with every gust of cold wind would fade in and out of sight.

Raz couldn't help but smile. This place was so *different*, so far gone from the arid lands a week's hard ride to the south. Even the Cienbal couldn't bring to life the land in the way this new place could. Though the chill still bit him through his furs, and the hard-packed ground hurt his clawed feet, Raz took in every detail, marveling.

If the rest of the North was anything like the forest around him, he thought he might like this realm very much.

After a half hour on foot, something caught Raz's eye along the road ahead. Two small obelisks, carved from old, dark granite about knee high, stood on each side of the wide path. Reaching the closest one, Raz bent down to get a closer look at it. On one side, facing the direction he'd come from, was engraved a single large *S*. On the other, in the direction he was going, was the letter *N*.

Straightening up again, Raz stood over the border marker for a long moment, staring at the *S*, following its curving form. It reminded him of the sand dunes and the waves of the Garin when its waters were caught by the desert wind. In his mind's eye he could see the infinite, beautiful, empty vastness of the Cienbal stretching out to the horizon in every direction, an entire world cut in two by red sand and blue sky.

Then Raz took a step forward, leaving everything he'd ever known far behind.

II

"What is for the best? To live a sheltered existence in the infinite confinement of these cursed mountains, or to seek out a way to better the lives of our people? The latter, you say? I agree, but what if the hunt for that better life meant putting them all in harm's way, or putting yourself in harm's way? What if it were a gamble regardless, with so much to lose and so little chance to gain…?"

—Shas-ronah Rhan, Last-Queen

"He is no longer within my sight, Hana."

"Which means what? He leaves? He dies? I swear upon the light of the First-One, Uhsula, if the boy is not returned to me, I will—!"

"Calm yourself, child. Your hatchling yet lives, and as strong as ever. No, he merely passes into the Cold. My sight does not extend beyond the sands. I can see nothing now."

Shas-hana Rhan sat hard on the stone dais that surrounded the dark throne carved directly into the wall of the cave. Her tail snaked nervously over the ground, clawed fingers rubbing her temples. The slim crown of black obsidian glass, a glittering circlet that usually rested comfortably over her brow between her webbed ears, suddenly felt as though it carried the weight of the mountain above her head. Pulling it off and placing it gently on the stone beside her, Shas-hana sighed in frustration.

"So he's actually done it…"

Beside her, Uhsula nodded slowly. The old seer had not taken the recent years well. If she'd been ancient before, she was practically defying death now, almost half again the age of the average female when they passed. Her eyes, once pale and opaque, were now orbs of a watery white, so distinct in the dim light of the Under Caves that Uhsula often opted to have her acolytes cover them with a long piece of dark cloth that wrapped around her head. The membranes of her ears had caught the rot long ago, leaving only tattered fragments to cling along their bony spines so that it often looked as though a great spider were hugging the back of her skull. She could no longer walk on her own, requiring the aid of two other females who had been tasked with watching over her, but even with their help short trips left her weary, and everyone but the Queen usually went to her rather than forcing her to come to them.

As much as it pained Hana, though, she could offer no such kindness. Sassyl Gal, the royal spymaster, was reporting more than a little disgruntlement within the Under Caves of late. There were only so many eyes and ears they could risk pervading the world of man, and a lack of news meant nothing good. The atherian had no way of knowing what was happening in the world above, no way of knowing how Hana's plan—already frowned upon in certain circles—was unfolding.

"Thank you, Uhsula," the Queen breathed after a moment. "And I'm sorry I keep getting upset with you. Recently I've started to question this idea of ours…"

From where she sat on the steps at the base of the stone dais, facing away from Hana, the old seer laughed wheezily.

"Child, if your first doubts about this come twenty summers into the process, I'd say there is little to bear worry for."

Uhsula picked up the wood-and-bone staff at her feet and tapped it against the ground. At once her handmaids appeared out of the dark, dressed in black loincloths that modestly covered the only parts of their bodies the atherian felt needed to be covered. They helped Uhsula to her feet gently, desensitized to the creaking and popping of her weary limbs as she stood.

Taking a moment to catch her breath, the seer turned to look with blind eyes at Shas-hana.

"Stand firm in your decision. It has been a long time coming, but finally we see hope that something may come of this great gamble of ours. Do not falter now. There is nothing we, or any of our people, can do to change what is to come. If you hesitate, Hana, there are those who will take the opportunity to shake your foundations until they see you crumble. Be strong, and the rewards for your years spent planning and worrying might just be reaped."

Then she nodded to her acolytes, and the pair led the old female gently out of the chambers, disappearing into the shadowed tunnels of the mountain.

For a long time Shas-hana stayed put, her mind turning over a hundred different things as she picked up the obsidian circlet and toyed with it aimlessly. As usual, Uhsula's visit had left her feeling odd, both partially sated and more discontent in the same space of time, like a child promised a toy but having to wait for it to be made.

The seer's last words rang true, though, and the Queen looked up at the dark ceiling, that cursed prison of roughhewn stone.

Now *was* the time to be strong, if ever there was one.

III

"Above all other actions come from our faith, it is often the great projects undertaken by the Laorin Priests and Priestesses of each new generation that gain us the appreciation, respect, and trust of the people of the vast North. Temples are a means of shelter and safe haven for the good of heart, the faithful a source of protection and guidance for those who need them most, and Laor an entity of comfort and spiritual warmth to the ones lucky enough to stumble into his arms. And yet, above all this, it is the broader ways in which we seek to improve life that the masses appreciate most. Eret Ta'hir did everything in his power to extend the Lifegiver's benedictions as far as they would go, even encouraging expeditions into the South and lands beyond. Talo Brahnt—my cherished partner—fought to end the oppression and exploitation of the poor and unlucky within the desperate valley towns here in the North. And Syrah, well... Syrah Brahnt has no need for expounding. Her conquests—once she found her own better half—outmatch anything I've managed to dig up in the great archives here in the Citadel, and certainly outdo anything in recent history."

—*Studying the Lifegiver*, by Carro al'Dor

... it is therefore with some desperation, my dear friend, that I've sent you this letter. The temple here in Azbar is a small one, and with only a few dozen of the faithful at my disposal I regret to say that we do not have the influence required to maintain order in this torn place. The town's Chairman, Tern, has reopened the Arena under the guise of attracting travelers and coin, and in many ways I cannot say I blame him. While we do not suffer the attacks of the mountain clans that the communities closer to the ranges do, this past freeze took a great toll on us, and we are hardly recovered. By the time this message reaches you, I hope to have made some headway with restocking our supplies and getting the Chairman and his council to see sense, but with every passing day more blood is spilled in that pit than I bear to think about.

In truth, I do not hold high hopes for my success. Tern is not his father, and he does not share the man's distaste for the Arena.

I may be attempting to coax reason from a man who has no intent or desire to see it.

I beg your aid, Talo. I understand that you have suffered your own losses in the past months, and that Cyurgi' Di is in process of preparing for the coming winter, but if you have any help to spare it would be desperately appreciated. I fear for the people of this town, for as the prisons empty and the volunteers dwindle, where will the council look to fill the Arena if not from within its own borders? I do not mean to prod at old wounds, dear friend, but I'm sure you recall a time when those slain were guilty only of substantial debt or minor crimes.

I can no longer do this alone.

Yours,
Kal Yu'ri

Talo sat for a long few minutes, rereading the letter in his hands. The candle he'd lit almost an hour ago was burning dangerously low, but he didn't bother taking flint to a fresh one. His fingers shook as he put the parchment gently down on the desk at long last. He leaned back in his chair, turning to look out the diamond-paned window set into the round wall by his bed at the edge of the room.

His life's work was coming apart at the seams.

He'd long known it had been bound to happen. It had taken a great number of his younger, fitter years to make even the slightest headway with the Arena Doctores and the towns that profited richly from the gladiator fights they offered, and a deal longer before he'd managed to push through a universal ban of the pits altogether.

He'd been a middle-aged man by the time that happy day had come, in fact.

The prohibition of bloodshed had been a tentative thing, though, and if he was being honest with himself, Talo was surprised his work had lasted this long. In a place like the North, any means of survival was a good means when the brutally bitter months of the freeze took hold. The Arenas offered men an opportunity to make a name for themselves, to win purses that would feed their families, to revel in glory that actually had its uses if they made it long enough to retire from the fights. Gladiators who fought well often came to be recognized, and upon leaving the Arena were often offered jobs as private escorts for traveling merchants, or even officer positions in the mercenary groups hired out to protect the valley towns every winter.

Essentially, on paper the Arenas had their benefits.

But it was the other side of the story, the results that the documents rarely showed, that made Talo sick to his stomach. The Arena, in reality, was a business that fed off a city, a place where desperate men were pitted against each other until one or both lay dead. Farmers who'd lost too many crops to the winds and snow signed their lives away with little more than a pitchfork to protect themselves. Criminals—yet people despite their convictions—were used as fodder for the enjoyment of a bloodthirsty crowd, thrown into the rings as a distraction, often unarmed. When the dungeons and prisons were empty, though, when the lines of willing recruits died away, the Arenas did exactly what Kal Yu'ri, High Priest of Azbar's Laorin temple, had made mention of:

They started finding excuses to round up the citizens of whatever towns surrounded them.

Damn it all, Talo cursed silently, leaning forward again and resting his forehead in the palms of his mammoth hands. His straight waist-length ponytail, long since turned more gray than brown, fell across his shoulder as he thought.

What was he going to do? It was too late to send significant aid to Azbar. The magics had already warned the Priests and Priestesses of Cyurgi' Di that the freeze was promising to be as brutal as the previous year's. Within a week the temperatures would plummet, and the snows could start anytime within the month after that. The Citadel needed all the bodies they had available. There was little enough time left as it was to finish stocking the cellars with enough food to make it through the next ten months.

But maybe there was another way…

While it wasn't *impossible* to make the journey to Azbar through the winter, it would certainly be more difficult a trek than it would have been had Kal's letter arrived even a single week earlier. Still, it was a feasible idea, especially if the group remained small.

Say… two people?

Lifting his head from his hands, Talo extended a finger and started moving it in small, concise circles. As he did, the air began to glow, and within seconds a thin, silky wisp of vibrant white light appeared, twirling around his finger until he sent it off with a gentle flick of his hand. He watched the graceful trail of light zip away, splitting into three identical bands that disappeared beyond the room's only door in a flash, two under the base and one through the keyhole.

Satisfied that his summonings were sent, Talo pushed himself to his feet, groaning as his bad knee protested the motion. Ignoring the pain, he crossed to a small oak cabinet beside his bed and opened its doors, pulling out another candle. With a thought it flared to life in his hands, and not a moment too soon as the dying flame on the desk behind him finally gave up with a last sputtering wink.

Smack!

"Ow!" Reyn Hartlet yelped, laughing. "What was that for?"

"*That* was for putting your hands where they don't belong, sir," Syrah Brahnt giggled from her place on top of him, straddling his naked hips.

"Well, you didn't seem to mind that much last night, did you?" Reyn growled, sitting up suddenly and flipping the woman over onto her back so quickly she gasped and laughed.

They were in Reyn's room tonight. As he'd selected to take on a permanent position in the Citadel as soon as he'd received his staff, his chambers were slightly larger and more lived-in. He had a small unframed mirror hanging from a nail on one wall, and a pile of books on a plain timber desk pushed up against another. Candles hung from the ceiling, suspended in thin metal cups, though none were lit.

Most importantly, though, was the fact that the bed was a good half width larger than Syrah's in her current room.

Syrah laughed again as Reyn bent over her and nuzzled her neck, kissing it lightly as she fought playfully back. It was dark in the room, neither of them seeing any need for light, but he still managed to find her wrists and pin them on either side of the pillow above her head. Her laughter ended abruptly, replaced by a tantalizing "*mmm*" of pleasure as she arched her back, pressing herself against his bare chest.

"Every day you seem to learn something else I like, don't you?" she whispered seductively into his ear.

Reyn chuckled, pushing himself up so that he could look her in the face through the dark.

"Not very hard, is it? You seem to like pretty much anything."

"Guilty as charged," Syrah breathed, and she lifted her head suddenly to reach his lips, kissing him roughly. He kissed her back just as passionately, letting go of one of her wrists so that his hand could stray down her arm, then her breast, reaching for the buttons of the simple nightgown draped over her slim form…

Then something darted into the room from under the door, and a small corner of the floor lit up with bluish-white light.

"Wait," Syrah gasped, breaking off the kiss as she turned to look at the disturbance.

Reyn, noticing it too, didn't protest, twisting off of her so that she could sit up and scoot to the end of the bed.

The narrow band of light was like a strip of thin silk, suspended magically in the air as it danced slowly in a gentle circle, casting a bright glow that oddly seemed only to fill the tiniest part of the dark room. Getting to her feet, Syrah made her way carefully towards the object and knelt beside it, extending a hand. The shining trail floated slowly forward, settling into her palm, where it hung for a moment.

Then it faded, and the room was dark again.

"Who was that?" Reyn asked through the black.

"Talo," Syrah told him, standing up and reaching out to feel the nearby wall. The disappearance of the message had left her completely blind. "I have to go, I'm sorry."

"It's alright. Go. I'll see you in the morning."

Syrah nodded to the shadows, made her way carefully to the door outlined in the pale glow of the candlelit hallway, and opened it just enough to slip through.

Blinking and squinting as her sensitive eyes struggled to get used to the sudden light, Syrah turned and started walking, wondering what Talo could want at this hour. It was nearly midnight, and though she knew her former mentor was well aware of her and Reyn's dynamic, she liked to think he would at least give her the benefit of the doubt and *assume* she was asleep right now.

Which meant that whatever he needed to see her about was important enough to wake her.

Putting a little rush in her step, Syrah followed the familiar path towards the High Priest's chambers. She'd been back at Cyurgi' Di well over a month now, and her memories of the old halls—a little foggy when she'd first returned—were fresh in her mind again. It had been years since she'd been consecrated into the Priesthood and left for the western ranges, intent on working out a peaceful solution between the wild mountain tribes of the Vietalis and the valley towns of Metcaf and Harond below. Now, being home, it was as though she'd leapt bodily back into her time as an acolyte spent under Talo's wing.

She couldn't have been happier.

It was a few minutes before she was knocking on the wide door of the High Priest's rooms, and she quickly flattened her white hair and checked that all the buttons of her nightgown were clasped as her former mentor's voice boomed "Come in!" from the other side. Pushing it open, Syrah stepped inside. Talo stood behind his desk, Carro al'Dor and Jofrey al'Sen across from him, and all three turned to look at Syrah as she walked in.

"There you are," Talo said with a smile, motioning her forward. "Come. I was just informing these two about this."

As Syrah moved to join Carro and Jofrey, Talo picked up what looked like a letter from the desk in front of him and held it out.

"Kal Yu'ri, the High Priest of one of our faith's smaller temples and a close friend of mine, has requested aid from Cyurgi' Di. What do you think of it?"

Taking the letter, Syrah read it over quickly. Then she cursed.

"If only we'd heard from him sooner," she said, biting her lower lip before handing the parchment to Jofrey to read. "We could have helped him then. As of now, though, I don't really see how, unless we only send a few… But that would be useless, wouldn't it? I don't see how three or four more of us could do much to change the minds of Azbar's council and Chairman if a whole temple hasn't already been able to handle it."

"It would depend on who was sent," Carro responded quietly, blue eyes on his partner as he stroked his braided blond beard thoughtfully. "You're not thinking of doing what I think you are, are you?"

"You know me best, don't you?" Talo responded fondly with a gruff laugh. "What do you think I'm thinking of doing?"

There was a silent moment in which Syrah looked around at all three older Priests.

"Am I missing something?" she asked finally. Before either Talo or Carro could respond, though, it was Jofrey who answered the question. Reyn's former Priest-Mentor had an oddly concerned look on his lined face as he spoke.

"He wants to go to Azbar himself."

Another moment of silence, and Syrah gaped at Talo.

"You want to do *what*?"

Talo, surprisingly, cringed under his former acolyte's angry outburst. From Syrah's left, Carro laughed out loud.

"My thoughts exactly. She keeps her head on straight, this one. You taught her well, Talo."

"Maybe too well," the High Priest muttered under his breath jokingly.

Syrah, however, was less than amused.

"You can't be serious." She put both hands on the desk in front of her and leaned over it angrily. "You want to leave on a fool's errand to the middle of nowhere *just* as the freeze picks up again? Never mind that you can barely make it to the dining hall for meals on that leg of yours! What about your responsibilities? Eret entrusted you with the Citadel, Talo, not anyone else. You would be leaving just as winter hits, and we aren't even properly stocked yet. We have a week left to finish what we need two to do! You *can't* leave now."

"I wouldn't bother, handsome," Carro cut in with a chuckle as Talo opened his mouth to argue. "She's got you nailed to the wall, and I'm with her on this one. Mind you, I'm more worried about your knee than anything else. Knowing how things have been the last few years, you're liable to trip and fall down a mountain-height of stairs before you even made it to the Woods. Where would we be then?"

"I think he should go."

There was a moment of absolute silence in which Syrah, Talo, and Carro all stared openly at Jofrey in surprise. Fortunately for him, it was Talo who recovered first.

"Thank you, Jofrey," he said quickly, holding up a hand to stop the angry outburst he could virtually see building on Syrah's pale lips. "I'll admit that of anyone I thought you might attempt to be the voice of reason, but I am grateful nonetheless."

Jofrey chuckled, nodding his head in thanks at the compliment.

"I *am* being the voice of reason. You two." He looked at Syrah and Carro. "While I admit you both bring up valid concerns, I would point out that Eret did leave Talo the mantle of High Priest for a reason. You should trust his judgment as a leader before you question it as a friend.

Talo has been handed a situation that requires his attention, and in my opinion has found the best solution to deal with it. By only sending a few the journey will be quicker *and* the toll on Cyurgi' Di's manpower will be minimal, not to mention that the harvesting is already in motion and requires only supervision. As for the High Priest's duties, Carro can handle them while he is gone. Beyond that, Talo's history with Azbar could have great impact on the situation there, given the right circumstances. As I said: the best option."

For a full five seconds Syrah and Carro continued to stare at the old Priest, open-mouthed.

"I-I suppose it's possible," Carro spluttered finally. "I still worry about your knee, Talo. And as for taking over, I'm sure there are other Priests better suited to the task of—"

"You needn't worry about either," Talo interrupted with a grunt as he sat down in the wingback chair behind his desk. "You're coming with me. Jofrey, I would like you to handle things in my absence."

It was Jofrey's turn to stumble over his words.

"M-me?" the Priest demanded, shocked. "Talo, surely you can find someone more worthy of taking over. Priest Jerrom maybe, or Petrük. Laor knows that woman would love a chance to—"

"Jerrom is approaching the Lifegiver's final embrace and has deserved his rest, and Valaria Petrük is a venomous cow who, if she had her way, would run this temple as a military outpost and see the return of hanging disobedient acolytes by their ankles in the furnaces. No. You are my pick, Jofrey. That is my final word."

Talo's sudden seriousness caught them all off guard, but they paid careful attention as he continued.

"You, Syrah," he said, placing his elbows on the desk and leaning into them, "will ensure that the harvest remains on schedule, and will assist Jofrey in any way you can. I don't plan on being gone more than three-score days, but if that doesn't happen I still expect you both to be able to take care of things while Carro and I are away. Is that clear?"

"I know we haven't had much time to ourselves lately, Talo," Carro stepped in, "but this is a little over the—"

"Carro," Talo sighed, "as much as I look forward to spending a trip alone with you, the reality is that you are both one of the best healers in this temple and our most talented scribe. I'll need both skills to make it to and from Azbar in one piece, and likely to help me with the council. These are simple people. You would be surprised what a clever letter or intelligent phrase will do towards making them see reason."

He turned to look at Syrah.

"You have my faith that everything will be in order when I return," he said quietly. "Can I hold you to that, Syrah?"

The Priestess was quiet for a moment, considering the question carefully before speaking.

"Safe travels, Talo. Don't get eaten by a bear. The poor thing might have indigestion."

IV

"It was an odd thing to watch him grow, to witness how his actions shaped him into the half-man, all-beast creature he became. Killing was more than a profession; killing was an obsession, and one which I say with no shame that I played my part in fueling. But you should have seen his eyes that first night he found me… For all his strength, all his speed, all his ferocity, they were the eyes of a broken soul…"

—Allihmad Jerr, master smith

Raz was in trouble.

He'd known it for the last two days, but as his sixth night spent away from the Southern heat broke a late dawn, he was realizing just how much trouble he was actually in. The temperatures had been constantly falling with each passing day, plummeting so low after sundown that he'd had to keep a fire burning through each of the last three nights. This morning, though, as he stood up next to the smoldering remains of the previous evening's fire, he swore silently to the surrounding trees.

It was barely any warmer now, as the Sun came up, than it had been for the hours he'd lain on his back studying Her Stars through the entwined branches.

He could *see* his breath misting in front of him. He was familiar with the concept of vapor. It wasn't uncommon for the contents of a drinking trough to disappear in the space of an hour around the Cienbal, but this new phenomenon was something else entirely. Raz took a deep breath, then exhaled slowly, marveling at the geyser of steam that rolled from his mouth and nostrils, fading quickly into the crisp, chilly air.

Despite the cold he couldn't help but do it twice more, smiling at the sight.

But he had to get moving. He could already feel his feet stiffening against the cold ground, and his wings, their thin membranes shielded only by his roughly hewn fur cloak, weren't much better off. Kneeling by the remains of the fire, he took a stick and prodded it back to life, enjoying the wave of heat that washed over him as he uncovered the embers under the built-up ash. There was no end to kindling. Everything from dead branches to whole felled trees were as common as stones and hills in these woods, and within five minutes Raz had another happy blaze crackling warmly. Sitting down and extending his wings around the flames, he sighed in relief as the heat soaked into him, loosening every tight muscle. Reaching out for Ahna's haft, he dragged her and his supply sack towards him, pulled it open, and rummaged through it for the remainder of his dried meat.

"Third time's the charm, right, sis?" he asked the dviassegai with a chuckle, eyeing the last four strips of dried flank he pulled from the cloth wrappings. "We'll get a foal today. That, or just starve to death."

By "foal," Raz meant the strange, agile four-legged animals he kept running across as he made his way haphazardly through the woods. He had no idea what they were called in truth, but as they had a similar build to what he thought of as a very small horse, he'd decided "foal" was as good a name as any. This wasn't an ideal title, of course. The creatures were tan with splotches of white across their fur, prancing about on slender legs, broad ears flicking in every direction as they grazed. A few times now Raz's quick eyes had even caught a glimpse of what looked like oddly branching horns adorning a few of their heads. *Males and females*, he'd decided. Not that it made a difference. Twice now he'd tried to sneak up on one of them, hoping to get close enough for a clear throw with his dagger, and twice the animals had bolted before he'd even thought himself close enough to be noticeable.

"I'll do better next time, Ahna," he said out loud, patting the weapon's haft. "Promise."

Within a minute the meat was gone and, his meager breakfast finished, Raz got to his feet, kicking dirt over the flames and watching sadly as the fire died with a lingering trail of smoke. Tucking his wings in tight under the cloak and pulling his hood over his head, Raz threw Ahna over his shoulder again and started heading northeast, the designated random direction of the day. With no map to go by and the road being too dangerous to follow, Raz had little choice but to hope the North wasn't as barren and empty as his father's old stories had often made the realm out to be.

Not that the haphazardness of his situation bothered Raz. It was oddly pleasant, in fact. For once he had no plan, no desperate urge to get something done and do something quick. Even before the war with the Mahsadën, Raz had always been *doing* something. There had been no shortage of work in the underworlds of Miropa, and even on the rare occasion that jobs were sparse he'd always felt the nauseating urge to get on with it, to find someone to hunt. There were always more bad men somewhere begging for a good thrashing, after all.

Here, though, and for the last week of his life, Raz had felt no such need. If it weren't for the blistering cold and the occasional blasts of icy wind that had replaced the cool breeze mere days after his border crossing, Raz was fairly convinced he would have enjoyed his stray journeying quite thoroughly.

Unfortunately, though, reality was a bitch to be wed to, and Raz pulled his cloak as tight around his shoulders as he could, holding it closed over his body with one hand as he made his way carefully down the steep bank of a mossy hill.

The way he was seeing things, he had three options. The first: turn around and hope he made it to warmer climates in time to escape the winter, which seemed to have decided on an early show this year. Second: hole up for the next ten months and wait out the freeze. He'd come across a few spots that might do the trick, mostly shallow caves in the hillsides or rock overhangs he might be able to build shelter around if he hurried. Third: find some sign of civilization, as dirty and downtrodden as it might be. After the slums of the desert fringe cities and this icy emptiness of the woods, any place with a bed would do the trick just fine.

Raz snorted as he ducked under the lowest limbs of a blue pine. *If only things were that easy.*

His first option was a suicide mission. Partially because he very much doubted he would be able to make the Southern climates in time, but mostly because half the South was in a frenzy hunting him down, and would be for some time. Regardless, he was a dead man. His second option was better, but only slightly so. For one thing he would have to learn how to hunt—and soon, by the looks of it—but even this aside he had to find suitable shelter to get through months of weather he had no idea what to expect from. Even though he liked to think he could manage it, he would have to find a way to stay warm, and struggling with that for ten months was not going to be easy…

No. His best option was to push through for as long as he could, even if it was only a couple more days. With any small amount of luck he'd manage to stumble across something or someone that could help him find his way to more agreeable environments. He'd been traveling for *days.* In the Cienbal that was one thing, but in a place as green and rich as these woods there had to be some sort of community nearby somewhere. Worst case, if he didn't make it, he'd build a bonfire to keep warm until he could go through with option two.

Raz grimaced at the image of himself hunting foals, or whatever the damn animals were called, in a foot of snow in the middle of winter. He'd never seen snow, but Agais had made it pretty clear that it was both wet and cold, a miserable, *miserable* combination.

For the love of all that is warm and living! Raz prayed half sarcastically, half desperately to the flashes of bright Sun he could see through the trees. *Give me SOMETHING better than a frozen death!*

"*Arrun*! W-wait! I-I can't—can't keep up!"

Arrun Koyt stopped running and turned around. Lueski was

struggling along behind him, one hand pressed against a stitch in her side as the other pushed off every tree she passed to gain her a moment's rest. She was gasping for breath, but so was Arrun, and his rush to his younger sister's side was more fueled by desperation than anything as he lifted her into his arms.

"Come on, just a little more! I'm sure we've almost lost them!"

It was a lie, but as he took off again, carrying the exhausted girl, Arrun knew it was the only thing he could say. They'd been running for three days now, barely stopping to rest or eat, and for a while he thought they'd gotten off free.

Then one of the dogs had found their tiny campsite, and they'd been forced to abandon what few supplies they had been able to make off with and start running again. Arrun had managed to lose the dog, but that didn't mean the others wouldn't pick up on their scent soon after.

"Only a little more, Lueski," he whispered quietly as they ran. "Just a little longer."

The girl, too tired to respond properly, nodded sluggishly. Barely eight years old, she was as adorable as they came. Her blue eyes and black hair had caught the attention of many a customer along their little bread tables in Azbar, and her child's smile almost always ended with an extra copper as a tip.

She was too young to be cut down as cheap entertainment.

Arrun, though… Arrun couldn't care less what happened to him. *He* was the idiot who had gotten them into this mess. When money had started getting tight in the middle of the last freeze, it was he who had decided to go to the loaners and borrow the gold necessary to get through the last few months.

I could have worked harder, he cursed himself. *I could have done SOMETHING. Instead, I do this…*

They were running because of him. He'd tried to offer himself up willingly, but the council had decreed that his outstanding debt demanded the recruitment of both he *and* his sister.

Lueski, who wasn't even old enough to understand exactly why they were on the run.

"Over my dead fucking body," Arrun had told them, and he and Lueski had taken off before the guards could come to collect. Kal had taken them in, even insisted they stay until everything blew over, but Arrun had insisted on running.

Just another thing he'd messed up.

"Just a little further, Sis," he said again in between gasps of breath. "Almost there."

It was an endless flurry of forest. Trees whipped by to their right and left, spiny leaves catching the pair across chests, arms, and faces as they ran. Great boulders blocked their path in many places, and the slope of hills was far more common than flat ground, resulting in more than one stumbling trip. Lueski was sobbing outright now, but just as Arrun opened his mouth again to comfort her, he heard it.

The baying of the hunting hounds, devilishly close behind them.

"*Run*, Lueski!" Arrun screamed, halting and dropping the girl on her feet, shoving her forward as he snatched a thick branch from the ground nearby.

"N-no!" Lueski yelled, turning to her brother. "You can't! Arrun—!"

But she stopped. Arrun was standing with his back to her, legs set and both hands shaking as he held the branch stiffly before him, brandishing it like a sword. For just a second he looked over his shoulder and gave the best smile he could.

"Go," he said, throwing her a roguish, sad wink. "I'll catch up when I'm through here."

Lueski could feel the tears streaming from her eyes, stinging the cold skin of her cheeks. She would have argued, but the look on her brother's face as he turned away from her told her it wouldn't matter. He was willing to make a stand here so that she could live, and she wasn't about to let him throw away his life in vain.

She gave the smallest of smiles towards the boy's back.

"I love you, Arrun," she said. Then she turned and fled, dashing through the trees again. She was too far away to hear it by the time her brother's broken voice responded.

"I love you too, Sis."

Raz was seriously reconsidering his earlier choice. Even though the temperature had actually risen a few degrees since that morning, his feet were so cold each step had progressed from painful to agonizing, then numb of all feeling, a sensation he didn't enjoy in the least. His wings and hands weren't much better off, and he shivered as he pulled the thin cloak tighter around his lean, scaly body.

"Sh-should have taken the time t-to make this a little warmer, huh, Ahna?" he muttered to the dviassegai still slung over his shoulder with a laugh. "W-would have been worth the d-delay."

I've become that fool who talks to himself in the streets, Raz thought with a snort, carefully navigating around a narrow brook that already had hints of frost biting at its shallow edges. *Or the woods, rather. Damn it all, how could it possibly get colder than this?*

But he knew it would. The Arros had educated all their children well, and Raz understood fully that water froze and snow formed only once the temperatures dropped past a certain point. And, as he'd seen no snow and the few rivers and streams he had seen were still flowing strong, it meant that this was only the beginning of what Raz was starting to think was going to be a *very* long few months for him.

"By the time I c-crawl out of my hole, I'll be t-trying to bleedin' *feed* you," he muttered to Ahna, annoyed. "Don't get me wrong, you're a great listener, Sis, but your ability to h-hold a conversation is somewhat l-lacking."

I'm going mad.

Raz laughed out loud at the trees, then cringed and swore as his numb toe caught an extending root and shot a hot bolt of pain up his left leg.

"DAMN. IT. ALL!" he yelled, dropping Ahna and the supplies and limping to lean against the trunk of the pine who'd abused him. "I thought I would enjoy this? Really? If this is what you have to offer me, you—!"

Raz let out a fluid stream of every curse he knew, including the few old desert ones he'd once conned the Grandmother into teaching him. His rant went on for nearly a minute, and he was so busy venting to the empty woods that he almost didn't notice the sounds that eventually tore him away from his anger. It was faint at first, the source still a ways away, but Raz froze to listen harder as he realized what it was.

Someone, or something, was running full tilt through the forest right at him.

In a blurred instant, Raz "the lost and angry wanderer" disappeared, and Raz i'Syul Arro came rushing to the surface. Kneeling down without taking his eyes away from the direction in which the noises were approaching, he opened the supply sack and grabbed the handles of his gladius and war ax, pulling them out. He would have preferred Ahna, but as she was tangled up in the straps of the bag he didn't have much of a choice. As he stood up, though, Raz realized the smaller weapons were probably a better choice anyway. His hands were so cold he could barely hold on to the grips with enough strength to wield them efficiently.

Combine that with the dviassegai's weight, and it might have spelled bad news.

Pushing those thoughts away, Raz cocked his head to the side to listen. Whatever it was that was coming towards him, it wasn't slowing down. He couldn't tell how big it was, nor if it was human or animal, as it was thrashing around too much for him to make sense of its bearing. As it got closer, he started to hear fast, rasping gasps, and after another few seconds thought he heard whimpering.

Is it injured? he thought, relaxing a little as he continued to scour in underbrush in the direction the thing was coming from. *Maybe some wounded animal trying to escape…*

Whatever it was, as it got closer and closer, Raz was almost positive it wasn't human. No person could make that much noise unless they were sprinting absolutely haphazardly through the trees, running *through* anything that got in their way rather than dodging around it.

Maybe it's a foal! a sudden, oddly elated voice piped up abruptly in the back of Raz's mind. Shoving it back, too, he waited, hood up and weapons raised in a defensive stance, ready for the worst.

It was therefore that, when a little girl about half his height came crashing out from between the trees, Raz was taken so off guard that he let her plow right into him.

The girl screamed as she bounced off his waist, tumbling to the ground and sobbing.

"No! NO! DON'T TAKE ME! PLEASE DON'T—!"

And then she stopped yelling, because she'd looked up enough to see the face that hid under Raz's hood. There was a pause where the look on the girl's features shifted from terrified shock to utter horror, and Raz knew what she was going to do the moment before it happened.

"No, don't—!" he yelped, dropping his weapons, but too late.

The girl opened her mouth and shrieked, a sharp, keening screech so loud a group of winter crows pecking about in the nearby shrubbery took off in fright.

V

Raz fell to one knee by the screaming child and clapped a hand over her mouth firmly, shutting her up.

"SHH! SHHHH!" he whispered urgently. "If someone is chasing you, the last thing you want to do is *lead them straight here*! SHH!"

It had occurred to Raz before, when his plans to escape northward first started to form, that there were some flaws to his schemes. Chief among them: he doubted many people in the North had ever dealt with or encountered the atherian.

This meant that he wouldn't have the same familiarity with the strangers he met in the forested scapes of this realm as he did with those of Miropa and the other fringe cities. While he was despised by as many people in the sandy plains as by those who appreciated his work, he did, at least, have a reputation there which meant he avoided the awkward exchange of introductions.

Awkward exchanges exactly like this one.

"My name is Raz," he whispered hurriedly. "I know I probably frighten you, and that you've likely never seen one of my kind, but I'm not going to hurt you. I'm atherian. Do you know what atherian means?"

The girl hesitated, her bright blue eyes frozen on his amber ones. Then, slowly, she nodded.

"Good," Raz breathed. "Now, I'm going to take my hand away, but only if you promise me you won't scream again. Do you promise?"

This time the hesitation was only brief, and she nodded again. Slowly Raz lifted his hand from her mouth, letting go of her completely. Immediately she started sobbing again, but held her word and kept the noise to a minimum, curling up into a ball on the mossy forest floor and wrapping her arms around her legs. Raz scooted back a step, still on one knee, just to make sure she knew he wasn't there to hurt her.

"Are you all right?" he asked after a moment. "What happened? Why were you running?"

The child shook her head rapidly, sobbing a little louder.

"No!" she hissed at no one in particular, squeezing her eyes shut tight. "No!"

"It's fine, you don't have to tell me," Raz said quickly. "I just need to know if you were followed. Are there men chasing you?"

This time the girl nodded once, very briefly, like she was trying hard not to think about whatever Raz's questions were prodding her towards.

"Are they trying to hurt you?"

Another nod.

"How many are there?"

A shake.

Raz sighed, standing up and listening again. He couldn't hear anything nearby, but the trees made it harder than he was used to. The only reason he'd made out the girl was because she'd been thrashing through the underbrush like a madwoman.

For good reason, apparently, Raz thought, looking back at her. She was shaking, still huddled in her tiny ball. Her clothes, once a decent set by the looks of them, were ripped and muddy. Dirt spattered every inch of her bare skin. Leaves and twigs stuck out from her messy black hair, and her fingers were somewhere between white and blue from the cold.

She must have been out here for as long as I have...

Raz's eyes narrowed as he tried listening harder, but still nothing, not a hint of trouble, snuck through the thickness of the woods. He was about to turn around, intent on grabbing his things to make another fire, when the girl spoke of her own accord.

"Help..." she whispered, so quietly Raz doubted he would have heard had he been human. "Help... please."

Moving to kneel beside her again, he tilted his head to look her in the face evenly.

"I'm going to," he said softly. "Let's get you warmed up, okay? I'm going to go find some wood. You just—"

"No," she interrupted, opening her eyes and looking up at him. "My brother... Help my brother."

Raz was quiet for a moment, studying her face before speaking.

"I can try, but for that you need to tell me *exactly* what's going on. Do you understand?"

The girl nodded. After another moment she seemed to calm minutely, letting go of her knees to push herself shakily up.

"L-Lueski," she started, her voice breaking. "I-I'm Lueski. My brother Arrun and I had a shop in A-Azbar, but we didn't have enough money so bad men from the town took it. They were going to take us, too, but Arrun wouldn't let them. H-he—"

"Wait," Raz cut in. His body had experienced a jolting chill that had nothing to do with the cold. "What do you mean, 'take you'? What was the town going to do with you?"

"The Arena," Lueski whispered in a frightened hiss. "They take the people who don't have enough money and make them fight each other. I don't like it... I don't want to fight!"

For just a moment the world went silent as the girl started to cry again, and Raz could hear the blood rushing through his ears, hear his breathing in his chest.

A little girl... They would use a little girl for pit fights? What kind of place had he come to? He'd left the South to *escape* this sort of horror.

Just as he felt the balance tip again, felt that fragile conscience he'd spent the last two weeks piecing back together start to crack, Raz shook himself free.

"Your brother, Lueski," he said urgently. "What happened to your brother?"

The little girl hiccupped and rubbed her eyes, trying to stop her crying.

"They sent men after us. Big men. Angry men with mean dogs. Ar-Arrun stayed back to try and stop them."

She looked up at Raz, her eyes swimming.

"He's gonna die!"

There was another moment's silence as Raz contemplated her words. He didn't have as many details as he would have liked, but if the child was right, then they didn't have a lot of time. Standing, Raz moved to pick up his gladius and war ax from the ground where he'd dropped them. Turning them over in his hands, he loosened stiffened wrists.

"Lueski," he said, "you need to take me to him."

"You think we're daft, boy? We know there was two of ya' this mornin' at that camp of yours! Where's yer sister? Spit it out!"

There was a smack and a cry of pain through the trees, and Raz got his hand around Lueski's mouth just in time to keep her from gasping in fright. He was listening, trying to make out as many details of the scene just beyond the tree line as he could without showing himself.

They'd traveled fast, Lueski guiding him back surprisingly well. He'd have liked to bring Ahna and the last of his supplies, but the need for haste had forced him to leave them, marking the path to find them later.

Listening now, he knew he'd made the right call.

"I told you," an exhausted, falsely fearless young voice retorted. "I don't know where she's at. Lost her two hours ago at the river. Stupid girl probably drowned for all I care."

"He's only trying to set them off track," Raz whispered as Lueski's eyes grew wide and hurt. "He just doesn't want them to find you."

"Right…" the first voice, an older man's, picked up again sarcastically. "Which is why Morty here's picked up a trail headin' south an' west. Ain't that right, Morty?"

In response a dog snarled, and at least three or four men laughed as the second voice, Lueski's brother, yelped.

"Just tell us where she's goin', Arrun," the bounty hunter's voice growled in wicked amusement, "and I promise I won't set the hounds on her when we catch up. Deal?"

"Lueski," Raz whispered sternly. "Stay. Here. Do *not* move. Got it?"

The terrified girl nodded and, as soon as he was sure she wouldn't budge, Raz stood up to make his way through the last few paces between the pines. The dogs must have smelled him first, because they started growling in unison before he even stepped into the small clearing the group was standing in.

A young man with blond hair—Arrun, Raz assumed—was on the ground, right leg torn and bloodied by one of the hunting hounds, his back pressed against the stump of a tree that had rotted away years ago. Three men and their hounds stood nearby, dressed in thick trapper's furs with an assortment of swords, bows, and daggers hanging from backs and belts. A fourth stood over Arrun, the meanest looking of the lot. This man turned at the dogs' warnings, his own animal held by a chain wrapped around his hand, and Raz took in the scruffy beard and scarred face at a glance.

The bounty hunter reminded him of the sarydâ, in a way...

"What the—?"

Raz stopped moving just inside the ring of trees, his hood pulled down to reveal his serpentine features. He had no patience for theatrics at the moment.

Nor for unnecessary banter.

"All of you," he hissed. "Leave. *Now.* It will be my only warning."

There was a moment of shocked silence, and then one of the group off to the side spoke.

"By the Lifegiver," he whispered, clearly shaken. "Raz i'Syul."

Raz, admittedly, was surprised.

"You know me?" he asked, looking over at the man, who nodded.

"Aye, sir. I do," he replied quickly, raising the hand that wasn't gripping the leather leash of his dog up in a sign of peace. "Did some work in the Southern desert towns a few years back. Saw ya' fight once, too. We want no trouble, sir. We'll be leavin' soon as ya' let—"

"What the shit are you blatherin' about, Shrith?" the man standing over Arrun cut in suddenly. "We're not going anywhere. You move and I'll skin ya myself."

"Boar, trust me on this one," the man called Shrith said, not taking his eyes off Raz or lowering his hand. "We're wantin' to leave. Now."

"Don't be a fuckin' coward, ya' doe," Boar growled, spitting on the ground before returning his attention to Raz, pulling his dog's chain tight. "An' *you.* Ugly bastard. Lizard-kind, ain't ya'? What the blazes you doin' so far out of your hole, scaly?"

"Boar—" Shrith tried again, but the leader shot him a look so venomous the man shut up at once.

"Anyhow," Boar continued, eyes moving slowly back to Raz, "*I* ain't heard shit about you, so I'll be damned if'n I'm a' let some sharp teeth and snake eyes cheat me outta my twenty gold for this one and his sister."

Boar kicked Arrun's injured leg and laughed as the boy cried out in pain.

He did shut up, though, when Raz's neck-crest rose to fin the back of his head.

"You should have listened to your friend," Raz said calmly, pulling his weapons out from where they'd been tucked in the back of his belt. "Too late now, though."

Boar's eyes narrowed, and he spat again.

Then he dropped the chain of his hound.

"Git 'em, Morty!" he yelled, spurring the animal into a forward rush. With a snarl it leapt, jaws wide as it went straight for Raz's throat.

Raz's clawed foot found it first, catching it in the chest and cracking several of the dog's ribs as he kicked it a solid three or four body lengths away. It fell to the ground and rolled twice before coming to a halt, whining and whimpering as it struggled to breathe.

"My dog!" Boar screamed, eyes livid, drawing the longsword at his side. "I'll kill you, ya' damn snake!"

"BOAR, NO!" Shrith yelled, but too late. The bounty hunter was already charging, blade pointed straight for Raz's heart.

Raz counted the man's steps as he approached, waiting for the moment. Four... three... two... When Boar's sword was barely a foot from his chest, Raz's war ax whipped upwards, catching the length of the blade. Even as the ax redirected the blow, the gladius in Raz's other hand was moving, a steely blur as it sliced cleanly through the man's wrist, severing Boar's sword hand. In a fraction of a second, though, Raz brought the blade full circle and struck again, horizontally and a little higher.

Boar's lost his head before he'd even had the time to register he'd lost his hand.

In all of a few seconds the fight was over, and the man's decapitated body fell to the ground at Raz's feet with a thud. Leaving his weapons drawn, Raz turned his eyes on the rest of the group, looking directly at Shrith.

"*Run*," he snarled.

The only sign left of the three and their animals ten seconds later was distant crashing through the woods. Even Morty, the injured dog, was dragging itself away in a hurry.

Raz waited until he was sure they were far gone before relaxing, tucking his wings into place, and letting his crest fall around the back of his neck again. Stowing his ax and gladius back into his belt, he took a step towards Arrun.

"Stay back!" the boy yelled, scrambling away on his rear despite his injured leg. Running over a big stone, he pulled it from the ground and brandished it one-handed as he held himself in a sitting position with the other. "Don't come near me! I'll kill you!"

Raz snorted, ignoring the threat as he continued his approach.

"Is that how you treat every person who saves your life, or just the ones that look like me?" he asked, a little annoyed. Arrun didn't put the stone down, though, so Raz sighed and stopped, turning to yell over his shoulder. "Lueski! It's safe. Come out!"

"Lueski?" Arrun asked, suddenly confused. "Wha—?"

But that was all he got out before the girl's small form came bolting out of the woods, crashing into his side.

"Arrun!" she cried, wrapping her arms around his waist so tightly the boy gasped. "Arrun! I thought you'd be gone! I thought you'd be taken or, or…!"

She stopped talking, sobbing into her brother's chest.

"Shh," Arrun hushed her, rubbing her back. "Shh, Sis. I'm alright. We're alright."

Raz's jaw tightened as he watched the pair of them. Arrun was a good bit older than his sister, maybe fifteen or sixteen judging by the shadow of a beard along his jawline. His hair was sandy blond rather than the raven black of Lueski's, but his eyes were the same shocking shade of blue. After a minute he turned to look back at Raz.

"Thank you," he said hoarsely. "Thank you for finding her. But w*ho are you*?"

"Raz," Raz replied shortly, pulling his cloak around his body again as the winds picked up once more. "For the moment let's just say I'm as much of a runaway as the pair of you."

Arrun nodded. Lueski was still hugging him so tightly she shook, sobbing into the torn cloth of his vest and shirt. Raz watched the two of them for another moment, then turned away and started making his way back towards the trees.

"Wait, where are you going?" Arrun called out.

"I'll be back," Raz said without looking over his shoulder. "I have a sister, too."

VI

Evening found the three of them seated around a roaring fire a good few leagues from the small clearing Arrun had been cornered in. Though he doubted the hunters would return after the bloody spectacle he'd made of their leader, between Boar's body and the openness of the area Raz had decided to get moving as soon as possible. Cleaning Arrun's injured leg carefully and wrapping it with most of the bandages from his supplies, he'd gotten them on their feet in fifteen minutes, guiding the pair through the woods, Ahna back over his shoulder. When night started to fall, though, and it became too dark for Arrun to travel by with his wounds, Raz had finally called them to a stop. He and Lueski set up a quick camp, clearing a spot on the ground for the fire, and within a half hour they were all huddled around the life-giving flames, soaking in the heat in relative silence.

At long last Raz allowed himself the relief he'd been holding back all day, too on edge listening for anyone following them to think of much else. Confident they were safe for the time being, though, now he allowed himself a smile.

Maybe we won't be stuck in this frozen hellhole all winter after all, he thought as he cleaned the blade of his gladius with a rough cloth.

Raz had considered himself something of a misanthrope for a long time, ever since the day Prida Arro had disappeared from their small shared home without a trace. Despite this—whether it was because he'd been on his own too long or because he was at least used to *some* arbitrary interaction in the crowded streets of Miropa—he was not unhappy to be around people once again. It was interesting, watching the siblings. Arrun had a good measure of self-control, but his sister—young and still a little unclear on propriety and the rules of social nuances—couldn't help but stare in open astonishment at Raz for most of the night. She took in his clawed fingers, thick tail, and reptilian snout with childish wonder now that she knew he wasn't going to eat her, and when Raz extended his wings around the flames to warm their thin membranes, she leaned towards her older brother.

"Can he fly, Arrun?" she whispered into his ear.

"Hush, Lueski," Arrun told her quietly. "Don't be rude."

"It's alright," Raz replied with a chuckle, making them both jump. Obviously they'd thought they were being quiet enough for him not to make out their words. He pointed at his ears.

"I hear better than you do. But no, it's fine. At her age it's understandable to be more than a little curious. Feel free to ask me anything you'd like, Lueski. As for being able to fly…" he glanced at his leathery wings, "…I'm honestly not sure."

"You're not sure?"

It was Arrun, this time, who asked the question, and Raz hid a smile.

So it's not just the sister who's curious.

"I'm not sure," he repeated. "I somewhat managed it once, for a few seconds, but that was in a very special situation, and I haven't tried it since. I've been a little preoccupied to think much about it."

He watched the flames of the fire, remembering the inferno of the burning bathhouse crashing around him the night he'd somehow managed a few brief moments of flight.

Odd how fond memories could mix so well with bad ones.

"Does your tongue hurt?"

Raz looked up at Lueski, perplexed.

"My… tongue?" he asked.

"It's cut in half," the little girl said matter-of-factly, pointing at his face.

"Lueski!" Arrun hissed, but Raz stopped him as he laughed again.

"It's *fine*, Arrun. No, Lueski, it doesn't hurt. It's how my tongue is, see?" He stuck his forked tongue out so she could look, wiggling it around.

Lueski giggled, winning a smile from her brother, who relaxed a little. For a while after the group didn't speak. More than once each of their stomachs growled in hunger, but as none of them had any food to spare they didn't voice their discomfort. Instead they sat in silence, appreciating the rare warmth of the campfire until Lueski fell asleep, her head in her brother's lap. Raz watched her from across the flames, remembering how Ahna used to fall asleep the exact same way.

"Our parents passed when she was six," Arrun spoke suddenly, and Raz looked up at him. The boy was watching his sister sleep, smoothing her hair with a gentle hand. "I was fourteen at the time, old enough to take care of things, at least according to the laws of the town. I took over the shop until Lueski could help, and we'd been working it ever since until this past winter."

There was another brief silence.

"Arrun," Raz asked quietly, "why were there hunters after you? Your sister told me something about money, and that they were going to drag you off to an arena?"

"*The* Arena," Arrun corrected him. "There are a few throughout the North, but Azbar's is the largest. They're technically illegal, ever since the Laorin managed to pass a ban on them twenty or thirty years ago, but recently they've started opening again. Last year's freeze was tough for a lot of people…"

He was quiet again then.

"So… what?" Raz pressed. "They were going to make you fight?

Because that's what Lueski made it sound—"

"They were going to make us die."

The sentence hung in the air as Raz blinked.

"They were going to make us die," Arrun repeated. "Sure, they say you have a fair chance, but it's bullshit. They give you a rusty sword and send you out in packs into the pit. They don't need us to fight. They have gladiators, volunteers with experience and training who get armor and better weapons. Sometimes they'll be matched against each other, but it's usually one or two of them against three or four of us. It sounds fine, until you realize that they know how to fight and the people who often get forced into the Arena are either petty criminals or farmers who couldn't pay their taxes. The gladiators rarely lose, but even when they do the victors are usually wounded so badly they die on the surgeon's table later anyway. It's a bloodbath is all, but it's a lucrative one. People come from all over to watch the fights, and those with money even bet and gamble on the outcomes. Ever since the Azbar Arena opened up again, things have been going better for the town, but the price isn't worth it. People are scared. The town's prisons were emptied within a couple months of the fights starting up, and after that the council and Chairman Tern decided to go after anyone that gave them an excuse to throw them in the pit. They're desperate to keep the money flowing through the Arena gates. It's gotten so bad they'll claim anyone old enough to hold a sword, so long as they can still bleed."

It's the Cages all over again, Raz thought, his eyes back on the fire as he listened to Arrun's story, *only instead of slavery they get handed a blade and get told to save themselves.*

"When I heard they were coming for us, I wouldn't have it," Arrun continued. "I told Lueski to grab anything she needed fast, and one of our parents' old friends helped sneak us out of the city. We've been on the run ever since. We aren't the first to make a break for it, but everyone else I've heard of doing the same has ended up being caught or killed by groups like the one you chased off. I think we're the first ones to get away."

"You aren't done with it yet," Raz told him. "You won't be until you can clear your name. Trust me, being on the run may sound appealing compared to being thrown into this 'Arena,' but it wears at you if all you're ever doing is picking up and moving."

"Speaking from experience?"

"A lot of it. If you think things are bad here, I can tell you it's nothing—*nothing*—compared to what's going on in the South. Slavery is as close to being legalized as it can be. People are being dragged out of their homes and tortured by the men they pay taxes to and trust to defend them. The governments are nothing but puppets to the underground societies that actually control everything… Believe it or not, as much as you'll hear me complain about the cold and as much as you can hate your own people for what they are doing with these Arenas, you're better off."

"You sound like you know more than most," Arrun responded, giving Raz a pointed look.

Raz nodded. "In a way. For a long time I conned myself into working for the wrong side. I made myself believe what I was doing was for some higher good. In reality, though, I was as much a puppet as anyone else."

"So you ran? Are you being chased, too?"

Raz smiled slowly. It wasn't a happy smile, but he could feel the satisfaction there, tucked away in some darker corner of his conscience.

"I'm running because half the Southern realm is after my skin," he said. "It's what happens when the puppet murders those holding the strings."

"You killed them?" Arrun hissed, shocked.

"You sound surprised," Raz told him, smirking. "After what you saw today, you thought that wouldn't be the case?"

"N-no," Arrun stuttered, "I just… I don't know… You killed *all* of them?"

"If only. But no. I didn't. The Mahsadën—the men I was working for—are too big a beast to slay on your own, even for me. You would need an army. I cut off its head, but by now I wouldn't be surprised if it's already started to grow a new one. In reality I think I only wanted to prove to myself that it *could* be hurt, because for a long time I was convinced it couldn't."

"And now they're after you, and you came here, of all places."

Raz shrugged, picking up a branch from the small pile of kindling by his side and poking the flames with it. He followed the spiraling dance of the sparks as they drifted upwards into the air, watching them disappear into the gusty night.

"It was as good a place as any, and better than most. To get to Perce or the Seven Cities, I would have had to cross the Cienbal, the Southern desert, and I spent enough time there as a child to know I wouldn't have managed that alone. I might have made for the West Isles and looked for a ship to stow away on in Acrosia, but the ports are controlled by the Mahsadën. If I'd been caught I would have been done for. The South's other fringe cities are in their pocket just as much, so that wasn't even an option. The North was my best bet, and with the seasons changing I'm hoping to catch a break and get a head start on anyone who's after me."

"So you're laying low in the woods?" Arrun asked him.

"I'm in these woods," Raz snorted, "because I'm lost. There's no point in laying low. I'm not going to spend the rest of my life hiding, and even if that was the intention my features aren't exactly akin to those of the average Northerner. I just have no idea where I am, nor had any idea to begin with. I figured if I had no plan, then anybody on my ass would have less to figure out and go by." He shivered, scooting closer to the fire as he prodded it again. "Now I'm starting to see the problems with my 'no-plan'-plan."

"Well I'm going to do you a favor and say if you get stuck out here, you're done for," Arrun told him with a nod, and Raz looked up again. "I'm not taking a shot at your skills as a survivalist. Obviously you can handle yourself, but if this is your first freeze coming up then you need to find shelter. It can snow so much in these woods that even the deer sometimes get stuck and freeze to death. And the winds—"

"Wait, the 'deer'? Is that what you call those horse-things that I always see leaping off through the trees? Some of them have horns?"

"I wouldn't call them horse-like," Arrun said tentatively, looking amused, "but yeah, that would be them. And they're called antlers, not horns. But I guess you wouldn't know that, would you?"

Raz shook his head.

"What else is out here?" he asked, looking around. Now that he was warm again, he could feel that original sense of elation and excitement start to creep back. Everything was so *new* here. "Do you even have horses? And what about snakes? Or scorpions? I hate scorpions..."

Arrun's eyebrows rose in surprise at the sudden stream of questions as Lueski twisted on his lap in her sleep.

"We have horses, yeah. As for snakes, not many, and only a couple dangerous kinds. You want to watch out for anything with an arrow-like head. But scorpions? What are scorpions?"

"They're big, ugly, spiderlike things with pincers that—" Raz began, imitating the creature with his hands. Then he stopped himself, dropping his arms. "You know what, if you've never heard of them, I'm going to do you the kindness of not telling you what they are. But I'm glad you have horses, at least. Good to know some things are still the same."

"If you say so... Do you have bears? Black and brown ones are pretty common and aren't usually dangerous, but if you get way north of here you run the chance of crossing an ursalus. Big, *big* things, half as tall again as you and twice as wide, with white-and-brown fur that makes them hard to see in the winter. Stay away from them."

Bears Raz had heard of, and he nodded.

"Moose?" Arrun asked, and Raz shook his head. "Now those you would call horse-like, but bigger. They're mean, even though you wouldn't think so looking at them."

"Everything is mean where I'm from."

"Well you shouldn't have to worry either way," Arrun insisted. "I'm not pulling your leg when I say you *can't* spend the freeze out here. It gets so cold it's not even possible to find water. Even in town we have to melt blocks of ice by the fires sometimes, and that's in a place where our walls block out a majority of the storm winds. You think these trees fall by themselves?" He motioned towards the pile of wood by Raz. "They get *blown* down. We get gales and blizzards that can knock down a house if it's not built properly. Even if you *can* fly, it won't help you."

He motioned to the swaying collage of pines around them.

"Unless your plan is anything short of digging a hole in the ground and staying there for the next ten months, you'd be better off finding another way to get through the freeze."

Raz sat for a long minute, pondering the advice.

"Then where would I go?" he asked finally. "What's the closest town from here?"

Arrun didn't respond at that.

"Arrun?" Raz pressed.

"Azbar," the boy answered reluctantly. "Lueski and I ran in a circle, hoping the hunters would get tired and return home since they were so close. We're less than two days away but—"

"Can you take me there?"

"What? No! Have you not been listening? If we get caught in that place we're as good as dead. They'll *chain* us to the Arena walls just to make sure we don't run again!"

"Arrun," Raz said quietly, "I promise you, if you take me to Azbar, I will make sure no harm comes to you. That goes even more so for Lueski. I'll throw myself in the Cages before I let a girl her age step into a place like the Arena."

"The Cages?" Arrun asked, confused. "… I don't understand."

"It's not important," Raz told him, pulling his hood up and lying on his side as he wrapped a wing over his body for warmth. "But you have my word. Take me to Azbar, and I will see to it that you and your sister can stop running for good."

VII

"Adventure is the essence of life. What would we be were it not for excitement, for that bold sense of daring and pleasure? It is not mankind's place to sit idly back in the comforts of our communities, but rather to take hold of Laor's gift of life and experience it to its fullest. Shameful is the man who has never felt the sand of the Southern desert under his feet, or experienced the rush of the Northern winds atop a mountain. Shameful is he who does not wish to ford a neck-deep river, or witness the sun rise over the eastern horizon of the Dramion Sea. We have been blessed with life, blessed with the ability to make and hold on to memories till and beyond our deathbed. What would we be if we did not take advantage of these wonderful gifts, and instead let opportunity pass us by?"

—Xaviun Fuerd, High Priest of Cyurgi' Di, c. 550 v.S.

It was a rare day for being so close to the freeze. Talo looked up from his place in the saddle, smiling at the shining sun he could only barely glimpse through the trees. They'd been on the road for three days now, but today was the first he and Carro had been able to shed their thick deerskin mantles and stuff them away into their packs. They rode now in typical traveler's attire: sleeveless fur-lined leather jerkins, layered wool pants, and heavy boots. While he felt oddly uncomfortable outside the customary white robes of his faith, Talo couldn't help but enjoy the freedom as they made their way through the Woods, his steel staff lying lengthwise across his lap. It had been a long time since he'd left the Citadel with it, and as he took a deep breath he reached down, feeling the strength of the metal between his fingers. It reminded him of decades long past where he'd spent years at a time away from anyplace he might have called home, adventures after he was first granted his consecration. He remembered climbing the ragged slopes of the Vietalis Ranges, fending off ambushes by the winter animals and the wild mountain men along the way. He remembered the western coastline, trailing leagues and leagues of pebbled beaches textured with bleached driftwood logs and shiny pearly shells. He remembered the heat of the South in summer and bitter cold of the Northern valley towns in full clutch of the freeze.

Talo did not resent his place amongst the Laorin. The Lifegiver had seen to grant him just reprieve for his hard time of servitude in the form of the High Priest's mantle, and it was a comfortable life for an aging man. But Talo had never been one to sit idle when his hands could aid in the work that needed to be done, and he often pined for the days when it was *he* who was set off into the world, and not the younger Priests and Priestesses he set off himself.

How I've missed you, old friend, Talo thought privately, rubbing a thumb against the roughhewn steel of the staff as he watched the patched dirt and grass of the forest road pass beneath them. *More than I've ever let myself realize, I believe.*

"You could do it again, you know?"

Talo blinked, shaken from his brief musings. Turning in his saddle, he looked back to find Carro watching him closely.

"What?"

"You could do it again," the Priest repeated, clucking his horse into a trot until he was riding beside his partner. "You don't have to bear the title if you don't want to. It is not a forced position. You have the right to pass it on anytime you see fit."

Talo sighed, turning his eyes back to the road.

"Am I so obvious?" he asked. A moment later he felt a hand rest gently on his knee. Carro had pulled his horse close enough to Talo's to lean over and reach.

"Not to those who do not know you as well as I," Carro said gently, giving him a small smile. "But barely a fraction of the year has passed and already I see you tire of it. Your energy is gone. You seem... unhappy."

Talo hesitated, then moved to lace his fingers overtop Carro's.

"If you are concerned about us..."

"*No,*" Carro said with a laugh, pulling his hand away and moving his horse to the other side of the path once more. "I'm concerned about *you.* I can't read your thoughts, Talo, as much as I'd like to, but it's as plain as a black bear in the snow to me that you sometimes wish the title had been given to someone else. Why not hand it off? No one would think less of you, considering you've done well even in the brief time you've held it. We could say this trip was a chance to see how Jofrey handles the title. If he does well, he could replace you."

Talo thought about it. If he renounced the High Priest's position, he'd have full freedom to personally address the matters he cared about. The last few years had been one thing. Tending to Eret and making sure the old Priest's affairs were all in order had been an all-consuming detail. He hadn't felt the nagging desire to be more than a man behind a desk during that time, content with aiding his former mentor with whatever the ailing man had needed. Now that Eret was held in His embrace, though, things were different...

Talo had *hated* having to argue with Syrah about leaving the Citadel. For one thing he hated arguing with her because the woman was like a daughter to him, one he'd even given his family name to, and she was as intelligent, calculating, and kind as he could ever have hoped his own children might have been had Carro and he had that option. The fact that she'd disapproved of his decision was saddening. Not because he felt betrayed in any way, but because her disapproval had reason.

It was that fact that had bothered Talo the most about his departure. The concept that taking matters into his own hands was not the best method of dealing with a situation was foreign to him, and he wasn't sure he liked it. All his life Talo had been a man of action, even *before* finding the Lifegiver, and sitting back as others carried the burden was not a natural part for him to play. It was a part for people like Petrük, that insufferable viper, who claimed good intentions while truthfully only seeking the comforts such positions allowed.

Perhaps I could step away… Talo thought, coaxing his horse back onto the trail as it swerved towards what must have been a particularly appealing patch of grass. Hearing himself think, though, he smiled.

"Carro al'Dor, you shameful bastard," he said with a laugh, looking at the Priest. "What kind of influence have you become to me? You've got me dreaming of long roads and open skies."

Carro grinned mischievously, shrugging.

"I merely blew on the budding flame. The dreams were already there, as I'm sure you know."

Too true.

Talo nodded. But was it worth the worry, really? He thought of Eret—a man much like himself in so many ways—and of all the things he had achieved as High Priest. Eret had found a way to transform the title into something ideal for his manner of handling the responsibilities the position presented, so why couldn't Talo do the same? Was he really thinking of giving it all up just for the chance to step into the sun again? His knee barely let him walk on a good day, and managing the winding steps down the mountain path had been a painful and time-consuming ordeal. If he were being truthful, Talo doubted he had much time left before he'd have to choose between Carro casting a permanent splint over his leg, or be satisfied with a life lived from his ass, which would be planted firmly on his bed.

"I think it's something to think about another time," he said after a while, turning to look at Carro. "For now we have more pressing matters to attend to before we can worry about any of mine."

"Unfortunately," Carro said sourly. "I've heard of this Quin Tern, Talo. I know you dealt with his father a long time ago, but between what you've told me of him and what I've gathered of his son, they are as far apart as can be."

"Markus was a good man, despite his decisions," Talo replied with a nod. "He was fairly easily swayed away from the temptations of the coin the Arena was bringing in, and even became an advocate for the shutting down of others when he realized Azbar could stand on its own two feet without the fights."

"Which would make his son the black to his white," Carro said insistently. "This is not a man to see reason unless it can be counted and spent. I understand that the towns suffered much this past freeze, but if *half* the things I've heard from the Azbar temple are true, then storms were less a reason and more an opportunity for Tern. He *leapt* at the chance to reopen the Arena. You'd think a decision like that, made by a rational man, would at least merit some period of contemplation."

"Unfortunately, the reality is that most of these are not 'rational' men," Talo responded, pushing aside an overhanging branch with his staff and ducking beneath it as he passed. "Of all the people I dealt with the first time we took on the Arenas, Markus Tern was probably the most level-headed. Did it surprise me? Not in the least. Anyone who plays any sort of hand in the popularization of such carnage is a different kind of person, Carro. *I* was a different kind of person. You have to have an appreciation for the violence to enjoy the fights, so you'll pardon me if I say you'd best stay clear of the stadium once we reach Azbar."

"Not a problem," Carro said quickly, his face abruptly green. It was an amusing air, contrasting the man's bulk and beaded blond beard that made him look so much like one of the savage mountain clansmen. Despite his tough exterior, the Priest had never had much of a stomach when it came to blood.

"It makes you the better man," Talo said. "If the council was so eager to jump on board with Tern and risk crossing the Laorin by going against the ban, then they will be a mix of the same kind of people."

"Then how are we going to deal with them?"

Talo sighed. "Unfortunately, the answer to that question is 'any way we can.' I'd love to think at least some of those responsible will be close enough to faith to hear reason in a discussion with Priests, but sometimes they are simply too far gone. From there it's negotiations, arguments, compromise… I wasn't short of bribing and threatening in my younger days, but I had a name amongst those people then."

"You don't think they'll remember the Lifetaker?"

Talo's breath caught short, and he tensed.

"A title I'd as soon forget, Carro, if you please."

"Unwise," the Priest said, stepping his horse around the glassy surface of a wide puddle as they came to a curve in the road. "If we are returning to a world you left, you'd best be prepared for what you're going to find under the cobwebs, handsome. Should we end up facing off with them directly, it may serve some use if these men have an idea who you were, and may at least shield you against insults some are undoubtedly going to throw our way."

Talo was silent for a time.

"Lifetaker," he spat quietly. "I was so *proud* of that name once, can you imagine that? The irony… Did you know I used to despise the Priests and Priestesses who would come around every summer, trying to spread the good word of Laor? I ran a fair share of them out of the town myself. Even Kal a time or two. It's the reason I took the name. Just to spite them and their 'life-giving' god."

"You said it yourself: you are no longer that man," Carro insisted, reaching out again to touch his partner's shoulder as they crossed a shallow riverbed, their mounts' iron shoes clopping over the old stonework of the narrow bridge beneath them. "You are far changed and far come. The Talo Brahnt I know has nothing shared with the Talo Brahnt of the past, as anyone who knows you now can attest to."

He swept an arm around, motioning to the Arocklen's trees.

"Look at this place," he persisted. "Would the man you were half a century ago have been able to be here now, enjoying a conversation with a one such as me?"

Talo grunted.

"Laughable," he said.

"*Exactly.*" Carro smiled. "I know you've long since come to terms with what you were and what you've done. The weight of the good you've worked for the people of this world heavily outdoes the burden of the pain you wrought. There is nothing left of the Lifetaker in you, so accept the fact that his name might serve, and realize it won't drag you back to a place you would rather never return to."

"You're too wise for a man your age," Talo said, reaching out to shove the Priest teasingly as their horses got too close again. "Anybody ever tell you that?"

"They have," Carro said, raising an eyebrow. "Twenty or thirty years ago, when it was true."

The two men shared a laugh at that, then rode on in silence, appreciating the merciful weather as the winding road continued its misshapen path south through the Woods.

VIII

"It is a wise man who avoids entangling himself in circumstances he knows little of. There are unfortunate situations in which it is a necessary risk, but these moments are few and far between, and as dangerous as they are rare. Not knowing is to not be prepared, and to not be prepared is to barrel headlong into moments in life better avoided."

—Jarden Arro, Champion of the Arro clan

Azbar was unlike any place Raz had ever laid eyes on. Many of the fringe cities of the South were surrounded by walls on all sides, but those were built of plastered mud and brick, mending their innate weaknesses with sheer bulk. Azbar's walls were made of mortared stone blocks, darkened by lichen and time, and were half again as tall as even Miropa's defenses had been. Ovate bastion towers stood every hundred-and-fifty paces along the line, their monolithic forms stuck aggressively out from the wall into the quarter-mile stretch of open field that partially ringed the town, each topped with a heavy dark banner embossed with the crossed antlers and sword that could only be the city's emblem. As if that weren't enough, the place was cleverly built with its back to a sheer cliff, a great ravine cut out of the earth by a rushing river that still flowed several hundred feet below. A smaller tributary ran straight through the community, bisecting it, and fell off the ridge in a misty waterfall Raz had made out from miles away as they'd crested a clear hill barely an hour's walk from their destination.

Now that they were practically at the gates, though, Raz couldn't help but gape at everything else laid out before him.

Azbar was less town and more metropolis, a city hidden in the woods. It was built along sloping earth, so even a hundred paces from the wall, Raz, Arrun, and Lueski could see much of the place, peaking at a steep cliff that hung out and over the canyon. A great stone-and-timber mansion of some kind was the only building at the top of this tall protrusion, almost foreboding in the way it looked out over the rest of the town.

"The town hall," Arrun told Raz, following his eyes to the singular building in the distance. "At least technically."

"Technically?" Raz asked, tearing his eyes away from the place as he shifted the heavy sack he had gathered up in his left hand. As they'd entered their final few miles, he'd freed Ahna from the straps, wanting to be prepared for anything on their approach

He'd sworn the siblings their safety, and he intended to stick by that promise.

"The Chairman uses it as his personal estate," Arrun answered, making sure Lueski's hand was held tight in his as they continued their approach on the gate. "He's taken up residence there, and no one tries to stop him. They're too afraid of the pit."

"Sounds like a charming man," Raz muttered under his breath, pulling his hood up to hide his face. His tail was already tucked away and his wings pulled in tight. "Now be quiet. They've seen us."

Sure enough, a figure was peering out over the wall top at them from the ramparts above the wide arch that was the town's southern gate. Raz's sharp ears made out the piercing whine of a warning whistle, and two more heads appeared by the first. They were still too far away to make out what the guards were saying, but soon one of the men nodded, and all three dropped out of sight. At once the iron portcullis, the great grate that blocked off the archway on its outer end, started to lift with the clanking of well-oiled machinery.

"Arrun…" Lueski whispered in fright as five men ducked under the rising gate onto the dirt road, identical longswords belted at their waists, and all attired in matching maroon and brown uniforms. The girl's brother shushed her, though.

Wisely.

"Halt!" one guard—an officer of some kind, judging by the single gold stripe over his left shoulder—called out. "Traveler, you are to state your name and business before proceeding! Also, be advised that you are in the company of two runaways wanted by the town of Azbar's court of law. If you've come to collect on the reward, we will—"

"I've come to make a deal!"

They were close enough now, barely a dozen yards apart, that Raz could see the mixture of surprise and curiosity pass over the faces of the five men as they heard his harsh voice.

"A deal?" the officer demanded. "What kind of deal?"

"I would have Azbar clear the names of my companions," Raz listed, putting a hand out to stop Arrun and Lueski as he continued to move forward, "as well as credit them the remainder of their debt. I want documents drawn up that guarantee their safety and freedom, as well as secure passage out of town at any time they so choose."

There was a roll of laughter from the five guards. Silently Raz thanked the Sun for choosing to shine so brightly at least one last time on that day. None of the men could see his face yet under the hood, even as he kept walking forward.

"And in return you offer what?" the officer asked through a mocking chuckle. "A chunk of the moon and a barrel of bear piss? The cold's getting to your head, stranger! You don't really think the council will—?"

Barely six or seven paces from the group, Raz reached up with his free hand and pulled off his hood.

As one, all five of the guards took a step back, a couple inhaling sharply, eyes wide as they saw his face.

"What in the Lifegiver's name...?" one of the men on the end hissed, shocked.

Raz had partially hoped that luck would favor him again, and that out of the five one might recognize him and caution his companions against a reckless move. Maybe he'd even have been able to manage a fair bargain without resorting to methods he'd rather have avoided if it could be helped...

Not surprisingly, though, like lightning, luck never struck the same place twice.

"Atherian? This far north?" the officer demanded, perplexed. "You're a fair bit mad to come such a ways from your heat, lizard-man. And you speak? I didn't know animals could talk."

"Insults are not recommended, Officer," Raz said simply, narrowing his eyes and extending his neck crest slowly, like the building warning of a rattlesnake. "As for your question: I offer myself to the Arena in place of my two companions."

"Wha—?" a shocked voice erupted from behind him. "No. Raz, you can't—!"

"*Be quiet, Lueski!*" Raz snapped over his shoulder, not taking his eyes off the group in front of him. Lueski shut up. Raz could hear her start to cry again, and he almost sighed in exasperation.

He'd been mulling it over the last two days, contemplating the options as the three of them had been making their way towards Azbar. He had no money to bargain for their life with, all of it having gone towards his escape from Miropa, and even had he kept some significant sum, he wasn't sure what gold crowns were worth to Northerners. His armor and weapons could fetch a fair price, but Raz would lose his head before he let himself part with any of them.

In the end, all he had left to bargain with was himself.

Not to mention there might just be a way to work such a play to his favor, too...

"You?" the officer asked, bravely ignoring Raz's bodily warnings and stepping forward, placing a hand on the crossguard of his blade. "You're big, atherian. But big doesn't necessarily mean you're worth shit in the pit. Nay, we'll take the boy and his sister, and you should be glad we don't just drag you along and throw you to the gladiators for sport."

"Take another *step*," Raz snapped, pointing a clawed finger at a guard who had moved towards Arrun and Lueski at his commander's words, "and I'll tear your eyes from your head and let you wander blind off the edge of the canyon."

The man, apparently a great deal more intelligent than his officer, backed off at once.

"Threatening an enforcer of the law is punishable by a fine of up to a hundred gold, lizard," the officer said gleefully, starting to draw his sword. "Men, take him and—!"

He didn't get to finish his sentence.

Raz—a blur of muscle, scales, and steel—caught the handle of the man's sword with his free hand and set a foot firmly on the guard's chest. Shoving him away, Raz watched the man stumble back, falling and landing hard on his rear.

The sword, though, stayed in Raz's hand.

"GET HIM!" someone yelled, and the other four came at him in a rush.

Predictable to a fault, Raz snorted inwardly.

They were well trained, though, and even as they dashed forward they moved to separate, giving one another the room needed to strike without the risk of lopping each other's arms off. It was a smart move, one that would have forced any other opponent to fight all four of them simultaneously from different sides.

For Raz, though, it just meant his targets were farther apart.

Throwing himself forward, Ahna still resting on his shoulder, Raz rolled under the horizontal slice of the left middle man, landing on one knee directly in front of the surprised end guard.

Shlok-shlok-shtunk!

In less than a second the flat of Raz's stolen sword landed on the outside of both the man's knees, the pommel catching him in the abdomen as he fell. Already turning, Raz leapt to his feet, catching and redirecting the overhead swing of the guard whose strike he'd avoided first. Whipping his blade in rapid circles, dragging his opponent's with it, Raz flicked the steel suddenly. The guard lost control of his weapon, and was still gaping at the blade as it flew through the air towards the gate when two controlled kicks to his stomach and shoulder sent him tumbling to the ground, winded.

The last two, thinking they were catching on, came at him significantly closer together, and Raz finally lifted Ahna from his shoulder. Dropping the borrowed sword, he lunged forward to catch them unprepared, whipping the dviassegai's head in a T-shaped slash, striking both of the men's extended swords with such force that one blade snapped into two pieces, and the other flew out of its owner's hands still ringing. Without bothering to slow down, Raz twisted Ahna so that he held her horizontally in front of him and shoved her haft hard directly into the hips of the two men. As they instinctively curled over the handle, the breath rushing out of their lungs in identical gasps, Raz roared and strained.

Before they knew what was happening, both men were suspended in the air, hooked by their own weight over the weapon's haft as Raz lifted them straight off the ground and held them over his head. His blood-red wings, kept relatively disguised until that moment, flared out to their full extent on either side of him. The guards' faces blanched at the sight of the winged atherian holding them both up in the air without so much as blinking under the effort.

"Take your friends and leave," Raz snarled in their terrified faces. "Then send out someone who isn't a complete waste of my time."

Twisting Ahna to the side, he let the two men fall in a tangled pile on top of each other. At once they scrambled to their feet and bolted for the open gate, completely ignoring their companions, of which only the officer had gotten to his feet. With one last shocked look at Raz's winged form, the man fled as well, disappearing into the safety of the archway.

"If I see or hear more than one person tonight, I'll kill them all!" Raz called after him. "No guards! You hear?"

There was no reply, unless you count the groans and wheezings of the two men still left laid out in the grass, but Raz didn't care. He'd been theatrical this time, but it had been necessary to make his point.

And he was *sure* it had been made.

Tucking his wings back under his fur mantle, Raz dropped Ahna once more onto his shoulder and turned around, making his way back to the two figures still huddled together a short ways down the road.

"Lifegiver's saggy balls… I've never seen anything like that!" Arrun shouted, eyes as wide as fists as Raz approached, just like his sister's. "Where'd you learn to fight like that?"

Raz cuffed him lightly, picking up his sack as he walked past, smirking.

"Watch your mouth around your sister, Arrun," he said semi-jokingly. "And half of that was self-taught, the other half by a man the Moon claimed years ago. Now come on. We're heading back to the tree line until they send someone out."

"He must have been some teacher…" Arrun breathed, pulling Lueski along as he ran after Raz.

That he was, Raz agreed privately, feeling the familiar white wood of Ahna's haft under his palm.

It was almost midnight by the time Azbar's representative finally made their appearance. Raz had left Arrun and Lueski a short ways into the woods, far enough so that the flames of their fire couldn't be seen from the town's walls, but close enough to make out any sign of trouble.

His own camp he'd made up right at the edge of the forest, the light of his fire a distinct beacon of orange and yellow beneath the trees as he heated the last strips of cooked venison from his pack. Arrun had shown him how to bait the deer in close using certain kinds of plants, and they'd managed to spear a small doe with a crude wooden javelin Raz had whittled to a point with his knife.

Meat had never tasted so good.

Azbar was not quick in its response, a fact that surprised Raz considering the elaborate show he'd put on at the town's gates. He worried more than once that the leaders behind the wall were trying to band together a hunting party for his small group, but in the quiet of the night he was fairly confident he would be able to hear the warning cranks of any of the gates if they opened. Therefore, since not once until well past dusk did he make out anything but the crackle of the fire, he relaxed and watched the flames dance, his wrists on his knees as he waited.

Finally, several hours after a bright half-Moon started her arch through the clear night sky—attended by Her Stars much further south in the sky that Raz was accustomed to—he heard the portcullis lift in the distance and the hoofbeats of a single horse approaching. A minute or so later the rider came to a halt, pulling the horse to a stop just outside the light of the flames as the mount whinnied.

"I'll admit," Raz called out from his seated place by the fire, not bothering to look up, "I expected to hear from someone sooner."

"Apologies for the delay, Master Arro," a woman's calm voice responded, and there was the thump of boots on earth as she dismounted. "As is with any important decision in a community as large as ours, it required some deliberation."

The speaker stepped into the light then, pulling off her leather rider's gloves as she did. Tall for a woman, she was of moderate build with a fit, muscular figure obvious even beneath the layers of cloth and fur she wore to fend off the returning cold. Her hair was black as the night around her, like Lueski's, but streaked with stripes of gray and white, and Raz realized the woman was not so young as to be expected to calmly meet a stranger who had just bested five of Azbar's trained guard without so much as a drop of drawn blood. Her skin was creased around her eyes, and she held herself with a bearing that spoke of a hard life well handled, hawklike green eyes taking in Raz's reptilian face without missing a beat.

"Join me," he said, motioning to the other side of the fire. The woman nodded her thanks, accepting the offer. As she sat, Raz noticed something else: a scar, barely missing her right eye as it curved out and around it, angling inward again to stop at her upper lip. It left her with an ugly, tugged half smile that marred what otherwise might have been an attractive face.

It was the kind of scar only a blade could make…

"So you've figured out my name," Raz said, ignoring his budding curiosity about his strange visitor.

"We have," the woman replied with another nod, holding her hands to the fire to warm them, eyes on the flames. "A group of our bounty hunters returned yesterday absent their leader. One tried to feed us some rambling story of how they'd somehow managed to run into a Southern legend in the middle of the Northern forests."

"You should thank the man. He can consider himself the only reason he and the others didn't suffer the same ending as Boar, or whatever his name was."

"Chairman Tern doesn't reward returning without promised captives," the woman said simply. "The only reason the remaining hunters weren't thrown into the pit was because they had valuable information regarding you."

"I hope your Chairman took the time to gather more than what *they* could tell you," Raz said with a humorless chuckle. "Otherwise, you don't really have much to go on."

"You're a former hired sword for the Southern underworld," the woman said at once, her eyes flicking up suddenly to his face. "You broke off your partnership, though we aren't aware why, and went on a spree that left well over a hundred dead and innumerable wounded. You're running, and there are a dozen different rewards offered from any given city for shipping your head back to the South in a basket."

She's testing me, Raz realized, staring the woman down coolly. *What manner of messenger is this…?*

"I would be interested in finding out how, exactly, you know all this," Raz responded nonchalantly, allowing his scaled tail to curl closer to the warmth of the fire, "but otherwise, yes. You are correct. What else do you know?"

"The rest is all boring history," she responded with a convincing shrug, but her eyes never left his. "Something about a lizard-kind infant found in the desert and raised by men. Then of a family butchered in their sleep, their homes burned to the ground with the living still inside. In all honesty it sounds like a bad bedtime story, though, doesn't it?"

The cold night air seemed to swallow Raz whole as he stared across the rippling dance of the flames, meeting the woman's gaze. He wasn't surprised by what she knew, honestly. It wasn't hard to piece together that messages, probably sent by bird, had likely beaten him north, warranting his arrest or execution. From there it was likely the bounty hunter Shrith who had filled in the details. Raz's history was common knowledge to most anyone who'd spent any amount of time in the fringe cities of the Cienbal.

Still, it was some small shock to have his past find him so quickly here, in this new world…

"You've no words for me?"

Raz blinked, then cursed silently. The woman was still watching him, her face immobile, but he could tell that she was getting something from the pause in their conversation. She was clever, this one. Dangerously clever. He could only hope she'd deduced that the silence meant Raz was capable of deep thought as much as the next man.

Regardless, he didn't have the patience for games at the moment.

"What use would words be when you already seem to have all there is to know?" Raz asked after a moment. "You seem happy enough figuring it all out on your own, after all. Tell me, were you ordered to come piece together the puzzle that is Raz i'Syul Arro, or is this just an annoying pastime of yours?"

It was the woman's turn to blink, and Raz smiled inwardly.

"Oh, was I not supposed to know?" he asked with false concern. "Do most men not see it, or is it that you're out of practice? Because if you know so much about me, you'd realize I've spent enough time in shady places to perceive pretty quick when people are trying to figure me out for their own devices."

There was another silence, this time not on Raz's account.

"They don't see it," the woman responded finally, straightening up, her eyes no longer boring into him. "But I suppose it's to be expected with your reputation. I apologize again. As Doctore, it's my responsibility to assure that—"

"As what?" Raz cut in.

"Of course," the woman said in realization. "You wouldn't know…"

After a second's hesitation, she stood up. Crossing her right fist over her heart, she gave a small bow towards Raz, speaking as she did.

"I am Alyssa Rhen, Doctore of the Azbar Arena, handler of the gladiators that compete within. I manage the discipline and training of the fighters deemed worth keeping in good health, and prepare them as best I can for the pit. It is my honor and obligation to supply satisfying entertainment for the crowds."

"Ah," Raz said slowly, cocking his head to the side and speaking with a venomous dose of sarcasm. "So *you're* the bitch who teaches men how to slaughter the helpless. Bravo, madam. You've successfully earned my utmost respect."

Rhen's jaw clenched at the pointed insult.

"I'd heard you were strangely honor-bound," she said, crossing her arms as she looked over the fire at him. "But then again, the whole phrase used to describe you also included the term 'insane,' so I hope you understand if I tell you I wasn't really sure what to make of it. Would it be so hard to convince you that there are others who share your distaste of the Arena, no matter how close they might seem to it?"

"It would," Raz growled. "Don't feed me your bullshit, woman. Or maybe you still think I'm an idiot? Your comfort around someone like me? Your scar? The manner in which you hold yourself and the fact that you are master of a group of trained, proven fighters? There is only one way the gladiators you discipline hold enough respect for you to heed *your* words, a woman of your age."

He lifted a hand, pointing directly at her chest.

"You were one of them, once. And a damn good one, if I'm not mistaken."

"You are clever, aren't you, Master Arro?" the woman drawled. "Although that deduction could have been made by a beggar sick in the head. Yes, I fought once as well, years ago before the Laorin shut down the Arenas in the first place. And yes, I was good. Does that necessarily mean I still approve of the way they are run?"

Raz was silent. Then he decided to give her a chance.

"Explain," he said shortly, sitting back on his hands.

Rhen knelt by the fire. "The code of ideals upon which the Arenas were first built some three hundred years ago was far different from the code they follow now. Back then, the pit was a method of dealing judgment and assigning punishment. Everything but minor disputes were handled with fists or blades, depending on the severity of the issue, and the victor of the fight was deemed blessed by the Stone Gods—older deities whose faiths have mostly died out, except in the tribes—and was awarded his demands by a jury of spectators. The system was not without its faults, but, when controlled, the Arenas kept a good balance in places where law and order were often thought of as things you needed to look somewhere else to find."

She picked up a burning stick from the fire, watching it go out and following the wafting smoke upwards into the dark.

"The first problems occurred when bets started being made on the outcomes of the trials," she continued. "Few were ever on a jury at once—maybe eight or nine selected individuals at most—but the winner and loser of the fight were always announced to the public. It made gambling easy. From there, you can imagine how the problem grew. The curious and wealthy started bribing the town council to grant them position on the juries so they could watch the fights. Then other seats started being sold, advertised as 'witness slots.' After that it wasn't long before the system grew into what it is today: a source of entertainment for people whose lives see too much hardship to find excitement in anything but brutality and blood."

"So you're claiming you were around when the Arenas still had some dignity left in them?" Raz asked her skeptically.

Rhen laughed. "Laor knows, no," she told him, shaking her head. "If the ledgers are at all accurate, the Arenas barely made it half a century before becoming what they are today. Believe it or not, I'm not *that* old."

Raz was somewhat pleased to hear the humor in her voice—otherwise nothing but business until that moment—but he didn't show it.

"Then you've yet to tell me how this makes you anything but the murdering hag I'm itching to think of you as," he said, plastering a false smile over his alien features.

"Oh, murdering hag I am many times over," Rhen said with a harsh laugh. "I might give your body count a run for its money, in fact, and I promise there is more innocent blood on my hands than on yours."

Raz's smile faded, and his neck crest pricked upward slowly.

"Then, *Doctore*, I challenge you to give me one good reason *not* to add your name to my ever-growing list. And don't try too hard, please. The more I listen to you talk, the more I feel we have less to discuss than you seem to claim. And I get bored quickly."

"My reason, Raz i'Syul Arro, is that if you struck out to eliminate every person who has ever made poor decisions in their life, you would find yourself alone in an empty world when you were done, with your blade at your own throat."

Raz paused at that, and the woman continued.

"Time," she said, waving upwards at the passing Moon. "Time is my one reason, and much of it has passed since my years as a champion of the crowd. I was a young woman then, and hungry for many things, though not what was generally expected of me. Instead of a husband or home, I wanted strength and glory. Instead of seeking an apprenticeship under a baker or basket weaver, I sought to feed myself through the winnings I made in the pit. It wasn't unheard of for a woman to partake in the fights, not even for one to become a successful gladiator, but no one had come through the Arena with my skills in living memory. It made it hard to stop, and I likely wouldn't have, had I not received this."

She traced the scar along her right cheek with a finger.

"It was the first time I think I ever realized I could die at any moment. Even if I was better, faster, and smarter than my opponents, they could always get lucky or I could get unlucky. As soon as the physician stitched me up, I announced my retirement from the fights. The Chairman at the time, though, Markus Tern, knew I had nowhere to go, and he offered me the position of Doctore and a place in his home until I found my own."

For the briefest of moments, Raz thought he saw the woman's harsh face soften with something close to sadness.

Then it was gone.

"It was the middle of the freeze, and I had little choice," she kept on. "Still, he could have left me to die in the snow, but he didn't. Why, though, I have no idea. I always got the sense that Tern had a hidden distaste for the Arena that he didn't share because of how it bolstered Azbar's economy. He didn't come to the games much—particularly any of the fights involving women—and when he did he never joined in the cheering. I didn't think he held much respect for me. I don't blame him, though… It was years before *I* could even respect myself."

"What do you mean?"

Raz admitted it to himself: he was intrigued. This was not a woman pouring her soul out to some stranger. He had only to take one look at Alyssa Rhen to get the sense that she was a stoic person, one who likely disliked the idea of talking when *doing* was an option.

Which meant that she had a point, if she was divulging this much to him…

"I mean," the Doctore replied, "that it all caught up to me one day."

She was silent then. For a long moment the woman sat, watching the fire with distant eyes. Raz didn't interrupt her thoughts. He knew well the signs of a mind reliving past actions, considering he was more often a victim of it than most.

"I woke up one day," the woman continued eventually, "and every face of every person I had ever killed was suspended between each of my thoughts. I could see them watching me, even when there was nothing there, and for the first time in my life I looked back and realized what I had done…"

Another silence. Rhen's face was still, and she hadn't taken her eyes off the fire.

Then, all at once, she seemed to break free. Her face grew hard again, and she looked back up at Raz, who was still studying her silently from across the flames.

"In short, it took me a long time to come to terms with myself," she said quickly, as though eager to wrap up the story. "The woman you see before you is what came out the other side. I can stand the fights now. There was a time when they made me sick and I had to put up a front for my fighters just so they wouldn't turn on me. That's gone, but it doesn't mean the way I feel has changed."

"Then why did you stay?" Raz asked her curiously. "Why are you still here?"

"Markus," Rhen responded at once. "The Chairman gave me everything, kept me alive when I would have been done for. I owe him."

"Not anymore you don't, assuming he's dead, since another—I'm assuming his son?—is in control of his seat."

"I owe his name," Rhen said. "I owe it to him to see Quin through whatever trials he brings upon himself, no matter how much of an ass the man is. A child growing into something further from his father, I have never seen."

"Fine," Raz replied, waving the discussion away. "Then I only have one more question. If you dislike the fights as much as you claim to, even if you won't leave your position, then why would you add more to the mix? Why would you take Arrun and Lueski?"

"If those two were what the town wanted, I wouldn't have bothered coming personally. The Chairman would have sent a regiment of guards out after you instead, considering you seem unwilling to part with the pair, but I'd bet my horse you'd be gone before they got close enough to figure out where you were hiding them. No… I'm here to discuss the terms of your deal."

"Ah," Raz said with a humorless smile. "Now I understand. Doctore, trainer of gladiators, here to get a feel of what she might have to work with."

Alyssa Rhen smiled.

"Exactly."

IX

"Foolish boy, you'll be the death of me. I should have had you beaten as a child. Maybe then you'd have grown up a decent man."

—Markus Tern, Azbar council Chairman

"You're sure this is a good idea?"

Quin Tern laughed, his pudgy jowls bouncing as he plucked a fresh frostberry from the bowl on the balustrade by his elbow. Popping it into his mouth, he picked up another and tossed it to Azzeki Koro, who caught it. The Captain-Commander of the Azbar guard stood beside the Chairman, looking out over the midnight horizon from the front palisade of the town hall estate. At the edge of the firelight-dotted hill that was the walled town, they could make out the indistinct shouting of the south gate guard yelling back and forth to each other.

"No, I'm not," the Chairman managed to get out between sucking the bitter juice from his thick fingers, each well adorned with at least one silver- or gold-set ring. "Call it a calculated risk."

"If the bounty hunter is right—"

"Let's hope he is." Tern smiled gleefully. "Can you imagine? Think of the notice, the attention. It's a shame the lizard had to show up on the brink of the freeze. Still, I'll bet you a thousand gold we'll have people coming from all over the North to see him!"

They could make out the metallic clanking of chains and the keen of protesting wood now, and though they couldn't see it, the two men knew the distant gates had been lifted.

Alyssa had returned from her errand in the woods.

And by the looks of the flaring trail of candle- and firelight as shop and homeowners threw open their doors and windows, she hadn't come home empty-handed.

Spitting the pale berry seeds out over the side of the porch, Tern stepped back towards the warmth of the building.

"Wake the council. It's time we go meet our guests."

Raz felt as though he was being paraded, like a sideshow in some freakish caravan. It wasn't an unfamiliar feeling. He could still remember how he'd been a major source of attraction the first few times his parents had allowed him within the walls of the Southern cities, how people had flocked to their camp and stalls to catch a glimpse of the "tame lizard."

Still, that had been out of necessity. Agais Arro had decided it would be safer for the world to know Raz existed rather than attempt to hide him and let the desert-folk speculate on their own.

This, though… this was something else.

Despite the late hour as they made their way up the winding cobbled street—Rhen in front, leading her horse by the reins—people were peering out at them from every open door and cracked window. Refusing to meet any of their curious gazes, Raz pulled his hood a little further over his head, hiding his face completely.

It irritated him, this little charade. It was just past midnight when the Doctore had led them into town under the pretense of wanting their arrival to be kept quiet, but clearly word had spread. Arrun and Lueski, huddled together a little to the side and in front of him, were certainly a source of fascination all their own in this unprecedented voluntary return. Still, Raz doubted the siblings were the reason so many of Azbar's citizens were wide awake when by all rights the town should have been dark and quiet. Judging by the lack of surprise from their escorts—a handful of officers uniformed in the same maroon and brown as the gate guard from the previous afternoon—Raz couldn't quite bring himself to believe the Chairman had ever intended their entry into town to be quiet.

Thoroughly annoyed, Raz distracted himself by taking in Azbar itself, looking around and marveling once again at the contrast this new world had to the one he'd left just weeks ago.

There were no mud-brick huts here, as far as he could tell. Granted, he doubted their retinue were taking them anywhere near the poor quarters of the town for the sake of advertising their presence to the right people, but even so. The buildings were solid timber and stone, decorated with wood carvings and simple pebble murals. Moss clung to walls and hugged the jagged lips of slated rooftops. Thin smoke from a few late-night fires furled here and there out of short chimneys. Evergreens towered above them in places where the space between structures allowed them to grow, making it feel like they'd never truly left the woods. Even the cobblestones beneath their feet were patched with narrow grass. Raz soon forgot about the eyes staring at him from every direction, half-hidden behind shutters and cracked doors. He was lost in that feeling again, that splendid revelation of discovery, opening his mouth to taste the crisp Northern night air.

This place… This place is wonderful…

Ahead of him, Arrun turned his head to look over his shoulder.

"What are you staring at?"

"Everything." Raz dropped his gaze to look down at him. "This town… I've never seen anything like it."

Arrun nodded but didn't reply. He had one arm wrapped around his sister's narrow shoulders, eyeing every unlit corner as though half expecting someone to jump out at them, rattling chains and leather bindings. Lueski seemed even more terrified, and as he watched the pair, Raz heard her whimper and duck even closer to her brother.

It made him sad, this contrast between their feelings and his own. Raz couldn't help his spirits from dampening a little as he turned his head to look around again. Somewhere out there, hidden in the twilight shadows of what to him was this magnificent fairy-tale city in the woods, something much darker slumbered. It wasn't just Arrun and Lueski that he felt the fear radiate from. The people, too, now that he looked, were watching their little party with mixed parts curiosity and fright, ducking away from the torchlight as it crept over them, only to poke their heads out again once they'd passed.

And here we thought we'd be getting a chance at a fresh start, huh, sis?

Ahna bumped up and down on his shoulder with each step, and Raz frowned again, watching a mother shoo her two young girls away from the open door. She glanced back at the guardsmen in fright before shutting it with a snap.

It all reminded him too much of the broken souls and ragweed-wasted street runners of the South. To find that same fear here, in this fresh green world… It was disheartening.

They walked for twenty minutes or so, following the road Raz quickly realized must have been the main thoroughfare from the south gate to the center of town. Sure enough, not long after his toes had started to go numb from the coolness of the stones beneath their feet, the streets opened up and split into a wide ring. In its center, abruptly visible from where it had been hiding against the dark sky, a great stone structure towered towards the heavens.

"Sun take me," Raz hissed, tilting his head back to look up.

The Arena was a colossal thing. At least eight stories high, it towered so far above most of the town Raz couldn't think how he had possibly missed it when they'd first seen Azbar sprawling across its hill from a distance. There were no carvings or murals here. The walls were weather stained and worn, and somewhere in the back of his mind Raz noted that Rhen had not been lying about the age of the place. It had the look of a giant who'd withstood many beatings from the elements and still held strong to withstand many more. Wide stone arches ringed every few floors, and he made a mental note to climb to the top if he could, and look out over horizon. Maybe he'd better understand the lushness of this cold land if he could take it all in as a whole.

"No! No!"

Raz looked away from the soaring walls of the Arena to find Lueski hugging her brother so close it was hard to tell them apart in the flickering of the torchlight. He was about to ask what was going on when he realized that Rhen was busy tying her horse to a hitching post at the bottom of a wide set of stairs leading up to a vaulted tunnel entryway.

Ahna was in Raz's hands in a blur, his armor-filled pack crashing to the ground at his feet.

"What are you playing at?" he demanded, stepping forward so that he was between Arrun and Lueski and the majority of their escort. "I warned you, woman. I'd think twice of crossing me."

"I assure you I'm playing no game, Master Arro." The Doctore raised her hands disarmingly. "You had terms, and I intend to see them held. But to do so, you'll have to meet with the Chairman, who"—she indicated the Arena behind her and continued with surprising distaste—"has requested you sit down with him here."

Behind him, Raz could hear Lueski start to cry into her brother's chest.

"Bastard," Arrun snarled under his breath.

"Quiet," Raz told him without looking back, his eyes not leaving Rhen as he addressed her again. "If Tern desires a meeting with me, he can come out here. I won't have Arrun and Lueski set a foot in this place."

The Doctore opened her mouth to respond, but Raz cut her off.

"That was not an offer for negotiations," he growled, tightening his grip on Ahna threateningly.

There was a tense moment in which the woman took Raz in with an intensity he had yet seen. She looked less than accustomed to taking orders, but seemed to realize he wasn't about to be moved on the subject. After a second, she finally nodded.

"Beck." She spoke to the officer nearest to her. "Tell the Chairman that Master Arro wishes to meet outside the Hall. And be quick about it."

The man took the steps two at a time before hurrying through the gloomy tunnel, the torch in his hand lighting it up like some great fire-breathing maw for a few brief seconds. Then the light vanished, and the rest of the group was left to wait, Raz never shifting from his place in front of the siblings, his eyes traveling over each of their guard one at a time. Either the men hadn't believed the story of his little exposition at the gates earlier that day, or they somehow thought it was beyond them. They met his gaze levelly, unflinching, one after the other. It was an unfamiliar reaction, almost impressive. He wasn't used to such defiance.

Brave little fools, aren't they, Ahna?

It was a few minutes before Beck returned. The officer stopped at the top of the steps, torch held high, so that their shadows formed long trails behind them.

"The Chairman says he will meet the atherian in the high box, but that he does not insist on the company of the Koyt brother and sister. They can wait here."

"Like I would let you—!" Raz began, but it was Rhen's turn to interrupt him.

"Master Arro will meet him," she called up to the officer before looking back at Raz. "I will vouch for the children's safety."

Raz hesitated. Ahna was still at the ready, hefted in both hands, but as he met the Doctore's keen eyes he sensed that same honor and respect he'd made out in the woman when they'd first met around the campfire.

"I have your word?"

Rhen nodded.

Raz hesitated. Then, deciding, he relaxed, tossing Ahna back over his shoulder. Turning around, he looked down at Arrun.

"Will you be alright?"

"Not much choice," the boy snorted. Then he nodded. "Aye, we'll manage till you get back. Watch your ass, though."

"And you watch my bag," Raz replied over his shoulder, already heading for the stairs.

He'd just taken his first step up when Beck blocked his way, hand on the cross guard of his sword.

"Your weapons," he said sharply. "You can leave them here."

Though he was two steps above him, the officer still had to look up a little to meet Raz's eyes. This fact seemed to hammer in some sort of realization, because he suddenly looked much less confident in himself as Raz's neck crest twitched and spread a fraction above his head.

"Doctore," Raz hissed without looking away from the man. "May I have permission to demonstrate to your men why it's never—and I do mean *never*—a good idea to get in my way?"

"That won't be necessary," Rhen said quickly. "Beck, stand down."

"I don't take orders from you," the man spat at her, clearly attempting to salvage what little composure he could.

"You do if you want to live," she snapped right back. "Let him keep his blades. The Chairman has his own guards already posted, and Azzeki is with him. Stand *down*."

These facts, coupled with the subtle urgency in her voice, seemed to get through to the officer. After a pause he let go of his hilt and stepped aside.

"Smart man," Raz growled sarcastically, brushing past him.

He didn't bother with a torch. Enough light was left from the town and the Moon above for him to see by just fine, even through the gloom. He crested the stairs and stepped into the tunnel, instinctively searching the shadows of the archways on either side of him.

As he did, Raz realized that the space was, in fact, less a passage than an elongated chamber, widening outward from the entrance until the ceiling above was so high and dark even he had difficulty making it out. Life-sized sculptures of greened iron and rough bronze lined the walls every few yards, postured atop stone pedestals and depicting men and women in different combat stances holding aloft all manner of weapons and shields. Their names were etched in wooden plaques that hung below their feet, and—suddenly realizing he had no idea if the written word of the North was anything like the Southern dialects he'd grown up with—Raz took a step towards the nearest of these. The metal woman was kneeling, the bow in her arms drawn to its fullest extent at some distant target, her chest and legs strapped with light armor. The letters below her boots were slightly varied, with more accents and stresses than he was accustomed to, but with some measure of relief Raz found he had little trouble making out the words.

Serëna Aymon, he read silently, *Queen of Arrows. Retired: 613v.S.*

He paused, taking the figure in, admiring the work for a moment before moving on to the next one. It depicted a tall, lithe man in a ribbed helm, arm drawn back in preparation to launch the long javelin gripped firmly in his hand.

Buron Heys. Death: 676v.S.

They continued like this all the way till the end. The name, their title if they had one, and the dates they'd retired or died. Evëna Uthrah, the Ax Maiden. Garrot Gros. Sylar Kern, Retribution. One by one Raz passed the former greats of the Arena, taking them in. They filled the room with a sense of impressive intimidation, and he could understand the buzz the crowds must have felt pouring through the hall on fight days.

He paused when he reached the last sculpture, its base barely two paces from the bottom of a steep stairway that led back up into the night. This one was strange. There was no plaque to be found, and the statue itself seemed to have been partially demolished. Where once a triumphant figure might have stood, there was nothing left but a pair of legs cut off just below the knee, revealing the hollow metal mold. The sandaled feet appeared to be crushing what looked like the skulls of a half-dozen men and women, all empty and vanquished. With no plaque there was no name, but it seemed someone—or perhaps several someones over time—had carved something into the stone at the base of the skulls. Reaching out and running a claw through the grooves, Raz made out the word.

"Lifetaker," he said aloud.

He pondered what had happened to the sculpture for a moment, but shrugged the curiosity away. The chamber was fascinating, he admitted to himself, and he would have to make it a point to come back in the day to see the statues in their full glory, but he had more important things to take care of before he could satisfy any of the questions this Northern city was enticing in him. Leaving the iron heroes behind, he hurried up the stairs, hugging his furs close against the returning winds.

The vast interior of the Arena was even more impressive than its exterior, illuminated by the Moon hanging like a lantern in the dark sky high above. Raz had emerged onto a small flat pavilion along the bottom of sloped stands built straight into the stone. Decorative arches—more than a handful falling apart under the weight of time—topped the highest seats like a great crown encircling the entire structure. Tattered banners hung between these, those that he could still make out bearing the crossed antlers and sword of Azbar. Raz could see in his mind's eye ten thousand men and women, all on their feet, clapping or jeering or roaring their approval.

And, directly in front of him, nothing but a heavy chain supported on iron rods blocked him from stepping off the edge of the high sloped walls that ringed a wide circular patch of uneven dark earth.

The pit was a filthy, sodden thing. It was trampled and uneven, with patches that formed puddles of dirty water here and there. The walls were stained with muddy splatters, and there were grooves and whole chunks missing from the stone where blades and heavier things had smashed against them. A dozen small braziers hung on narrow chains all around the ring, snuffed now but undoubtedly ablaze for warmth and light when fights were being held. The winds abated for a moment, and suddenly Raz could taste the iron reek in the air. He wondered how much blood of how many men, women, and children could be churned up into that damp earth.

Then he wondered how many of the streaks and handprints on the walls weren't mud at all…

A flicker caught his eye, and Raz looked across the pit to see bright firelight illuminating a large covered pavilion that stuck out above and over the opposite stands. Shadows flickered against the canopy, and he turned and started making his way towards the light, climbing the stands as he did. It wasn't long before he could make out the strong smell of cooked meat, well mixed with the bouquet of fruits and warm bread. Chattering voices and laughter picked up when the winds died again for a second, and Raz even heard the sweet thrum of a lyre plying its way through the conversations.

When he was halfway up the stands and level with the high box, Raz paused, taking in the scene. A dozen or so men were seated on lavish chairs and benches around a massive fire contained in a rectangular metal trough. Dressed in fine furs and thick clothes, they seemed to be guffawing at the antics of an oddly attired character twirling around them. He looked like one of the street performers Raz had so often encountered in his old life, all flourish, with colorfully striped pants and shoes, and a shirt that was laughably too large for his thin frame.

The jester was dancing and boasting a story with exaggerated gestures to the tune of the lyre, but Raz drowned him out. Instead he took in the other men, noticing as he did yet another group. Beyond the light of the fire, tucked against the back wall, a solid line of guardsmen stood shoulder to shoulder, bearing silent witness to the scene. Taking a quick count, Raz tallied a minimum of ten that he could see.

"At least someone seems to be taking us seriously," Raz muttered, thumbing Ahna's whitewood haft. "But I guess they couldn't all be fools, could they?"

As he spoke, one of the guard broke off from the wall and approached a laughing man sitting in his own great chair, a wide fur-covered throne, directly at the head of the fire. He was an atrociously fat figure, with bouncing jowls and thick fingers that sparkled with jeweled rings. His blond hair was long and well kept, giving him an almost girlish look, and he nodded when the guard bent to speak in his ear before waving him away.

Quin Tern, Raz decided, was as unpleasant on the outside as he was likely rotten on the in.

Satisfied, Raz started moving again. It took a minute or two more to get all the way around the ring, and he paused one last time to check that his gladius, ax, and knife were all within easy reach in case things turned sour.

Then he stepped under the alcove, and the lyre struck a poor note before stopping dead.

X

Not a soul moved under the firelit canopy. Only the cracking wood in the trough and the cold wind held barely at bay by the flames made a sound. Every face was turned to look at Raz, more than one of them barely masking a healthy dose of fear. He met every gaze impassively. Only when he finally saw movement in the corner of his eye did he speak.

"Chairman." He addressed the man he'd deduced to be Tern. "Tell your guard to keep their weapons sheathed and their hands where I can see them. I assure you, if I wanted any of you dead you'd already be so, but I'm not opposed to another demonstration if they insist on it."

Tern didn't look away for a second, as though sizing Raz up to assess if there was more to him than the seven feet of muscle and steel. Raz was a little surprised to see something more than greedy gluttony in the man's gaze. There was intelligence there, a cold edge of intellect he'd seen before.

Tern's blue eyes held the same cunning look about them as Ergoin Sass' had…

"Azzeki," Tern finally spoke, looking around at the dark-skinned man in the shadows, whose hand had drifted down to the hilt of his thin blade. "Calm yourself. I doubt Master Arro is here to cause us any harm."

He turned back to Raz, indicating a wide log seat at his right hand, covered in what seemed to be wolf pelts.

"Please. Sit."

Raz accepted, taking his place by the fire. He rested Ahna's pointed tip against the stone between his feet, tucking her between his crossed arms.

"We have terms to discuss."

Tern blinked. Then he started to laugh, the others joining him at once as though on cue.

"Right to it, I see!" the man exclaimed, still chuckling, reaching out to punch Raz's shoulder like they were old friends. "Calm down, man. Calm down. Let me introduce you to our town council first! This is Mâgus Vyn"—he indicated a thin man with a pale-blond beard in reddish furs at his left. "He owns and maintains the majority of the inns throughout our good city. And beside him is Eles Terovel, who has been—"

"You'll learn very quickly, Chairman, that I don't give two shits about details that don't pertain to me or my intent."

Raz let the vulgarity settle in. While he truly cared nothing for who the men were and what they'd done to buy themselves such prestigious positions, he also made it a point to read every one of their faces in the brief moment of shock his interruption provided. Most of them were true trims, timid cowards who flinched, appalled, at his words. A couple, though, were harder men, their faces darkening and their gazes sharpening.

Surprisingly, though, Quin Tern only laughed harder.

"So I've heard, so I've heard," he chuckled finally. "Very well, as you clearly will not be dissuaded." He indicated the rest of the council. "We are listening."

"You've been given my conditions?"

"You made them hard for the poor men of my guard to forget, given how you practically beat it into them."

"I had a point to make."

"And it was well made," Tern nodded. "As for the terms, I think we can come to an agreement. The Koyt siblings will be cleared of their remaining debt, and I will have our scribes draft up the necessary documents guaranteeing their safe passage from the town at any time they choose. In exchange I expect you will—"

"There is one more thing I require."

For the first time since he'd sat down, Raz saw Tern look angry. The fat man masked his face at once, changing it into a politely curious expression, but he couldn't completely hide the hint of frustration from his pudgy creases.

"And what might that be?" he asked in a tone of forced courtesy.

"The immediate release of all your pit fighters convicted of minor crimes, and further guarantee that you will cease to sentence debtors and petty criminals with what you and I both know to be nothing less than a death sentence."

There was the briefest moment of quiet.

And then every man around the fire started talking at once.

"What business of yours is it how we punish—?" the first man Tern had tried to introduce began.

"After we offer you a chance to come to terms? Insulting, I say!" another figure, almost as fat as the Chairman, spoke up from the far corner.

"Out! Get out! We won't have you insulting—!"

"ENOUGH!"

The council fell silent at once. Tern was holding a hand up, and his voice was commanding when he spoke again, further separating him from his appearance.

"I would like to know the reasoning for this request," he continued. "Let him explain."

Raz did not like the man. He had the rank stench of luxury, a mix of sweat and sex and wine, and that nasty edge in his eyes. But, as Tern looked around at him, Raz grudgingly admitted he held some respect for the obese Chairman.

"So please," Tern spoke firmly. "Tell us why we would do this, Master Arro."

"How much have you been offered for my head?" Raz asked at once.

Another sudden quiet.

"How much?" he insisted, looking around at the other councilmen.

"Ah… T-ten thousand Southern crowns," the thickly bearded man on Raz's right stuttered. "Equivalent to slightly more than twelve thousand gold of our own currency."

"And you've sent word to the fringe cities that I am in Azbar?"

"No."

It was Tern who spoke this time. His many chins were resting in the palm of his hand, and he was watching Raz speak with genuine interest.

Apparently this was not a discussion he had anticipated having.

"We thought it best to see what you had to offer us before we made a decision," he sighed, as though unaccustomed to this amount of honesty in a conversation. "Ten thousand crowns is a sum, admittedly, but between admission fees and gambling, the town can make near that amount in a good couple weeks through this Arena."

Tern waved a thick hand out at the darkened stands.

"I am curious, though," he continued, still watching Raz. "Did you think we'd sent birds south?"

"No… But I think you should do so."

To a one, every member of the council looked blankly surprised.

"Do so," Raz repeated. "While the roads aren't completely overtaken by snow. The sooner the better."

"Why would we do that?" asked one of the hard-faced men across the fire. He had two fingers missing from his left hand and looked like he could use the heavy ax that sat against his chair. "More importantly, why would *you* suggest we do that?"

"To bring them here."

It was not one of the council who spoke. Instead the guard Tern had addressed earlier—Azzeki, Raz thought the Chairman had called him—stepped away from the wall into the firelight. He was tall and well built, and for the first time Raz realized he wasn't wearing the standard colors of the Azbar guard, but rather was dressed in light leather armor that had been dyed completely black. Even the rope-bound hilt of the sword at his hip was smoke-blackened. He had dark hair and even darker skin, with pale eyes that glinted in the light as he looked down at Tern.

A Percian, Raz realized, somewhat surprised. *Seems we're not the only outsiders around, are we, sis?*

"The lizard means to bring the bounty hunters here," Azzeki said aloud, though he seemed to be only addressing the Chairman. "He plans on standing his ground, luring them each in turn into fair combat, rather than keep running."

"I'd gathered," Tern responded quietly, watching Raz bristle at the slur. "And please watch your tongue, Azzeki. There's no need to dredge up your personal feelings here."

The soldier didn't respond, instead choosing to stand at attention slightly behind and to the side of Tern's chair, refusing to meet Raz's eyes.

"Excuse Captain-Commander Koro, Master Arro," the Chairman said with a disarming smile. "He has been with us for many years, and yet somehow has not seemed to shake off his old life entirely."

"My kind aren't often seen as more than property where he comes from," Raz said simply, still staring up at the Percian, daring him to look down. "I take no offense, Chairman, though I do hope Azzeki here decides to try his luck at collecting the ten thousand crowns for himself..."

"He *won't*," Tern assured Raz, giving Azzeki an indicative look over his shoulder. "But, as we are back on the subject of your bounty, I would still like to hear this alternative plan of yours. Our method has worked out very well for us thus far and—"

"Your 'method' has left the entirety of your town fearing for its safety," Raz growled, feeling himself grip Ahna's haft in anger. "What's left of it, that is. You're lucky to have come across me in the unique position I am currently in or, I promise you, Chairman, you *would* already be dead. I've cleansed one city of its foulest, and I would be obliged to repeat the endeavor if you continue to tempt me."

The motion was so quick it even took Raz by surprise. He was on his feet in a fraction of a second, towering up to face Azzeki, his gladius hissing from its sheath as Ahna fell to the ground. The dark-skinned man's gaze had finally found his, a curved saber held threateningly before him. As they squared off, each eyeing the other with silent contempt, Raz noticed an utter stillness in the Captain-Commander's form. There was a discipline there, a preparation of mind and body.

Raz realized suddenly that there was vastly more to Azzeki Koro than he might have ever given the man credit for.

Then Tern's voice rose over the gasps and exclamations of the other councilmen.

"I said ENOUGH!" he spat, waving them down from his chair, which he'd never left. "Arro, sit. Azzeki, away with you. If I've need of you, I will *say as much*."

Neither Raz nor the Captain-Commander moved for a good few seconds. Then Azzeki spat into the fire, sheathed his curved blade, and turned on his heel towards the back wall. Raz watched him walk away, only sitting down again and laying the gladius across his knees when the man had returned to his space against the stone.

"You have made your distaste for our ways clear," Tern told Raz, and again he seemed to be having difficulty keeping the anger out of his voice. "But, while we are all quite aware of your exploits in the South, we also know that the freeze is upon us and you have no place to go. Not to mention your apparent affection for the Koyt brother and sister. So, if you are done making empty threats, Arro, I would like to *move on with this conversation.*"

Again Raz was surprised—and, resentfully, somewhat impressed—by this fat little man. He had *no* fear. Perhaps it was a life of wealth and luxury that had deluded him into thinking he was untouchable. Or maybe he just felt safe in the situation, his company outnumbering Raz nearly twenty-five to one.

Whatever the case, it was an irritating confidence.

"I was suggesting you send messages to the fringe cities in the South," Raz started again, looking away from Tern to address the council as a whole. "And the other Northern towns, come to think of it. If you received word from the Mahsadën, then I'm sure you're not the only ones. Tell them I'm here. Tell them the price on my head is up for grabs to any man or woman that wants it, and that you will guarantee that I am kept within the walls of Azbar until they arrive."

"To what end?" one of the councilmen demanded.

Beside Raz, Tern snorted impatiently.

"To fight, obviously," he snapped. "Old fools. Arro believes he can take on a world's worth of bounty hunters and mercenaries, it seems."

"On an even playing field, I can take on this world's and the next's," Raz snarled. "I offered myself to fight in the place of Arrun and Lueski, and you accepted that. The only change is that I am now offering myself in exchange for the rest of your town. You think people will always want to see your trained men slaughter a handful of farmers and baker's hands with nothing but a rusty blade to their name? The appeal will wear off, not to mention the obvious issue that you are *butchering your own people.* Eventually you'll have no one left to throw in your precious pit. You're tearing yourself apart from the inside, you fat trim, and you're blinded by the gold you're making hand over fist."

He raised the gladius, letting it shine impressively in the firelight.

"I'm offering you a way out of all your problems. What have you got to lose? You said yourself you can make ten thousand crowns in a few weeks in this place. Even if I only last a fight or two, you're bound to make up the lost bounty on sheer hype and skimmed profits from the bets. And if I live up to what I promise? If I thrash every sad excuse for a fighter you throw at me? How much do you stand to gain?" He was staring at Tern intently. "How much am I worth to your Arena if I'm as good as I claim to be? As good as you've been told I am?"

He was playing on the man's greed, the only thing he was still positive held some sway on the Chairman. Sure enough, he could see the words sink in, see the avarice and desire shine in those mean blue eyes.

"Worst case?" Raz finished finally. "You make your twelve thousand gold, I get myself killed, and who's to stop you going back to your old ways then. Best case? You make dozens that amount, and you stop poaching from your own people. You cannot lose."

He knew he had convinced them before he'd even stopped speaking. All around the fire the councilmen were muttering amongst themselves, and Raz could tell from the words he caught over the flames that they were intrigued. In what Raz was starting to feel was his usual fashion, Tern was not looking away from him, taking him in as though again trying to discern if there was more than what he could see directly in front of him.

"And the freeze?" one of the other men asked. "The snows could start within the week. Your plan is all well and good, Master Arro, but it would have been better proposed as summer started, if not earlier."

"Is it impossible to travel through snow?" Raz asked. It was both a sincere and rhetorical question. Though he assumed the answer was no, he had very little concept of what snow actually was, so he was gambling.

"Well… not exactly…" the councilman replied hesitantly. "But if you expect many to travel through the freeze just to—"

"I do," Raz cut him off. "You might have your own concept of how much money ten thousand crowns is, but that notion is relative. It's more than many men could accumulate in several lifetimes. If it *is* possible to travel during the freeze, they will come. I assure you."

"Even so, that could take weeks," the man on Raz's right threw in. "We have fights scheduled in those times. Are you suggesting we cancel them?"

"If I could convince you to do so, I would." Raz sighed. "Sadly, I get the feeling that's not going to happen. I've met the Doctore. She's informed me you have gladiators you keep on retainer. Pit me against those."

"So you can kill our prized fighters?" the hard-faced man with the missing fingers interjected. "Not likely!"

Raz thought quickly.

"Then pit me against two or three of them at a time, unarmed. I can only imagine the bettors in the stands will shit themselves over that, and you'll only profit more. And I *swear*"—he held up a hand to stop the aged councilman from interrupting again—"your men will survive unscathed… relatively."

The old man blinked, then smirked as though Raz had let slip some lewd joke.

"I wasn't concerned for them. I was going to ask if you seriously expect us to believe you can take on our gladiators, unarmed, and come out on top? *And* without killing any of them?"

For a response, Raz reached up and undid the chest buckle of his gladius sheath. The scabbard fell to the floor, followed by the blade itself. As he drew his war ax from its belt loop, he looked at Tern.

"Chairman, can I assume your guard are as well trained as your gladiators?"

Tern watched Raz tug his dagger free from its sheath and put it on the ground beside his other weapons before responding.

"They're trained well enough. Why?"

Raz undid the clasp of his cloak and stood up again. The entire wall behind him was cast into shadow as he stretched his wings to their fullest extent, smiling at the paling faces of the council.

"Because," he replied casually, looking around at the uniformed men along the back wall, "I truly feel there is no better method of convincing a man than by example."

Raz appeared a half hour later at the mouth of the Arena, mud soaked and freezing, but smiling. Ahna was thrown over one shoulder, his gear all strapped back into place. As he started down the steps towards the square, he saw Rhen catch sight of him, halting in her hushed discussion with one of the officers that had escorted them into town. Arrun and Lueski, sitting huddled together on the bottom steps with their backs to the Arena, saw her movements and looked around.

Lueski was first on her feet, stumbling up the stairs in a rush to throw her arms around Raz's waist.

"Didn't know if you were coming back," she mumbled, her voice muffled as she pressed her face into his cloak which was, mercifully, still dry.

"Promised you I would, didn't I?" he told her softly, reaching down to pet her head. She looked up at him, her eyes red but no longer tearful.

"Can we go home?"

Raz nodded, and he looked past her to Rhen. Reaching around to pull a thick roll of parchments from the back of his belt, he tossed it to the Doctore.

"They say that Arrun and Lueski can return to their properties, clear of debt, and are assured a small sum for expenses until I pay it back with any winnings I might make," he called to her as she caught them, taking Lueski's hand and leading her down the stairs. "They also guarantee me lodging, food, and drink in any establishment I choose, though I think I'll be staying with these two for the time being."

He let go of Lueski so that she could run and hug her brother, who was holding on to Raz's pack as promised. Behind them, Rhen was scanning the documents quickly, flipping through them one at a time.

"They also say you're to report to me at dawn in three days' time for your first match," she said as he came to stand beside her. "Three days, huh? I'm surprised they gave you a night, let alone that much time."

"I was convincing," Raz told her simply, watching Lueski dance around her brother as the boy laughed. The little girl looked happier than Raz had yet seen her. "They didn't refuse me much of anything."

"Well, let's hope you're as convincing come time to fight," Rhen replied, rolling the parchments up and handing them back. "I'd hate for it all to turn sour for those two the moment things finally start to go their way."

Raz looked sidelong at her. The woman, too, was watching the children, but there wasn't a hint of sarcasm in her voice or scarred face as she spoke. Instead, she looked sad.

"I convinced the council to stop conscripting for the lists from within the town," Raz told her in a hushed tone, still watching her. Rhen blinked, then whirled on him.

"Wha—! How?"

"You'll see. Like I said… I was convincing."

Leaving her dumbfounded, Raz moved back to the siblings, grabbing his heavy pack from Arrun, and shooing them on.

XI

"There is yet beauty in the cruelness of winter. It takes a true love of the world to look beyond the freeze, to look beyond the wind and snow, but if you can manage it you will see the serenity that lies hidden there. As I sit here beneath the wide limbs of great trees, I must say I have found a rare moment of true peace. The silence of morning, the warmth of some measure of sun clashing with the icy chill of the season air… Now, if only Talo would stop muttering in his sleep."

—private journal of Carro al'Dor

Talo was dreaming of warm water and hot food. He was in his rooms back in the Citadel, enjoying a soak in the High Priest's private bath chambers. Great wooden trays stacked with all manner of cooked meat, steamed vegetables, and toasted grain were floating around him, and he was thoroughly enjoying picking at anything that came within easy reach. He was far too comfortable to move, but fortunately the water seemed to be flowing just right, so that every few seconds another tray with a different tasty morsel would slip close enough to grab. He sighed, reaching beneath the surface to scratch an itch on the bottom of his foot.

"Delicious." He spoke to no one in particular, merely addressing his own delightful satisfaction. "Mouthwatering. Absolutely hits the spot."

He tossed a fat grape into his mouth, lounging back against the tiled wall of the bath. *How could I have ever desired to leave this?* he asked himself. He was so comfortable, so content. It was a rare commodity to be able to live like this. Why had he ever wanted to leave in the first place?

He reached down again to scratch the bottom of his foot. Suddenly, it was less of an itch and more of an odd throb.

Talo closed his eyes, breathing in deeply. He felt the warm vapor pleasantly muddle his thoughts. He wanted to sink below the hot water and never come up. He would never be cold or hungry again.

What *was* that annoying sensation?

Talo opened his eyes again and looked down. It took him a second to blink away the water that trickled from his forehead, but finally he made out his foot.

Was that a boot kicking him below the surface? And… wait…

Why in the Lifegiver's name was he fully clothed?

Talo awoke blearily. Something was knocking harder and harder against the bottom of his foot. Groaning, he turned over under his thick swaddle of furs.

Carro was grinning down at him, kicking the bottom of his boot.

"Rise and shine, old man. It's past time to get going."

Talo groaned again, but sat up. They were camped out beneath the lowest branches of a massive pine, the ground around them a soft layer of brown needles. The air was chilly, still smelling of the thick Arocklen Woods they'd left behind only the day before, and the winter winds had finally started in earnest. They were under the last of the trees before the Dehn Plains, and from beneath the canopy Talo could just make out the distant greenery of hills and valleys.

It was beautiful, this place.

But it was also as cold as the freeze's arse.

"I was having—quite possibly—the most wonderful dream a man could ever conceive in our current position," Talo grumbled, throwing the furs off and shuddering as the cold morning air whooshed over him.

"You'll have plenty more nights to continue it," Carro snorted at him, bending down to fold up his bedroll. "We're still a week out, and if we don't get going we could get caught in the open if the snows start."

"Bah," Talo muttered sourly, but he got to his feet, flinching at the spasm in his bad knee. The remnants of the previous night's fire still smoldered at the foot of his bedding, radiating vestiges of warmth, and it was with some regret that Talo extinguished them with a flick of his hand.

"Come on," Carro called from outside the tree, where he was strapping his packs back on his horse. "If we make good time we'll reach Ystréd before nightfall."

Ystréd was one of the few towns along the road to Azbar, and the thought of an actual bed and a hot meal was all Talo needed to galvanize himself into action. Not a quarter hour later the pair of them were leaving the camp behind, hoods pulled up and hand-spun-wool scarves wrapped loosely over the lower halves of their faces to fend off the wind.

The Dehn was truly a magnificent place. Steep hills rose up around shallow riverbeds that glittered in the cloudy sun. Everything was dark green, the earth grown thick with tall grass that made the world look like it was shifting and moving as the winds changed. Short waterfalls pooled into shallow depths where fish glimmered along the bottom, hardly moving as they prepared for the coming cold. Deer leapt across the hilltops in groups, and once Talo caught sight of a lone wolf eyeing them, seated at the mouth of its den beneath some stony outcrops.

Leaving well enough alone, though, it didn't move to follow.

It had been years, Talo realized, since he'd been this far south. The Arocklen he'd still ventured through on the occasional summer days when his knee would allow it, but even then he could only ever explore the few miles that hemmed the great mountain stairway without making camp. Not to mention that as High Priest—and before that as Eret's caretaker—he hadn't the luxury of such freedoms in quite some time.

Now, though… such scenery was half the reason he had wanted to make this trip in the first place.

Talo smiled behind the wool scarf, looking out over the plains. He couldn't help the memories rising up unbidden from past years. He remembered taking this very road—little more than a pair of tracks through the grass torn up by years of wagons and horses—with Syrah, Reyn, and Jofrey, winding in and out of the hills as they made for the grand dry deserts of the South. And before that, when he'd first brought Syrah back to the Citadel. She'd been such a little thing…

"What's so funny?"

Carro was looking around at him, raising his voice to beat the wind. Talo realized he was still grinning behind his scarf. He raised an eyebrow.

"Please," Carro laughed. "You think I need to be able to see you smiling to know when something is amusing you? Go on. What is it?"

"Not amusing," Talo told him, pulling his horse up side-by-side. "Just… It goes by fast, doesn't it?"

"What does? This little quest of ours?"

"No, no," Talo chuckled, waving a hand out at the horizon. "Time. Life. The years… It's there, and then it begins to pass you by just as you start to figure out what you're supposed to do with it."

"Oh."

Carro turned away from him. He, too, took in the Dehn, and for a second looked like he was lost in his own memories.

"It does." He nodded after a moment. "I remember the first time I came through this way. My mother finally got tired of seeing my father's reflection in my face. I must have been six or seven, I can't remember. She didn't tell me where we were going."

"A sad story with a happy ending."

"True enough." Carro nodded again.

They rode on in silence for a few minutes, lost in the past, letting the horses wander a little off the road to graze.

"I remember bringing Syrah through this way," Talo said after a while, reaching down to pluck a purple flower that was swaying above the grass. "When her parents first gave her to the faith. She fought me tooth and nail all the way from Stullens until we got here. It was the end of the freeze, but still the trip was as horrible as you can imagine. She was miserable, and I wasn't much better off. Here, though, we got lucky. A few days of no storms and calm winds. Have you seen the Dehn under snow?"

Carro shook his head.

"You can't imagine it." Talo held the flower up to look at it. It was frost-tipped in the cold. "There is no end to the white. It was like walking across a new world that had never been touched. We were the only ones for miles and miles."

He opened his hand and let the flower be picked up and whisked away by the wind.

"Who knew what she'd become?" he said softly.

"I'm sure you did," Carro told him, and Talo could tell he was smiling. "You know best that great people can come from unexpected places."

Talo snorted, pulling his horse back onto the road. They crossed a narrow stone bridge suspended over a shallow river that was already icing along its borders.

"I found Laor in the pit. I didn't have him thrown upon me."

"Still, you weren't born into the Priesthood, like most of the others. Take Valaria Petrük. She claims her family has been among the Cyurgi' Di's residents since it was taken over by the faith and she's—in your own words, mind you—a 'venomous cow.' So why would you assume Syrah would have been any different from you?"

"If you'd seen how hard she fought me up until these plains, you'd have wondered the same thing," Talo chuckled. "I swear I thought that girl had gladiator blood in her. Did I ever tell you about how she almost ran away from me in the forests between Drangstek and the Fehlons?"

"I don't believe so," Carro laughed. "But that's a story I *have* to hear."

"Well," Talo began, remembering back, "she'd been fighting me all day, and it had been raining nonstop, so I was in no mood. I was seriously considering tying her to the bags, but then…"

As he told the story, elaborating to Carro how a young Syrah had daringly escaped from him by climbing a tree and hiding in an old owl hole for a night, Talo remembered other things. Looking out over the Dehn as they trotted along the crest of a particularly high hill, he remembered his own first trip across the plains.

And he remembered, for the first time in years, that feeling of starting over. Of walking into a new life.

It does go by fast…

They made excellent time, just as they'd hoped, but it was still an hour or two after nightfall when they rode into Ystréd. A larger village whose low wall cut up and down the hillsides, the town was dark and quiet as they passed beneath its only gate, heading for an old inn frequented by the traveling faith in too much of a hurry to claim lodging at the local temple. The Red Bear was bright in the night, raucous laughter and the comfortable clatter of dinner plates and flagons on wood rolling from the open doorway.

Talo and Carro dismounted, tying their mounts to a nearby post before shouldering their travel sacks and making for the warmth inside. The inn was a simple two-story structure, the rooms on the top floor while the ground level was taken up by a high-ceilinged common area and bar. Torches, candles, and a large hearth fire in the right wall filled the place with cozy light and heat, and a number of patrons were scattered around three long tables perpendicular to the door. A few more were seated at the counter, behind which a barkeep was cleaning dirty glasses with a worn rag, laughing and talking with a big man swaddled in old furs.

It was this man who noticed the Priests first, and the surprise on his face must have caught the attention of the barkeep, because he too looked around. It didn't take long before the entire common room quieted down, most faces turning towards them as Talo and Carro started for the bar.

Laorin weren't uncommon in the North, but it was still a rare sight to see two Priests, staffs in hand, come strolling into the local tavern.

"Peace, friends," Talo said loudly, pulling the scarf down off his face and raising a hand as he laughed. "Return to your drinks. We aren't spreading the word today."

A few of the patrons chuckled, then turned back to their own business.

"Get you something, sirs?" the barkeep asked, putting down his glass as Talo and Carro took a seat just down from the man in old furs. "Mead? Frostberry wine?"

"Wine for me," Carro told him, reaching into his pack for a few coppers to pay.

"And me," Talo said, doing the same. "And two plates of whatever you have that's hot."

The barman nodded, disappearing through a narrow door in the back corner. He reappeared shortly after, skillfully balancing a pair of dented plates steaming full of what looked like beef stew, and two large goblets filled to the brim.

"I assume you'll be headed for the mountains?" he asked, placing their dinners before them. Talo, already reaching for the wine, let Carro answer.

"Coming from, actually." He accepted a wooden spoon as it was handed to him. "You haven't heard word about the weather south, have you? We're hoping to make Azbar within the week."

"Azbar?" a brusque voice asked suddenly. "You two lookin' ta' see the fights? Ain't you lot banned from tha' sort a' thing?"

Both Priests turned to look at the big man down the counter from them. He was an older fellow, maybe a few years younger than either of them, but his furs were well used and dirty, as was the leather pommel of the longsword strapped at his hip. He was eyeing them curiously.

"Name's Abyn," he said gruffly, extending a hand over the empty chair between them. Talo shook it briefly. The man's palm was calloused from what could only have been years at the sword.

"Beg pardon me manners, jumpin' in like tha', but Solva and me"—Abyn indicated the barkeep—"were just chattin' 'bout the news."

"We're banned from partaking, yes, but not from watching," Talo said calculatingly, putting his wine down. "We heard Azbar had opened up its Arena again, and wanted to see for ourselves what the fuss was all about."

He could tell Carro was about to say something in surprise—he was, after all, not the least bit interested in seeing the fights—but nudged him in the ribs with an elbow.

Something the man had said had piqued Talo's curiosity. News? What news? What had Quin Tern come up with now that could spark muttered conversations in tiny pubs hundreds of miles from Azbar itself?

"Aye," Abyn nodded solemnly. "S'not just a few who are curious, I 'spose. Ten thousand Southern crowns ain't nothin' to sneeze at."

"Ten thousand crowns?" Carro asked.

It was the barman, Solva, who responded.

"Bounty that's been promised, along with a victor's purse, to whoever can slay the new champion." He picked up another glass and eyed it disapprovingly. "Rassiyul, Rassisule, or something like that."

"Wha—? Raz i'Syul?"

The barkeep blinked in surprise at Talo's sudden outburst, as did Abyn.

"Aye," he said, shifting over to sit beside the Priests and leaning in. "Ya' heard of him, have ya'? Scourge a' the South, they're callin' him now. They say he killed a thousand men and butchered the slave rings in Miropa 'afore they chased him northward. There's a price on his head, and it sounds like Azbar sent birds out to anyplace that might have a man what wants to try his luck at claiming it."

Talo was stunned. He sat in shocked silence, staring at nothing as Carro looked between him and the other men.

"Raz i'Syul?" he asked, confused. "Who is he? I've never heard of him."

"Southern sarydâ, apparently," the barman told him. "Desert mercenary. Word is he's the only atherian to have made a name for himself in civilized culture. I've had all kinds coming in and out for the last day or so, trying to beat the snows to get to Azbar. Some to fight, and more to watch the fights."

"Atherian?" Carro looked shocked. "Lizard-folk? I thought they were beast-men, that they didn't even venture into man-made cities."

"Raz i'Syul did."

They all turned to look at Talo. While he was still staring emptily at his stew, he seemed to have regained the ability to speak.

"He was taken in by one of the nomadic trading families, back when the caravans still crossed the desert." It was easy information. All he had to do was repeat the facts he'd come across all those years ago. "He was raised by the Arros, one of the largest families, and learned the Common tongue, not to the mention the desert culture. A talented fighter, but I'd heard he was a good man… I thought he was a good man…"

His words trailed off for a moment, but suddenly he looked up at Solva.

"He came this far north?" he demanded. "You're sure? The slave rings are hunting him?"

"The Mahsadën themselves, the word is," the barkeep nodded. "You seem to know a lot about him, Priest…"

"A gladiator," Talo muttered under his breath, ignoring the comment. "What madness possessed him to do that…?"

"Talo, what—?" Carro began to ask, sounding thoroughly confused, but Talo stopped him with a hand.

"A room," he said abruptly to Solva, pulling a silver piece from his pack and tossing it onto the counter. "And please have the rest of our meal brought up to us."

The barkeep blinked in surprise, but reached into the pocket of his apron to pull out a long copper key.

"Second door on your right up the stairs," he said, holding it out. "But what about—?"

"Thank you," Talo cut him off, snatching the key from the man's hand and giving Carro a significant look. At once Carro jumped off his seat, grabbing his own gear.

"Pleasure meeting you both, have a lovely evening!" he said hurriedly to the two men, rushing to follow Talo up the stairway and leaving the bewildered pair at the bar.

When they were upstairs, Talo unlocked and opened their room door at once, closing it quickly behind them. It was a small space, barely wide enough to fit the two beds that largely filled it. Ignoring it all, though, Carro whirled on his partner.

"Talo, what in the Lifegiver's name was that all about?" he demanded. "Who is Raz i'Syul?"

Talo looked up at him. "Do you remember, six or seven years ago, the mission Syrah and I took with Jofrey and Reyn Hartlet? The one that took us south?"

"You came back early," Carro nodded, but he sounded suddenly suspicious. "Syrah was mugged, or something like that. You felt the town you were in was unsafe."

"That's not exactly how it—That's not what happened. Carro… Raz i'Syul Arro is the only reason Syrah made it out of that city alive."

XII

"I cannot aptly describe the feeling in the air these last two weeks. Word has spread. People are whispering in the streets. Places amongst the stands in the Arena are always valued highly, but not since I was matched with the Lifetaker have I known every single seat to be sold off in advance. The stories they say about him... I'd heard a few obviously, before they sent me out to meet him in the woods. But what I've been told since then, what larger truths seem to be mixed in with the rumors and tall tales... I can't help but wonder what kind of beast we've let into our home..."

—private journal of Alyssa Rhen

Raz was cold. Raz was wet. Raz was so muddy he doubted he looked like much more than a shapely pile of filth with eyes.

But Raz, unlike his opponents, was at the very least standing on his own two feet.

"Come on, then," he growled, circling the collapsed brothers as they struggled to free themselves of the icy muck and each other. "You call yourselves fighters? Maybe I should consider asking your Doctore if she'll let me take on the next group unarmed *and* blindfolded."

It was meant to taunt the two gladiators.

It worked like a charm.

"Damn lizard!" Ajuk Rothe, a heavy man in a half helm and iron breastplate, cursed as he managed to shake himself free of his sibling. He had only one sword left of the two he'd started with, but regardless he charged Raz head-on, bringing the blade up with two hands for an overhead slash. Aiming for the vulnerable space between neck and shoulder, he let the steel fall, slicing down, going for the kill.

What he found instead of flesh and bone, though, was air and dirt.

"Too slow," Raz growled from beside him as the man stumbled forward behind his own impetus.

Before Ajuk could fall again, however, one clawed hand caught the back collar of his breastplate, the other slamming up to take the man in the abdomen. Sweeping the gladiator's feet out from under him with a leg, Raz shoved upward, tossing the man into the air even as he continued forward.

The result was a cumbersome front flip, ending when Ajuk crashed hard to the pit floor on his back, from which he didn't rise again.

By now, though, the other fighter was back on his feet, and Raz turned to face him bare-handed. Smaller and leaner than his brother, Brüg Rothe had the brains not to attempt to take his faster, stronger opponent in a rush. Instead he held back, finding good footing and hefting his long pike before him defensively.

"Ain't coming to you, ya scaly bastard!" he shouted after spitting out a mouthful of mud. "You feel like bein' skewered, you're gonna have to come do it yerself."

"I appreciate the warning," Raz said with a shrug, following Brüg's movements as the man started making a careful circle around him. "I've been poked full of holes plenty of times before, though. Don't think another couple more is going to matter much."

Then he shot forward.

For a minute or two he let the gladiator believe he had a chance. For all intents and purposes the man *was* good with his pike, taking full advantage of its reach to keep a good distance between Raz and himself. Raz, for his part, dodged left and right and down as needed in rapid repetitions, allowing the iron point of the weapon to sneak within inches of his belly, legs, and shoulders. Had he had Ahna in his hands, or even his gladius, the pike or its wielder or both would have lost their head any number of times.

While the blood might have won some people over, though, such a rapid end would have done little to please the crowd.

Still, eventually the theatrics had to come to a close. As Brüg began to tire, Raz knew his dance would get obvious and boring. Therefore, the next time the pike was thrust outward a little too far, Raz stepped around and forward, making good use of old footwork to close the gap between their two bodies in a blink.

His extended arm caught Brüg below the neck, clotheslining him so abruptly he hit the pit floor with no less force than his brother had. The pike followed a moment after, and the fight was done.

Sound returned suddenly and sharply to Raz's world. What he'd droned out during the fight came back in a single wave, riding along with the explosive cheering, hollering, and applause of ten thousand bodies taking to their feet in the stands above. Raz looked up, gazing into the crowd that commended him so fondly.

All the while wondering if there might have been a time in his life, even not so long ago, that he might have enjoyed their praise.

When the chanting started, Raz didn't fight the frown. These men and women of the North didn't know him well enough yet to read his mood by his face, but even if they had he doubted they'd notice or care. Still, when the word became clear, rising in volume with every repetition, he felt the familiar angry tension building within him.

"SCOURGE! SCOURGE! SCOURGE! SCOURGE!"

Over and over again they shouted it, feeding off the title and their own bloodlust. When he finally had enough, when he felt the anticipation had built to the point of bursting, Raz raised a single hand in silent acknowledgement. The crowd exploded again, their roar trailing behind Raz as he turned his back on the pit, leaving behind the Rothe brothers' unconscious forms as he made for the rising portcullis that led to the Arena's underworks.

Men and women alike stepped smartly out of the way as Raz reached the bottom of the uneven earthen gangway that led down from the Arena floor. He was in the waiting chambers, the series of large dirt-and-timber rooms where gladiators were housed as they awaited their moments of glory, as well as the wild animals sometimes used as complements to the entertainment. Heavy iron sconces bearing torches along the walls supplemented what little grayish light made its way down through the arched gateway at the top of the ramp, illuminating the mass of people scattered around the room. There were no beasts today. A week ago a number of half-starved wolves had been chained to one end of the chamber, but they'd been killed off in a well-publicized fight that had claimed the life of one of the Doctore's prized gladiators, as well as the arm of another.

Now the only things in the waiting area were fighters themselves, a few preparing for the two or three encore matches that would follow Raz's series of theatrical fights, but most nursing minor wounds and bruises. A number of these looked up when Raz passed, spitting on the ground as he went by or else cursing him in a variety of languages he didn't often recognize. They were men and women of every culture and ethnicity Raz had ever heard of, and many he hadn't. Azbar's Arena was—as anyone involved in its newfound success was quick to repeat—the largest of the Northern fighting pits. Even after hundreds of Azbar's own had volunteered to learn and train under Alyssa Rhen and her subordinates, dozens more had come through the city gates over the summer from every corner of the known world. Imperialists and Islers from the West. Southern sarydâ—*true* Southern sarydâ—along with many a Percian and former soldier from the armies of the Seven Cities. There were even a handful of mountain men from the range tribes throughout the North, big, burly figures with long hair and beards who fought just as well with their fists as they did with the massive axes and war-hammers that had accompanied them down.

The only thing most of the Arena gladiators had in common, in fact, was a mutual and distinct hatred of Raz.

Nothing new there, Raz thought humorlessly as he made his way through the chambers towards the heavy wood-and-iron door set at the very back. Reaching it, he took a moment to bang most of the mud that caked his armor and furs free, shaking his wings to clear them of the offending muck, then pulled it open.

Inside was a smaller chamber, cut into the earth with a lower ceiling. Raz had to duck to make it under the door, and the tops of his ears hit the wide timber crossbeams that held up the packed earth above his head. The air was warmer and brighter here, though, alight from the orange flames that leapt from the well-ventilated fireplace dug out of the wall at the back of the room. It lit up the collection of old tapestries, maps, and oil paintings spaced evenly around the chamber, and outlined the heavy carved bureau that took up the middle of floor.

It outlined, too, the shape of the woman who stood over the desk, contemplating a series of narrow parchments she held flattened upon the wood.

She looked up when Raz entered the room, shutting the door behind him. As he approached the desk he allowed his wings to extend a few feet to either side of him, bathing them in the warmth of the fire. As one week had turned into two, the temperatures—even during the brightest parts of what sunny days they were still getting—had continued to fall. Raz was acclimating as best he could, learning how to layer furs on leather and always keep moving to stay warm, but it wasn't easy. Any opportunity he got to stand near a fire, he took it. The only time he didn't think about the cold, in fact, was when he was fighting in the pit, or else home with Lueski and Arrun.

"How did it go?"

Alyssa Rhen stood straight as Raz came to stand over the desk. The firelight did nothing to ease the edge of the scar on her face, but as always she held herself with such stolidity it demanded a sort of respect.

"First two fights were smooth," Raz said with a shrug. "Pynus, Garrut, and Sofia need to learn to coordinate better. I had them split away from each other within a minute of the gates lifting, and it actually took some work to make it entertaining from there. The next pair were better for a while, but impatient. I had to end it fast after Boten nearly cleaved Dakker in two with that bastard sword of his. I hope you got him to a surgeon in time. He needed sewing up, and Boten needs a smaller sword. He's good, but doesn't have the strength to wield a hand-and-a-half properly."

"I'll speak to him." Alyssa acknowledged the advice with a nod. "What of the Rothe brothers?"

"The best you've thrown at me so far. Both have talent, but Brüg has discipline his brother lacks. He would be much better off paired with a different partner or group. Maybe the shield-bearers you had me face last week? Or that other spearwoman you had matched up with the two mountain men a few days ago—what did she call herself?"

"Esha the Raven," Rhen replied with half an amused smile. "And I agree, but Brüg won't fight with anyone other than Ajuk. Family ties and all that."

Raz shrugged. "His loss. Maybe when Ajuk gets himself killed, Brüg will see sense."

"Let's hope, but in the meantime"—Alyssa waved a hand at the curling papers on her desk—"you have other things to worry about than the welfare of men who would kill you in your sleep if I let them."

Raz chuckled, but reached down and picked up one of the sheets, pulling it flat. Numbers lined the left side, paralled by a long list of names he could barely make out.

"Your scribes need some work on their handwriting," he grumbled after a moment. "What is this?"

"Your handiwork." Rhen moved to take a seat in the padded leather chair behind her desk. "The result of your birds."

That caught Raz's attention. More carefully he perused the list, trying to make out the names.

"So, the gamble paid off," he mumbled, still peering at the scribbles. "I assume Tern is pleased."

"Ecstatic, though I'm not so sure you're actually winning the gamble. That's the first part of the records the gate guard have compiled based on reported comings and goings. These are the other three"—she crossed her legs and put a finger on the short stack of parchment before her—"comprising some three hundred hopeful combatants so far."

For a moment she paused, watching Raz continue to peruse the list.

"Some of those are undoubtedly fake," she continued eventually. "Titles of old legends, ancient warriors."

"Retribution," Raz nodded. "Queen of Arrows. Lifetaker. I've seen those before, and unless the dead and decrepit are rising from their rest for a chance at my head, I'd say you're on the mark."

"Let's hope." Alyssa leaned back in her chair. "Sylar Kern would have given you a run for your money, and my own gold would not have been bet on you if you'd gone toe-to-toe with the Lifetaker. Still, even with the fakes looking for their shot at wealth and glory, there are names on there that should concern you. Bounty hunters, assassins, even an exiled former admiral in the Imperium's flotilla. The men and women under my wing are good, atherian, but we both know they don't pose much threat to you one way or the other. *These* names, on the other hand"—she indicated the sheets again as Raz placed the parchment he'd been examining back on the desk—"are of a different caliber altogether."

"Let's hope so," Raz nodded with a half smile of his own. "I imagine your crowds would eventually get bored of watching me embarrass the gladiators they've considered their pride and joy for months now."

The Doctore didn't so much as flinch at the underhanded slight. Instead, she shrugged.

"Most likely. Then again, let's not pretend you care in the least what the crowd thinks and feels. The better your opponent, the less likely the next man is to pick up the sword when he falls. You've thought it all out, atherian, and I give you credit for it. Spill enough of the blood of legends, and eventually they'll stop trying. Isn't that the plan?"

Raz smiled again, giving the woman a sidelong look.

"As always, Doctore," he said as he turned away from her, making for the wall and shelf where Ahna, his gladius, war ax, and dagger rested innocently, "you see far too much."

Often, as he started his walk home, Raz felt there were more admirers *outside* the Arena than in the stands themselves. He'd given up any attempt at guile or disguise, as no matter by which way he left there always seemed to be a group of enthusiastic spectators waiting for him to regale in that day's glories. Not once had he ever sated their shouts for tales regarding his past adventures, or answered requests to reveal Ahna or his other blades to the crowd. He didn't even acknowledge the groups with a wave anymore, as he had the first few times, because even this small gesture of appreciation seemed to galvanize the mob into greater excitement and made it all the more difficult to escape them.

Instead, head bowed under the heavy black-and-silver-fur mantel that also covered his still-dirty armor and weapons, he made his way briskly through the crowd, Ahna thrown over one shoulder. The throng of hopefuls were not so foolish as to stand in his way as he moved, preferring rather to shout their admirations from a safe distance when it became clear Raz was once again in no mood to delay. Neither did they follow him past the edge of the wide cobbled ring that surrounded the Arena on all sides. Once Raz ducked into the narrower alleys of the town proper, they generally left him to his business.

Once Raz had ducked into the narrower alleys of the town proper, he could breathe easy again.

As he picked his way south along the familiar path through the maze of homes, shops, and buildings, Raz considered his fans. Not for the first time, either. Fighting in the Arena was nothing like when he had worked for the Mahsadën. Then, he'd always been torn. He'd deluded himself, sure, but there had been some part of him that had always pulled away from his decision, some fragment of the conscience the Arros had worked so hard with him to build. In the Arena, he felt no such inner battle. Even when he considered how he would likely return to killing rather than incapacitating soon enough, he didn't feel the doubt.

Taking the heads of the men and women who had come to Azbar for a shot at claiming his own seemed fair enough, after all.

But still, despite his clear conscience, it felt odd to be so openly praised for his actions. It was not a completely new experience—he'd won plenty of public duels, challenges, and plain old fights in his time—but while the admiration of *those* crowds had been genuine, it had always been grudgingly granted. In the South, Raz had always felt his skills were considered rather similarly to how one might view the venomous bite of a sandviper: respected, but not necessarily appreciated.

Here, Raz felt his skills were all *too much* appreciated.

"Guess it's a good problem to have," Raz muttered to the dviassegai by his cheek as he descended a narrow, curved stairwell that lined a small hill of tall fir trees. "Can't say that a year ago I would have complained about a little glory. Should be a nice change of pace…"

Still, maybe it was more than the alien concept of appreciation that put him at odds with the Arena spectators. While Raz didn't consider himself a peaceful man by any measurement, he wasn't sure he qualified as an innately violent one either. His methods might speak volumes otherwise to some, he was sure, but he had never really taken pleasure in his work in the true sense of the phrase. He felt pride for his skills, sure, as well as a twisted sense of content in his reputation. Perhaps it could even be argued he garnered satisfaction in his success, a sort of perverted fulfillment in his campaign to free the world from the grasp of those who built perfect lives for themselves on the backs of the downtrodden and helpless.

But pleasure? Never. Not when he had torn Corm Ayzenbas limb from limb for the butchery of the Arros. Not when he had sent bits of one of the šef to the man's colleagues in gift baskets. Not when he had speared Imaneal Evony through the heart, effectively cutting off the head of the Miropan Mahsadën, if only for a while.

Pleasure had never been part of the deal.

How, then, could pleasure be such an integral part of the Arena, whose muddy floor was soaked with more blood than Raz thought he could spill in a hundred lifetimes?

He stopped, pausing in his pursuit to get home before dark. After following a cobblestone road for several minutes, he'd come to a bend in the track, the curve of which was blocked by no building, and opened up the world. Down the hill, towards the outer wall where he was headed, Azbar was alight once more as evening fell. Though it was not aglow with points of orange-and-white flame, as it would be once night came in truth, there was something distinctly taking in the way smoke furled over a thousand slate and wood-slat rooftops, each a different shade of gray, brown, or reddish green. Beyond that, the wall itself cut across the scene like a dark stroke, separating the town from the open plain and heavy woodlands beyond. Rolling like waves on an ocean, the great greenery of the trees rode their hills and valleys, rising and dipping in layers across the land. As distant winds licked at them, Raz could see the whole forest ripple and sway like a field in the breeze. Above all of it, the sky churned gray with clouds, a lingering storm that never actually broke. Every so often the heavens would shift enough to let the Sun peek through, and for a brief time one could watch daylight dance down in faded rays, moving across the hills and trees until the clouds closed up once more.

Standing on the edge of the road, looking out over the scene, Raz almost chuckled to himself. In the South, the blood and battle had seemed an appropriate way of life, an angry and harsh way matched so well by the unforgiving sands and endless glare of the Sun.

But not in a place like this, Raz thought, feeling those distant winds finally reach him, shifting his heavy furs around him as he continued to watch the faraway roll of the mountainous horizon. *Not in a place like this.*

XIII

It wasn't quite dark by the time Raz reached the Koyts' little home on the very outskirts of town, but it was late enough that the streets were mostly empty and the lamplighters had started making their rounds. As he climbed the uneven stone steps to the house's front door, Raz watched one such man, fascinated as the lighter reached up with a long rod of thin wood, capped by a burning candle, to set a street lantern ablaze. While Raz couldn't imagine it was fulfilling labor, the fact that such work existed at all was nearly beyond him. There was no such concept in the fringe towns around the Cienbal, just as there was no concept of loggers or trappers or any number of other occupations.

Smiling to himself, he reached up and knocked on the door.

"What's so funny?" Arrun asked him at once as the boy pulled it open, seeing the look on Raz's face.

"Just trying to imagine what your market squares would look like with elephants and snake charmers," Raz replied as he ducked into the house.

Lueski and Arrun's residence was a palace by most Southern standards, but in Azbar it wasn't much more than a small home, once doubling as a bakery. From the outside one could make out its two stories easily enough, round windows cut into mortared granite on both floors, with a solid wood stand built street-side around and along the lowest part of the outer wall. Arrun had explained proudly that, at one time, their parents—Warren and Marta—had had all manner of breads and baked goods on display through all hours of the day, selling to regulars and passersbys alike. Every third day Arrun and his father would go into market weighed down with heavy loaves and cakes, trading them to the larger bakeries for flour and ingredients.

Arrun had finished the story quietly, explaining how, after the freeze had claimed their mother and father, though, it had become much harder for he and Lueski to keep the storefront afloat.

On the inside the home was a bit blander than one would presume initially. The siblings had sold off nearly all of the accoutrements one would expect to find in a family setting. There was no furniture to speak of save two thin feather mattresses on the floor by the fireplace. The wide hearth was unadorned, with nothing left to place or hang along its frame. Mirrors, silverware, tools, jewelry—anything that carried value of any kind was long gone, first sold off to the well-respected dealers along the markets, then to the less reputable pawners one could find crawling about the alleys of the paupers' quarters.

By the time the Koyts had nothing left to sell, their house had gone from a lived-in family space to an empty shell of a home. When they'd arrived back for the first time after Raz had dealt with the Chairman, they had been greeted by a thin layer of dust, and cobwebs along every corner. Most of the next day was spent cleaning, then buying food from the market with the advance Raz had been granted by the council.

They hadn't bothered with furniture, yet. No one talked about it, but Raz knew Arrun was putting real consideration into taking advantage while they could and leaving Azbar behind for good.

The market streets had been an enjoyable experience. While the narrow, intersecting roads possessed an order to them that was utterly lacking in the bazaars of the fringe cities, Raz had found himself almost grinning at the familiarity of the bustle, the push of the crowd. No one shouted aloud save to find families lost in the throng, but the general hubbub of the people droned constantly, giving the roads and their shops that spark of life that no other place in the city could have. It brought Raz back years, and he couldn't help but wonder what the Arros would have made of the place, this strange city in the woods, all gray and black and green from stone and earth and tree.

It had been a pleasurable trip, but a short one, and before long they'd been back in the emptiness of the Koyts' home, now two weeks later just as it had been then.

"So whose ass did you whoop today?" Arrun asked with only half-masked enthusiasm, closing the door behind Raz.

"I think I've told you enough times," Raz grumbled over his shoulder as a small voice squealed from the corner by the fire, and Lueski came pelting towards him, "to watch your mouth around your sister."

Arrun chuckled, then stepped around him to allow Lueski to leap on Raz and hug him around the waist—a well-formed habit now—heedless of the knife and ax beneath his furs.

"Did you win?" she asked him excitedly, looking up at him with lake-blue eyes through black hair. "Did you beat the bad men? Did you? Did you?"

Raz smiled back.

"Well I'd had to have, wouldn't I?" he told her, gently disengaging from Lueski's arms as he leaned Ahna in her usual spot against the wall by the door. "Who else would have stories for you, otherwise?"

He almost laughed as Lueski positively bounced with excitement.

"Go help your brother with dinner," he told her, turning to hang his mantel on an old iron peg by the door. "I'll be down as soon as I've washed up."

Lueski bounded off at once. After he'd pulled his ax and knife free of his belt, leaving the gladius strapped over his shoulder, Raz made his way upstairs to one of the three small bedrooms on the second floor. He'd claimed the middle one—Arrun's old room—for his things, and once he'd closed the door behind him he started undoing the clasps of heavy steel plate around his arm and leg. The largest of the chambers would have served him better, but Raz had felt claiming Warren and Marta's former room would have been heartless.

Before long, Raz was mud-free, every inch of himself scrubbed clean in the warm water Lueski had already prepped in a bin for him. After that, his armor came next, caked earth knocked off as best he could before wiping everything down with a damp cloth. Once he'd hung everything to dry and changed into clean clothes—leaving his dirt-soaked ones in a pile against the wall for Lueski to clean in the morning—he made his way back downstairs, gladius still on his back.

Arrun and his sister already had dinner ready, plates—one of the few purchases they'd made other than food—set out by the fire to warm. Accepting one from Arrun as he made his way to the hearth, Raz sat down as close to the flames as he could stand, basking in the heat.

For a time the three of them sat in silence, content in the meal and heat and company. Arrun had prepared a hearty spiced soup for he and his sister, but for Raz he hadn't bothered doing more than searing a pair of large trout steaks that barely fit on the platter. The meal had become a quick favorite of Raz's, who'd only ever had silverfish from the Garin growing up.

When dinner was almost done, though, Lueski looked up expectantly. Arrun, too, seemed a little on edge, but hid it better. Tilting his head back to swallow a last mouthful of fish, Raz chuckled.

"I suppose you'll be wanting to hear about my day, then?" he asked.

Lueski nodded fervently, and Raz smiled.

It had become a ritual for them, and as Raz threw himself into the details of his day's fights—leaving out certain unnecessary details Lueski didn't need to hear—he felt the comfort of routine take hold of him. It had been too long since he'd been able to stay in once place for more than a few nights at a time. He remembered his old room at the White Sands with an odd sense of loss, but shook it off.

Despite the bleakness of the house, despite the precariousness of his situation, despite the weight of the shadows he could feel dancing around him, moving steadily closer with their knives and swords and axes wielded aloft, it had been many years since Raz had felt so content. It was something to hold on to, something nearly tangible for which he fought. This peace, this satisfaction, bore the comforting weight of a heavy coat, fighting off the cold that was all the other horrors waiting for him out there in the world.

And I won't lose it.

It was with this thought that Raz put Lueski to bed later that night, tucking her thick feather-stuffed blankets around her mattress by the fire. It was this thought that pulled him down into sleep a few minutes later, laid out on his bedroll before the front door, one wing pulled over him under his own quilts.

And it was this thought that had made him draw the gladius free of its sheath before doing so, laying it out, bare and ready, between his body and the door.

XIV

In twos and threes they'd face the beast,
each thinking themselves worthy.
In twos and threes they fell like wheat,
while the beast was hardly dirtied…

—"The Monster Come North," by unknown minstrel

"Spectator or combatant, sir?"

Carro blinked.

"I beg your—" he started in alarm. "What do you mean, 'spectator or combatant'?"

They stood outside the east gates of Azbar. Talo had left Carro to deal with gaining them entrance to the city, standing a little ways back, horse reins in hand, allowing himself to gaze up along the high stone wall that loomed over them like a sleeping giant. It reminded him of the walls of Cyurgi' Di to an extent, but with a sinister ambience that lacked in the defenses of the High Citadel. There the sleeping giant seemed a calm sort, peaceful in its slumber.

The walls of Azbar, on the other hand, felt more like the titan could wake at any moment and crush Talo where he stood.

"Do you declare yourself spectator or combatant, sir?" the officer at the gate was asking impatiently, quill poised over the pages of the open booklet on the narrow desk he was sitting behind. "Are you here to watch the fights, or take part?"

Talo, glancing behind him, couldn't blame the man's ill-tempered demeanor. Though the snows had yet to come—an odd blessing for what promised to be a hard winter—the cold had arrived in force. Frost tipped every blade of the grassy field that surrounded the town, giving the green of the pasture a smoky tinge. The ground of the path beneath their feet—in the summer churned soft and muddy by the comings and goings from the gate—was hard and sharp, frozen into whatever wear it had shown when the freeze descended. The Priests had long since abandoned their traveling tunics for the warm layers of their faith's robes once more, but even so the chill still bit at them now that they had stopped moving.

And yet, despite this bitter cold, behind Talo the line of men, women, carts, and horses trying to get into the city extended halfway between the wall and the woodlands across the plains. Most of the figures seemed harmless enough, travelers come from afar to see the fights, judging by their packs and wagons, but there were other sorts mixed in among them. Some—like the unsavory fellow directly behind Talo in line, wide frame slouched over the old dappled charger he rode atop, clothed with tattered furs and with a massive two-handed claymore hung from the side of his saddle—were of a different make altogether.

"I—well I—" Carro stumbled over his words, obviously taken more than a little aback by the officer's query. "I—that is to say *we*—"

"Spectators," Talo interrupted at last, deciding to put his lover out of his misery. "Come to see what's become of the Arena since last we were here."

The officer glanced between the Priests, giving Talo a particularly hard look, then nodded. Not bothering to write anything down in his little book, he waved them through.

"What was that about?" Carro hissed after he'd taken his horse from Talo and they were safely through the gate. Talo, in response, put a finger to his lips and kept walking a few paces into town, then led Carro and the horses around the corner of a natural slate fountain that had frozen over in the cold. There he stopped, hugging the wall so that he was half-hidden by the stone, and watched the gate.

"Spectator or com—" the officer began, but the haggard, hard rider than had been behind them in line cut him off.

"Combatant," he growled at once in a gravelly, hoarse voice.

The gate officer, choosing to ignore the interruption, looked the man and his horse up and down.

"Name and occupation?" he said after a moment, dipping his quill into the ink well at the corner of his desk, set up next to a couple of lit candles to keep it from hardening.

"Wehn Galen," the rider replied. "And my occupation is none a' yer business."

The officer, obviously a great deal more patient than Talo had given him credit for, didn't bother responding. Instead he jotted something down in his little book, pulled a sealed letter from a small drawer to his left, then gestured towards the gate.

"Make your way to the town hall and present this"—he held up the envelope—"at the gate. A few of you have already passed through today, so it won't be long before the Captain-Commander comes to fill you all in on the details of your agenda and agreements. Keep the peace of the town, stay away from other combatants, and report to the Arena at your assigned day and time, or forfeit your fight. Lodgings you will need to procure for yourself, and know that none of the inns and taverns in town are accepting credit as payment."

Finally, as the officer stood and held out the envelope for the rider to reach down and grab, the man allowed himself something of a vengeful smirk.

"Few of your kind are expected to live long enough to pay the debt, you see."

The rider muttered something unintelligible in reply, then pulled his horse around, kicking it into a trot through the gates. As he rode by their little corner, Talo turned away, not wanting to be caught eavesdropping.

"Seems our friends in Ystréd weren't exaggerating," he muttered, looking around at Carro. "They're padding the lists."

"Lists?" Carro asked, peering around Talo towards the gate again.

"Fight lists. The pool of names they can draw from for the pit."

"Ah." Carro frowned at the gate for a moment, then turned to face the city. Though most of it was hidden by the buildings, walkways, banners, and rooftops that immediately surrounded them, the highest points of Azbar were visible in the distance. At its apex, cresting the cliffs that hung over the gorge at the city's back, the town hall watched over all. Though they couldn't see it, both men knew the Arena was somewhere below it, dark and hungry and waiting.

"A list of dead men walking," Carro said sadly after a moment, then sighed. "So much blood spilled. It seems such a waste, Talo. You may have left a good man in the South those years ago, but if Arro is responsible for this butchery, I'm not sure he's deserving of our help."

Talo didn't reply. They'd left Ystréd in too much of a hurry to find out more about the situation in Azbar. They'd debated asking around and trying to find out more on what was going on, but had decided against it. In part they couldn't really afford to delay their arrival, but there was also the fact that they couldn't risk word of their nosing into the city's business reaching Azbar before they did. Given what Kal Yu'ri had told them in his letters, Talo wouldn't have put it past the new Chairman to have the entirety of his guard alert to their coming.

Whether the soldiers would be instructed to merely block them from entry, or deal with them through less peaceful means, he wasn't so sure about.

Still, despite the evidence to the contrary, Talo wasn't just ready to pass judgment on Raz i'Syul Arro. Most like it was nothing more than the sense of debt he felt he owed the man, or maybe the memory of how many had judged the Lifetaker a bloodthirsty beast in his own time, but something held Talo firm in his conviction that Arro should have the opportunity to explain himself.

The aging High Priest thumbed the steel of his staff, cool even with leather gloves between skin and metal.

Conviction, after all, he thought to himself, *has an endless value all its own.*

"Let's find Kal," he said finally, turning to lead them north, deeper into the city.

Azbar's Laorin temple was a pitiful thing by most standards. In comparison to the fortress that was the Citadel, it was particularly ramshackle, a hunched, unadorned building sheltered in the hugging canopies of the evergreens that rose up on either side of it. Its entrance was a plain stone archway, stained with lichen and moss, set into a crumbling hip-high wall surrounding the temple and the gardens beyond in its entirety. The grounds were meticulously cared for, tended undoubtedly by the heedful hands of the temple's limited population of Priests, Priestesses, and acolytes. Despite the freeze, the paired plots on either side of the slate walkway that led to the temple itself were alive with late-season flowers, weather-resistant shrubbery, and vines that had browned in the cold but continued to climb handsomely over the walls of the building. In the summer the place would be abloom with all shades of greens and blues and whatever brighter colors the flowers of the warmer season would bring along with them.

Leaving their horses tied at the archway, Talo and Carro followed the narrow path right up to the heavy oak doors of the temple. As Carro reached out to knock the head of his staff briefly against the wood, Talo looked around them, thinking of the first time he'd set foot on the ancient reed mats they stood upon, right in front of the entrance.

It doesn't change, this place, he thought as there was a clunk of a lock bar being shifted out of the way, and the door swung open with the quiet grind of well-oiled hinges.

A face appeared in the entrance, youthful and curious. At once Talo got the distinct impression that unannounced visitors did not often frequent the temple, because the boy eyed them with a mixture of suspicion and excitement as he took in their garments and the paired steel staffs.

Then he spotted the thin line of unassuming black along the ridge of Talo's white hood, and he blanched.

"High Priest!" he exclaimed at once, leaping forward to tug at the second door, swinging it wide. "Please, come in! High Priest Yu'ri made mention we might have visitors, but I don't think he was expecting you for some time."

"He made it clear the need was urgent," Talo told the acolyte with a nod, stepping into the temple after Carro. "That, and the road wasn't as harsh as it might have been."

"And thank the Lifegiver for that," Carro muttered, pulling his traveling packs from over his shoulder to set down beside the door.

The interior of the temple was just as unadorned as the outside walls, but at least it was warmer. They'd entered directly into the great hall, much of the slate floor taken up by a single long table with several dozen mismatched chairs pushed under it on either side. Above them the roof jutted upward, angled sharply in order to shed the unforgiving snow that would bear down in due course. Curved rafters cast odd shadows against the incline of the ceiling, shifting about in the light of the massive fire that burned in a wide hearth jutting out of the wall at the end of the hall. Heat washed in waves over the room, and the flames outlined a large huddle of figures sitting and standing around the fire, talking in quiet murmurs to one another. As one the group looked around when Carro and Talo were let in, and almost at once a figure broke away, hurrying towards the door.

"Talo! God, man! Has Laor seen fit to give you wings? It's been barely three weeks since I sent the bird!"

"Kal," Talo greeted the smaller man fondly, accepting his embrace with one arm, his other hand still holding tight to his staff. "No wings, sadly. Though I hear there are more of them in this town than last I was here."

Kal Yu'ri chuckled, breaking away to step back and take them in. He was a slight man, with darkened skin he'd inherited from a Southern father. His eyes were still the same blue of his Northern mother's, however, and the crinkling around them—only hinted at the last time Talo had seen the man—was deep and sharp, but kindly. His High Priest's robes, bearing the same single black stripe as Talo's, were frayed and patched in places, but still crisp and clean. All in all he looked like a man worn by time and responsibility, but carrying it all well.

"Yes," Yu'ri nodded, still smiling and turning to Carro, "Raz i'Syul has certainly been making waves, to say the least. And you, sir, I can only assume must be Priest al'Dor."

"In the flesh, though not for long in spirit if we don't get nearer to that fire of yours, Priest Yu'ri." Carro returned the smile easily, accepting and shaking the High Priest's offered hand. "And please, no need for formalities. Carro is fine, if I may do the same."

"By all means!" Kal waved them towards the fire, where the group he'd left still waited. "I don't know about your Citadel, but I think you'll find formalities only go so far in the valley towns."

"I remember," Talo chuckled, following Kal's lead as they made for the far end of the hall, his staff clinking on the slate. "It seems not so long ago your mother was scolding me for my 'appalling choice of verbal diction.'"

"Ah, Mother," Kal said sadly as they reached the group. "Yes… the Lifegiver saw fit to return her to his embrace some dozen years ago now, and she left me with the High Priest's mantel. I like to think it might have gone to my father, but he'd passed a few years before her. Don't let the woman fool you, though. I once heard her tell one of the other Priestesses in secret how amusing she found your 'gutter language.'"

"Hard woman, gentle soul," Talo agreed with a nod before looking around at the figures gathered before them.

The group was an odd mélange of sorts. Talo was relieved to see that Kal had understated their number somewhat in his letter, but there still couldn't have been more than two score men and women around the fire. Among them, perhaps a dozen wore the robes of consecrated Priest and Priestess. About the same number wore the plainer robes of acolytes, pressed and clean as Kal's own despite being in varied states of shabbiness. The rest wore plain clothes of all styles, marking them most likely to be followers of Laor, men and women of faith who came to the temple to pray and seek guidance. Such people made the occasional pilgrimage up to Cyurgi' Di during the highest points of summer, but aside from that were rarely seen in the Citadel.

"My friends," Kal announced, stepping through the ring into the firelight, motioning Talo and Carro to follow. "Allow me to introduce High Priest Talo Brahnt and Priest Carro al'Dor, come from the High Citadel. They've traveled hard to get here in such short time, and undoubtedly would appreciate a moment's rest before delving into the matters at hand. I think it best if we end the morning's discussion for the time being, to be resumed once I've brought our friends up to speed."

There was a stirring among the crowd. Many of the individuals—mostly among the Laorin—were looking at the pair of them with rapt attention and interest. A few, however, had harder looks, specifically among the members of the city itself. Talo was unsurprised to see that these gazes were reserved almost solely for him, and came mostly from those about his age or older.

Not for the first time, an old sadness touched surface, stroked to life by the fingers of bad and bloody memories. Talo imagined each of the men and women watching him with barely veiled dislike were feeling some similar form of those same emotions.

Sadness, he thought, watching as the group dispersed, the town's faithful heading for the door and the members of the temple going about their duties, *or perhaps worse.*

Once the hall had all but emptied, Kal breathed a deep sigh.

"With every week we see less and less of the faithful come to discuss Azbar's situation," he said sadly, motioning to a triad of chairs that had been vacated, set up near one side of the hearth. "You should have seen this place when Tern first started claiming debtors for the pits. We couldn't fit everyone inside the temple! People were clamoring to have us stand up to him, begging the Laorin to put a stop to the madness."

"What happened?" Carro asked, helping Talo ease into the middle chair before taking one beside him. "I didn't count more than fifteen from the town."

Kal sighed again, claiming the last chair, and nodded.

"Much and more." He shrugged, then thanked a small girl in acolyte's robes as she appeared and presented him with a steaming cup of some strong tea smelling of herbs. As the girl offered a cup in turn to Talo and Carro, promising to return with bread and cheese from the kitchen, he continued.

"For one thing, the longer it goes on, the less people care. We see it every year during the summer months. For the first week or so the town clamors to help those most affected by the freeze. Collapsed roofs are fixed, the hungry are fed, clothes and blankets and firewood are donated in droves. After that week, though, the help slows. The donations become less frequent, until they stop almost altogether. Within the month even the hungry are invisible again."

"It becomes part of the life they live," Talo said with a nod, swirling his drink absent-mindedly as he listened. "The desire for change is enacted by change, not by a lack of it. When things shift, there is a natural outcry, a desire for a shift back. Sometimes this is a positive reaction, sometimes not. Regardless, once that shift becomes the new normal, that desire to effect dissipates and is eventually forgotten."

"Exactly." Kal brooded for a moment before continuing, watching the fire flicker as he sipped his drink. "And such has it been with the Arena. Not immediately, mind you. There were enough volunteers to last for a while, so no one was immediately alarmed. By the time I started to think I should reach out to you, however, things were already slanting towards bad. Those guilty of violent crimes were being offered a chance at freedom if they fought. Soon after, they weren't even given the choice. From there it only got worse. The prisons were emptied, the woods around the town hunted free of bears and wolves and any other dangerous game that could provide some form of entertainment. Minor crimes suddenly became punishable by bouts in the Arena. Dozens died before the only criminals left in the city were the ones too smart to be caught."

"And that's when Tern started claiming debtors?" Carro asked.

"It is," Kal nodded. "For the first week or so they tried to make do with deathless fights, using the gladiators the Arena keeps for true entertainment, but that didn't last long. People are bloodthirsty at heart. The crowds demanded murder, and the Chairman was happy to sate them when he found his answer. Men, women, even children. If you could die, you could fight."

Talo felt his whole body still. He'd been in the process of raising the cooling tea to his lips, but froze instead. After a moment he lowered the cup slowly, hard-pressed to keep his hand still.

Beside him, Carro's face registered much of the emotion Talo was feeling.

"Children?" he hissed in fury, one hand gripping the arm of his chair so tight the old wood looked liable to break. "Tern is having children thrown to the pit?"

"He was." Kal frowned. "That was when we attempted to make our voices heard in truth. We'd tried before, mind, but nothing overtly aggressive. Public displays of intolerance. Petitions for the closing of the Arena, and then—when that didn't work—for the banning of fights involving anyone but trained gladiators. We had some success for a time, but eventually Tern had the guard break up our gatherings, citing us for 'disruption of the peace' of all things. When it became clear he had no conscience for *who* he threw in the pit, so long as they bled, though, we had to act. I took the matter to Tern and the council directly. I pleaded, begged, even threatened. I warned them of the wrath of Laor they might incur for spitting so casually on His gifts, of the wrath of man they would bring upon their heads if they kept tearing families apart and butchering the innocent in the name of the law."

"I'm assuming that didn't go over as well as you would have liked," Talo said, leaning back in his chair, still listening raptly.

"They laughed." Kal's jaw was a hard line, clenched and tight as he fought to control the anger in his voice. "These men who claim to seek nothing but the good of the town and its people. These men, many of whom I have consoled through life and loss and hard times, telling them to seek the Lifegiver. They laughed, called me an old fool with outdated morals, and had me thrown from the town hall. When I tried to go back the next day, I was barred entry under suspicion of 'seeking to harm one or more members of the council.'"

There was a moment of heavy, seething silence. Talo absorbed it all, eyes on the fire, letting everything sink in and take hold.

Children, he thought numbly. *Not even in my time did the Arena allow children into the pit…*

Eventually, he turned back to Kal.

"What happened, though?" he asked. "You said 'he was.' You imply Tern only allowed these fights to go on for so long. Why? Was the Arena failing to draw the crowds?"

Kal snorted.

"Failing to draw the crowds?" He laughed. "No such luck. If anything, fights between commoners or criminals drew greater attention to the place than ever before. It seems there's nothing quite like witnessing two parties of equally lacking skill and knowledge have it out in a desperate battle for survival."

"The feeling of power, of control," Talo nodded absently. "It's what drew the crowds in truth the last time, the only thing that kept the gold flowing in earnest once the spectators got mostly bored of gladiators and wild animals having at it."

"Then it seems your Arena of old was missing Raz i'Syul Arro."

There was another pause.

"i'Syul?" Carro said tentatively after a moment. "… You'll have to explain."

"The atherian is the reason." Kal drained his cup of tea, then set it carefully on the arm of his chair. "You asked what happened? What changed to make Tern stop claiming minor criminals and debtors as fodder for the pits? Then I tell you: Raz i'Syul Arro. The man appeared out of thin air, a week or so after I'd sent you the bird. No one is sure how or why, but one day everything is normal, and the next morning there's a Southern lizard-kind wandering the streets of Azbar. Took some getting used to, to say the least."

"And he… what?" Talo pressed. "Convinced Tern there was nothing to be gained from stealing men and women from the populace? What did he have to say that you didn't?"

"It's not what he had to say that made the difference. It's what he had to offer. It's not all clear, but the rumors say i'Syul was able to make an exchange for the freedom of the captives. He bargained to have them set free, and Tern hasn't claimed a single man or woman from within the walls of Azbar since."

"But what did he bargain with?" Carro demanded, obviously shocked. "What could he possibly have had that would press the Chairman away from a lucrative system already in place?"

Kal opened his mouth to speak, but Talo beat him to it. The High Priest was gazing at the far wall, putting together the pieces as they clicked with what he'd known of the man beforehand.

So that's why he's doing it. That's why he's thrown himself to the pit…

"He bargained with the only thing he had, and the one thing that might be more valuable than the lives of debtors and criminals," Talo said.

Then he turned to look at his partner.

"Himself, Carro. Raz i'Syul gambled his life for theirs."

XV

"Though the Tundra beyond the Northern Ranges is vast and largely unexplored, I cannot imagine it a more unforgiving place than these mountains in winter. Despite our shelter, family, and warmth, beyond the comfort of these great walls the world rages with the fierceness of titans. Even as I sit here, scribbling away in the faded light of my lantern, I hear the wind ripping against the stone. I will not sleep well tonight, I fear. And if I do, I imagine dreams of winter demons will plague my slumber."

—private journal of Eret Ta'hir

The battlements of the High Citadel were among the few places in the great temple one could be truly alone. The Laorin had no use for them, after all, and few thought to explore the tops of the keep's walls when they were quite content simply staying within them.

For those among the faith who were not so fulfilled, however, they proved sometimes to be a place of freedom in a world otherwise caged in stone.

Syrah's boots crunched in the thick layer of snow built up over the parapets as she walked. The storm had passed, the winds shifting to carry the blizzard south, but not before framing the world and all its vast entirety in gray and white. Had Syrah looked in either direction as she walked, she might have been dazzled by how the snow had softened the hard edge of the surrounding mountains. Rather than teeth seeking to devour the sky, for now the ranges seemed more like the tips of reaching fingers, curious to touch and feel the clouds and darkness beyond.

As it was, Syrah saw nothing but the snow beneath her feet, her mind preoccupied with the letter clenched in one gloved hand at her side.

When she reached the most southeastern corner of the wall, she finally stopped. In truth it was less a corner and more the rounded lip of a bastion jutting out over the cliffs, a suspended mass of worn granite hanging over empty air. Overtop of its crenellations, the world was laid out for Syrah, an intricate patchwork of woodland beneath the wisps of low-hanging clouds. In the clarity of the day, the Arocklen sprawled from the base of the mountain, weaving and dipping over land carved by time and nature. A great blanket of white and green, it stretched almost to the lip of the horizon—a substantial ways, considering Syrah's vantage. At the very edge of view, a thin, broken line of paler green marked the end of the woods and the start of the Dehn, the great plains beyond.

It seemed such a peaceful world. So tranquil in the stillness that followed every storm. It seemed that nothing could shatter the quiet, the utter silence broken only by the occasional lazy gust of late wind, or the distant shriek of a cliff hawk somewhere in the ranges below.

Syrah, though, knew better. The fragile parchment in her hand crunched and crumpled in her clenched fist as she looked out over the false calmness of the North.

The letter had come as she was breaking her fast, presented to her by Priest Jofrey so calmly she'd known right away something was wrong. Her thoughts had immediately gone to Talo and his foolish haste southward, but as she'd opened the letter a whole different set of fears came rushing forth.

She knew that handwriting. She'd seen it scrawled many a time on little notes she had found the mornings after their relations, each one charming and clever. The young captain of Harond's night- watch had certainly not been her only lover in her years out in the world, but he'd been her favorite and—Syrah liked to think—she his. That had been nearly a year ago now, though, and in truth she hadn't thought of the man much since coming home. On the one hand she'd had duties to return to, more than ever since Talo had run off to patch the mess up in Azbar, leaving Jofrey in his place. On the other, she and Reyn had become closer and closer of late, spending more and more nights in each other's beds than their own individually. Syrah had rarely given in to fanciful thoughts of settling down, always knowing she would leave and move on when Laor called her again. When she did, though, she'd even chanced to think of what Reyn would be like as more than a simple bedmate…

It was odd, therefore, with such things weighing on her mind, to be handed a letter, scrawled in the distinct hand of a former lover, bearing such grave news.

Metcaf was burning.

Abruptly, fury rose up in Syrah like hot water brought suddenly to boil. It raged through her unchecked, the kind of fiery wrath that can only be brought on by the loss of something so meaningful it becomes a part of the soul.

Like one's greatest accomplishments, and the peace between two peoples.

The feeling reached full measure, and Syrah sucked in a breath of icy mountain air. She released it in a keening scream of anger that rang out, echoing over the mountains. There was a flash and *whoosh* of flames, and the letter in Syrah's hands turned to ash in a glister of white fire. In the same moment the snow around Syrah's feet vaporized in a blink, vanishing into eruptive mist in the brief onslaught of heat she released with all her fury.

"FOOLS!" Syrah yelled to the sky. "BASTARDS! ALL OF YOU! BASTARDS!"

Breathing hard, she listened until those echoes faded away. Then, at last, she took another deep breath, and calmed herself.

Fools, she thought again, though privately. *Idiots. What do they have to gain? What is there possibly to gain?*

The letter had been obviously rushed, but it had given Syrah all the information she needed. Three years she'd spent hammering out treaties for mutual peace and prosperity between the Sigûrth tribe and valley towns of Metcaf and Harond. For three years she had toiled on both sides of the line—often at great risk—to end the age-old war between the raiding mountain men, who knew no other way of life, and the retaliating towns, who had found only fire could fight fire.

And in the space of a few months, she thought, turning her palm up to look at the grayish soot that clung to the wool of her gloves, *it all turns to ash.*

Emhret Grahst, the old Kayle of the tribe whom Syrah had dealt with extensively, was dead. Killed in ritual combat, he'd been succeeded by his murderer and nephew, Gûlraht Baoill. Syrah had only seen the man a few times, but each experience had left her with a distinct understanding: had Baoill had his way, she would have been as a victim of "the old ways"—impaled alive outside the burning walls of her home, or kept as a slave to be used and raped as was seen fit.

Grahst had had his own respect for the customs and traditions of his people, but he'd also been no fool. With the onslaught of the last freeze, more brutal than any recorded in a hundred years, he'd known he'd had the choice to bow to a new way, or risk the doom of his people altogether. The old Kayle had made peace with the towns, returning captives and slaves, trading pelts and mined gems, and signing guarantees that the raids would end and that the Sigûrth would find another means to survive in their mountains. In exchange, Metcaf and Harond had provided the tribe with the firewood, wool, food, clothing, and tools they'd needed to make it through the winters. It hadn't been easy, and there had been obstacle after obstacle right up until the signing, but the alliances had come to fruition in the end.

Now… those same treaties probably burned with the valley town.

Twenty-five thousand.

The number was staggering to Syrah. That Baoill had amassed himself an army was unsurprising. If he were indeed intent on returning his tribe to the old ways, he would need a force to match his ambition. But the new Kayle had descended on Metcaf with a force of *twenty-five thousand* hardened mountain warriors. To amass such a group, Baoill would have had to have spent the entirety of the summer and early winter challenging the other tribes and conquering them. He'd allowed the treaties to hold, at least for a time. The towns hadn't even been told that Emhret Grahst had been deposed, to keep the ruse intact.

Bastard, Syrah thought again, turning her back to the battlement wall and sliding down to seat herself on stone, now cleared of offending snow. *Clever, evil bastard.*

But clever he was. There was no denying it. And it concerned Syrah more than she was willing to admit. Gûlraht Baoill had never seemed overtly stupid, to be fair, but neither had he demonstrated any overarching inclination towards intellect. Apart from a blatant outrage as his uncle had shifted away from tradition, in fact, Syrah had always had the impression that Baoill had little to offer in the form of opinion or advice, preferring to sit quietly while the others discussed and argued.

Now, though… Now Syrah realized that saying nothing and having nothing to say were—while presenting similarly—two very different concepts.

He's thought it through. He's planned and plotted in detail. Months of preparation, of bolstering his troops with the warriors of other tribes. He was so ardently opposed to bending knee to the treaties, yet he didn't attack right away…

It showed patience, above all things, something Syrah had not come to expect from the mountain tribe in more than small quantities. Patience and cunning.

Syrah tilted her head back to rest it against the stone, looking up into the endless blue of the sky. The moon was visible, as it was on occasion during the day, a mere shadow of itself, so brightly outshined by the sun it shared the heavens with.

What would he do next? What was Baoill's plan? It didn't seem plausible that the burning of Metcaf was his ultimate goal. The letter had spoken of atrocities the likes of which the mountain tribes hadn't partaken in years. Slaves driven away in droves into the ranges with nothing but the clothes on their backs. The elderly burned at the stake, deemed infirm and unworthy of keeping. The children too young to survive the journey ripped from their parents' arms and left to the elements and fires.

Worst of all, the bodies of the city guard and any citizen who had raised arms against the Sigûrth, quartered and strung from chains over Metcaf's walls, or else impaled as gruesome keepers around each of the city's gates.

Such tactics were meant to send a warning, and what sort of general sent warnings if his campaign was already over?

No. Baoill had only begun, and Syrah had been relieved to read in the letter that Harond was in a fury fortifying itself in preparation for assault. With the freeze now at their door, Syrah didn't know what Baoill would do or when he might do it. Would he press immediately east for Harond? Maybe south in an attempt to reach fairer weather, making for the smaller towns of Stullens and Drangstek along the Fissûr Ranges? Maybe he would even make camp for the season, holing himself and his army up to wait out the winter?

Whatever his decision was in the end, the only thing Syrah was convinced of was that Gûlraht Baoill had raised an army for a reason.

Gûlraht Baoill had raised an army for war.

XVI

"I have long admired the council of Azbar for their choice of scribes. Quite apart from a detailed and accurate—if often fraudulent—account of tax revenue, trade, and lawmaking of the period, the men and women selected to attend and record the battles of the Arena during its brief reopening in the 860's have in particular my deepest admiration for the license and creativity they took in the work. Their descriptions paint well the picture of the time, place, and people. I can almost feel myself there when reading their stories, standing tall in the stands, fists in the air, screaming my encouragements into the pit."

—*The North: Ancient Tradition and Culture*, by Agor Kehn

Talo had heard it said before that smell was the most potent of methods for drawing up old memories. To inhale the familiar wafts of a person or place, they so told, could bring to mind things one had thought beyond recollection, or simply didn't know one remembered.

Standing outside the great arched mouth of the Arena entrance, Talo was realizing some things were best left forgotten…

Even beyond the walls he could make out the iron stench in the air. He doubted anyone else in the crowd thronging by on either side of him and Kal noticed it, but to Talo it was as familiar—if not as fond—a memory as the earthen scents of the halls of Cyurgi' Di. Bits of scattered recollections flashed across his mind with every breath he took, like parts of some great painting shredded and left to the winds. Faces, feelings, sights, sounds. The image of a quivering young man, watching the shifting light of the outside sky through the wooden crossbars of the portcullis as it opened for him for the first time. The same man, older and taller, reddened blades thrust above his head in a twin salute to the roar of the crowd as he turned a slow circle in the mud. The same man again, head bowed and face hidden behind long straight hair, kneeling over the still form of a woman whose life was slipping away like the blood from the great wound across her face.

This time there were no swords. They'd been thrown into the crowd in an attempt to deafen the hateful cheer of victory.

"Talo?"

Talo came to abruptly. The harsh rumbling of the crowd they divided returned in a rush, the memories slinking back into the dark place they'd been hiding. He turned to look at Kal, who was eyeing him in concern.

"Are you sure you want to do this?" the man asked for what had to be the tenth time that day.

"I'm sure," Talo answered yet again and, leaning heavily on Kal's offered arm, he took the first step upward, into the maw of the Arena.

They'd been in Azbar for five days now, collecting themselves and gathering what information the Laorin hadn't been able to provide already. Talo had been more than a little relieved to be proven right in giving Raz i'Syul the benefit of the doubt, but it wasn't until he heard it from the town itself that the truth sunk in. The atherian seemed to have been in Azbar for some time, yet still the streets were abuzz with little else. Tales of his fights in the pit. Stories of his battles against the Southern criminal rings. Even rumors that he had come to the city to rid it of the Chairman and his council. Talo and Carro had had trouble getting much else out of anyone, in fact, as no one seemed inclined to speak of anything but the Southern legend who had come from nowhere to grace their Arena. Eventually, though, some people opened up, pointing them in the direction of what the Priests were looking for.

What they found was beyond any description Kal or the other residents of the Azbar temple had been able to put into words.

Along the markets they found groups of begging orphans the locals had dubbed "the Arena's children." Dirty, shivering wretches, they huddled together against the cold, their parents long dragged off and never returned. Around one of the wells in the eastern parts of the city, a man had approached them, trying to sell off any of a dozen empty properties in the area whose families weren't alive to need them anymore. He'd been desperate, unable to shake the fearful waver in his voice as he followed them around the square, dropping price again and again in what became clear was a hard-fought effort to keep himself—and perhaps his own family—afloat. Along the western edge of the outer wall, the burned frames of a half-dozen homes still stood, swallowed up in a blaze set by a crazed and desperate woman who had preferred to end her family's lives on her own terms than that of the Arena's.

Trinkets and coins littered these ruins, leaving the wooden skeletons glittering in the sun, one for every other within Azbar's walls who had preferred to take their own life than lose it at the end of a stranger's sword.

"Is this what it was like, then?" Carro had asked in quiet shock when they'd found out what the tributes were for, standing in the road along the morbid remains of the buildings. "Is this how it was, when it was open before?"

Talo hadn't had the heart to answer him truthfully, to tell him that, in so many ways, it had been far, far worse.

And now, climbing the last steps into the Hall of Heroes, he faced the proof that he had played his fair part in creating that broken world.

Both he and Kal were dressed in common clothes today, not wanting to draw more attention than was necessary. Patched cloth tunics with thick overcoats were covered with heavy brown mantles, wide hoods lined with fur to beat the snow that hadn't seen fit to fall just yet. The winds were brutal, though, ripping through the Hall so that everyone bowed their heads against it, yelling to be heard by their companions. No one seemed much bothered to pause and take in the life-sized statues that flanked the long chamber on either side, warriors frozen in metal, their names engraved in plates below their figures. There were some Talo would have liked to pay his respects to but—in the interest of staying inconspicuous—he and Kal moved with the crowd, if a little slower. It didn't seem word had reached Tern of his and Carro's stealing into the city, and giving the Chairman any cause to find out just didn't seem like a good idea.

Despite this, though, Talo couldn't help but stop when he reached the final pedestal, the only new addition to the Hall since he'd last seen it nearly thirty years prior.

The base was of unadorned marble, like all the rest, but the nameplate had been torn away. The hollow iron molds of paired feet mounting a pile of human skulls were all that remained of the statue itself. Even had he not seen the title illicitly carved into the top of the stone, Talo knew whom it meant to represent.

Lifetaker.

"They tore it down nearly as quick as it went up," Kal said with a frown, looking down at what remained of the statue. "Markus Tern had it put in a few years after you left, once it became clear you weren't coming back. Six months later word reached Azbar that you were trying to ban the fights across the North." The man laughed unexpectedly. "The mob was so mad, I wouldn't be surprised if they ripped it apart with nothing but their bare hands."

"A shame," Talo said quietly, reaching out with the hand that wasn't wrapped around Kal's arm to trace the carved name with a finger. "I may have deflated my ego somewhat since my youth, but I admit I would have liked to see it."

"I doubt it," Kal said with a snort, smiling slyly. "It was naked."

At that, Talo straightened bolt upright.

"It was *what?*"

"Naked," Kal repeated, chuckling now at the look of abject horror on Talo's face. "Stark, stripped, and stitchless. Raz i'Syul may be a living and breathing Southern myth, but we have some of our own. There were tales that said the Lifetaker could take on an army of fighters with nothing but his swords. The sculptor"—Kal waved at what remained of the statue—"apparently took the stories a little literally."

Talo mouthed at the air like a fish, lacking any fitting response to this unpleasant imagery.

"Naked," he finally managed to gulp, looking back at the desecrated pedestal. "For years all I dreamed of was a place in this Hall, and when I finally get it, I'm naked."

"There's a lesson in there , I'm sure," Kal said with a smile, turning to start leading Talo back towards the stadium stairs, "but for now we'd best find seats. We don't want to be among the unfortunate left to stand."

Talo allowed himself to be guided away, but kept his eyes on the statue for another few moments even as he walked. He would have liked a minute to reminisce, but Kal spoke true enough. His knee wouldn't do well to stand for through the fight they had come to see.

As they managed the last of the final stairs, stepping out from under the arching ceiling into the Arena proper, Talo's first impression was that not a thing had changed about the place. The great stadium looped ahead of them in either direction, ancient stone worn by time and weather, but no less impressive in the meticulous deliberation with which it was carved and placed. The stands stretched upwards for five full floors of seats, capping along a flat ring where the unfortunate latecomers could stand for as long as the fights would last. Thick decorative arches crowned this topmost level, some standing tall despite their years, others crumbling into various states of ruin. Worn gray banners depicting the crossed antlers and swords of Azbar hung from these stone loops, like cloth doors to the sky. If one was brave—or inebriated—enough, they had only to step over a narrow chain barrier and push the banners aside to witness the city in all its splendor from one of the highest vantages in town.

Despite this, though, what truly drew the eye of every man and woman in the Arena was at its center. There, perfectly circular and gaping like a hungry mouth, was the pit itself.

It was not a pretty thing, as one might assume if judging by the rest of the Arena's carefully manicured architecture. The pit, instead, had been built to serve a purpose which had nothing to do with aesthetic pleasantries, and everything to do with brute and simple violence. The walls were of plain stone and mortar, mottled in color and texture and scarred by old gouges and blows that marked where steel had missed flesh. Fifteen feet high, they had a slight incline to them that allowed all spectators except for those in the topmost seats a fair view of everything that was going on even when the fight was happening right below them. The muddy floor itself was not smoothed or prepped, and old footprints could even be made out in the frozen ground, lightly covered in a thin blanket of morning frost. Fifty paces across, it was small enough to keep even duels interesting, but large enough to host an all-out melee of ten to twelve if desired.

To the spectators around them, the pit spoke of excitement and the promise of entertainment. To Talo, it whispered only of death.

"This way," Kal said, pressing Talo to the right. Ordinarily, men and women of the city guard would bar them from leaving the Hall of Heroes without paying the entrance fee to the stands. When the fights started, a few lucky street urchins might be allowed to watch from the top of the stairs leading back down into the Hall, peering over the heavy chain barrier into the pit, but otherwise the chamber would be cleared until the end of the matches.

Today, though, the council had seen fit to offer free entry to any and all who wished to come.

Today, after all, was opening day.

Two days prior, Quin Tern had made himself a popular man indeed when heralds appeared in each of Azbar's main squares, announcing what they had dubbed "the Chairman's Tourney." Talo, Carro, and Kal had been together to witness one such proclamation, and the enthusiasm it had been received with was disheartening to say they least. The promise of true violence, of blood and gore and death, had certainly dredged up a crowd, but it was the declaration that the first day of the tournament would be free to all, the stands of the Arena filled until they were at capacity, that had stirred most into a frenzy.

"A gift from the Chairman to the great citizens of Azbar," the herald had boomed in closing over the excited heads around him, standing on his wide stool as guards flanked him on three sides, "in thanks for their patience and patronage as he has prepared the Arena for this grand spectacle of might and madness."

"Madness is right," Carro had muttered in disgust. Initially, Talo had only agreed with him, nodding along as he considered the announcement. Now, though, as Kal led him through the crowd around the inner ring of the Arena, he was realizing something else.

Tern is gambling it all on success, Talo thought, considering the coin they *hadn't* had to fork over to be there. *He assumes he'll make up the loss, in the end.*

"Kal"—Talo had to almost shout over the excited buzz of thousands of spectators already in their seats despite the fact that the fights wouldn't start for nearly an hour—"is he that good? i'Syul? It seems to me your Chairman has a lot riding on these games of his, and to be convinced to stop poaching from the prisons and town… I would think it took a lot."

Kal nodded, but didn't reply immediately. Taking a set of narrow steps between sections of the seats, he helped Talo climb a few levels and carefully circumvent a wide basin-like trough from which great leaping flames spewed heat in all directions. There were dozens of these massive sconces throughout the stadium, even along the upper floor, each burning hot and steady on the careful supply of oil and wood fed to them by attendants over the course of the day. Aside from life-giving warmth, the fires provided a certain edge to the atmosphere, adding to the simmering excitement that bubbled in the air

It wasn't before he'd led them both towards a couple open spaces, tucked away along the fourth row up from the bottom of the stands, that Kal finally answered.

"I haven't watched him fight myself, obviously," he said, helping Talo ease himself onto the plain stone, "but ask anyone who has and they'll swear the man is practically some old god of war."

"Have you ever seen him?" Talo asked. He'd intended to question Kal about the atherian at some point, but priority of the mission at hand always claimed dominance. Most of their time had been spent discussing the legislature and public reaction, identifying what could realistically be done about the Arena in the moment, and what would have to wait.

They hadn't come up with a lot of options on either end.

"Once," Kal said, then snorted. "And I'm quite sure I made a fool of myself."

"How so?"

"He's… Well, he's *big*, Talo. Very big. Oh, you and your man are sizable specimens yourselves, I know, but not like i'Syul. I was at the markets when I saw him, and I'm almost ashamed to say I stared. Completely forgot myself, taking him in. The way he moved…"

Kal paused, sitting back to lean on his hands, considering his words.

"I've heard people talk of him as though he's a mountain among men," he continued eventually, "but I don't think that's the most appropriate comparison. He doesn't lumber or plod along like some giant. He's more… I don't know… elegant, maybe? No, that's not the word. Graceful? Maybe he's—"

"In the world of mercenaries and fighters," Talo said loudly as a group of fat men swinging about tankards of some frothing drink erupted into laughter below them, "the term is 'conservative.'"

Kal blinked, then looked around at Talo again.

"Yes," he hissed, as though making some great realization. "Conservative. Exactly. Smooth, clean, quiet. For a man built like a tower, it was astounding. The way he eased through the crowd, as though he were barely there. I don't think i'Syul saw me himself, but I must have seemed a real idiot to the rest of the market, what with me standing with my mouth hanging open like some buffoon."

Beside him, Talo couldn't help but chuckle.

"What's so funny?" Kal asked, frowning at the man.

"Syrah once told me a very similar story." Talo was still laughing to himself, watching the restless crowd around them. "And I wouldn't worry about the crowd. If i'Syul is anything like you and Syrah describe him, I'm sure you weren't the only one staring."

Kal seemed about to respond, but paused, considering.

"… I suppose," he said after a moment, looking back down into the pit thoughtfully. "I don't know. If you or Carro had been there, I doubt you'd have been caught frozen in place."

"You obviously don't know Carro yet," Talo said with another laugh. "As for me, well… I've seen a great many interesting things out in the world, Kal. I've seen a great many interesting things in this very Arena, in fact." He waved a hand to indicate the stadium around them. "But in truth, coming across a seven-foot-tall lizard-man while shopping for my morning bread might top most of the surprising experiences even *I* can think of."

Kal snorted, then grew quiet. For a time the two High Priests sat in silence, looking about as the throng thickened with every passing minute.

After a while, though, Kal spoke again.

"Talo… You say you've seen things in this place. Tell me then… Why are we here?"

Talo turned to look at him, eyebrow raised curiously.

"I thought it fairly obvious," he said with half a smile. "We're here to see the fights."

"Yes but—but why?" It was Kal's turn to wave a gloved hand at the pit below them. "This place. The things you must have witnessed. 'Interesting' things, you said, but I don't think that's what you mean… As long as I've known you, as many letters as we have exchanged over the years, you've never been keen to revisit this part of your past. So I ask again: Why are we here?"

For a moment, Talo did nothing. He watched Kal, silently mulling over his answer, reflecting on the words he could not seem to say. Turning away, his eyes found the pit Kal had just been indicating.

The pit where he had spent so much of his life…

In truth, Talo wasn't sure he could explain himself to the High Priest. He wasn't even sure he had explained himself well to Carro that morning when the man had asked him—somewhat green at the thought of the fights—the same question Kal was inquiring on now. He'd tried, of course. He'd done his best to put words to the convoluted feelings and emotions that had been crashing over him since he'd first received Kal's letter, vestiges of which he'd been feeling for decades before that. In the end, Talo wasn't sure he had aptly explained the simple fact that, when all was said and done, he needed to witness with his own two eyes the newfound freedom of the dreadful beast he'd fought so hard to cage in the first place.

A beast which, before he'd been able to see the world through the eyes of the Lifegiver, had bought him his own freedom and given him reason to live.

"It wasn't easy," Talo said finally. "It wasn't easy, locking away this Arena, banning it, then all its counterparts, from the North."

Kal—who seemed to have thought he wasn't going to get a response—sat up straight.

"I know," he said with a nod, leaning to rest his elbows on knees, hands hanging between his legs. "I was there for much of that fight, remember? For the first decade of it we—"

"No," Talo cut him off. "I mean it wasn't an easy choice to make. To *keep* making. Every day I fought to close this stadium, every decision we made in order to do so. I was fighting with myself as much as we were fighting anyone else."

Kal said nothing.

"This place," Talo continued, looking up into the stands opposite them, gazing into the crowd, "it's taken so much from so many. It's claimed lives, limbs, loved ones. It's stolen hope and happiness."

"But not yours."

It was a simple statement, but it took Talo completely by surprise. He turned once more to look at Kal, eyes wide. Even Carro hadn't been able to understand…

"Exactly," Talo said, not looking away from the man. "No. Not mine. Never mine."

Kal nodded.

"It gave you much, this Arena," he said. "I understand. What you feel is base gratitude. Every man falls prey to it, even—no, *especially*—the best of us. We of the faith are grateful, for example. We are grateful for life. We are grateful to Laor for His gift."

"A gratitude we share now, yes, but not then. Then you prayed to your god for life, and I prayed to mine for death."

Kal nodded again.

"Fair enough, but you were still grateful. Grateful for something. Reason, purpose, meaning. Whatever name you choose to give it, it doesn't matter. You carried that with you in the ring, and you carried it beyond when you came into the faith."

"I do still."

At this, Kal paused.

"Ah," he breathed. "I see now…"

Talo frowned.

"You do?" he asked, unbelieving.

Kal shrugged a shoulder nonchalantly, then lounged back again, looking up into the sky almost lazily.

"I do." Without looking away from the pale rolling of the graying sky, he continued. "Doubt. Hesitation. Regret. All by-products of decision, of action. All men doubt. All men hesitate. I'm not so sure all men regret, but perhaps they should. Tell me, do you regret the end of the Arena?"

"No."

That answer was easy. Once Talo had made the decision, it had been final even in his own mind.

"But you doubt? You hesitate?"

"Did," Talo said. He, too, turned to look up at the overcast sky. The great walls of the Arena shielded the stands themselves from much of the wind, but even so a faint breeze kicked about them, teasing loose strands of long straight hair around his bearded face. "I did doubt. I did hesitate. Then the time for both was done and the choice was made."

Talo sighed, watching the minute outline of a pair of crows cross the stadium far overhead, their distant calls lost to the noise of the crowd.

"It wasn't an easy choice, like I said. That pit took everything from many, but gave as much to some. To turn my back on it, to betray the stones that had given me life and purpose… It wasn't easy, but it had to be done. Now though, that choice, that impossible decision that I had to make and did make… it's all coming undone."

"There is no shame in gratitude, Talo," Kal said wisely.

"Perhaps not, but it isn't shame I feel now. Once, maybe, but I've long since come to terms with it. Now… Now I feel fear. Now despite all you have told me, despite everything Carro and I saw as we explored the city… Now I feel disbelief."

Kal nodded.

"Your life's work," he said thoughtfully. "A time full of hard decisions and even harder fights. I can understand. A man, told of the death of his son, does not believe until he holds the body in his hands."

It was Talo's turn to nod.

"Exactly."

"And you have to see it for yourself."

Now, Talo took his eyes from the sky, away from old thoughts and memories. Once more he looked down into the pit, that circular scar of blood and mud. Once more he smelled the tang of iron and death in the caress of the wind.

"And I have to see it for myself."

XVII

"Before they enter the ring, every gladiator is different. Some are calm, composed, though often falsely so. Others make no attempt to hide their fear, shivering and whimpering in the dust before the gates that they suspect wholeheartedly will open upon their demise. Some pray. Some check steel one last time. Some practice footwork, or mutter encouragements to themselves. The only thing they all have in common, every man and woman among them, is that they do something. Even in exhibition matches, where little blood is ever spilt, we are unable—or perhaps simply unwilling?—to bear complete mind to the battle at hand."

—private journal of Alyssa Rhen

Raz leaned against the dirt-and-timber wall of the Arena underworks, wings stretched slightly to either side of him to keep them from getting uncomfortably pinned. His head was bowed, eyes closed, with one clawed foot on the ground and the other bent up to rest on the wall itself. He had his arms crossed with Ahna tucked in the nook of one elbow, the higher part of her haft resting against his shoulder. Her blades were bare, their leather sack left in the Doctore's quarters along with his furs and cloak to be retrieved after the fights were done, though some would bet he wouldn't be alive to do so.

Privately, without looking up, Raz smiled.

"Something funny?"

Raz opened his eyes at the question. A contingent of ten guardsmen, hands on weapon hilts, stood around him in a half circle, effectively cutting him off from the rest of the fighters in the chamber. All around them, much like any other day beneath the Arena's stands, men and women were milling about tending to armor, oiling their weapons, or sparring in preparation. These figures, though, were of a different sort than the gladiators Alyssa Rhen had under her care. Rather than being whet under careful guidance and training, they were hardened by life and honed by hardship. These were rough people, many among them undoubtedly as cruel as they were dangerous.

And each and every one of them was in turn giving Raz looks that left nothing to the imagination as to what they intended for him and the ten thousand crown price on his head.

Raz turned to look at the guard who had spoken, the furthest to the left, and the youngest of the lot. He was a freckly youth, well built and handsome, with curly blond hair that fell in ringlets from beneath his plain soldier's helm. He had green-brown eyes that might have been attractive any other time, but right now were ugly with disdain as he looked over his shoulder at Raz.

Raz said nothing. Instead he looked directly at the man and smiled wider, revealing every one of his white, needlelike teeth.

The guardsman blanched, but turned angrily to face him, opening his mouth in doubtless preparation to spit some insult meant to goad Raz into doing something stupid. The man to curly's right, however, stopped him with an outstretched hand and spun the youth back around to face the chamber.

"Leave it, Wylson," Raz heard him mutter. "It'll be a job enough protecting the lizard from these bastards *without* wondering if he's gonna take a bite out of my arse while my back's turned."

Chuckling at the image, Raz looked back over their heads into the rest of the busy room.

Quin Tern certainly knows how to make a message heard...

According to the last count given to him by Rhen, some five-hundred and fifty odd had beaten the snow to Azbar and signed up to fight. Half a dozen of those were dead by Raz's own hand already, being fool enough to risk the Chairman's wrath and take him on in broad daylight in the streets. When it became clear anyone who tried to take Raz by surprise didn't *live* long enough to face said wrath, though, the attempts ended.

Still, even after another score had been thrown from the city for brawls and other such hassles, that left well over five hundred capable men and women within the walls of Azbar to fill the Arena's lists. So many, in fact, that the council had been hard-pressed to figure out what to do with all of them.

In the end they'd decided on simplicity, and the Chairman's Tourney had been conceived, an endless series of consecutive four-day events. Bouts of thirty-two matches would run over the first two days, each with four brackets of eight fighters. The third day was a gap, in order to allow recovery of the finalists, during which Arena gladiators and the bounty hunters alike could vie to participate in matches for the pleasure of the crowds, winning themselves favor and gold in the process. On the fourth day there would be exhibition matches of a similar style, then the four winners of the tournament days would face Raz together, as individuals, or in any combination they saw fit. If they chose to band together, Raz would be allowed his full gear. If they split into pairs, he would have his gladius.

If they chose to take him on individually, Raz would be granted nothing more than his armor.

Raz had been there when Tern had made these announcements to the hundreds of bounty hunters, speaking down on them from his Chairman's box as they stood in the stadium of the Arena. He'd caught many self-assured smiles and exchanged glances of glee between old friends and comrades-in-arms.

He had every intention of making them realize how premature their confidence had been.

Today was the opening day. Tomorrow the tournaments would start in truth. For now, though, Tern had wanted something special to captivate the massive crowd he had gathered for the experience. He'd evened the odds of the matches, crafting only four branches of four fighters for today's opening battles. The four winners would be given brief reprieve while Arena gladiators kept the crowds entertained, then they'd return to the ring to face Raz in what the Chairman had called a "special event."

Raz couldn't be sure what the man had meant, but he knew one thing: though Tern gained nothing from letting him die this early in his tourney, the man was clever enough to make even guaranteed survival look interesting.

"Let me through."

Raz looked around. Alyssa Rhen was passing between two of his protective detail, stepping towards him. The Doctore wore dyed crimson furs over her leathers today, along with a thick black scarf she was pulling down off her face as she approached.

"How's it look?" Raz asked as she stopped beside him.

Rhen looked over her shoulder, past the guard into the crowd of fighters. Her brow creased in annoyance.

"As bad as ever," she said without looking around. "Nothing new to you, though. Same as your bouts last week. The ground is frozen and the puddles are ice. Use both to your advantage. These idiots won't know the pit, so if you're smart you'll get through without much trouble."

Raz chuckled, shifting into a more comfortable position on the wall.

"If I didn't know better, I'd say you were worried about me, Doctore."

Alyssa sighed, crossing her arms. The scar along the right side of her face tugged angrily at her lip as she turned back to face him.

"Worried for you and worried for your intentions are not necessarily mutually exclusive, Arro. If you fall, then what you've managed to pull together here falls with you. All of it."

Raz nodded. "I don't plan on falling, least of all anytime soon."

"Then why this farce?" Alyssa hissed indignantly, indicating the bounty hunters beyond the ring of guards. "Between the tournament fighters and the exhibitionists, there are at least two dozen men and women down here who want nothing more than to see you dead. If you think even *you* could fight your way out of that, I should reconsider my wagers on grounds of insanity."

"You're betting on me?" Raz laughed. "I'm touched. But don't worry, your money is safe enough. Tern is a bastard, but—whether fortunately or unfortunately in the long run—he's far from stupid. He knows there won't be any fighting down here. Here, if I die, it's on a man's word who delivered the killing blow. Even if it's true, it leaves him with a target on his back for whoever wants to claim the bounty for themselves. No. They'll wait. They'll wait until they have ten thousand witnesses to corroborate their claim."

"Thirteen today," Alyssa snorted. "Tern's not charging entry, to build up the excitement. There are thirteen thousand spectators in those stands right now."

"Well then," Raz said as a horn sounded above them, echoing down through the portcullis at the top of the gangway, "we'd best not disappoint, should we?"

"No," Alyssa said. Then she smiled slowly. "And speaking of… The reason I came down here. I need to borrow Ahna, if you don't mind."

When the horn blew, calling for the attention of the spectators, Talo suspected he might go deaf from the noise. As one, thousands leapt to their feet, bellowing and hollering in tumultuous excitement. For a minute his view was partially blocked by the backs of the men in front of he and Kal, so he didn't notice the arrival of the fat man until the throng finally calmed and started falling back onto their seats.

Quin Tern was as unlike his father as it was possible to be. Whereas Markus had been tall and slim of form, Quin's girth seemed to take up most of the open terrace that led back into the alcove of the Chairman's box. He wore heavy silver robes that swirled around his great form as he moved, and Talo could see the distinct glint of gold on the hand waving for quiet over the stands.

When silence finally fell, the man's strong voice echoed out over the stand.

"Friends!" Tern boomed, extending an arm to the crowd. "Citizens and honored guests! It is my distinct pleasure, as Chairman of this grand city, to welcome you this day! Through hard times and cold winters Azbar has stood as a shining pinnacle in the North, a bastion of culture and civilization, tall and strong among the wilds of the woods. Our ancestors of old built this great Arena, and many more after them stood on the very stone beneath your feet. Blood and iron are the ways of the North. Steel and hardship are our kin!"

Tern paused then, thumping a fist to his chest, where it rested across his heart.

"Here today, though, men will sacrifice so that your burden might be lessened. Today, many will bleed so that you do not have to. The gates of the Arena are open once more, and Azbar no longer suffers as it did. We of the council have risked the wrath of the Lifegiver Himself in this endeavor, but it is our own small gift to you. Winter knocks anew at our door, but no longer will you be hard-pressed to pay for the wood to keep your houses warm, or the bread to keep your families fed. From within these walls"—Tern spread both arms wide to indicate the great circular expanse of the stadium—"Azbar will grow firm again. By the blood shed on this earth"—he pointed imperiously down into the pit before him—"we of the council pledge ourselves to your unending protection, that you might never need fear again."

Tern stopped again as the crowd erupted at that, many leaping to their feet once more. Talo and Kal exchanged dubious glances.

"However," Tern continued at last as the stadium quieted once more, "that pledge is not just made on *any* blood. It is not made on the blood of our brave gladiators, fighting so hard for you and your entertainment. It is not made on the unworthy lives of criminals, whose deaths were no more than vindicated punishment doled out for your pleasure. No, our pledge is made on the souls of *true* warriors, hard men and women from every corner of the North and beyond! Azbar called, and they came, beating even winter in their pursuit of glory. You have seen them among you, witnessed their fierceness with your own two eyes. They come hungry, savagely desirous of one thing and one thing only!"

At this, Tern half turned to gesture behind him. At once two servants in pale-gold robes hurried forward, both clearly straining to keep hold of each end of what they held in their arms.

"I present to you," Tern roared as the crowd once again erupted at the sight of the thing, "Ahna, the great spear of the fiercest warrior our world has ever seen, the Scourge of the South, RAZ I'SYUL ARRO!"

If Talo hadn't been going deaf before, he was certain he would now. This time, though, he couldn't really blame the hysterical screaming and jumping of the masses. The weapon the two men hefted up for the crowd to see was a magnificent thing, as beautiful in its simplicity as it was terrifying in design. More than seven feet long from the heavy point on one end to the tips of its twin, gently curving blades on the other, the spear looked to have a wood haft, but by the weight it seemed to carry—judging from the shaking of its bearers—there was more to it than that.

"Steel born of the fiery Southern gods," Tern continued, turning back to the crowd even as he continued to gesture at Ahna. "So heavy two men can hardly lift her. Today her presence is our benediction, our reminder of what it is the men and women you will see before you are fighting for. Her master is meant to be their prey. Will they manage it? Will some of the fiercest warriors in our great lands hold up to the savagery of our Monster?"

To this, the response was tumultuous denial. All screamed and shouted their "no"s and "never"s, aggressively waving downward-pointing thumbs in contradiction.

"*Our* Monster?" Kal hissed in outrage. "Well, you can't say Tern doesn't know how to win himself a crowd."

Talo nodded, but didn't reply as the Chairman's voice picked up once more.

"You think not? You think our Southern legend will have what it takes to fight the best we have to offer? Very well! Then let this spear be as much a symbol to him as it is to us! Let his Ahna be displayed to remind him that he does not fight for himself today, with all the advantages the world has to offer. No! Raz i'Syul, for the first time in his life, fights for another. He fights for you, fights for this Arena, and fights for the IRON SPIRIT OF OUR GREAT CITY OF AZBAR!"

Tern's final words rang strong and clear, and one last time the crowd applauded him with a roar. Turning away from the stands, Tern nodded to the men holding Ahna aloft. At once they lowered her to the ground. For a brief moment Talo and Kal couldn't see the weapon as the attendants fumbled around with something. Then they were picking the spear up again, and Talo saw that loose rope nooses had been looped around both of her ends. As he watched, the men began lowering Ahna over the edge of the Chairman's box, careful to keep her haft even and balanced. When they finally stopped, tying the ropes off somewhere beyond Talo's scope of vision, the spear hung symbolically below the Chairman's box, suspended what must have been just short of twenty feet in the air above the muddy pit floor.

Unable to help himself, Talo chuckled.

"Clever bastard."

Kal turned to look at him. "What's funny?" he asked.

Talo was about to answer, but was interrupted by the trumpeting of yet another horn.

"You'll see," he said simply, eyes back on the pit as a row of men and women in well-worn gear of all kinds marched their way into view from the raised portcullis in the west wall. They were of the same sort as the man who had followed the Priests into Azbar nearly a week ago—Galen, Talo seemed to recall. All of them, even the three or four women among their sixteen, looked tougher than their boiled leathers and colder than the steel of the swords, spears, and axes drawn and bare for the enjoyment of the crowds. A pair of heralds stepped forward to replace Tern in the alcove opening as the Chairman drew back to a heavy throne-like timber chair to watch the fights. In turn they announced the names and titles of the fighters, pausing between each to allow the mentioned man or woman to thrust weapons in the air and for the crowd to have its approval heard.

When the last of the names were called, the trumpet sounded again, and most of the group strode back out of the pit into the Arena underworks once more. When they were gone, two were left.

"First bout!" one of the heralds called loudly out over the stand. "Manoth Corm"—he indicated a bald, heavy man in dented plate, a two-handed maul clenched tightly in mailed fists beneath his thick beard—"to challenge Barsyn, Hunter of the Dehn!"

The other man, slighter and far younger than Corm, raised sword and round shield to the crowds as he turned in a circle, throwing a handsome smile to the women in the lowest seats. On the other side of the pit, Corm hadn't so much as glanced up as the stands had cheered for him, spitting impatiently on the ground at his feet and hefting his weapon in preparation.

"The big man is done for," Talo muttered as the men squared off.

Kal raised a brow. "Are we to bet on the matches, then?"

Talo snorted at that. "I think the Lifegiver might frown on me stealing your gold off the backs of dead men. No. Still, as I said: Corm is done for."

"No bets then," Kal agreed. "But I think you're wrong. Corm has the weight and reach on the boy."

Talo hitched a shoulder in half a shrug. "I suppose we'll have to see," he said as the herald vanished into the Chairman's box.

For the first time since they'd sat down over an hour ago, silence gripped the stadium, all eyes on the Chairman. Quin Tern leaned forward in his chair, gazing down upon the men ready to kill for him below.

"Begin."

And so it did.

Manoth Corm—as Talo suspected he might—charged forward at once, bellowing a war cry as he ran. His maul swung up and over in a two-handed slash, bearing down on Barsyn's head, well above any defensible angle. For half a heartbeat Talo thought the boy would let himself be crushed. Then, at the last possible moment, Barsyn stepped out of the way, striking at Corm's exposed side as the older man's maul smashed into frozen earth, sending icy mud flying.

Sword hit heavy plate, though, and the blow was fouled.

Barsyn leapt clear even as Corm took a heavy swipe sideways at him with a mailed fist. Then the maul was out of the ground, and Corm lumbered forward once again.

For some time the fight continued like this. Corm charging in with heavy blows, trusting in his strength and weight, obviously under the impression he could bull his way into a win. Barsyn, in turn, would dodge left, right, and back, avoiding the bulk of the maul's strikes by leaping aside or deflecting them skillfully with angled parries of his shield. Occasionally, when the opportunity presented itself, he would attempt to sneak through Corm's defense, aiming for angles and weak points in the plate. Corm, though, was obviously experienced enough to know what the boy was attempting, avoiding steel with quick twists and shifts that left Barsyn's sword ringing against solid iron each time.

By all accounts, despite the differences in their size, age, and style, the two were well matched. Talo had to appreciate, with some reservation, the skill of whoever was in charge of pairing the bouts.

For a few minutes more the crowd gasped and "ooh"ed as the combatants went about playing their game of cat and mouse. Ordinarily the elongation of such repetitive engagements might have bored them, but the air itself was so thick with excitement and anticipation of the day that Talo wouldn't have put it past the men and women of the crowd to have kept cheering if the fight lasted another hour.

Fortunately, though, it didn't.

It was a sudden mistake, easily avoided if Corm had troubled to keep mind of his surroundings. As it was, the older man—as Talo had known and, he suspected, Barsyn as well—was too focused on chasing the Hunter of the Dehn around the ring to be bothered with watching his footing, intent on crushing the boy with superior size and strength. It was sadly predictable, as it was the mindset of most larger fighters. Trusting in their mass worked for them in general but, when it failed them, it was their end.

That, Talo supposed, and the slick patch of ice that found its way under Corm's left foot.

The big man went down, crashing onto his left side, momentarily pinned under the weight of his armor. In a blink Barsyn was on him, sword flashing once in the sun, going for the one place where there was no armor.

Steel found the crook beneath jaw and neck, hiding under Manoth Corm's thick beard, and the older man died without a sound, windpipe severed along with the thick veins in the flesh paralleling the spine.

Barsyn raised his bloodied sword to the heavens, and the crowd rose to their feet in a frenzy, cheering and applauding with renewed gusto.

"Such a waste," Kal said sadly, having remained seated beside Talo. He watched as a handful of footmen in plain brown-and-gray uniforms hurried onto the field to start dragging away Corm's motionless form. Barsyn, still waving and beaming into the crowd, followed the body down beneath the Arena.

"'Death is the beginning of new, just as birth is the end of old,'" Talo quoted, echoing past words of Eret Ta'hir. "Somewhere in this world,

Corm will return soon enough."

"Then let us pray his next ending isn't in a place like that," grumbled Kal, pointing down into the pit. "Still… how did you know he was going to lose?"

Talo half smiled at the question. "Surviving a duel is as much about being able to wield and control your own strengths as it is knowing an opponent's weaknesses. Corm never learned that. You could see it in his bearing. He was itching to end the fight as soon as possible. The big ones usually are."

"*You're* big," Kal retorted with a chuckle. "Is that how you did it?"

"Fortunately, no. I figured out as much of my own strengths and weaknesses as I did my opponents'. Each match I learned all over again when to strike, where to strike, and how to strike. They can teach you how you're *supposed* to do something, but showing you how to adapt when what you've been taught is more likely to get you killed is another beast entirely."

"And I suppose you adapted," Kal said with a whistle.

"I suppose I did."

XVIII

"Only so many of the statues that once stood in the Hall of Heroes remain intact today. Among them, though, is an oddity. While all the others comprised of carefully cast bronze on a heavy marble pedestal, there is one that is made of cheap iron, bent and hammered into its rough but unmistakable shape. Though Raz i'Syul Arro was—for numerous obvious reasons—never deemed worthy of standing among the other greats by the leading parties of Azbar, it seems that there were plenty among the city's people who thought otherwise. So many, in fact, that when the crude depiction of his form was set among the Heroes, one must venture that the council knew better than to order it removed."

—*A Comprised History of the Arenas*, by unknown author

The fights took most of the day. From his place on the wall, Raz watched the pairs take the gangway, one after another. He started to play a game with himself, attempting to guess who would survive and who the Arena's attendants would roll down the ramp as a corpse at the end of a bout. On a few occasions no one died, one combatant having yielded to the other in the hopes of living to fight another day.

On one occasion, both were rolled.

Raz had to give the Doctore her credit. She knew how to judge the men and women she'd been presented. Most often he guessed correctly who would walk down the ramp and who would tumble, but not always. There were a few surprises here and there. A thin, dirty fellow wielding nothing more than a pair of daggers beneath his tattered cloak strode unscathed behind the bloody body of man in leather armor, a man Raz had been quite sure could handle the curved saber he'd had strapped to one hip. Later, an older woman with a scar that split the dark hair along her left scalp had to be helped down the gangway by the attendants, having bested a spearman Raz would have put his money on. Then again, judging by the darkness of the cloth she clutched against her abdomen, glistening wet in the light of the underworks' torches, he wasn't so sure he'd been that far off.

The day went on, Raz watching from behind his assigned guard, the crowd of fighters thinning out with every hour. He had thought he'd get bored, but the sound of the matches above coupled with the waxing and waning commentary of the crowd kept him thoroughly entertained. The metallic stench of blood was fresher now, accented with oiled leather and sweat. Before long, Raz even felt the edges of true excitement brushing against his conscience, the kind he used to get when handed a contract that demanded the head of a slaver. By the time attendants brought him food at midday—seared venison and some sort of spiced vegetable stew he didn't bother with—Raz was hard-pressed to stop himself from demanding how much longer he would have to wait. He loathed the Arena and its spectators. He would never have given them the blood that they wanted, never oblige to the butchering of the innocents and gladiators Tern and his council would have thrown to him as fodder in an instant if they thought it would turn them a profit.

This, though… These hunters had come with every intention of seeing him dead. They would take any and every chance they could to separate his head from his shoulders and ride it south to Miropa.

Yes… This blood, Raz could give to the crowd more than willingly.

"Final bout," the high voice of one of the heralds called out eventually. "Athur the Goat Man to challenge Lelan val'En. Combatants… BEGIN!"

Raz droned out the ensuing clash of steel on steel, already almost drowned by the thousands of cheers so loud it was hard on his ears even down here in the underworks. Instead, Raz stepped away from the wall he'd been leaning against once more and stretched his wings. Then, one limb at a time, he began to loosen up, not wanting to be stiff for what lay ahead.

"Any man can lose to any other man," Jarden Arro had once told him. "Only a fool doesn't consider the fact that every fight, any fight, might be his last."

Raz rolled his long neck, loosening it with several distinct pops that made a couple of his guard glance over their shoulder. Next he rolled shoulders and stretched wrists, opening and closing fists to ensure cold fingers stayed strong and ready. By the time he finished all of his little exercises, the crowd's volume had reached new heights, and a minute later the portcullis at the top of the ramp was raised once more.

In life, Athur the Goat Man had been nearly as round as he was tall. In death this served him well—or at least the Arena attendants tasked to ridding the pit of his body. The man needed little more than a half push before he tumbled down of his own accord, hitting the underwork floor with a muffled thump and the crunch of adjusting dirt. The attendants scurried behind him, huffing and grunting to shift his massive form so that they could roll him away into the side chamber that housed the bodies of the other defeated until they could be disposed of.

After them, the Southerner Lelan val'En strode imperiously down the ramp, broadsword and dagger still drawn, both reddened to the hilt. He was a tall man with large shoulders and long arms that let him use his paired weapons to great effect. He had a pinched face, though, the kind that made him look as though he were always staring down his nose at something. It didn't go well with his darker complexion, and it didn't endear him to Raz at all.

Nor did the raising of his sword to point in Raz's direction.

"Like tha', scaly?" val'En spat, waving the dagger in his other hand to indicate the body of the Goat Man the attendants were still struggling with. "Enjoy the show. Ain't nothin' keepin' me from dumpin' your carcass in the pile with the rest of them, now."

"Oh," Raz replied with a smile, "I can think of one or two things that might make it difficult for you, val'En. You're one of four, don't forget. A few of the others might have something to say about you claiming the price on my head all for yourself."

"Just gotta promise you I'll get to you first, then, ain't I?"

This time Raz allowed a little of the excitement he hadn't been able to temper leak out into his smile. It must have shown, hungry on his reptilian features as the red crest on his neck flared half-erect, since val'En seemed to lose a little of the Southern bravado in his dark eyes.

"I hope you can keep that promise, Southerner. Because if you don't get to me first, I swear on the Sun above I'll get to you last."

To his credit, val'En recovered his composure well. Seemingly choosing not to dignify Raz with an answer, he spat once more and strode off, wiping his blades clean on the side of his thick cotton pants as he walked. Raz watched him go until the man turned a corner in the underwork tunnels and disappeared.

There goes one we'll enjoy taking a chunk out of, huh, sis?

Raz shivered, opening and closing his hands again. He had enough faith in the Doctore to have entrusted her and her helpers with Ahna without much pause. Still, he felt bare without the dviassegai at his side. Anytime she wasn't within reach, in fact, he felt much the same. Now, not knowing where she was, the bareness was accented with a tinge of loss.

Funny enough, though, Raz had the distinct impression he would be seeing Ahna again soon.

About five minutes after val'En's departure, the gladiators of the Arena began forming along the gangway. They would provide entertainment for the next half hour while the four finalists rested and had any minor wounds stitched up and cared for. Then all would be called back to the Arena, and the finale of the Chairman's Tourney's opening day would begin.

For the first time since that morning, Raz finally grew restless. The combat he could hear above seemed to draw little more from the crowd than the occasional cheer or—more often—jeer. The herald kept up a lively commentary that helped paint the picture a little, but from the sound of it the spectators seemed barely satisfied with the entertainment offered during this brief interlude.

And Tern knows that, Raz realized, watching the misting gray light descend in rays through the wooden crossbars at the top of the ramp. *He's teasing them just enough so that, when the main course finally shows, they'll be starving for blood.*

At long last, after what felt more like half a day than a mere half hour, the herald announced the conclusion of the exhibitions. There was relative silence as the gladiators gave their formal thanks to the stands for their attention and patronage, and then the men and women under Alyssa's care marched back down into the underworks, sparing Raz more than a few glances of loathing on the way. Not a minute after them, three men—including val'En—and a woman crossed before Raz's guard to gather along the ramp. While val'En wore light leather over striped cloth, the other two men—Wellen Ryvers and Tymoth Barse, if Raz remembered correctly—wore a mixed fit of studded leather and plate over chain. Each had won their branches of the tourney decisively, not letting any match go longer than a minute. In one hand, both men carried a tower shield. In the other, though, Wellen preferred a flanged mace to Tymoth's longsword. Had it not been obvious by their matching skill and equipment, the whispered conversation they were having a pace from the other two only confirmed the pair knew each other.

Something to keep in mind, Raz thought as he turned his eyes on the woman.

Sona, she'd called herself simply. Unlike the others, the woman was there partially by luck, having won her final bout by default when her would-be opponent succumbed to wounds he'd received vying for his shot. Despite this, Sona was also the one Raz thought most likely to take him by surprise. A heavy cloth cloak hung over and around her shoulders, and he'd seen nothing of her body except for pale Northern legs over furred boots slip through the slit in her cape as she walked. Her bouts had been surprisingly quiet, and faster even than Ryvers' or Barth's. Judging by the response of the crowd, though, whatever she'd done had been entertainment enough to forgive her the speed of her kills.

"Combatants! Up the ramp! The gate opens in one minute!"

Alyssa Rhen had appeared again, showing up for the first time since Raz had seen her that morning. She looked weary, the age in her face more pronounced than ever.

"Something the matter?" Raz asked as she passed through his ring of guards again.

"You try explaining to a score of men and women, all armed, why the crowd—usually so fond of them—barely gave them so much as a whistle as they fought," she said angrily, coming to stop before him and crossing her arms.

Raz shrugged. "Your spectators have a taste for blood. They've been teased all day. Did you expect it to go any better?"

Alyssa shrugged, raising one hand to press on her eyes. "No, of course not, but *they* didn't. Nor did they want to hear that. You robbed three hundred gladiators of a majority of their livelihood when you showed up. They're keen on any reason to blame you, these days."

"My, I'm so shocked," Raz said dryly as the herald called out again. "However will I live with myself now?"

Alyssa smirked, looking over her shoulder to watch the portcullis lift.

"Spectators!"

It was no longer the herald, but Tern now, who addressed the Arena once more.

"Friends! You have witnessed today some of the finest blades in the world! You have picked your winners and placed your bets! Cheered for your survivors and mourned your lost! Now, though, the true entertainment begins. In a moment's time you will meet again the brave warriors come to slay the great Scourge of the South, the four who fought hardest, survived longest, just to win and keep your affections!"

The crowd roared in unison, screaming their approval.

"They had best prepare, though," Tern continued in a theatrically hushed tone that still managed to carry through the stadium. "They had best be ready, for what comes out of the gate after them is more than man, more even than beast. Raz i'Syul Arro has claimed more lives than any ten you saw today combined. He has fought—and won—many battles in this very Arena. He has no blades, armed only with steel claws and teeth stained by the blood of the murdered. He comes with no intention of dying, and every intention of feeding your hunger."

The crowd was quiet now, hanging on to the Chairman's every word.

"So!" Tern's voice picked up again, climbing back into an excited pitch. "Who will you choose? Will you cheer for the brave four, come to slay the Monster and claim their reward? Or will you stand behind your champion, a being more savage than anything to have ever walked this earth? Whatever you decide, it is time to PLACE. YOUR. BETS!"

Over the boom of the stands, the herald began calling the names of the four finalists. Raz didn't make out the first two, but watched as val'En and Ryvers disappeared through the gate. Sona was next, and he heard the distinct cheers for her name as she stepped out into the gray sunlight. Barth went last, and finally Raz was alone, with only Alyssa and the guard standing between him and his turn in the pit.

"I guess I don't need to tell you to watch your ass?" the Doctore said half sarcastically, half warningly.

"If you did, I doubt we would ever have gotten this far," Raz laughed, stepping forward.

With only a moment's hesitation the guard parted, and he started to climb the gangway. The cold of the outside air clawed at him almost immediately as he got close to the gate, chilling the steel of his armor and tips of his fingers and ears. He kept moving, though, eyes on the dim glow that was the Sun in a cloud-darkened sky above.

Perhaps it was good the Twins couldn't see what would happen here today.

"Now," the herald shouted, cutting over the crowd, "it is time to meet the challenger. Men and women of Azbar, stand in welcome of your champion! Enter, RAZ I'SYUL ARRO!"

XIX

Raz blinked away the momentary blindness of stepping back into the day. When he could see normally, he had to actively deny himself the temptation to stare openmouthed into the stands.

Never in his life, not even in the thriving mass markets of Miropa, had Raz ever seen so many people.

His fights before today had drawn the crowd, even selling out the Arena, according to Rhen. Now, though, the masses flowed like ants, an ocean of colored furs and cloth that undulated unnaturally, as though blown by a hundred different winds in all directions. They numbered so many that Raz could literally feel the heat of their bodies in the moderate coolness of the air that—by all rights—should have been frigid.

So this is what thirteen thousand looks like, he thought to himself, standing in the pit at the mouth of the portcullis that had already begun to lower behind him. *Who knew there were this many people in the world?*

As he looked around, a form directly across from him caught his eye. The Chairman sat in a great throne-like chair, scooted very near the edge of his box. His eyes, clear cold blue even from this distance, were watching Raz expectantly, though he demonstrated no such inclination by any other indication. Beside and behind him, an ever-present shadow almost invisible in the shade of the alcove, Azzeki Koro stood watch. The whites of his dark eyes were on Raz as well, though Raz imagined there was more hope for failure in them than the Captain-Commander would ever let his master see.

And there, below them both, suspended by ropes against the stone wall some seventeen or eighteen feet above the pit, was Ahna.

Raz couldn't help it. He smiled.

Clever fucking bastard.

"Ready to die, lizard?"

Raz looked away from the dviassegai. Though no one had called a start to the fight, the four finalists were already spread out to encircle him. They held their ground for the time being, but Raz could see the itch in their forms, a longing to bear steel down on him. His back was barely a foot from wooden crossbeams, and he had nowhere to run.

Still, he kept smiling, turning his attention to val'En who had, naturally, posed the question.

"One day, Southerner," he answered, setting his body into a defensive stance as Tern heaved himself to his feet above the pit. "Tomorrow even, possibly. But not today. I hope you remember my promise."

val'En looked none too pleased with this response, his already pinched face twisting into an even uglier snarl. He was the middle left of the half circle. Ryvers and Barth flanked Raz on either side with their shields readied before them, and Sona held middle right. She appeared the distinct weak link of the lot, her smaller form still covered by the wide mantle. Raz watched her size him up, eyeing him from behind a crop of dirty-brown bangs. Her gaze rested momentarily on every part of him. Legs, shoulders, chest, head. She had the look of someone prepping themself for a split-second decision.

Abruptly, Raz thought he knew what was beneath that billowing fur cape of hers, and decisions snapped into place one after the other. He didn't take his eyes off her even as Tern stepped forward, out of the shade of his box, into the dim light.

"COMBATANTS!" he boomed, raising a hand in the air, where it paused, holding the stillness of the day.

Then, like the blade of a guillotine, it dropped.

"BEGIN!"

All four converged on Raz at once, clearly hoping to rush in and finish the job quick, but he was already moving. The moment Tern had spoken he'd taken off, making a line right for Sona, the "weak link" of the group.

The weak link who knew all too well that was what she looked like, just as Raz knew every other fighter she'd faced today had thought. His theory was confirmed when the barest hint of a smile crossed her hard face, and she brought both hands up from beneath her cloak.

Had Raz not had his suspicions, the heavy crossbow she had tucked against her right hip would have been the end of him.

As it was, though, the massive bolt, rather than taking him squarely through the chest, whizzed harmlessly over his back as he rolled under it. He thought he heard the woman start to curse, but she hadn't managed to finish the word when his steel gauntlet hammered into her gut, bearing with it all the weight of his body as the momentum of his roll carried him forward, out of the controlled little pocket the four of them had set up.

Sona herself flew backwards, tumbling and sliding over the slick ground, coming to a rest huddled and wretching a few paces from the wall beneath the Chairman's box, the crossbow still clenched in one hand.

Right where he wanted her.

val'En and Ryvers yelled as Raz ran, calling him coward and other names when he bolted away. Only Barth, the mace wielder, realized what he was doing.

"No!" he howled. "Don't let him get to—!"

But it was far too late. Raz doubted even Sona—struggling to her feet again as he whipped past her—would have had a prayer of getting a bolt in him as he leapt. Eighteen feet straight up would have been impossible even for him. The first jump, though, got him ten feet in the air, where his clawed feet found good purchase on the incline of the rough wall meant to allow the spectators to see from every angle.

The second got him the other eight.

One hand found Ahna's haft, and even through the battlefog Raz made out the roar of the stands at that. Letting her bear his weight for a moment, Raz tucked his legs beneath him on the stone. Then, in one motion, he slashed her weighted tip clear with his free hand, twisted her blades out of the noose of rope at their base as he started to fall, and pushed off the wall with all his strength.

Below him, Sona had only just gotten back to her feet, still heaving, one hand clutching her abdomen. She barely had time to look up and try to make out what the other three finalists were screaming when Ahna took her through the shoulder, falling with all the weight of heavy steel and an eighteen-foot drop.

Almost at once, Sona hit the ground again.

This time in two parts.

"Oh, Lifegiver's fat arse!" Kal bellowed, bounding to his feet with the rest of the crowd as Raz i'Syul leapt clear of the wall, bearing his great spear down in a massive overhead arc as he fell. "No! Dear god, don't do—"

His plea cut itself short, though, as the woman, Sona, fell to the pit floor, head, left shoulder, and left arm to one side, and the rest of her to the other.

"God," Kal mumbled, falling heavily back into his seat. "Laor save us all. That beast—"

"Is not for us to judge," Talo finished for him. His eyes never left the pit, watching the atherian get to his feet over the body of his first victory. "There's little of Laor's light in that one, I grant you, but I think we would have been deluding ourselves if we expected otherwise. Consider *why* he is doing this before you condemn him for doing it. For a man like that, there is little but the belief that there is no other way."

As some of us know better than others, he finished the thought privately.

Beside him, Kal was quivering, seemingly unable to look away from the pit. Leaving him to his shock, Talo gave his full attention back to the fight.

Raz i'Syul hadn't done more than stand up since he'd landed, letting the three tourney victors left make their advance. They knew better than to separate, now. With his spear in hand, the atherian would pick them off one by one without so much as blinking if they spread too far apart.

Despite this, Talo got the distinct impression they were only delaying the inevitable.

He had never, in all his years, seen anything like Raz i'Syul Arro, in the Arena or out. He was not, though it was hard to believe, the largest he'd ever come across—the Lifetaker had faced off against a mountain man once who'd been more giant than human—but he was by far the fastest. From the moment Tern had said the word, the atherian had been little more than a flash of dark scales, red wings, and silver steel. Though stories would embellish it to great lengths by nightfall, Sona and her crossbow had fallen within fifteen seconds of the start of the match.

The crowd gasped. The shield brothers, Wellen Ryvers and Tymoth Barse, were demonstrating their superior experience fighting together. Leaving the last finalist, Lelan val'En, to his own fate, they'd collapsed on each other and rushed i'Syul, shields side by side, weapons held high in preparation of a quick strike. They'd assumed the atherian would fall back at the onslaught, as any other warrior would, leaving them the momentary opening of the retreat to attack.

What they had not expected was for i'Syul to stand his ground, using his two-headed spear's superior reach to swing wide and around, attempting to catch Ryvers from the side. The man's quick shift, rolling his shield left, was all that saved him from being cleaved mostly in half.

Then again, it did nothing to defend him from the atherian's armored fist, once again bearing every ounce of i'Syul's mass behind it as he bolted forward, too quick for Barth to catch him with his mace. Sharpened plate steel collided with temple, and what looked like most of the inside of Ryvers' head sprayed a dozen yards across the pit.

Barth, to his credit, tried to correct as best he could. One clawed foot caught him a massive kick in the side before he could bring his shield around, though, and the man went flying. He hit the ground hard, shield and mace skidding away until they *thunked* against the wall of the pit.

Before he could so much as move to stand up, the great shadow of Raz i'Syul Arro crossed over him, a dark form leaping some eight feet in the air, bearing Ahna's twin points down with driving force.

The blades took Barth through the chest, cutting through flesh, bone, and earth alike.

The crowd was in an uproar. Had he not been so focused on the fight, Talo might have thought to cover his ears to save them from ringing later. Instead he watched the atherian stand, leaving Ahna where she was, pinning the dying Tymoth Barth to the pit floor.

"He left the spear?" Kal demanded, confused. "Why would he leave it? There's still one standing!"

To Talo, though, it made perfect sense.

"To set an example," he explained. "To prove beyond a doubt that he is not one to be trifled with. I would have done the same thing, in his place, had I been capable of it."

"Do what?" Kal shouted, eyes wide as the atherian turned to face Lelan val'En, the last of the finalists left alive. "What's he going to do?"

"I would say watch, but it might be best if you covered your eyes for this part, Kal. And don't mention a word of it to Carro tonight."

Kal look half horrified, half fascinated, but he did not look away. Instead he watched Raz bear down on val'En with a terrifying calmness, the sort of deadly grace one might find in the fine edge of a new sword, wings half spread to either side, tail snaking along behind him.

Talo even thought the atherian seemed to be smiling, though it was hard to tell on those reptilian features.

val'En, on the other hand, had lost all nerve. Blades held before him, both sword and dagger shaking violently, he was retreating with every step Raz took in his direction. When his back hit the wall, such terror framed the man's Southern features that Talo could make it out even from his place in the stands.

Raz, though, stopped moving within easy reach of val'En's blades. He stood, unflinching, even as the crowd screamed for blood. val'En, seeing what he thought was his one opportunity to live, took full advantage of the opening.

Just as you're meant to, fool, Talo thought with a frown.

Sure enough, his first strike hit nothing but empty air. His second and third did no better, missing the atherian by inches each time as i'Syul dodged and weaved out of the way. For about thirty seconds val'En was allowed to fight for his life and, in doing so, demonstrate to a crowd of thirteen thousand that it would take more than skill and steel to bring down Raz i'Syul Arro, the Scourge of the South.

Then the thirty seconds were up, and val'En's fight ended brutally.

As the man's sword came around for a wide sweep, Raz caught the wielding wrist in one hand, and broke it. As val'En screamed, Raz stripped him of the sword, twisted, and ran the man through the belly with it.

The blade ripped through him, hit the stone behind him, and snapped with the sort of ringing crack only shattered metal can make.

val'En staggered against the wall where he stood for a few moments, utterly shocked as he gaped at the hilt and three inches of steel protruding from his gut. Then he began to wail, dagger dropping from his left hand as he fell to his knees, hands scrabbling at the blood pouring from his wound.

Raz stood over him for a time, watching. Then, bending down, he picked up the abandoned dagger from the ground.

"Look away, Kal," Talo warned.

Kal at last tore his wide eyes from the scene to look at him.

"Why should—?" he started to ask, but Talo cut him off.

"Look *away*, Kal."

Kal hesitated a moment more. Then, though it seemed hard for him to do, he tilted his head up to look beyond the pit, beyond the crowd, and into the gray sky above.

Below the heavens, Raz was toying with the knife. val'En still knelt before him, screaming his life away in fear and pain.

End it quick, Talo prayed. *Let him end it quickly.*

He prayed, knowing full well it was in vain.

Slowly, almost caringly, i'Syul's hand reached out. For a moment he gripped the dying man's shoulder, steadying him. It seemed that i'Syul said something to val'En, there in the break.

Then the steel claws leapt from shoulder to encase the man's whole face like a cruel spider. Bulging eyes peered from between the atherian's fingers, and the crowd gasped as Raz stood slowly, lifting a squirming and kicking val'En clear of the ground with one hand, sliding him up the wall behind him. There was a pause in which the crowd held silence, every man, woman, and child fixed in terrified rapture.

Then the stolen dagger came up and, with such delicate precision it might have been a surgeon's blade, slid slowly into val'En's right eye.

For ten horrible seconds the man's screams outdid anything else Talo had heard that day. They pierced the air, adding a tangible edge to the chill that hurt down to the very bone. Though he never looked away, Talo could tell that Kal was quivering beside him again, shivering against the pain of those screams, still staring up into the sky.

When i'Syul gave the dagger a final little twist, the scream pitched for half a heartbeat.

Then val'En was quiet at last.

Talo would have liked to be able to say, at that point, that the stands were hushed, their hunger for death stilled by the atrocity they had just witnessed. He would have liked even to say that, somewhere in that crowd, voices rose to curse and spit on Raz i'Syul's cruelty.

The truth, of course, was that such mercy had long fled the fiendish boundaries of the Arena.

As one the crowd surged to its feet around the Priests. They boomed with such ecstatic pleasure, Talo was almost jealous of them and their thrill. In truth, though, he felt ill. Thirteen thousand voices called out nothing more than endless praise for the butchery they had just witnessed, and it turned his stomach.

He didn't seem to be the only one, though. Through the gaps in the leaping bodies, Talo watched Raz i'Syul release Lelan val'En's still form, letting it slide down the wall to rest in a slumped half-sit against the stone. For a long time the atherian didn't look away from his bloody work, staring down at the man in silence.

When he finally turned his back on the corpse, though, the look on his face lit again that little light of hope Talo still held for the man.

Raz i'Syul was no longer smiling, as he had been during the fight. There was no joy, alien or otherwise, to be gleaned on his face, no pride or excitement or pleasure. In fact, as the man looked up into the cheering crowd, Talo was quite sure the only emotion he could make out was complete and utter disgust.

"MONSTER OF KARTH! MONSTER OF KARTH! ALL HAIL, THE MONSTER OF KARTH!"

The call ripped Talo from his thoughts completely. He twisted around in his seat to try to make out the shouter, but whoever it was was lost in the crowd. The words carried, though, and a chant began to spread throughout the stands.

"MONSTER! MONSTER! MONSTER! MONSTER!"

It rippled across the Arena, building with every second as a hundred new voices picked up the call. Before long it was the only thing to be heard, louder even than the wind.

"MONSTER! MONSTER! MONSTER! MONSTER!"

"Monster of Karth?" Talo hissed. "Did I hear that right? Monster of *Karth*? Why in the Lifegiver's name would they call him that?"

At last Kal looked down from the clouds, turning to Talo. He seemed shaken, face dark and mouth half-open, his mind clearly still on what he had just witnessed, eyes averted or not. After a moment, though, he seemed to lift himself from his horror, taking a breath as his face cleared.

"Monster of Karth." He nodded. "Yes, it's one of his titles, though whether that's by his choosing or another's I couldn't say. You didn't hear Tern calling him 'Monster' earlier, when—?"

"I thought it was just a description!" Talo exclaimed, cutting the man off. "But why? Why Karth? Why that place?"

Kal blinked. "You don't—? No. No, of course you wouldn't know. How could you?"

Kal frowned then, looking back down into the pit at the atherian. i'Syul was now crossing the frozen ground to retrieve Ahna from where she still pinned Tymoth Barth's corpse to the earth. After what they'd just seen, Talo fully expected to see judgment, even disgust on his friend's face.

When Kal looked back at him, though, he realized all he saw was sadness and pity.

"That man has darkness in his past, Talo," he began to explain. "I don't know everything, mind, but I can at least tell you—"

"SILENCE!"

Quin Tern's voice cut across Kal's words, echoing over the hubbub of the crowd. Both Priests looked to the Chairman's box, as did every other eye in the Arena. Men and women returned to their seats slowly, eager to hear what more their Chairman could possibly offer them.

"Ladies and gentleman of Azbar," Tern boomed. "Friends and honored guests of our great city. You came for blood, and you came for battle. You came to see what the skill and training of man could do against a creature born to savagery. You came with the hopes of entertainment the likes of which you have never dreamed of experiencing. I HOPE YOU HAVE NOT BEEN DISSAPOINTED!"

The surge of screamed agreements rang for a long moment, echoing over the roll of heavy applause that accompanied it.

"Today, however, is only the beginning!" Tern continued once it had died away. "Sixteen entered the ring this day to fight for their chance. Sixteen were defeated. Not even the best of them could stand to your Monster, your great Scourge. But there are others. Indeed, there are *five hundred* others! Will one among them be the slayer of your champion? Will one among them wield the blade meant to end Raz i'Syul Arro's life? Come! Witness the fights for yourselves, and we. Shall. SEE!"

With those final words, Tern bent himself into a surprisingly graceful bow for his size, then turned away from the stadium. The crowd was whipping itself into another frenzy, clapping and stomping, but through them Talo could see once more the indistinct shape of Raz i'Syul, his great spear thrown over one shoulder, making for the pit gate as the portcullis rose once more.

"Come on," he told Kal brusquely, heaving himself to his feet and ignoring the throb of a bad knee left unmoving too long. "We need to go."

"Go?" Kal asked in surprise. "Go where?"

"To speak to the Arena's new favorite!" Talo yelled back over his shoulder, already limping down the steps, hurrying to beat the rush of the exiting crowd.

XX

Talo was very glad Kal had roused him early that morning. They'd barely been standing for a half hour now, fringing the throng of spectators that hovered around the heavy double doors in the outer south wall of the Arena, and already his knee felt ready to give. Pain had yielded way to numbness some five minutes before, and Talo didn't move for fear that his leg would refuse to go with him if he did.

Had they spent all day on their feet in the upper rings of the Arena, like the latecomers, Talo rather thought he'd have been ready to beg Carro to just take the limb.

He stood side by side with Kal, leaning against the wall of a wide alley directly across from the doors. Beyond the encircling protection of the stadium the wind had grown cruel again, but no one seemed to mind. The people before them swirled excitedly, murmuring amongst themselves in anticipation. Every here and there children bounced up and down, trying to see above the crowd. Minor fights broke out every couple of minutes as individuals tried to push closer to the doors, settled by the guardsmen roaming through the group.

All waiting impatiently for the appearance of Raz i'Syul Arro.

The doors they crowded around led to the Arena underworks. It was the entrance of gladiators and animals, fighters and fodder alike. Talo had barely been able to take his eyes off them the entire time he and Kal had been standing there. He kept losing himself in old memories, images from long years ago of those doors opening up to him for the first time, and then of the crowds that awaited the Lifetaker after some great victory, just as they awaited Raz i'Syul now.

Maybe he's smartened up, though, Talo thought. *Maybe he'll find himself another way out.*

He hoped not. He and Kal were standing in the wind and cold of the gray afternoon in the hopes of catching the atherian as he left. There were things to be said, questions to be asked, and Talo wasn't sure when he'd get another chance, if he'd get one at all. Kal had already tried to talk him out of it, calling i'Syul "unchecked" and "wild," and Talo had the distinct impression that he wouldn't hear the end of any desire to speak to the man if Carro got wind of what they'd witnessed today.

Despite himself, Talo had to crack a smile at the image of his partner, green faced and clammy, attempting to hear out his and Kal's description of the fights.

"They're opening."

Talo blinked at Kal's words. Sure enough, the doors were swinging slowly apart. He didn't allow himself to get too excited, though. Twice they'd opened already, each time for attendants wheeling out narrow wagons piled high with the remains of the fights, the dead barely covered in the same old cloth, stained red and black. Talo had no interest in sharing the crowd's peaking thrill at these grim reminders of the day's violence.

This time, though, the only thing to step from the doorway was a massive figure, face and body mostly hidden under a heavy black-and-silver fur mantle, great spear thrown over one shoulder as he walked. It was fascinating, watching i'Syul cut a swath through the throng. Many screamed and shouted his name as he passed, but none were fool enough to reach out and touch him, much less get in his way. On the contrary, even as they cheered him the men and women of the group seemed to retreat from the man, pulling away as though repelled by his proximity, then falling together again to follow. As a result, the atherian was clear of them in seconds, never looking left or right as he walked, not even when he passed in front of Talo and Kal, heading down the alley they had sheltered themselves in.

Nodding to Kal, Talo pulled himself off the wall and took the man's offered arm. Together the pair started limping after i'Syul as fast as they could manage.

For some time they followed him, trailing the atherian's dark form around corners and bends, down main fairways and side streets alike. Azbar passed them in sullen silence, the city's spirits dampened by the gray of the winter day. What few people they came across didn't bother giving the disguised Priests a second glance, preferring to turn and watch i'Syul until he was out of sight.

The atherian had been in the city for weeks, but it seemed the fascination with his presence was far from dissipated.

They were heading south all the while, cutting through market and residential districts alike as they walked. i'Syul seemed in no hurry to get wherever he was going, bearing a steady pace through the buildings and trees that grew every here and there where spaces between the walls allowed. The wind cut in and out around them as they took turns and hills, sometimes blocked by stone for a minute only to be channeled by it the next, ripping in an angry howl through the narrowest lanes. Several times Talo had had to raise a hand to shield his eyes from the chill gusts, worrying in those moments if they would lose the atherian as he moved. It had been their ambition to wait for the right moment to call out. They had no desire to draw a crowd, but were just as intent not to make the man fear he was being ambushed on some back road.

After about ten minutes of tailing him through the city, though, the atherian took away all say they had in the matter.

They'd just finished struggling down a short set of rough-hewn stairs, weaving their way through a few empty streets at their base, when they turned a corner to find that all trace of the man seemed to have vanished. As though he'd simply blinked out of existence, i'Syul had disappeared into thin air. They stood along a tapered path that slanted slightly uphill, the cobblestone beneath their boots inclined inward to allow for rain and snowmelt. The whole space was barely wide enough to accommodate them both side by side, and penned in by the back walls of the two- and three-story buildings jutting up to tower over them like silent witnesses.

It was the stillness of these walls, the emptiness of the alley and heavy silence of the sky above, that caused both men to jump when a dark shadow plummeted from the rooftops to crash onto the cobblestone behind them.

"Most know by now," a throaty tenor growled, "that it's a very bad idea to follow me."

Together the Priests whirled around. Talo managed to compose himself, hands up to make it clear they were not armed.

Kal was not so calm.

Perhaps it was the scene of the fights they'd witnessed only an hour before, or maybe it was just the heavy form of Raz i'Syul Arro looming above them now, great spear held before him, its blades naked to the icy afternoon. Regardless, Kal's hands whipped upward. There was a flash of light, and ivory flames lined his palms and fingers, ignoring the wool of his gloves or the edges of his robes.

The change in Raz i'Syul was instantaneous. Whereas in one moment his reptilian face had held nothing more than confident disdain towards the strangers who had been tracking him through the city, in the next it was hard and cold, golden eyes taking in Kal's flames with a calculating intelligence the likes of which Talo had rarely seen. He could make out lithe muscle bunching beneath what little dark skin was left exposed to the elements between armor and cloth. The red webbing along the back of i'Syul's neck flared up, bright as a setting sun against the somber palette of the city. Steel claws gleamed in the white sheen of Laorin magic, red in places where blood still caked the metal.

Abruptly, Talo realized how close the High Citadel and the temple of Azbar were to requiring new leadership.

Raz i'Syul, though, didn't charge. He barely moved, in fact, the only adjustment in his form coming as his thick tail shifted in the air behind him, suspended over the cobblestone. His eyes never left the flicker of Kal's flames, and after a few seconds an odd change came over the man.

His face darkened, his grip on the spear spasmed, and his lips pulled back in an ugly snarl, revealing every inch of narrow, wicked teeth.

"*Priests?*"

The hissed question did not seem directed at anyone in particular. In fact, Talo had the distinct impression that the exclamation was merely a manifestation of whatever realization had suddenly gripped the atherian, voiced in something like disbelief.

Talo decided then was as good a time as ever to make himself heard.

"Kal, calm yourself," he said quietly. Beside him Kal opened his mouth to argue, but Talo gave him a pointed look, and the man hesitated.

Then, after a moment, he let the magics go, and flames dissipated in a glimmer of white as Kal's hands fell to his sides.

Talo breathed a quiet sigh of relief, then looked to the atherian again.

"Raz i'Syul," he said with a nod, letting his own hands drop now that it seemed i'Syul wasn't about to tear them apart just yet. "I apologize for the secrecy, but we deemed it a necessary precaution. I am Talo Brahnt of the High Citadel, Cyurgi' Di. This"—he indicated Kal—"is Kal Yu'ri, of Azbar. Obviously you are correct. We are Priests of Laor, though I'm quite surprised you know of us. I would have thought it unlikely, considering where—"

"I know more about you than you think, *Priest.*"

Talo was taken aback by the harshness of the words. i'Syul had his eyes on him, now, and something burned there that took a moment to recognize. At first he thought it might be fear, but that made no sense. It wasn't hate either. Talo had seen hatred in all its forms over the years.

No, he realized finally. What he saw in the slit pupils of the atherian was nothing less than pure, unbridled fury.

"I know of your beliefs," i'Syul hissed. "I know of your god, your 'Lifegiver.' I even know of your magic, if that's what you call it. The Grandmother told me much and more, when I asked."

"Then you should know we bear you no ill will," Talo said, lifting his empty hands again and taking another limping step forward. "I hope that this 'Grandmother' of yours told you we are men of peace, of hope. All who speak in Laor's name seek to follow the righteous path. It's why we are here. The situation in Azbar has grown out of control. You know this, I know this, and every person in the city knows this. We also know what you've done—what you are *doing*—to make it better. We know you are fighting to alleviate the strain the Arena has placed on the backs of the innocent. As a man of faith I cannot thank you for that, given your methods. As a man of family and friends, though, I cannot thank you enough."

"I don't want your *thanks*," Raz spat, and once again Talo was taken by surprise by the venom in the man's words. "I don't need your approval, Priest. I don't care for your opinion of my 'methods,' as you say. I will protect mine and my own as I see fit, and you and your false god have no place seeking me out to tell me whether that is right or wrong."

"False god?" Kal exclaimed furiously. "Now wait just one minute, you—!"

"We had hoped"—Talo cut across the Priest loudly—"to discuss with you the future of this city, and what you intend for it. You seek peace, I believe. So do we. We may go about it in different ways, Arro, but at the end of the day I know you want an end to the killing as much as we do."

"There is no end to the killing," the atherian growled. "There is no end to any of it. The monster that is men like Quin Tern does not stop, even when its head has been cut off. I would know."

"You would know only that which you have experienced," Talo said gently. "You are at war, man, and in war there never seems to be any end. Only the next fight, only the next move..."

Raz's eyes narrowed at that.

"You claim to know much of war for a man of the cloth. Tell me, what does a Priest experience in his lifetime of hardships that would lead him to such conclusions? The bickering over the freshest bread and cleanest robes? Maybe disputes held in warm rooms about what light best holds the wonders of your holy relics? Don't give me that shit, Priest. What you learn in books is not enough to inform you on the ways of the world."

"For your information—!" Kal started up again, but Talo once more cut him off.

"I recommend," he said pointedly, giving the other Priest another look, "that you not attempt to judge a man's past by his present, Arro. It will often leave you a fool."

"And *I* recommend," Raz retorted angrily, "that you not assume a man knows nothing of what he speaks about. You think I don't know you? You think I don't remember you? You're older now, I'll give it to you, and I don't recall the limp. Your hair's changed, too. More silver now. Still, there's enough. There can't be many among your faith of your size, and none with your voice."

"My voice?" Talo asked slowly. He had the odd feeling he was not going to like where this was going.

"Your voice," Raz said with a nod. "I remember it. I remember *everything* about that day. '*Where have you been? I've been worried sick about you! Laor save me, I was about to go looking.*' I remember your inn, the Ovana. I remember the girl, the men, the empty house. Mostly, though... Mostly I just remember the fire."

Something cold was clawing at Talo, now, and it wasn't the wind. He didn't recall the exact words, but he trusted that Arro had them right. Vaguely he remembered hurrying out to Syrah, exclaiming outrage at her injuries only to have her insist she would explain, but that first they had to leave.

He remembered a shape on the rooftops across the street, vanishing before Talo could get a better look.

"You were there…" he said quietly. "I should have known, but I never really thought… I was surprised you didn't stay with her to guard her, though frankly I was more surprised you helped at all."

"I helped," Raz spat, "because I was raised to do for others what they could not do for themselves. I helped because your girl would have ended up raped or murdered or sold off to the rings if I hadn't. I didn't stay with her, because I was above, on the roofs, watching to make sure she wasn't being followed."

"She wasn't," Talo said. "We prepared ourselves for it, even as we packed, but no one ever came. We left as soon as possible, just as you'd instructed her, and no one tracked us then, either."

"No one tracked you, because the slavers I kept your acolyte from had decided *I* was the one more deserving of punishment than you."

The clawing cold took full hold of Talo then, pulling at his stomach and heart.

"What do you mean?" he breathed, wide eyes on the atherian. "What happened, child?"

Raz i'Syul stood silent for a long moment. Above them the wind was still picking up, its screams fading in and out, though it never dipped down into their narrow road. Had it done so, Talo thought it might have shaken the man from whatever place he had gone. The atherian's eyes were still on him, but they looked past him now, seeing nothing but whatever memories were forging their way through his mind. The fury in his features didn't fade, but with it now were other things, too. Hate and fear came in true, mixing with a sad sort of pain.

Grief, Talo realized.

After a time, i'Syul pulled himself back to the living world. Rather than answer Talo's question, though, he stood straight, letting his spear hang loose from one hand.

"Come near me again, and we can find out how committed your god is to keeping you alive," he said roughly.

Then he turned away from the Priests, moving back the way they'd come. As Talo and Kal watched him go, he took a corner at the end of the alley and vanished once more from view.

"Lifegiver's mercy," Kal breathed, sounding as though he'd been holding his breath the whole time. "I wasn't sure we were going to make it out of that one…"

Talo didn't respond, watching the turn in the road where the atherian had disappeared. The cold inside him wasn't fading. Instead it weighed on him, pulling him down until he wanted to press his back to the wall and slide to the cobblestone.

"Talo… It's not a good idea to go after him."

Talo grunted. "Not like we have a lot of choice. I don't think he'll let us follow him again, even if we were stupid enough to try. We'll have to find another way."

This last statement Talo said more to himself than to Kal. There was much that the atherian had said that didn't sit well with him, every word binding together to form this entrapping hold that made him feel almost ill.

"So you're going to try again?"

Talo hesitated, then nodded.

Kal sighed. Then he took a few steps forward and offered up his arm.

Talo looked around at him. "Home?" he asked.

Surprising him, Kal shook his head.

"You're not going to let this go," he said. "On top of that, I get the feeling your man would have my head if I so much as implied I intended to leave you to your own devices when it comes to Arro, especially after he hears about the fights."

Talo raised an eyebrow, but took the offered arm. "Where to, then?" he asked.

"First to a woman I know who has a talent for toy making, then somewhere you can get the answers I can't give you," Kal said, starting to walk in the direction Arro had just gone. "Though I think I might actually have a few."

"You do?" Talo asked sharply. "Wait. Why toys?"

Beside him, Kal nodded, then seemed to hesitate. Again Talo saw the inexplicable sadness on the man's face, the same sadness that had been there when Kal had looked down on Raz i'Syul in the pit.

"As for the toys, you'll see. But Talo… Your trip south, the one you took with Syrah… What year was it?"

Talo frowned, confused, but thought about it.

"854?" he muttered after a moment as they took the same corner the atherian had vanished around, heading south once more through the streets. "Or '55. I don't recall exactly. Why?"

Kal frowned, then nodded.

"Going on eight years," he muttered to himself. "I guess it would make sense…"

He looked up, gazing into the winter sky. The clouds patchworked the heavens like a great gray quilt, lumpy and dark as it shifted overhead.

"I never finished telling you," he said quietly, "how he got to be called 'the Monster of Karth…"

XXI

"What happened, Raz? Where did our family go? Where did they all go?"

—Prida Arro, 857 v.S.

Raz felt as though he'd been knifed in the gut. As he made his way south, his feet taking their familiar route home without so much as a conscious thought on his part, the only thing he could feel or think about was the stabbing ache just below his chest, too hot and too deep. It wasn't an unfamiliar pain, by any means. He knew it well, in fact, having lived with it for months, even years.

But it was a pain he'd hoped was long forgotten.

Damn Priests, he thought bitterly, turning onto the road home and feeling the sensation twist at the memory of the two men he'd left in the alley. It was a corrupt feeling, laced with directionless fury and hate, the kind of sensation that had led him dangerously close to madness once in his life already.

It wasn't fair to blame them. He knew that. The fault of the massacre of the Arros was on the armed mercenaries who had poured into the caravan's camp that night, swallowing the lives of Raz's family like a black tide. It had taken him some time to come to that conclusion, to let go of the guilt and self-hate that had plagued him the years following Karth, but eventually Raz had managed it. The weight of those crimes fell on the heads of the men and women wielding the blades.

Men and women who were dead to the last, butchered one after another over the next few days, until the only one left had been Crom Ayzenbas.

And Ayzenbas had taken a long, long time to die.

But if the Priests hadn't been there, it would never have happened.

That was a fair thought, Raz convinced himself. If the Laorin had stayed out of the South, keeping to their own business in these frigid Northern hills, then Raz might never have known they existed, much less had to intervene on their behalf. And if he'd never intervened, then Ayzenbas might never have sentenced the Arros to die.

Then I have reason to feel like this, Raz told himself fiercely. *I have reason to hate them. It's their fault. It's THEIR FAULT.*

No. It's not.

Raz stopped short. He realized dimly that he stood at the base of the steps of Arrun and Lueski's little home, looking up at the heavy timber door. What he was seeing, though, was a face he only rarely thought of anymore.

Turning away from the house, Raz kept walking as though he'd never paused. For several minutes he continued on, ignorant of the cold and wind.

When he got to the stairs, he took them three at a time.

The steps were worn slate on lime, built into the city wall itself. At the top one could see the woods that spread south, west, and east, the land a cascade of rippling hills.

Raz, though, turned his back on the forests to face the city, and with a running start leapt from the wall itself.

He landed with a light *crunch* on the rooftop of an old granary, kicking loose a couple wooden slats as he found his footing. He balanced there for a moment, two feet and a hand on the incline of the roof, Ahna held snug over his shoulder with the other.

Then he ran.

Raz was not as familiar with Azbar as he had been with Karth all those years ago, not to mention he'd never been carrying the dviassegai. Several times he had to correct himself in a split second, leaping and rolling to avoid plummeting to the roads below, or dodging left, right, and over as dips in the roofs and chimneys added obstacles to his path.

After a time, though, old habits returned, and even with one hand indisposed Raz made easy work of the unfamiliar skyline.

For nearly fifteen minutes he ran, jumping, leaping, soaring, rolling. Clawed feet and fingers found good anchorage in wood and the gaps between stone, swinging him from lip to lip, roof to roof. His tail whipped about instinctively, avoiding colliding with walls and windows, or else shifting to keep his balance along the narrow apexes and slanted edges. His body at last falling into the familiar cohesion he had never realized he missed so much, Raz ran as though he could outdistance his thoughts themselves.

When he finally stopped, the view he'd sought did indeed grant him a brief moment of reprieve.

There was no wall between Azbar and the canyon at its back. The fissure seemed almost endlessly deep in the fading light of the afternoon, and was wide enough by far to discourage raiders who might think to cross it for an easy sacking. Instead, the architects of the city seemed to have had a vision to conquer the chasm for their own enjoyment, extending semicircular platforms out at the limit of every road that ended along the lip of the canyon. Built into the cliffs themselves, the views from these little extensions offered the thrill of looking the abyss in the face, staring straight down to find the rushing river that raged far, far below.

Despite this, Raz thought he rather preferred his vantage.

He stood at the top of the highest building he'd been able to find along the edge of the fissure, a narrow five-story tower that—had it been made of mudbrick and mortar—would have made any Southerner curse the stupidity of the builder for shaping something so vulnerable to the winds. Raz didn't know as to what purpose it might serve, though he suspected it to be some sort of tannery, judging by the smell of oil and hide cast about him in the wind. Regardless, it put him twenty feet higher than anywhere else in the vicinity, opening up the world for him as he had not experienced it in a long, long time.

Yet more woodland clung to the far lip of the canyon. Trees of all shapes and sizes hung out and over the emptiness, their roots clinging to mossy earth so tightly they appeared like men desperate not to fall. As they did southward, the woods seemed to extend infinitely north, hushing the harsh edges of the world in green.

Beyond the endless trees, though, clawing at the lip of the horizon, the ghosts of white-capped mountain ranges were still visible beneath the gray of the sky.

It was as he followed the sharp outline of these distant titans that the face Raz had been running from finally caught up to him. The mountains were everything that was the North, just as she had been.

A pretty girl, with skin so pale it hurt him to think of the Sun reaching it, and hair so white it looked to have been painted to frame her deep, pink eyes.

A girl who had nearly vanished from the world for the simple fact that she was in the wrong place at the wrong time…

Just as we'd all been…

Gently, Raz eased himself down, tucking his mantle beneath him so as to have a warm place to sit along the highest edge of the roof. Ahna he placed beside him, hooking the bottom of her blades between the slats so she wouldn't slide away to plummet down on some unfortunate bystander below.

That's what we'd all been, wasn't it? Raz asked himself then, pulling what loose layers of his furs were left around him in an effort to beat the wind. *In the wrong place at the wrong time?*

If he was going to be angry at the unfortunate nature of man to be exactly where he shouldn't be when he shouldn't be, then Raz had more to blame than just the Laorin. The Arros should be at fault simply for being in Karth, not to mention rearing him to have the skills and willpower to intervene on the albino girl's behalf. Raz himself, of course, should be at fault for being in the market street that day, looking for food, wood, and a butcher's knife.

And the girl, in particular, should be at fault for tempting the slavers with her presence.

No.

As he sat there, high above the heads of the oblivious citizens of Azbar milling about below, Raz felt the wretched ache start to fade from his chest. He let it go, holding tight to a conviction he'd always had, but never acknowledged.

The girl was not at fault. Blaming her for the death of the Arros would be equivalent to blaming her for her own abduction. He might as well have claimed she was asking for it, dressed the way she was.

Raz snorted.

How utterly stupid.

No, the albino could not be made at fault for the wickedness of the men who had taken her. She could not be made at fault for the massacre, and—if she was not at fault—neither could Raz or the Arros.

Or the Priests, those men of cloth of Laor, whom the Grandmother thought had only been in such a doleful place as Karth so as to offer aid to the poor and needy.

Raz let this conclusion sink in, let it wash over him like the wind. As he did, he let go of the bitterness, of the rage that had swelled in him so abruptly upon encountering the Priests, in particular the man who called himself Talo Brahnt.

Brahnt was as the rest of us, Raz thought, this time with refreshing conviction. *Wrong place. Wrong time.*

It didn't mean he had to like the man.

Still, with the release of his anger, Raz felt the knife that had been twisting into his heart be drawn out in full. It left a sort of emptiness there, a hole that felt like it could not be filled, but Raz suspected it was a space that had been there for a very long time.

A space that had once been filled by the love of parents, and the love of a sister.

Raz looked up, then, away from the fissure and the trees and the mountains. It was more instinct than conscious act, but he realized as he did so that it had been some time since he'd sought out Her Stars, or looked for his family in the heavens. Even had there been clear skies, he doubted it was late enough for them to have appeared just yet.

He was surprised, therefore, when a glint of white caught his eyes against the gray.

"What the…?" Raz asked himself quietly, taking Ahna up in one hand and climbing to his feet.

He thought at first that the point of paleness was a trick of the light, or perhaps a minute shift in the clouds that would correct itself rapidly enough. The white didn't fade, though, and Raz followed it carefully, realizing it was moving in a lazy, swirling pattern, like a falling leaf.

In a silent dance it fell closer, until Raz—against his better judgment—reached out a clawed hand to catch it gently in his palm. The pale thing reminded him of a tiny fluff of cotton, like those his mother and the other women of the caravan used to work until they could be spun into thread and clothing. He brought it up to his face to examine it more closely, realizing as he did that the thing seemed to be shifting, moving in his hand.

No. Not moving. *Melting.*

Within seconds the little flake of snow was gone, leaving nothing but a tiny spot of wetness along the cool skin of Raz's hand.

XXII

By the time Raz turned back onto the road leading to Arrun and Lueski's home, he had realized two things. First: snow was wonderful. It flew and darted around, dueling wind and gravity, until it settled with utter silence upon any surface it reached. As more and more started to come down, the sounds of the world became hushed, easing away the dull headache that constantly threatened to bloom whenever Raz was around people and all their noises.

Second: snow was horrible.

Deciding to return home by way of the roofs, Raz nearly killed himself twice before realizing the roads were a safer option. The snow made everything wet and slick, turning what had been safe hand- and footholds only a half hour before into sly little deathtraps. More upsetting even than that, snow was *cold*. It clung to him as he walked, sticking to the line of his furs and rolling off the steel of his armor. Where it found skin was the worst, though, melting quickly and leaving Raz's feet and tail frigid and stiff. His wings were warm enough, for once, tucked and bundled beneath the heavy mantle, but the snow even managed to slip its way beneath his hood, wetting his cheeks and the tip of his snout.

"Good thing we didn't try our luck in the woods, huh, sis?" he muttered to the evening, watching the mist of his breath cut a swath between the falling flakes.

Reaching the house stairs, Raz took them carefully, not wanting to slip on the thin layer of white that had already started to build on the coolness of the granite. When he got to the top, he pounded on the door, then turned to look over his shoulder as he waited for it to open for him.

The world was gray and white, hinting at the green of the firs and pines scattered along the road. The lamp-men had already been by to fill and light the street lanterns, and the warm glow of the flames cut a staggered pattern through the quiet curtain of falling snow. Nothing moved, everyone having ducked into their homes to wait out the first storm of the freeze. Not even the wind spoke now, as though the world was intent on utter silence, if only for a night.

Raz was so taken by the scene that he nearly jumped out of his skin when the door screeched open behind him.

"Oh," said Arrun, his face falling as he saw the snow. "And here I thought we might go the whole winter without this shit."

"Arrun, how many times do I have to tell you to watch your mouth around—?"

Before he could finish the sentence, though, Raz froze.

As the warm air of the house rushed out to meet him, something unfamiliar came with it. He knew every smell of the Koyts' home, including that of Lueski and Arrun themselves. He was greeted by it daily, and it had become a comforting thing, a soft reminder of the peace and tranquility he could always expect when returning home.

But now something new twisted amongst the familiar scents.

"Who's with you?" he asked sharply. Without waiting for a response, he bulled past Arrun, nearly knocking the boy over in the process, and turned to face the room.

In the far wall the fire burned as always, filling the space with the sort of heavy warmth that eased its way comfortably into the body. Lueski's and Arrun's bedrolls had been piled up against the right wall, and the girl herself was sitting with her back to the flames, playing with what looked like a new doll, all colored cloth and dry straw. As soon as he stepped through the door she looked up, and the familiar smile leapt across her face.

"He's here!" she shouted with a laugh, clambering to her feet and running to greet him. "He's here! Told you he'd be back soon!"

She leapt and grabbed him around the waist, as was her fashion. Raz took her head gently in one hand, careful with this steel claws, and pressed her to him.

His eyes, though, didn't leave the two men standing together by the hearth, both turning to face him at Lueski's shouts.

"Perhaps I should have been clearer," he growled, "regarding exactly what would happen if you followed me again."

The Laorin exchanged a look. Talo Brahnt looked calm enough, though he had one hand on the edge of the fireplace to keep the weight off what Raz was sure had to be a bad leg. The other one—Yu'ri, if he remembered—looked less so, but despite this it was he who spoke up now.

"We didn't follow you," he said. "We didn't have to. I brought Talo here so that he could ask the questions he needs to, and to check on Arrun and Lueski."

At that, Raz blinked. At his waist, Lueski shifted, and he let go of her head so she could look up at him.

"Mister Yu'ri helped us when the bad men were coming," she said with a smile. "He gave us food and water and hid us so we wouldn't get caught."

For a moment, Raz could say nothing, staring down at the little girl. Then he whirled on her brother.

"*These* are the friends who helped you?" he hissed, waving at the Laorin. "*These* are the men who got you out of Azbar?"

Arrun nodded, half smiling. Apparently seeing Raz so taken aback was amusing, somehow.

"High Priest Yu'ri took us in when the warrant was put out for our arrest," he said. "Our parents were part of the faith. He wanted us to stay in the temple, but I was the one who insisted on running."

"Warren and Marta—Arrun and Lueski's parents—were members of my temple before their passing," Kal Yu'ri continued the explanation from by the fire. "The children got to us easily enough, but Arrun wasn't convinced the guard wouldn't be willing to disturb the Laorin to find them, just to set an example. I wasn't either, but the others we'd snuck out of Azbar hadn't fared well, so I was willing to take the chance. It was his right to deny it, though, and he did the best he could by his sister."

Raz looked down at Lueski again, who still had her arms around him as she smiled, serenely oblivious to the tension in the room.

"You might have mentioned all of this earlier," he said, patting the girl's head before extracting himself carefully from her hug. "Our prior conversation may have gone a little differently."

"I wasn't sure what your intentions were with the children," Yu'ri said with a shrug. "I admit that I don't find it easy to trust you, Master Arro, nor am I sure the Koyts should. As it is, though, it seems you've shown them no ill will, so I am inclined to give you the benefit of the doubt." He glanced at Brahnt briefly before finishing. "Would you grant us the same?"

Raz hesitated, his eyes shifting to the larger man. Talo Brahnt had a formidable figure, wide at the hips and shoulders, and tall enough that he reached Raz's neck, which was a rarity in and of itself. His hands looked better suited for throttling than praying, and there were scars there, Raz realized. They were old and pale, long healed and faded, but they nicked and lined his fingers and knuckles enough for Raz to second-guess his earlier assumption that both men had led an easy life among the faith. Kal Yu'ri, perhaps, had been raised for the cloth.

Talo Brahnt, on the other hand, seemed to have taken a more complicated path into the arms of his god.

Making a decision, Raz reached out to lean Ahna against the wall. His gladius and war ax came next, their harness undone and hung from the iron peg by the door where he usually hung his mantle. The furs themselves he kept, mostly because the falling snow outside had left him with a chill that hadn't quite faded.

But also because they helped to hide the knife still strapped above his right hip.

When he was done, Raz turned back to face the Priests. Though he'd said nothing, the two men seemed to take his disarming as an agreement, and they relaxed slightly.

"There are many words I owe you," Brahnt spoke first, blue eyes sad as they met Raz's. "About the Arros, about Karth, about you…"

Raz bristled at the sound of his family's name, but he didn't respond, resolving to let the man have his moment.

"I took Syrah from the city as soon as was possible," the Priest explained. "I barely had time to find out your name before we ran, making north again weeks before we had intended. I remember her worrying, how often she would look back the way we came. I remember telling her that you would be alright, that your head and heart were all you needed to make it in that harsh world."

He paused and swallowed. Through the haze of anger Raz was fighting to control, he allowed himself to realize that this conversation was clearly not easy for the man.

"Had I known—Had I even *suspected*—I don't know what I could have done. I would have returned, at the very least. I would have sought you out. I cannot aptly explain to you how much I or the faith owe you, Arro. Syrah was—Syrah *is*—as a daughter to me, and the woman she has grown to be will put any great name among the faithful to shame one day. What you did for us cost you greatly. It took from you what you held dearest, and I will bear the responsibility for it gladly. I should have been there. It should have been me watching over her. It should have been me—"

"You would have had to kill them."

Talo stopped abruptly at Raz's interruption, looking surprised at the words. Raz, for one, sighed and moved closer to the fire. He kneeled before the flames, letting the heat wash over him and into the steel of his armor.

"You would have had to kill them," he repeated after a moment, not looking up at Talo, who stood beside him now. "To keep them away from her, you would have had to end their lives. I admit I may not know as much about you as I claimed, Priest, but I do know some things, and I know you don't kill. You can't."

He watched the fire for a moment more, recalled the stale dry air of that little house, the settling of brick dust as he stood among the dead and dying.

"The slave rings don't accept defeat graciously," he said. "They don't take kindly to being thwarted. I killed four of the five men in that house, that day. I let the last one live, because your girl asked me to. Can you guess how they found out I was involved?"

Talo didn't respond, listening intently.

"If I'd finished the job, if I'd ripped his throat out like I'd wanted to, there's a chance my family wouldn't have died that night. Not a big one, mind. Someone was bound to figure it out eventually. But still, a chance…"

Raz looked away from the fire now, meeting the man's eyes.

"If it had been you there that day, Priest, would you have been able to stop them?"

Talo hesitated. Then he nodded.

Raz chuckled. "I thought as much," he said, glancing down at the man's scarred hands again. "Next question now… Would you have been able to kill them?"

A short hesitation. Then Talo shook his head once.

Raz smiled dryly at the response. "Then you would have been done for. Word would have gotten back to Ayzenbas—probably even faster—and within hours the city would have become one giant net. The girl would have been taken, as would you and the others if you'd given them half a chance. If not, they'd just have killed you and left your bodies for the slum runners to loot and violate as they saw fit."

"Ayzenbas was their leader?"

It was Kal Yu'ri who asked, almost whispering the question. Raz looked around Talo to see the other Priest and Arrun both standing there, listening raptly. Lueski seemed to have run off to play with her new doll again.

"He was," Raz nodded. Then he smiled wickedly. "Would you like me to tell you what happened to him?"

"No," Talo said gruffly, speaking for the first time since Raz had started talking. "And I don't think you would even if we wanted to, given we are within earshot of your new charges."

Raz lost his smile at that.

"Fair enough," he said, watching Talo again. Then he got to his feet, standing to tower over the big man, barely a foot from each other.

"I doubt I will ever be your friend, Priest," he said. "It should have been you and your ilk to fall beneath the blade that day, not my friends. Not my family. I'll never forget that. But I won't let you claim fault for it either. The men who are to blame for that are dead, though Ayzenbas could never suffer enough to atone for what he did, as hard as I tried."

Brahnt stood before him, unflinching under Raz's gaze, meeting his eyes evenly. When he spoke, though, his voice was hoarse, as though he were hard-pressed to keep the emotion out of his words.

"I would never ask you to forget it," the man said. "But can you forgive it?"

For a long time Raz stood over him, taking the Priest in. Here was a man who had lived a hard life. Raz was sure of it now. Despite that, there was a gentleness in Brahnt's bearing, a kind countenance that spoke nothing of softness or weakness, but rather of the pride and strength found in peace.

Here was a man who had sought, and found, his redemption.

"I will try," Raz said with a small nod.

At his words, something bent in the big man. Relief washed his bearded face, replacing what Raz realized had been the lines of hidden heartbreak and grief.

"You really had no idea, did you?" he asked quietly.

Talo shook his head at that, smiling sadly. "None. You might have made a name for yourself in the South, Arro, and have a good start on doing the same here, but I haven't heard a whisper of you since we fled Karth. Kal told me today."

"Word spread quick when you arrived," Kal spoke up from behind Talo. "The North knows by now, too. Quin Tern's birds will have seen to that."

"The birds were my idea," Raz said. "Your Chairman was smart enough not to take advantage of Miropa's offer until he saw the benefit of every angle. He's clever, Tern."

At that, Kal spluttered in anger.

"You *praise* him?" he demanded. "After everything he's done? After what he did to Arrun and Lueski! How could you—!"

"That wasn't praise, Kal."

Brahnt cut across Yu'ri's outburst. The big Priest was watching Raz with a new face now, not one cut from the grief he'd worn minutes before. This face was calculating and alert, aware of Raz's implication.

"It was acknowledgement," he finished the statement. "Arro was merely highlighting that the Chairman has his strengths."

"Precisely," Raz told Yu'ri with a nod. "It would do if you could stop jumping down my throat every other word I utter, High Priest. I don't care much for false friendship, but if we intend to work together, then civility is the least we can manage."

At that, Kal looked surprised.

"Work together?" he asked, as though he wasn't sure he had heard Raz correctly. "You mean… You would be willing to help us?"

Raz snorted. "I'd love to pretend that would be the case, but in truth I think it's *I* who is more in need of assistance. I'd hoped a month or two of blood would satisfy the crowds, or at least dissuade people from signing up to fight, but the bounty from the South is substantial, and Quin is only going to add to it as needed to keep interest in the fights going. At this rate I'm more likely to kill off half the North—and probably do myself in in the process—than I am to convince your Chairman he should abandon his aspirations for the fights." He looked to Talo. "It's my understanding that the faith has taken down the Arenas once before. What's stopping them now?"

"Timing," the man responded, taking a step around Raz to get his bad leg closer to the fire. "Manpower. The favor of the people. You name it. You think it's bad now? Wait until the Arena has been standing for a hundred years. Last time the Laorin took a stand, the people of the North had had enough of the blood, enough of living in fear that they might suffer the same fate of the unfortunates they jeered down upon whenever there was a fight. Here in Azbar, the leadership was different, too. Markus Tern tolerated the Arena because it was tradition, and because it was a primary source of capital for the city. He never enjoyed it, much less thrived on it, as his son does. When the opportunity came to ban the fights, when the Laorin presented him with alternative means for the town to support itself, he required little convincing. I doubt Quin will be as accommodating."

"It's certainly not likely," Raz said thoughtfully. "What were these alternatives, though? What were you able to offer the town that enabled them to abandon the Arena?"

"Well first, the Arena wasn't making near as much profit as the city claimed," Kal answered now. "Fees came in hand over fist, true enough, and the place looked nothing short of a goldmine if you only gave it a cursory once-over, but there was much more to it than that."

Raz frowned, glancing at Talo for confirmation. The big Priest nodded.

"Kal was a driving force the first time the faith took on the Arenas," he said. "He knows the political ins and outs better than I do, at the very least."

"*And* the financials," Kal said with a note of pride Raz found amusing coming from such a pious man. "Despite the gold it took in, the Arena was costing the city at least half its intake every cycle. Purses and prizes were an obvious loss, but there were others. Maintenance of the stadium and pit. Training of the gladiators. Training of the attendants. Cost per head for the hunters and poachers to bring back live game as sport. Fees to smiths and armorers throughout the city to make and repair weapons and gear. Smaller costs included paying off the physicians treating the gladiators, as well as the gravediggers and cemetery keepers for dealing with the dead. Still, even those added up over the months and years."

"What about now, though?" Raz asked, looking between the two Priests. "What's changed that's made people forget? If it's not as substantial a pillar to Azbar's stability, why was it allowed to reopen?"

"Time," Talo told him. "The likelihood is that little if anything has 'changed,' as you say. It's been decades since the ban was put in place, and longer still since the battle began to do so. Many alive then are gone, and the masses with the power to make change now were too young to have witnessed the discussions, to hear the reasonings. I doubt if one in ten who crowd the stadium have any concept of the things we are discussing, and fewer still would care even if they did. Beyond that, the last winters have been so brutal that the entirety of the city is willing to cling to anything that might make life a little easier during the freeze, and the

Arena does that, especially now."

"Now?" Raz asked.

"Now that you're here," Talo said with a shrug. "Even fewer are willing to make a stand with Tern and his guards no longer drafting their entertainment from within the walls of the city. Not to mention the profits the taverns and inns are seeing from outsiders coming to see the fights."

"So you believe I was mistaken to step in?" Raz bristled. "You're saying I should have let those people—some as young as Lueski!—face men and women who wouldn't think twice before murdering them where they stood?"

"*No.*"

It was Yu'ri, surprisingly, who spoke so vehemently.

"Please try to understand, Master Arro, that Talo and I are in a difficult position," he said, sounding frustrated. "We understand that you seek peace, and we applaud it. Where our disadvantage lies is in your methods. On the one hand, your business is one of death and violence and, in the eyes of the Lifegiver, such transgressions should be unforgivable. On the other, though… well…"

Yu'ri looked suddenly uncomfortable, as though he was having difficulty articulating his intentions.

"On the other," Talo picked up for him, "you single-handedly ended the harvesting of debtors and criminals from within Azbar. We of the faith hold no life in value above another, but we are not so blind as to deny the fact that the men and women who fall in the Arena now are all there by choice. I say, with a clear conscience no less, that you have done a great thing, here in this place."

"*Talo*," Yu'ri hissed, shocked, but the bigger Priest waved any further comment away impatiently.

"Until the day comes when He sees fit to end all wars, the Lifegiver is not unaware that violence will exist among His flock. Yes, no life may have greater value than another, Yu'ri, but are you honestly going to sit there and preach that there is *not* a difference between a life taken and a life given? We *will* bring down the Arena again, but in the meantime you cannot argue that Arro's way is a far lesser of two evils."

Yu'ri seemed to have no immediate answer to that, opening and closing his mouth as though biting back half-formed thoughts.

"Lesser or not," he finally managed to squeak out, "are we really going to condone this, Talo? I mean"—he dropped his voice to a low whisper—"did you *see* what he did today?"

"Three hundred and forty-seven."

Both Priests looked around at Raz, who was frowning.

"What?" Yu'ri asked, perplexed.

"Three hundred and forty-seven," Raz said again. "That's how many are left on the list—the bounty hunters who'd come to Azbar for a chance at my head. Before today, it was over five hundred. Exclude the ones lost this afternoon, and nearly a hundred withdrew their names after today's final match."

He watched Yu'ri carefully, judging the man's reaction as he continued.

"I'm not going to ask for your forgiveness for what I did to Lelan val'En. It was cruel and violent—evil, even—and I'm a long way from forgiving myself, much less seeking forgiveness from others. But I know I will. It may not be tonight or tomorrow or anytime in the next ten years, but I will. He would have killed me without a second thought, sure, so I don't have too much to regret, but it's more than that."

He held up a single steel-clawed finger for Yu'ri.

"I will forgive myself because, when it is all said and done, one death—val'En's one death—saved the wasting of a hundred lives."

For a long time Yu'ri stared at Raz's lifted finger. Then he looked at Raz himself.

"I may have misjudged you, Arro."

Raz snorted, then shrugged, letting his hand drop. "Happens more often than you would think," he said. He looked around at Talo, who was watching him with an odd sort of attentiveness, as though seeing him for the first time.

"What?" Raz asked.

Talo blinked, then shook his head as though to clear it. "It's funny..." he replied. "Have you ever heard of the dahgün, Arro?"

"The da-what?" Raz asked.

"Dahgün," Talo said again, spreading his arms wide. "The great dragons of the North, massive winged beasts crafted by Laor to rule the earth eons before man so much as spoke his first word."

At that, Raz snorted. "No, can't say I have," he said. "I'm not all that familiar with Northern fairy tales as of yet. Why?"

"Because," Talo told him, "the stories go that the dragons were violent creatures, incapable of peace and love, obsessed only with the destruction of all that surrounded them, particularly their own kind. To a last they waged war against each other, ravaging the world, carving out the valleys and mountains of the North, even scorching the Southern lands so terribly nothing was left but dirt and sand."

Raz said nothing, listening more intently than he might have admitted.

"It's thought," Talo continued, "that when Laor realized that His great creations were capable of nothing but fiery brutality, each one against the others, He razed them from the earth. Disgusted with their actions, He wiped them from existence, pulling them from the infinite circle of rebirth, reshaping the world and its creatures into ones more capable of peace and prosperity."

Here, some private thought pulled at the corner of Talo's mouth as he continued to look at Raz.

"Despite that, every few years you hear rumors about a backwoodsman or trapper returning home with tales of a sighting, stories of massive winged creatures in the clouds between the mountains, or circling high above the deepest parts of the Northern forests. There are hundreds of theories, stories and tales and farfetched reasonings as to *why* the Lifegiver might have spared some of the dahgün, shielding them from His wrath when it came. One theory, in particular, has always struck me, though…"

He smiled in full now.

"He saved the ones who fought only to end the fighting. He saved the ones who killed only in the hopes that they might end the killing. For all their flaws, he valued even those who battled, so long as they battled for peace."

Raz watched the Priest steadily for some time after he had finished his story. He didn't know what he was looking for, exactly. Perhaps a hint of sarcasm, or the lingering amusement of a joke made at Raz's expense. He found nothing, though, and when he looked to the other Priest to judge his reaction, he found Yu'ri watching him thoughtfully.

He wasn't sure what to make of it all.

"But it's only a story, after all," Talo said abruptly, finally ending the silence. "I just found the comparison interesting. And on the subject of stories, there will be one involving my head on a platter if we don't get back to Carro soon. Yu'ri?"

Behind him, Yu'ri jumped, pulled from whatever internal turmoil he was experiencing.

"Carro? Wha—? Oh! Yes!" He turned to Arrun. "Would you mind fetching our coats, Arrun? I believe your sister took them upstairs somewhere when we arrived."

"I don't envy your return home," Raz muttered as Arrun ran up the stairs. "Your Northern snow is an odd thing, to say the least. I'm not quite sure what to make of it."

"Well, the North as a whole isn't quite sure what to make of you, Arro, so I think you can call things even for now," Talo chuckled, watching Arrun return, weighed down with heavy overcoats and thick mantles made of some dark-brown fur. Taking his from the boy with a thanks, he pulled them over his broad shoulders, clasping the cloth about his neck as Yu'ri did the same beside him.

When he was done, he looked to Raz once more.

"There is much to be discussed, Arro, but it can wait the night, I think. It's my understanding you have a few days till your next fight, so we will be in touch. Don't come to the temple. Yu'ri has caused enough trouble for Tern thrice over to earn the Laorin a careful watch, and you visiting would no doubt get back to the Chairman. We will be in touch soon. In the meantime…" He paused, then held out a hand. "Take care of yourself."

Raz looked down at the offered arm.

Then he reached out his own, took it, and shook.

"And take care of them," Yu'ri said gruffly, indicating Arrun over his shoulder as Talo took him by the elbow. "They don't deserve any more trouble in their lives."

"No," Raz said quietly, watching Lueski reappear at the top of the stairs, drawn by the Priests' departure. "No, they don't."

"I'll have to send a bird come morning!" Talo said as the pair started for the door. "It's high time I sent the Citadel an update, and Syrah will be very happy to hear you're well. I know you've been in her prayers for many years."

And with that, and a final cordial nod from Yu'ri, the Priest opened the door and vanished into the black and gray of the snowy night outside.

"Mister Yu'ri's nice, isn't he?" Lueski called down from upstairs.

"Very nice, yes," Raz replied automatically, his eyes still on the door, mind awhirl.

The Priests had given him much to consider. If he was honest with himself, Raz hadn't been sure what his next move was going to be once the Chairman's Tourney was in place. His priority, when he'd offered himself to the Arena, had been clearing Arrun and Lueski from their debt and ending Azbar's enslavement to the pit. He'd accomplished that, proving to Quin Tern that there was a way to keep the fights going *without* harboring the ire of the cityfolk.

There, though, Raz's plan ended, favoring the hope that opportunity would eventually present itself, even if he had to cut down every bounty hunter in the North to encourage it.

But now… Now, other options were afforded to him. Now doors were opening he never would have even considered.

Now I'm not alone.

Raz allowed himself a small smile at the thought. His option of allies was limited, and perhaps not to his absolute preference—given the choice he would have preferred swords at his back over prayers—but he was no longer a solitary figure out there on the frozen mud, one against all, him against the world.

He had fought his war alone long enough. It felt good, for once, to know someone was out there doing the same.

"Lueski, put your doll away and help your brother with dinner," Raz said, moving to grab his ax and gladius from the peg by the door before retrieving Ahna from her place on the wall and making his way up the stairs. "I'll be down once I've cleaned up."

"Do we get stories about today?" Lueski squealed excitedly, bouncing up and down with anticipation as he passed her at the top of the stairs, heading for the room where he kept the washbasin.

"Of course," Raz said with a smile.

The girl squeaked in delight and bolted down the steps to help her brother.

"Though we might leave some of the details out, right, Ahna?" Raz added in a quiet mutter to the dviassegai, ducking into Arrun's old room.

Two hours later, Raz sat bare-chested with his back to the fire, wings half-spread around him so he could watch the dancing red light that washed through their thin membranes against the floor and far wall. One hand was absently stroking Lueski's hair, fast asleep on her bedroll beside him, belly full of buttered bread and spiced potatoes, her dreams heroically scripted by Raz's evening tales of the fights. Tales he'd adapted somewhat, crafting the events into something more age appropriate. Dreams were one thing.

Nightmares were another.

To his right, Arrun, too, slept. His bare feet poked out from beneath his layered furs, extended towards the fire. His breath came soft and quiet in slumber, the sort of deep, regular breathing that spoke the difference between someone actually sleeping and someone only pretending.

Knowing the difference had saved Raz's skin on more than one occasion.

But it was on neither of the Koyt children that Raz's thoughts revolved around now. Through dinner and most of the evening, Raz's mind had been preoccupied with Talo Brahnt and Kal Yu'ri, wondering what he might be able to accomplish with their help. Their Lifegiver seemed to have a place in the hearts of many, here in the North.

After today, Raz himself would have a place in the hearts of everyone else.

Can we do it? he had asked himself over their meal, so preoccupied with the question that he barely touched his fish, prompting Arrun to ask him twice if everything was okay.

In the end he had decided only the Sun and Moon could know the future's absolutes, and the best he could do was pray that he and the Laorin would find a way.

Now, though, Raz's thoughts had traveled elsewhere. Now they found themselves hooked around a realization he hadn't really registered until after the children had gone to sleep. Listening to them breathing, Raz could also make out the sounds of the winds beyond the house's stone walls. The night seemed to have given up its pretense of silence, preferring now to announce with gusto the storm that raged outside. The whining, dipping, and spiking shriek of winter air had made Raz wonder if Talo's bird would make it to this "Citadel" of his.

It was then that he realized he'd learned something else, that evening.

Again Raz pulled up the face in his mind's eyes. The pretty girl with snow for hair and pink, deep eyes that had taken him in without a wince of fear or suspicion. He remembered the strength in her form, the fierceness of her belief when she'd asked him to spare the life of a dying man.

He remembered the relief, the genuine solace in them, too, when he'd fatefully agreed.

Raz had rediscovered an old anger today, a fire that had burned low and cool, all but forgotten until he had been confronted by Brahnt and Yu'ri in that narrow little alley. Despite himself, even now he felt that fire leap a little at the thought of the Priests, his rage not totally sated by the events of the day.

When he thought of the girl, though… the fire only cooled.

Was it what he had seen in her? The truth he had witnessed in her convictions, the strength he had noted in her body, the gratitude he had seen in her eyes when he'd bent to her desire? Was it the fact that she was the catalyst for his forgiveness, at least what little of it he'd been able to find so far?

Whatever it was, remembering her face tempered Raz. Whatever it was, remembering her face seemed to calm his soul.

"Syrah…" he muttered quietly to himself, still absently stroking Lueski's dark hair. "Always wondered what her name was…"

XXIII

"It is often that I remember my late lover with fondness, but never with quite as much vigor as when I recall him calling Petrük 'a venomous cow.' Laor forgive me, but there are times—particularly when I take walks along the ramparts of our great Citadel—that I find myself amazed at how simple it would be to put an abrupt end to her unpleasantness, and claim simply that she slipped on the ice that has such a nasty habit of building up there along the battlements."

—private journal of Carro al'Dor

"You can't be serious."

"Of course I'm serious, girl. We should consider that this is all in the greater plan of the Lifegiver. When *I* did my pilgrimages to the western towns, it was easy to see that none of their people were ever touched by the light of Laor. This is His cleansing, His purge of the faithless and blasphemers."

"Just because they haven't taken the cloth doesn't make them blasphemers, Petrük! Much less deserving of genocide! They were good people made hard only because it's the only way of life they know, the only way of life that had ever let them survive the freezes!"

"Well, perhaps if you'd spent more time with your 'good people' of the towns rather than gallivanting around with your savages in the mountains, more might have found Laor and escaped His judgment!"

"Now listen here you insufferable bi—!"

"Syrah, that's enough."

Syrah turned furiously on Jofrey, who had cut across her outburst. She was on her feet, both hands curled into angry fists on the table before her.

"That's *enough*?" she demanded shrilly. "This woman"—she pointed a finger furiously at Valaria Petrük, sitting with a smug sort of smile across the table from them—"is saying that the massacre of two valley towns—the deaths of tens of thousands, and the enslavement of that many again—is all in line with Laor's will, and you're telling *me* 'that's enough'?"

"Sister Petrük is entitled to her opinion," Jofrey said firmly, not taking his eyes off Petrük herself, "however misguided and idiotic it may be."

That knocked the smugness from the old woman's face, leaving her looking like she'd run into an invisible wall.

They sat, all ten of the Citadel's most respected members, along the leftmost table of Cyurgi' Di's great dining hall, five on either side of it. Outside a new storm was raging, darkening the clerestory windows above their heads to near black despite the earliness of the afternoon, and rattling loose panes of colored glass in their iron linings. The hall itself, though, was warm and bright, heated by the old copper pipes pumped full of steam by the furnaces far beneath them. Pale candles were scattered along the center of their table—only the ones closest to and between them having been lit by helpful acolytes before the start of their meeting—and iron floor sconces held heavy lanterns that burned cleanly around the room, leaving the place smelling vaguely of fire and oil. It was an old scent, familiar and friendly to all, and for Syrah in particular it was one of the first memories she had of this great temple she now called home. They were alone in the hall, having claimed the chambers until the kitchens said they were ready to serve supper, which wouldn't be for another hour. It was a good thing, too, because Petrük looked ready to murder as she glared at Jofrey.

"Had He seen fit to spare Metcaf and Harond, Laor would have done so," the old woman said through gritted teeth. "He did not, so it's only fair to assume that there is a reason He has abandoned them."

"The Lifegiver grants His Gift of life, Valaria, but he also grants free will," Benala Forn, a Priestess only slightly younger than Petrük, said from two spots to her right. "It is neither fair to the people of those towns or Laor Himself to claim He has anything to do with these atrocities."

"But it is just as foolish to assume that He does not," yet another Priest spoke up from Jofrey's right. Behn Argo had a kindly face that hid a deceitfully sharp temper, and he was looking at Benala as though she had stroked it into life with her words. "He may grant free will, but Laor will impact the lives of His flock as He deems fit. It is only human hubris not to say that He would do no such thing."

"If you think any of us believe the Lifegiver is unable to affect us of this world, then you mistake our argument," Syrah said impatiently, still on her feet to Jofrey's left. "No one is claiming otherwise, Argo, but to say that Laor's will is what butchered those people is only one step short of saying He condones the methods used. Do you know what Baoill did, what the birds have been bringing word of? When Harond didn't open its gates for him, he had his men slit the throats of two hundred slaves they'd claimed in Metcaf. Then dumped their corpses into every well and river within half a mile of the city, choking them full, and waited."

Syrah held up a hand, lifting four fingers and showing them to the table.

"Four days. That's how long it took before Harond's waters were so fouled no one could draw from the cisterns. By six, thousands of the already sick were dead from tainted drink. On the eighth day Harond opened its gates in a plea for parlay, and Gûlraht Baoill took it as viciously as he did Metcaf. This time, though, he claimed no slaves, allowed the taking of no battle wives. Barely a handful of survivors were recovered.

Anyone living was put to the sword, then thrown to the fires. By the time help came from the southern towns, Baoill had had his men pile what was left of the dead under every gate leading in and out of the city. The letters from Stullens and Drangstek say they had to send scouts *over* the walls to get in, because no one would go near the black mountains of corpses. What they found was nothing but smoke and dying fires, charred frames of what had been the city buried in snow. Most of the remains of the men and women who'd fallen inside the wall had been left where they fell, abandoned to the crows."

Here Syrah paused, allowing herself a moment to keep her arms from shaking as she waited for the inevitable question.

It was old Priest Jerrom Eyr, the last living member of Eret Ta'hir's generation, who spoke, in a wheezing whisper.

"And the children?"

Syrah turned to look at him. It had been surprising how hard a time she'd had meeting Jerrom's eye when she'd first returned to the Citadel. His aged face was lined and marked by passing years, his beard thinning to catch up with the ring of white hair that sat, wispy and weak, around his head. In his eyes, though, there was still that depth, the endless vat of experience, hardship, and happiness, that one could often find in those of great age who had managed to hold on to their minds.

Looking him in the eye always stabbed at her, because they were the same eyes Eret had had. The same eyes she had never had a chance to bid farewell to.

And they were looking at her with the same resigned strength Eret would have had, if he'd been the one to have to ask her the question.

"The children met the scouts at the top of the wall," she answered reluctantly. "Hundreds of them lined up like sentries along the battlements. Baoill's men had driven spears and lengths of wood through them so they would stay propped up. Some had been dead when they'd been impaled." Syrah blinked away a sudden fury that threatened to bring tears to her eyes. "Others had not."

There was a long pause after Syrah's elaboration as she looked about at them. Even Petrük seemed to be at a loss for words, and old Priest Elber at the far end of the table could be heard whispering "Lifegiver have mercy" under his breath.

Finally, Jofrey broke the shock.

"By your silence it seems we are all in agreement that whatever the Sigûrth's new Kayle has been about these last months, it was not done with Laor's blessing. This is a man who must be stopped, before his warpath razes the North."

"Then we need to know what he's after," Petrük offered, sounding abruptly as though she'd had every intention of facing off with the man the entire time. "What is his end game? If Baoill was aiming to claim the North for the mountain clans, he would have done better to move south, making for Stullens and Drangstek. Instead, you tell us he kept east, into the Arocklen."

"Both valley towns are generally well defended, given their own trouble with the tribes in the Fissür Ranges," Cullen Brern, the Citadel's master-at-arms, spoke up from Jofrey's right. "Maybe Baoill thinks he would do better to seek out easier pillaging? Make for Ystréd instead? It's a smaller town, its walls not nearly as defensible."

"They're usually prepared, but Stullens and Drangstek both sent most of their forces north in an attempt to assist Harond." Syrah shook her head, thinking out loud now. "If Baoill had been fast, he could have gotten his armies east around Cayleb's Wash, making south again, and very likely slipped past the southern towns' support without anyone being the wiser. Why, then, did he march for the Woods?"

"To wait out the freeze?" Aster Re'het, the young Priestess in charge of educating the Citadel's acolytes, offered tentatively.

"For game?" Kallet Brern, Master Brern's younger brother and master of the furnace and forges, said. "Perhaps the army is running low on food."

"The element of surprise?" Jofrey himself offered up. "By making for the Woods, then cutting south through them and across the Dehn Plains, Baoill makes it much harder for Ystréd to know when the attack will come."

"He could even be coming here," Petrük practically squealed, not wanting to be left out of the conversation.

"Or Azbar?" Elber offered. "Given the city is practically the only trading hub the North has with the fringe cities in the South, perhaps Baoill is attempting to weaken our economies, making all the other valley towns easier targets in the long run?"

Syrah felt a twinge of fear as she thought of Azbar, with Talo and Carro believing themselves safe behind the high walls of the woodland city, dealing with their own troubles.

"Do we think he's that patient?" she asked, looking around. "A blow to Azbar could spell trouble across the board."

"Baoill waited a long time to make his moves," Jofrey said thoughtfully. "Metcaf and Harond weren't even aware that the old Kayle had been dethroned when the Sigûrth attacked… If you ask me, assuming Gûlraht Baoill does *not* have the patience for such an attack would be foolish. Still, if Azbar is his goal there are other paths to take that would make easier marching than through the Arocklen. Stullen's and Drangstek's armies made due north, going as the crow flies in the hopes of arriving in time to assist Harond. If Baoill had gone east around

Cayleb's Wash, like you suggested, the lake would have provided more than enough buffer between them. From there, carrying east is the Dehn, which might be hilly, but it would be a hell of a lot easier than getting an entire army through the Woods, especially now that the freeze is truly upon us."

Jofrey paused, staring at his hands as he thought. Then he looked up and around at Syrah.

"Is he still moving?" he asked. "What did Baoill do once he made it to the Woods?"

"As of now he's believed to have halted his march. The scouts Stullens sent after the army claim it's the snows. Apparently they lost a few men to the storms themselves."

"Unsurprising," Jofrey muttered. "If this freeze is anything like the last few years, anyone caught in the blizzards will be in trouble." He looked around to Aster Re'het. "There's a good chance Aster is correct, all things considered. There isn't much shelter this far north that could harbor an army of twenty-five thousand. Perhaps Baoill sees the Arocklen as the best option for weathering out the winter."

"Which means we are free of him." Petrük sounded relieved as she spoke. "If the savage is holing up for the freeze, we have nothing to be concerned for."

Syrah blinked, then turned slowly on the woman. Her anger, temporarily redirected, returned in force. She opened her mouth, set on to word her scathing derision, when Jofrey's hand touched her arm.

"*If* Baoill has paused in his march, it is a temporary thing," he said, eyes on Petrük. Syrah could hear the irritation in his voice, but he did a better job of holding his composure than she would have. "They are mountain men all, which means they will move again as soon as the freeze begins to wane. That gives us six months, seven if we're lucky. Before you decide Gûlraht Baoill isn't worth another thought, why don't you tell us how you plan to prepare in that time, hmm? What are you going to do to assist the remaining towns and cities to stop the Kayle? Because we are all eagerly awaiting your suggestions."

Again Petrük looked as though she had been hit, and again she seemed to have no answer. The old Priestess was a master of the silver tongue, but Jofrey's carefully crafted words had robbed her of any opportunity to be coy, to feign diplomatically away. Instead she sat silent, seething and trading her glare between Jofrey and Syrah, who ignored her.

"Syrah's experience with these tribes is by far the most extensive," Jofrey continued as though Petrük weren't there, looking about at the other Priests and Priestesses around the table. "Talo granted me authority in his absence as High Priest, and it is my recommendation that we follow her lead on this."

He turned to look at Syrah.

"So… what should we do?"

Syrah didn't respond at once, eyes on the table as she thought. No one pressed her now that Petrük had been shamed into silence.

Waiting out the winter? Is he, though? Baoill has momentum now…

That was the truth. By now word must be reaching the eastern towns about Metcaf and Harond. Baoill had the advantage of fear, of panic. Doubt and fright in the hearts of the men tasked with defending Ystréd and Azbar were bad enough, but when it was caught by the masses the results could be disastrous. It was what had happened in Harond, in fact. What few survivors had been found all said the same thing: it hadn't been the city guard or the defenders along the wall who had opened the gates for the Kayle and his army. It had been the people, an angry mob of panicked citizens who'd overrun the men and women tasked in protecting them, bent on deliverance from their poisoned city, of pleading with Gûlraht Baoill for their freedom.

Fear and panic alone had won the Sigûrth the city.

So what would it take for Baoill to give it up?

That answer was simple. The one thing the Kayle could not do without on his bloody campaign.

His army.

Even for men of the mountain, winter was a brutal foe. They were built for it, worshiped it even in the form of their Stone Gods. They believed the freeze was responsible for crafting boys into men and weeding out the weak from the strong. And yet, despite this, they often fell victim to it, defeated by the brutality of the forces they believed to be the judgment of harsh deities.

Baoill's uncle, Emhret, had insulted the old ways by asking the valley towns for help, and Baoill had killed him for it. But did that mean the new Kayle was fool enough to spit in winter's face?

No, Syrah realized suddenly. *To show weakness in the face of the storms was bad enough, but to claim one was better than them… That would be claiming one was better than the Gods. That would be true blasphemy.*

Even as she thought this, Syrah heard once again the rattling of the glass above their heads, buffeted by the anger of the storm.

Winter could claim Baoill's forces and he knows it.

"Baoill won't march through the freeze," Syrah said finally, and a few of the congregation who had been having whispered discussions in private jumped and turned to look at her. "Not in truth, at least. On clear days he may press forward little by little, but he won't push his luck. We already know he's not a fool. He will force himself to wait, lose what momentum he's gained, if it means allowing his army to survive the winter."

"And then?" Priest Jerrom asked, watching Syrah intently, as was the rest of the table.

"And then he will strike hard and fast, as he did in Metcaf. As he did in Harond. If we can't find a way to halt the Kayle before the winter's wane, then Baoill will stop at nothing to claim the North for himself and his tribe."

As they left the dining hall, Syrah walked with Jofrey. She could feel his eyes on her, but ignored him for a while, involved in her own thoughts. When it became clear he wasn't about to leave her alone, though, she sighed in exasperation.

"This is why I thought Talo was a fool to leave," she finally said out loud. "If he'd been here, we'd have had less of a time convincing them we need to act."

"You suspected a madman would descend from the mountains, wreaking havoc on the North and its valley towns, pillaging and burning everything in his path?" Jofrey asked her in a half-amused, half-weary tone.

Syrah snorted, turning a corner to ascend a long ramp that led higher into the mountain.

"Well obviously not *exactly* this situation, but it could have been anything. A High Priest's place is in the Citadel, with his people."

"A High Priest's place is with *the* people," Jofrey corrected her gently, keeping with her as they climbed. "A High Priest's place is where he is needed most to guard the lives of those he is charged with protecting. If you think Eret did his greatest work from behind a desk, I would be happy to correct you. Eret only ended his excursions into the world after Talo started to make a name for himself, doing much of the work his Priest Mentor couldn't shoulder anymore."

"Then Talo needed to take a knee himself, if you catch my drift," Syrah muttered, aggravated, as they reach the ramp's landing and turned right, their steps echoing along the curved walls of the spacious tunnels. "That leg of his will be his end, if he's not careful. And if he wanted to secure the fate of the world, he should have stayed to help with this mess."

"If trouble plagued the world one problem at a time, my dear, then there would be little need for those of our faith," Jofrey chuckled. "Does the sacking of the western towns outweigh the troubles in Azbar? Certainly. There's no argument there. But the Sigûrth hadn't made themselves known when Talo left, and he took advantage of the simplest answer to a significant problem in and of itself. You did not know Talo before he took the cloth, Syrah. In truth neither did I, but I met him shortly enough after to have a good sense of what his life was like before finding the Lifegiver. When a man takes part in such things, he becomes intimate with the atrocity of it. He shoulders blame not often due onto him, no matter what anyone else says."

Jofrey looked around as they walked. Lanterns hung every ten feet or so above their heads, casting bright patches of light to melt with the glow of the blue and white candles burning silently in their little alcoves, scattered along the wall at all different heights.

"The resurrection of the Arena is, to Talo, a failure he is driven to correct, just as their banning the first time around was the result of a different failure he was driven to correct. Not his alone, certainly, but his to bear. It is a trouble that weighs more heavily on him than it could any of us."

"I know that," Syrah said quietly. "I understand that. But the Sigûrth—"

"Will be dealt with," Jofrey finished for her with a nod. "And I very much doubt Talo will stay away long once he hears of this, if he hasn't already. For the moment, though, understand that there are parts of every man's past that we feel we must one day face head-on."

"Have you faced yours?" Syrah asked, half joking as they came to a stop before a massive timber door. Crafted from layered woods of many tints and textures, it depicted an artistic collage of geometries, shapes and lines that crossed pleasantly one over the other all the way to its utmost lip three feet above their heads.

Jofrey smiled. "A long time ago, before I ever joined the faith," he answered. "Laor found me in the midst of my own troubled past, child. That story, though, is for another day. Now"—he turned to face the door—"tell me what is it we're doing here."

"*We* aren't doing anything," Syrah said, sticking her tongue out at the man as she reached for the simple iron handle that had long ago replaced whatever ornate monstrosity must have preceded it. Despite its size, the door opened easily and without a sound. "You followed me here, remember?"

"Ah yes, my mistake," Jofrey replied with a smile, dropping his voice automatically as they stepped into the chamber. "How silly of me to think you might like some assistance in whatever it is you're scheming."

The great library of Cyurgi' Di was as grand as its door suggested. A massive circular room, its domed ceiling was held up by numerous twisting columns of carved wood, each unique in their meticulous detail. Between these, curved rows of high shelves extended outward from the center of the room, so tall that rolling ladders were attached to most of them, sliding this way and that as a hundred or so of the Citadel's faithful moved about the library, searching for new texts and tomes to peruse. In the very middle of the room, a knee-high wall of stone covered with soft cushions—upon which a dozen Priests, Priestesses, and acolytes were lounging, lost in their readings—encircled a round iron grate fifteen feet across. Beneath the grate, a shaft extended straight down, like a well. If one was willing to tolerate the heat for a moment, it was possible to peer through the intricate patterns cut into the iron and glimpse the orange and red of the furnace room far, far below, from which warm dry air rose in steady waves. The largest chamber in all of Cyurgi' Di—aside from the dining hall itself—it was common suspicion that the library had once comprised the private rooms of whatever lord had ruled the Saragrias Ranges from the comfort of the Citadel, long before the faithful had claimed its warm halls for their own.

Syrah cut across the smooth slate of the floor without looking left or right, leaving the others to their books. Jofrey followed behind, silent now. They had both passed beneath the ribbed curves of the ceiling two stories above them too many times in their years to be mesmerized by the artistry of its craft, but even so it was impossible not to feel a moment of bewitchment whenever one walked between the shelves. Large rectangular wedges of thick glass, resistant to the weight of built-up snow and hammering hail, had been patterned into the roof of the library, and had they looked up, Syrah and Jofrey might have taken pause to watch the storm rage thirty feet above their heads, silenced and kept at bay by the skill of long-dead laborers. They might even have stopped to examine once more—as all of the faithful within Cyurgi' Di did at some point or another—the blanketing murals, painted with careful hands, that colored every inch of the ceiling's smoothed stone. These, it was known, had been added in the years after the Laorin had taken up residence within the High Citadel. Each depicted some prominent Priest or Priestess going about the acts for which they were remembered. Painted light shown from the apex of the vaulting, reaching outward to bathe each of the Laorin, silhouetting them against their background.

They were beautiful works all, and every generation certain members of the faith made it their duty to maintain and restore the paintings, ensuring the history locked in those colors would remain intact for all those come after them.

Syrah made for the very back of the library, circling the heat well and ignoring the curious glances thrown her way by a few of the readers. Passing them and slipping through the other side of the rings of shelves, she reached the far wall, where a set of wide steps had been carved out of the stone, leading up. Running parallel to the wall, she took the steps rapidly, stepping onto the landing as Jofrey hurried along behind her. The second and third floors of the library weren't true floors. Rather, they were wide walkways that led all the way around the chamber, each inmost edge comprising of the wall of the floor below, giving the entire room a great sensation of growing as one looked up. Narrower halls led off the walkways, branching into smaller chambers secluded for private study.

It was towards one of these that Syrah made. Passing a young acolyte, maybe twelve or thirteen, she grabbed him gently by the arm.

"What's your name, boy?" she asked kindly. The acolyte blinked blue eyes at her, glancing down at the paleness of her hand.

"W-Willor, Mistress Brahnt," he stuttered.

Syrah smiled at him, dropping her hand and kneeling down so that she was face-to-face with him.

"It's nice to meet you, Willor," she said quietly. "Now, I have a favor to ask you. Can you run and fetch me as much clean parchment as you can find, as well as ink and a quill?" She glanced at Jofrey over her shoulder, and grinned mischievously at him. "Actually, make that *two* quills. Can you do that for me?"

Willor nodded furiously.

"Good. You can bring them to me in here." She indicated an empty study to her right, complete with its own thick-paned window, through which the snow could be made out, whirling against the gray and black of the mountains outside.

"Letters?" Jofrey groaned as the boy took off, then followed Syrah into the room. "Did I just willingly sacrifice my evening so I could spend it cooped up in a room with you writing *letters*?"

"Not letters, per se," Syrah said with a smile, plopping herself down on the thick cushion of one of the two mismatched chairs around the small table that took up much of the room's space. "More like a call to arms. Of course, if you have a better idea on how to coordinate our strategy with the remaining valley towns, I'm all ears. You know I was never much of a scribe."

Jofrey's resigned sigh was answer enough, and he took a seat in the other chair.

"Fine," he said, propping his elbow on the table and his chin in hand as he turned to look out the window. "Not much is going to get through this storm, though."

"We'll send them as soon as it clears," Syrah said with a nod, pushing a lock of white hair out of her eyes as she, too, watched the snow. "Mind you, between Talo, Carro, the valley towns, the smaller villages, and all the faith's temples, it could very well be spring by the time we finish up."

"Let's hope not," Jofrey mumbled sarcastically.

Then he groaned, because Willor had just appeared in the doorway of their small room, balancing two inkwells with quills on a stack of sheeted parchment so tall he was having trouble seeing over it.

XXIV

"Fear the Gods, my son. Revere them. They are the ones who granted you your strength. They are the ones who granted you your mind. When the time comes, Gûlraht, do not shun Them of Stone. For if They have the power to craft a man such as you, consider what manner of creature They will have to create in order to dole out your punishment for angering them."

—Tarruk Baoill's last words to his son

Gûlraht Baoill drank in the quiet like water offered to a man dying of thirst. Only once before had he known such peace in a place. It had been a cave, an abyssal cavern where his father had led him when he was a boy, blind in the dark through cramped tunnels and down slick climbs until they reached the place itself. Buried beneath all the weight of the mountains above, a world of light and life existed, a place where the walls themselves were alive with shifting greens and blues, shimmering like false reflections across the surface of still water. For hours they had sat together in silence, allowing the tranquility of that wondrous sunless world to steal away whatever fears and concerns plagued the world of man far above.

After his father's passing, Gûlraht had never been able to find the cave again.

That peace, though, he thought, looking up into the trees, *might still be found, it seems.*

He had heard that, in the midst of the freeze, the thick canopy of the Arocklen weighed so densely with snow that the light of day could not pierce its veil. He had heard that the forest floor of the woods was blacker than night come winter, secreting away the treacherous pitch and roll of hills and tricky footing. He had heard that monsters stalked between the great pines, barely allowing a glint of sharp eyes in the dark before dragging away the unwary.

So far, though, he had seen none of this.

Perhaps it was that he and his twenty-five thousand still hugged the outskirts of the great Wood. The trees grew narrower and scattered here, allowing snow to pile more thickly in certain places than others, and giving way to sunlight that cut down through the green, gray, and white of the winter woodland. Or perhaps the storms hadn't come heavily enough. The one or two he'd forced his troops through, trekking for the Woods, had certainly been troublesome, but they were nothing to the howling blizzards that would come with the true depth of the freeze, raging with all the force of the Stone Gods come to test man's strength and resolve.

Whatever it was, instead of the bleak portrait of gnarled wood, dirty snow, and oppressive darkness he'd painted in his mind, Gûlraht had found a world of solace beneath stoic branches, a place of calming seclusion that once again stripped the hardships of man from his flesh, lifting the heavy weight of leadership from his shoulders. He stood now in the largest clearing he'd been able to find within a minute's trek of camp, the space in the canopy above no more than a man's length wide, peering up through the trees. It was another clear morning, the heavens above a sheet of blue streaked with wisps of pale clouds. Gûlraht would call for a slow march soon, pressing steadily further into the Arocklen.

For now, though, he allowed his men their fraction of the restfulness he was seeking out himself.

No birds called out, no animals moved between the thick trunks, but the Woods themselves sang for him, a quiet, divine harmony. Wind snuck, cold but gentle, through the Arocklen, shifting branches so that they creaked in the breeze. Here and there snow slipped from its perch, freeing needled leaves to wave fluidly about. Looking upward, he could watch the tips of the great pines themselves join the dance, waving back and forth until the forest around him seemed a living thing, shifting with each intake of breath.

Gûlraht's blue eyes moved a little higher, though, and abruptly the burden of his intents came crashing down on him once more.

To the common eye, the Saragrias Range could not seem much different from any of the other mountain ridges of the North. It cut upward in staggered rows like teeth, black-and-gray faces only streaked here and there with white. The tips were capped in snow, so that on a cloudy day the mountains might seem to melt into the very sky. They towered upward, just north of the Kayle and his thousands, seeming to take up most of the world, like any mountain does when one stands at its feet.

To Gûlraht, however, there was little that was *not* different about the Saragrias. To Gûlraht, it seemed these mountains carved up the sky with evil ambition, marring the very face of the earth.

Gûlraht—as most men of the mountain tribesmen knew their homelands—was conscious of every mile of the Vietalis Ranges as intimately as one might know the body of a lover. Even leagues upon leagues away he could close his eyes and conjure the ridgeline in his thoughts, imagining it against the glow or rising and setting suns. *Those* mountains, to him, spoke of strength and power, of reverence to the Gods, and reverence to one's own purpose.

When he looked up at the Saragrias, on the other hand, Gûlraht saw only weakness, corruption of faith, and could almost taste the bitterness of betrayal.

Somewhere up there, thinking herself safe behind the wicked line of her mountains, the bitch hid from him.

"I'm coming for you, Witch," Gûlraht told the wind softly. "Let us see how your false god answers your prayers."

Then, in a whirl of leather and furs and beaded hair, the Kayle turned and started back for camp, leaving his tranquility behind.

XXV

"There are times—more and more often, I fear, as I grow older—that I wonder why Laor saw fit to place me as He has. Perhaps it was the ignorance of youth, that blind confidence which may just have served me better than most in my earlier years, but I remember a time when the choices were easy, when the decisions were black and white and I only had to stick to whatever I decided on. With the cursed experience and wisdom of age, however, I have lost that confidence. Every question has more than one answer. Every problem, a dozen solutions. Laor has granted me the comforts of the High Priest's mantle, but in the same breath has seen fit to challenge me with a lifetime of questioning myself and my actions. I pray only that I can bear this weight, and pray even harder that my successor can bear the weight of whatever mistakes I might make."

—private journal of Eret Ta'hir

"Talo, there is no *time* for this!" Carro nearly screamed in frustration, watching Talo and Kal pull on their plain heavy coats by the doors of the temple.

Talo frowned at that. "If there is no time for this, then there is no time for the people of Azbar. Are you asking me to abandon tens of thousands to whatever fate Quin Tern has in store for them? That man would grind every member of his populace into blood and bone if he thought it would turn him a profit."

"I'm loath to say it, love, but yes. I know it's not in you to walk away from a fight, but if we don't act soon there may not *be* an Azbar for you to fight for!"

"I am walking away, Carro," Talo said impatiently. "I said we would leave today, and we will. But there are things that need to be addressed. I can't leave him without cause or reason. He needs to know, to understand."

"Arro will survive," Carro hissed in exasperation. "He's made it this far, hasn't he? And he has friends here, the boy and girl. They will give him enough cause to keep going, even after we are gone."

"For the last two weeks the only thing we have been doing is preparing him for an end to his fighting. You've met him, Carro. Do you *truly* believe him to be a man that finds fulfillment in the blood on his hands? Do you think for a moment that he would be content to suffer the killings endlessly, without being told *why* we abandoned him?"

At that, Carro hesitated. The truth was that he *had*, for a moment, thought Raz i'Syul Arro found enjoyment in his actions, in the death and pain doled out by his hand. Carro nearly shivered as he remembered the first time he'd met the atherian, stealing away late in the night with Talo and Yu'ri, making for market quarters, their predetermined meeting place. They thought they'd been the first to arrive, stowing themselves in the shadows of the alleys on one side of the street, the scent of salted meat and stale bread from the butcher and bakery on either side of them mixing with that chill crispness of the air one can only find in a winter night.

So when a towering black shadow detached itself from the wall behind them, it had taken all Carro had not to scream.

Despite all description and warning nothing could have truly prepared the Priest for his first meeting with the "Monster of Karth." To Carro, Raz i'Syul seemed like some devil out of a children's storybook. All he saw at first was the glint of eyes beneath a heavy hood, glimmering over a black reptilian snout and a number of white teeth that stuck up and down between his lips. At seven feet tall he towered over all of them, making even Talo look suddenly small, which had frightened Carro more than anything. To him, Talo had always held an unbreakable quality, that stoic strength of a man not easily felled, like the wall of some great castle.

When he looked at Raz i'Syul, though, Carro suddenly realized just how frail even the strongest of men could be.

It didn't help that Arro seemed to have little interest in small talk, or friendly exchanges of any sort. He nodded briefly when Talo had introduced Carro as another Priest from the High Citadel, but had given no other greeting. Carro had only learned later why the atherian seemed unable to be anything more than civil towards them, and at the time had thought it base rudeness and reminiscent of every other mercenary and sellsword he'd ever met.

But then they'd started to discuss the plight of Azbar, and it didn't take long for Carro to second-guess himself.

They spoke for hours that night, their conversation covering everything from what Arro was hearing from Alyssa Rhen to what little headway Kal had been able to make before help had arrived. They spoke of approaching Tern again, of attempting once more to rile the population of Azbar itself into revolt, and even of reaching out to other towns for assistance in pressuring the Chairman into shutting the Arena down once more.

In the end they'd made little headway, but it was certainly no fault of Arro's. The atherian had listened to every postulation earnestly, taking in their ideas and offering his own when he saw fit. Not only were his suggestions good, but Carro realized after a time that each one seemed resolutely set around ending the fights as soon as possible.

"I've made my point," Arro had said. "I thought they would stop after a few fights, but Tern is raising the pot after every win to entice more to keep fighting. We need to find another way, and we need to find it fast."

This is no monster, Carro remembered realizing. *This is a man with skills he doesn't want to use.*

He'd looked at Talo then, and understood why his partner seemed so intent on freeing the atherian from his burden.

Looking at him now, he made that realization yet again.

"He's not you, Talo," he said quietly.

Talo froze at that, his back to the room now, already limping towards the door. It was a moment before he spoke, and even then he didn't turn around.

"I know that, but *I* was *him*. And if I'd been offered a chance to stop, then abandoned just as hope was offered, it would have been my undoing, Carro. The man has tasted madness once already, I think. I won't have a hand in dragging him back there again."

Then he pulled the door open and, Kal following close behind, disappeared into the gray of the afternoon.

Quin Tern heard the racing footsteps from the minute the runner entered the town hall. He listened to them hammer their way up old creaking staircases, echoing along with thrown open doors and startled servants in their rush to get to him.

What now? he thought, eyes narrowing, letting his arms drop and turning away from the low fire in the east wall of his room, causing a great chagrin for the manservants on either side of him. They'd been surging about him, dressing and powdering him in preparation for the day's tournaments. Whoever had selected his attire had done well today, choosing to layer him in sleek silver wolf furs offset by a black doublet with silver buttons. The clothes were tighter around his midriff than he preferred, but he was in a forgiving mood, pleased with the splendor of the robes. Quin was more than a little irritated, therefore, when the doors to his chambers flew open, revealing a breathless messenger in the uniform of the city, breathing like the bellows, a crunched letter held in one hand.

"Ch-Chairman, sir!" the runner managed to gasp out as he hurried into the room. "A message for you! Came by bird this morning. Sir… Harond is fallen."

The mood of the room changed abruptly. Where a moment before it had been a whirl of servants all attempting to keep about their duties of dressing him as the Chairman turned to face the door, in the next all was still. Every man among them had turned to face the messenger, eyes wide.

Even Tern himself took a second to recover.

"What?" he demanded in a hiss, lumbering forward and reaching out for the crumpled parchment. Ordinarily he might have had the man flogged for presenting the letter to him in such poor condition, but Quin hardly registered the wrinkling as he pulled the sheet flat, scanning it quickly. It wasn't a long message, but it was succinct. He didn't recognize the curved signature at the bottom, done in a woman's crisp hand. He'd heard the old High Priest of Cyurgi' Di had passed, but it was his understanding that Talo Brahnt—an acquaintance of Azbar in years past—had been chosen to take his place. The fact that it wasn't Brahnt, rather than this mystery woman, who was sending word made Quin suspicious, but such concerns were rapidly superseded by the contents of the letter itself.

So, the savages have claimed Harond, too…

They'd heard of Metcaf, of course. Weeks ago now. It hadn't caused much of a stir, though. The mountain clans of the North had been raiding for centuries, attacking every year and taking what was needed before vanishing like a fading fog back up into the cliffs. That they had razed the city completely seemed foolish, as nothing could be plundered from a place that wasn't allowed to rebuild, but when they'd heard that the clans were uniting under a new Kayle, Quin and the council had written it off to inexperienced leadership and the inability of their new master to control his troops.

But Harond, too, now… This changes things.

All at once, Quin felt cold.

"Get more wood on the fire," he snapped at a manservant attempting to fluff the cuff of his left sleeve as he read. "And someone find Azzeki."

At once a few of the men scattered, leaving the rest to wait with Quin, half-dressed with his letter. Again he read the words, as though taking them in twice would reveal some secret deceit, or perhaps even a bad joke.

But no. As much as his distaste of the Laorin ran deep, Quin had never known the faith to bring concern to anything that didn't deserve it.

And they think the man is moving south? Quin thought, alarmed as he again reached the passage regarding the Citadel's suspicions of the new Kayle's plans. *Why would he come so far from his mountains? What value would be gained in putting the eastern cities in his warpath?*

Quin wished suddenly that he had done a better job of paying attention to the historical instruction his father had put him through as a child. He'd taken well enough to mathematics and economics, but he'd never seen much value in the study of the distant past.

Why would he be pushing for Azbar?

A figure appeared in the room's open doorway, and Quin looked up to find Azzeki striding in, bedecked in his usual blacks, curved saber on his hip.

"You wanted to see me?" the Percian asked, revealing the gleam of white teeth against his dark face as he spoke.

Quin nodded. "Summon the council. Tell them I have need of them at once, and to be quick about it. I expect them here within the hour, and any who are late can count themselves replaced."

Azzeki, for once, looked taken aback. "Today is a four-day for the tournament. The lizard fights this morning. Most of them will like be heading to the Arena already. I thought you, too, would be—"

"Azzeki, when I tell you to do something I don't mean 'after I've convinced you to do it.' I mean *now*. And have a runner sent to Kal Yu'ri. I'd sooner spit on the man than let him in my front door, but there are things to be discussed."

Azzeki barely hesitated this time before nodding. Then, turning on his heel, he left the room, again at double pace.

For another minute Quin kept looking down at the letter in his hand, no longer reading the words, but going over them carefully in his head. Then he looked up.

"Well?" he demanded imperiously, looking about at the manservants now standing awkwardly around him. "What are you all waiting for? These robes aren't about to finish putting themselves on!"

XXVI

"Among the great cities of the old North still standing today, Azbar was arguably the largest. At its peak in the early 800's v.S., the valley town held a populace of nearly three-quarters of a million. Over the next two hundred years or so, as the citizens of the North sprawled out into smaller villages and began colonizing the woodlands and plains, the old writings tell us that those numbers dwindled somewhat, though never low enough to keep the city from being a major source of trade with the Southern fringe cities. With the development of our more modern sea trade and the paving of the Lands' Road leading north and south from the Tundra all the way to the Seven Cities, though, Azbar has lost much of its former luster. Today, the city struggles to survive on fees from its once-great Arena, as well as what meager timber it can collect from the rapidly depleting woodlands around it."

—*The North: Ancient Tradition and Culture*, by Agor Kehn

Blood ran in rivulets down Raz's right leg, but he ignored it. It was a narrow gash, granted to his opponent while Raz twisted out of the way, allowed in favor of letting the steel take him full in the side, either cleaving him in two or disemboweling him where he stood.

If I'm to die, Raz thought, almost amused as he leapt back, giving himself some room, *it won't be as an accidental homage to you, Sass.*

All around him, trampled snow had turned the pit from a serene circular field of white to a chaos of brown-and-black slush. Red dotted and streaked the ground even in places where winter's blanket hadn't yet been disturbed, and smooth lines crisscrossed here and there where bladework had brought the weapon low enough to nearly catch earth.

Raz glanced down at himself, grimacing. Apart from the wound in his right leg, he had a new dent in the thigh guard of his left, a shallow stab in his abdomen, and one of the chest straps that held the pauldron encasing his upper left arm would have to be replaced. It had been severed by a crossing sweep that had come far too close for comfort, leaving a thin cut diagonally across his chest, and even as he moved Raz felt the steel shift awkwardly on his shoulder.

"It's a pity," Raz said aloud, calling out in a raised voice as he reached around to undo the armor's remaining straps. "You're not unskilled with that thing, boy. Are you sure you wouldn't rather be making a name for yourself out in the world than die by it here today?"

Across from him, Breck Tilus stood a few paces away, his heavy breathing misting around youthful features. He looked exhausted, the curling black hair that snuck out from beneath his leather helm wet and plastered across his forehead, his wide form quivering as he fought to catch his wind. He looked content enough with the brief reprieve, pale brown eyes never shifting away from Raz.

Likewise, the tip of the heavy bastard sword he held in both hands never dropped below a defensible position.

Raz, on the other hand, had no weapon. It had been like this for nearly every fight in the last two weeks, in fact, since the gruesome results of the tournament's opening day. The victors of the tourney kept opting to face him man-to-man, having convinced themselves that without his blades—and most certainly without Ahna—Raz was an even opponent.

None seemed very considerate of the fact that the corpses kept rolling back down the gangway regardless, if just one at a time.

The boy smiled across the pit at Raz. It wasn't a sneer, for once, like the look most of his opponents cast his way, overly confident in their own skills and bearing the firm belief that there was no way he, some "lizard from the South," could best them.

No, it was a true smile, if a hard one, and it made Raz sad.

"I thank you for the compliment, Master Arro," Tilus responded between breaths. "But making a name for myself is exactly what I intend to do here and now."

Raz frowned. Then, with one hand, he pulled the useless steel from his shoulder and let it crash to the snow.

"Impatience is about to get you killed, boy," he said, starting to walk forward, ever ignoring the numbness of his scaled feet against the frozen earth. "Only the headstrong rush needlessly forward, and only fools do so with a sword in hand."

"My father told me the same thing," Tilus said with a laugh. "He told me that before I won my first fight, then again before I claimed my first bounty. He told me that when I joined the mercenary companies, too. You say I'm headstrong? At my age, aren't I allowed to be?"

"You are," Raz growled, coming to a stop a couple feet outside of the bastard sword's reach. "But you're also meant to have the opportunity to grow out of it, to grow older. If you do this… you're not going to get that chance."

Tilus paused then, and Raz thought he saw some of the boy's confidence waver. He hoped, for half a moment, that he'd gotten through.

But—as it is like to do in the thralls of youthful ignorance—vanity won over sense.

"Your advice does not fall on deaf ear, I swear it." Tilus brought his sword up to his cheek, pointing it right at Raz and taking an aggressive stance. "But as you say, I'm not unskilled with this thing."

And with that, he rushed forward.

At once Raz was on the defense again, as he had been for most of the fight. Every now and then the blows came around at angles that allowed him to deflect them carefully with the thick steel of his bracers, but mostly Raz spent his time dodging and weaving. He used the shape of the pit to his advantage, trailing the rounding of the wall so that he never got pinned with his back against the stone. He was careful as he moved, all too aware of the precision of the boy's strikes, the strength of his blows. All it would take was one slip, one mistake, and Raz was liable to lose a limb, maybe even a wing or his tail. He had to stay focused, stay calm, and stay as aware of his footing as he was of his opponent. After the first snowfall, the Doctore had allowed him access to the pit as much as he needed, giving him the opportunity to train himself, to adjust. It hadn't been easy, and he had his doubts that anyone was infallible on such unstable purchase, but he'd learned his strengths and weaknesses and adjusted accordingly.

So, though the chill and wetness of the snow bit at his flesh, tearing painfully into his skin, Raz had thanked the Sun often in the last week for having born him into the world with claws.

When both feet found ideal footing, winning good grip in furrows and divots in the frozen mud beneath the snow, Raz decided it was time to turn the fight on its head.

Tilus was not expecting the pounce. For a time during his charge, he might have been wary of a counterattack, but after a while all fights tend to settle into a rhythm. It is the primary weakness of inexperience, the true cost of youthful ignorance, though, that leads young fighters into embracing the pattern. For Tilus, paths like that would have always been in his favor, his superior strength and skill allowing him to lead the dance until he won.

When the dance is forcibly changed, though, such men are often left reeling.

The boy had just brought his blade up for another crossward blow when Raz was suddenly moving *at* him rather than away from him. To his credit he didn't hesitate in his strike, bringing it down just as he'd intended, aiming for Raz's newly bared left shoulder. Raz, though, closed the gap between them faster than any steel could fall. He was already beside Tilus by the time the blow would have reached him, and the sword—driven downward with all the hopes of a killing strike—dug into the snow and earth, sticking there. Before the boy had the chance to pull it out, Raz's foot collided with the back of his weight-bearing leg, bringing him to his knees. He still clung one-handed to the blade, his grasp at an awkward angle with the sword lodged in the ground. Without hesitating, Raz punched down with a mailed fist, crushing the boy's right shoulder. As Tilus screamed in pain, his hand dropping loosely from the bastard sword's handle, Raz reached out and pulled the blade free.

Then, in a single motion, he swung the blade around and dragged its razor edge across Brek Tilus' throat.

If one has never seen the force with which arterial blood can spray, it is a terrifying thing. A gush of red, misting in the icy air, erupted across the snowy ground and stained the stone of the angled wall beside them. Tilus didn't even have time to choke on his own blood. Raz had cut so quick and so deep that he was gone in seconds, allowing for only one bubbling rasp from his severed windpipe before he was still.

Putting a foot to his back, Raz shoved the boy so that he fell facedown into the slush and mud.

"Fool," he said sadly, watching the red creep into the brown and white of the snow. "Dead ears are no better than deaf ears."

Then he tossed the bastard sword aside, and looked up into the crowd.

The sounds of the world returned to Raz in a rush, as they always did after a match. Abruptly the dull throb of white noise that he had all but forgotten erupted into the ear-splitting cacophony that was the comprised roar of ten thousand spectators. The colored ocean of fur and wool waved around him like churning water as some jumped up and down in excitement, some applauded from their seats, and some waved fists about, cursing him for lost wagers. The great iron sconces along the stairs burned bright and hot, lining the sections of the stands so that each looked like a painting of mismatched color framed in fire.

It was a familiar sight, one he was becoming accustomed to, if no less appreciative of.

Something today, though, was not quite right…

Turning about, Raz peered up into the Chairman's box. He was used to the fleshy form of Quin Tern leering down at him after each victory, as pleased with himself as he was with Raz, outlined in the light of the flames behind him. He was used, too, to the dark form of Azzeki Koro there, half-hidden behind the Chairman's heavy throne. He was accustomed to their presence, and even more so to Tern's habitual post-fight monologues, praising "the Scourge" and "the Monster" for his skills and praising the people of Azbar for making such a wise choice in the selection of their champion.

So when the only silhouette to appear in the alcove's opening was the narrow frame of a herald, Raz got the distinct impression that something was wrong.

"Victory of the fifth branch of the Chairman's Tourney is given to Raz i'Syul Arro, the Monster of Karth, the Scourge of the South," the man announced in a carrying voice to cut over the still-shouting crowd. "Thus concludes our third week of tourney. Preliminaries for the sixth branch will start tomorrow for any who—"

As the herald continued to announce the schedule for the coming days, Raz turned away from the box, eyes on the crowd. Most were getting up now, rising to their feet and making for the Hall of Heroes, murmuring excitedly over the day's matches. Some, though, were keeping to their seats, too enthralled in their conversation to be bothered with the queues that led out of the Arena, or else waiting for the herald to finish speaking, in case he announced anything exciting.

If something's going on, Raz thought, still scanning the masses, *they'll be here...*

His eyes found the section he was looking for, the first on the left of the Hall. It was easy for them to blend into the crowd, pretending to be simply part of the throng. It was how they'd been in communication, how they'd agreed to make contact if they needed to speak. He'd met them a few times over the last two weeks, discussing strategy and options and what could be done about the cancer that was the Arena.

Sure enough, the Priests waited patiently for him to see them, seated as close to the pit as they could manage.

Raz met Talo Brahnt's blue eyes, and he nodded. The Priest returned the motion, then leaned over to whisper something to Kal Yu'ri. At once the smaller Priest stood up, reaching out to help Brahnt to his feet, and together the pair joined the line leaving the stadium.

Turning away from them, Raz bent down to pick up the pauldron he'd pulled off his shoulder, lifting it from the dirty snow. As he did, his eyes fell again on the still form of Brek Tilus. A pair of attendants were already ducking under the rising gate of the portcullis to Raz's left, making for the boy's body. When they reached it, each went to take an ankle, intent on dragging him away.

Fury spiked in Raz's chest, and the red of the crest along his neck flared into sudden brightness.

"Pick him up!" he snarled, causing both men to jump and quail away from him. "Carry him. And if I see you roll him down the ramp, so help me if your families find enough left of you to know what happened."

XXVII

A half hour later the great double doors from the Arena underworks opened for Raz, and he stepped out into the familiar wash of the crowd. Despite the fact that it had started to snow once more, frosting the hair, hoods, and shoulders of his admirers, the numbers seemed to have only increased yet again today. They moved about him, still smart enough to stay out of reach, except for one unfortunate, who must have been pushed across his path. He met the man's eye for a moment, then a few others, then moved on, scanning the edges of the throng.

Where are you?

He found them hugging the mouth of the alley directly across from the doors, keeping to the wall, just as they had on the day they'd first introduced themselves.

Raz moved forward casually, parting the flood of bodies around him, ignoring the screams and cheers as he passed. Finally ridding himself of his fans, he strode right past the Priests, making for the deeper parts of the residential quarters, where one could get lost in all the twists and turns.

For a few minutes Raz walked, picking his way haphazardly through the buildings. He didn't know where he was going, didn't suspect where he might end up. He just picked a direction and went with it, choosing a turn at every split, exploring an alley at every opportunity. It was never hard to find his way back. The citizens of Azbar were nothing like the Miropans of past years, who would spit at his feet or curse as he passed. Here in the North, when he asked for directions people tended to trip over themselves offering them up.

It was an odd—but not unwelcome—change.

When he'd gotten himself good and turned around, Raz finally stopped. The courtyard he found himself in was a pleasant little space, a sort of semi-private circular pavilion with a single gnarled fir growing in the middle, the earth it was rooted in elevated to about knee height and held secure by a flat-topped wall. It was here that Raz sat, brushing away the little buildup of snow that had accumulated on the stone, and tucking his furs beneath him.

Then he waited.

It never took the Priests long to find him. He wasn't exactly sure *how* it was they managed to track him down so quickly, but he had his suspicions. He'd seen one or two tricks of theirs so far, the power of their magics. He supposed he should have been impressed, but in truth what abilities they'd demonstrated thus far—though more tangible, perhaps—seemed somewhat lacking compared to the recurrent omniscience he'd witnessed growing up from the Grandmother.

They have their uses, though, Raz thought with a shiver, feeling his body start to tighten up in the cold now that he had stopped moving.

Sure enough, it wasn't more than half a minute before the staggered footsteps of Kal Yu'ri supporting a limping Talo Brahnt reached his ears, and only shortly after that that the pair turned a corner and made their way slowly down the snowy alley into Raz's little courtyard. On seeing them, Brahnt leaning as heavily as he always did on Yu'ri's arm, Raz frowned.

"I still don't see the value in all this cloak-and-dagger, Priest," he growled while Brahnt eased gingerly down beside him with a relieved sigh. "You're putting yourself through unnecessary strain. I should just come to you."

"If Tern got word that I was in town—much less that we've been speaking—it could spell disaster," Brahnt said with a shake of his head. Yu'ri stayed standing before them. "I can't impress that upon you enough. Now that the Arena is on its own two feet again, to the council of Azbar the Laorin are something akin to soldiers in a rebellion. It would not do well for you to be seen with us."

Raz grumbled under his breath, but nodded, reaching out to pull the furs tighter around his body.

"Oh!" Talo exclaimed in doleful alarm. "Pardon my ill manners. Here."

He waved a hand in Raz's direction. The air rippled, as though shifted by some blasting force, but instead of being thrown off his feet, Raz felt warmth seep into every inch of his body, pressing its way comfortably down into him. He relaxed, breathing his own sigh of relief as the stiffness of the cold left him.

The spell didn't ever hold more than an hour or so, but it was wonderful while it lasted.

"Thank you," he told the Priest with a nod. "Now, though"—he looked between Brahnt and Yu'ri—"what's going on? Tern wasn't at the fights today, and he's never missed an ounce of that bloodshed. The fact that you showed up tells me there's something I need concern myself with."

At that, Brahnt looked around at Yu'ri. "Tern probably received the same news we did," he said. "Syrah will likely have sent birds to all the Northern cities."

"Along with the other temples," Yu'ri said with a nod. "If she's convinced the Citadel to vie for an end to Baoill's atrocities, she's going to be looking for as much support as she can get."

"Undoubtedly," Talo agreed, before turning back to Raz. "What do you know of the mountain tribes?"

Raz shrugged. "Scattered bits," he said, thinking back to what stories

Arrun told him during his first couple of weeks with the siblings. "Not much. I can attest to their fighting skills, perhaps, but that's about as far as my expertise is like to reach. Who is Baoill?"

"A villainous bastard."

Both Raz and Brahnt blinked at that, looking at Yu'ri.

"Sorry," the Priest muttered, going red in the face. "Couldn't help myself."

Something like a smile pulled for a second at the corner of Brahnt's mouth, but it was a pained twitch, and Raz had the sudden impression he was not going to like whatever he was about to hear.

"Gûlraht Baoill," Brahnt told him, "is as dark a spirit as they come. He took power among the mountain men through combat, as is tradition. The old Kayle, though—what we might think of as a king or emperor—was the first in a long line of mountain chieftains willing to negotiate with the Laorin and valley towns towards peace and mutual prosperity. Syrah did a lot of work with him personally, in fact. For almost three years she traveled between the northern towns and the Vietalis Ranges above them, hammering out accords and treaties between the two peoples. Baoill, though, had no interest in keeping the peace. From the moment the crown fell to him he seems to have been gathering himself for something bold, bolstering the ranks of his armies for some great coup. He came out of the mountains with twenty-five thousand men, razing one valley town after another. Now he seems to have settled north of here for the winter, in the Arocklen Woods."

"Baoill," Raz repeated the name thoughtfully. "I've never heard of him…"

"You aren't likely to have," Brahnt said with a nod. "Not many had, until a few weeks ago, when he burned Metcaf to the ground."

"Along with tens of thousands," Yu'ri added sourly, his face darkening. "Though the ones he left to the flames were only those he didn't manage to chain and drive into the ranges."

Abruptly, the spell of warmth around Raz seemed to shatter. Though he knew it was there, could feel the caress of magic on his smooth skin, it felt as though the heat had suddenly gone from the air.

"Slaves?" Raz growled, his armor clinking gently as it shifted to accommodate the sudden tension in his form. "You have *slaves* up here?"

It was obvious that Brahnt and Yu'ri had noticed the change in him, because they exchanged a concerned glance before anyone spoke.

"*We* do not," Brahnt said pointedly. "The Laorin had all forms of indentured servitude banned in the settled North nearly three hundred years ago, and it stuck. The mountain tribes, though, don't fall under any governance or religious law. Prisoners of war are used as camp slaves, or claimed as battle wives. When the march is over, when the tribes return to their mountains, they are divided among the people like the rest of whatever riches each raiding party returns with."

Raz said nothing, sitting there on the low wall, watching the little flakes of snow fall around him, twisting away from his body as the warmth of the Priest's magic kept them at bay.

It was happening again. The sudden cold realization that the world around him, so grand and so green, was only a façade to cover up the ugliness that was beneath. He was growing to love this land of trees and snow, growing to tolerate the cold and wet and wind if it meant knowing the lushness of the woodland and the grassy bounty of the earth and mountains.

At the same time, though, Raz was also growing to realize that he would never be able to run fast enough to escape the corruption of man and his corrosive pursuits.

"Will it never end?" he growled somberly. "Years. Years I've spent trying to forge a dent in the world, and each time I feel I'm making headway I turn around only to realize the shadows I slew behind me have only been replaced by greater and deeper darkness."

"Or you look ahead and see the road you're on seems to have no light at its end," Brahnt said with a nod. "Yes, I'm all too familiar with that feeling, sadly. Then again… Imagine what the world might look like if we didn't fight to better it. Out there in the woods"—he waved a hand vaguely about them, indicating some distance place—"roads are cut through the trees, some wide enough so that carts can be two abreast, passing without colliding. There are men whose sole purpose is to keep those roads clean and unhindered, pulling up roots, moving toppled trunks, even rebuilding when too much stone and dirt get washed away in the summer floods. They toil every day, keeping the forest at bay. They know they would never be able to destroy it completely, to wipe every tree and hill and boulder from the map, but they do enough to keep the roads safe and intact. Can you imagine what would happen if one day they gave up? If one morning, tired of fighting a battle they could never really win, those men put down their tools and bent to the will of the woods? It would be a matter of weeks before the roads became ungovernable. Within the year nature would reclaim them completely, and in ten you might never have even known there was any sort of path in the first place."

Raz cracked a smile at that.

"So that's how you picture us?" he asked. "As glorified caretakers of a world too twisted out of shape to attend to its own troubles?"

"Sometimes I don't even think we qualify as 'glorified,'" Brahnt said with a snort. "But yes, in a word, though we go about it differently. It is a hard task, one that requires persistence and patience, sacrifice and a good head on your shoulders. But it is an essential task just the same."

Brahnt looked to the sky, then frowned.

"Still, that doesn't make it any easier. Especially in times like these."

Raz nodded. "So what are you planning to do?"

Talo sighed. "Baoill has twenty-five thousand, and his position in the Woods gives him great advantage. Ordinarily it's only a fool who goes beneath those trees in the freeze, but none of the usual dangers will pose any threat to the Kayle's army. Instead they will offer him shelter, game to survive the winter, and even some measure of freedom to keep his march moving, if slowly. Syrah believes he will be pushing east and south as often as possible through the freeze, and at first opportunity will break from cover and make for Ystréd, the only true town north of here. Once he's done there, Baoill will make for Azbar itself."

Raz nodded again. "Even the city walls won't last against an army that size."

"That's not even considering that it may grow," Yu'ri offered suddenly. "There are tribes in the Saragrias as well. It's unclear whether Baoill conquered or coerced the other mountain men of the Vietalis into joining him, but either way there are bound to be groups enticed by his assault on the cities. The clans have been raiding—and the valley towns defending themselves—for as long as anyone can remember. Even the old archives in the Cyurgi' Di imply that it's a vicious cycle with no likely or obvious end."

"But this Baoill seeks to end it through violence," Raz snorted, then looked at Talo. "Weren't you telling me of a similar story, a few weeks back?"

"If you're implying that Baoill and you are similar, you couldn't be more wrong." Talo shook his head. "Baoill seeks no peace through his actions. If he did, he would have built on the treaties Syrah drafted with the old Kayle. In fact, he wouldn't have challenged Emhret Grahst at all. No, Baoill is seizing power, looking to reclaim the Northern lands for himself and his people. Peace might come from it all eventually, true, but that's like saying the best way to end a fight between neighbors is to have one executed. There are infinite more opportunities to come to a less barbaric solution."

"And you intend to leave, so you can explore them."

Raz said it as matter-of-factly as he could.

Talo hesitated. It was clearly not an easy question to answer.

"We do," he said finally.

Raz nodded, unsure of what to say. The disappointment was more bitter than he would have admitted. He might not like the Priests, but he had to admit to himself that he had slept better the last few weeks, with their camaraderie easing the unpleasant weight of his role within the lumbering stone walls of Azbar.

"And I would like to know if you would consider coming with us."

Raz looked around so fast beneath his hood that he felt his neck pop. Yu'ri, too, was obviously surprised by Talo's statement, because he was gaping at the High Priest like the man had abruptly grown an extra head.

"Talo!" he finally managed to hiss. "What are you—? You can't really—!"

Talo cut him off with a raised hand. "You can keep your opinion to yourself this time, Kal. I would have asked in the long run anyway, but it seems our timetable has turned." He watched Raz intently. "Let me be clear: I do not *want* to leave. This battle, the one you have been fighting these last two months, is as much mine as it is yours. More so even, and I am loath to turn my back on it when we have only just begun. If I stayed, though, I would be staying for myself. Azbar's troubles are great, yes, but they pale in comparison to the brewing storm north of here, and I have a responsibility to the people of the land before I have a responsibility to the peace in Azbar."

He pointed northward.

"In Cyurgi' Di there are those among the Laorin who have experience in the arts of battle, of war. But we are few and far between, and at this time we are not nearly enough to face the tide of the Kayle's army. Whether we will ever be, I don't know, but regardless your experience could prove invaluable to us, should it come to that."

"But he's a *killer*, Talo," Yu'ri hissed, not even bothering to keep his voice down in his desperation to get his point across. "You cannot suggest we turn a blind eye on his—!"

"What I *suggest*," Talo said loudly, a note of anger creeping into his voice for the first time since Raz had met him, "is the exploitation of an advantage, Kal!"

"Yu'ri is right, though," Raz offered. "It's one thing to request my assistance, Priest. It's another to expect me to bend to your rules. Your kind can't kill, and I thought you were forbidden from condoning the death of others."

"I do not condone their death," Brahnt told him. "I do not condone your methods, or the means by which you meet your ends. But I condone your values, and your skills. And if you would ask me which I would prefer—the death of less or the death of more—I can give you an easy answer. As the world stands, violence is inevitable. No amount of prayer, of work, of missions or sermons or preaching will cure our lands of bloodshed overnight. Laor knows this. Laor understands this. So when He sees fit to offer me the opportunity to save what lives I can, I will take it. Even if *you* are that opportunity, Raz i'Syul Arro."

"And even if it means abandoning the work we've done here, in this place? The work *I've* done here?"

Talo's face darkened, but he didn't hesitate.

"Yes," he said quietly. "I've said it once today, and I will say it again. If Baoill is not dealt with, there may be no Azbar for you to protect come the summer seasons."

Raz watched him steadily for a moment, weighing the Priest's words. He considered his options carefully, attempting to fathom every detail, every outcome.

But this was not a fight. This was not a duel of fist and blades, and Raz realized quickly that he could not so easily see what lay ahead of him on either path.

On one hand, he had responsibilities here in the city. While he wasn't about to call the place a "home," it was at least home to Arrun and Lueski, and it was home to over half-a-million others. Others who had come to depend on him, whether they knew it or not. Others who had need of him, had need of his presence in that pit, a presence that filled the void left by their merciful absence. The Arena was a beast of endless hunger, and despite anything he might do or say, Raz had no clear concept of how to end—or even sate—that hunger.

On the other hand, though, war seemed to be plodding down on them from the horizon. Raz had never been at war. Not in truth, anyway. He'd waged his own battles, perhaps, fought for his personal vendettas and vengeances, but what seemed to be descending on the North from the mountains was a different sort of fight altogether.

And what good is one man in a fight like that?

Raz considered that question. Here, in Azbar, he had value. Real, *true* value. Here, with the death of three or four a week, he saved dozens. Here, his actions mattered.

The dark form of a pedestrian in some sort of hurry darted past the mouth of the alley, shifting Raz's gaze to it. No one else followed, everyone tucked away and warm in their homes, but Raz imagined what the streets of Azbar must be like in the summer, alive with energetic bodies anxious to enjoy the warmer months while they could. Here, in the city, Raz could do something to keep those people safe, to keep their thoughts on the mindless things people were supposed to think about. Here, he meant something.

Imagining being out there, in the world, against an army of twenty-five thousand and growing, Raz suddenly thought he had some small understanding of what it must have been like to be the smallest fish in a very, *very* large pond.

"No."

The answer passed Raz's lips before he even had a chance to articulate an explanation. He watched Talo's face fall, and sighed.

"No," he said again. "I won't come with you, though I appreciate the offer. I have more value here, fighting this fight we started, than out there against an enemy I know nothing about."

"But we could teach you!" Talo insisted. "I could teach you. *Syrah* could teach you."

Raz caught the spark of interest that flared within himself at the woman's name, quenching it before it had time to catch fire.

"I don't doubt that, Priest, but you and I both know I'm not meant to be a student. I'm not meant to be a councilor or advisor or whatever it is you intend to make of me. Furthermore, even if you and some select few would be willing to listen to what I have to say, there are others"—he waved a hand at Yu'ri, who frowned—"who would be much less inclined to take my advice to heart. I am a killer, after all. And—as I have no desire of taking the cloth, as you have—I don't imagine that's an offense so easily forgiven, especially since I have little intention to change the way I go about my business. If you needed a soldier, that would be one thing. But you don't need a soldier. Your kind has no use for soldiers. Here, though"—he waved about them, at the gray and white stone of the buildings, at the swaying of the tree above their heads—"*here* they have need of a soldier. Here, I have value."

Talo seemed to have no answer to that. He merely watched Raz for a time, clearly disappointed.

"I'd thought you would have wanted to come," he said finally. "I didn't even consider you might want to stay."

"You thought right," Raz told him with a nod. "I *do* want to come. I *do* want to be rid of the responsibilities I have here. I want the freedom of the road, the ease I had—if only for a time—when I first came to your Northern lands."

He set his arms behind him, feeling the coolness of the layered snow seep into the leather and steel of his gauntlets.

"But what I want and what I need are two very different beasts," he continued. "I want to go, but I need to stay. I want the freedom you offer, but I've made decisions here, pacts that I cannot cast aside just yet."

Again Talo was quiet, watching him, chewing over his words.

"It's funny you consider yourself a poor candidate for what I offer," he said sadly. "It's that sort of character I might find lacking when I seek advice on what to do about Baoill."

Raz smiled at that. "You and I have very different opinions of my value, it seems."

"Not different," Talo said with a shake of his head before gesturing to Yu'ri. "Divided. We each see one side of the same coin. You see the part of you that differs so drastically from our faith, whilst I see the part of you that aligns with every hope and dream Laor bears for His people.

You see death, violence, and murder, and you are not wrong to do so. But I see strength, honor, and the courage to do what must be done in order to ensure the safety of those you are responsible for."

He reached out to clutch Yu'ri's offered arm, grunting as he pulled himself painfully to his feet. When he'd gotten his balance, he looked over his shoulder at Raz, still seated beneath the tree.

"Carro and I will be on the northbound road for Ystréd, should you change your mind. After that, it's through the Dehn Plains and on to the Arocklen."

Raz nodded, but didn't respond. After a moment's hesitation, Brahnt allowed Yu'ri to pull him away, making for the road again.

They'd reached the mouth of the alley leading out from the courtyard when the Priest forced his companion to stop again. Looking around one last time, he raised a hand in farewell.

"Take care of yourself, boy."

Then he was gone, leaning on Yu'ri, limping down the alley and around the corner.

"And you, Priest," Raz said to the emptiness of the afternoon chill, tilting his head to watch the thickening snow spill between the branches of the tree. Reaching out a hand, he found Ahna's haft and dragged her across his lap.

"Just you and me again, huh, sis?" he whispered sadly. The dviassegai offered no obvious response, but as he ran a hand over her worn white wood, Raz found old memories flitting across his mind. His uncle's face, then that of his mother and father, then Ahna herself. Raz had always found that he had a better memory than man, but after so many years, even he had trouble recalling the details of their features. Their forms came now more as tanned skin, bleached and braided hair, and the shine of clan chains than it did with any particularity.

What did come clear, though, were the faces of a brother and sister, the former preparing dinner, the latter waiting anxiously for Raz to get home.

Smiling, Raz pushed himself to his feet and tossed Ahna over one shoulder.

Well, he thought, feeling the warmth of Brahnt's magic shift around him as he made for the alley himself, *maybe not just you and me.*

XXVIII

"It feels, at times, as though I might have always intended to surround myself with fools, Azzeki. The buffoons who have somehow coaxed themselves into my favor seem to demand more from me on any given day then I ever demand of them. To hell with advisors! They were my father's weakness. We have the guard on our side. What use have I of second-rate information from the council when I possess my own eyes and ears all over the city already?"

—Azbar Chairman Quin Tern to Captain-Commander Azzeki Koro

Trell Hamus ran as though some dark demon were hounding him. He wasn't so sure the idea was far off, because in the hush of the falling snow his imagination kept frightening him with the sounds of beating wings and the clink of heavy steel armor.

The Monster had caught a glimpse of him, Trell knew. He'd passed the mouth of the alley leading into the courtyard in his haste to get back to the town hall, and he was positive he'd seen the man's amber eyes on him, if only for a moment.

Even if the Monster didn't know Trell's destination, though, the guardsman couldn't help but imagine the atherian barreling up behind him, intent on finding out why he'd been eavesdropping and what he had heard.

He hadn't meant to, of course. He'd had no scheme, when he set out, to overhear anything. Trell had only been there because he knew the city best, and was the fastest runner the guard had to offer. The order had been given to him by the Captain-Commander himself, in fact.

"Find the High Priest," Azzeki Koro had said. "Tell him his presence is requested at once. The Chairman has need of him."

Trell had barely given himself time to nod and salute before he was off running, heading straight for the temple. He'd thought it the obvious choice, and had been surprised, therefore, when he'd been informed by the acolyte who had answered the door that High Priest Yu'ri was away, off to see the fights.

"The fights?" Trell had asked, as it seemed an odd choice. The boy, dressed in the plain white clothes of his position, didn't have much of an answer, merely shrugging and nodding.

By the time Trell made it to the Arena, the day's tournament was all but over. Figuring he would do better to keep an eye on the crowds as they left, funneled through the narrower walls of the Hall of Heroes, rather than risk missing Yu'ri in the Arena itself, Trell posted up and waited. When the day's matches came to a close, climaxing with a great roar of the crowd, Trell hopped up onto a stack of barrels and old wooden boxes along the wall of the blacksmith's shop directly across from the Arena entrance.

There, for the duration of the people's exiting, he waited, peering into the masses, looking for the signature white of the faith's robes.

Nothing.

When the last of the spectators finally wound their way down the Arena stairs, drunk on some spirit or another, Trell started to get worried.

The Captain-Commander was not known for his patience. Even less so was the Chairman himself.

For a minute more Trell debated taking the standard route back to the temple, hoping to catch the High Priest as he returned home, or at least find him back at the temple itself. When he saw the mass start to gather around the door of the underworks, though, he'd decided to linger.

If the High Priest held an odd penchant for the tournament, why wouldn't he hold a similar enthusiasm for the fighters themselves? Perhaps even the Arena's newest champion, the so-called "Monster of Karth"…

Trell himself had yet to see Raz i'Syul Arro. He'd heard stories from his friends, rumors and descriptions from the other members of the guard, but he'd never managed to pay himself a seat to see a four-day final's bout in the Arena for himself. Perhaps it was a bit of this curiosity—as well as the desire to leave no stone unturned—that led Trell to sift through the crowd waiting outside the underworks.

For a quarter hour Trell tucked his way through the mass of people shifting about impatiently. All manner moved around him, some shouting and cheering, others talking quietly amongst themselves. Each time the doors opened, everyone would shift their eyes to them, anxious to see what would step out from between them.

The first two times it was nothing but the corpse cart and some straggling gladiators who had made it through the day, and both times the crowd had returned to their business disappointed.

Almost as disappointed, in fact, as Trell was.

The High Priest was nowhere to be found. He'd gotten in among the crowd thinking that perhaps the man's white robes were covered by a cape or coat, making them hard to find from a higher vantage point. He had no more luck finding the man from the ground, though, and Trell was truly starting to panic. If he had to run all the way back to the temple for Yu'ri, Azzeki Koro would have his hide.

It was then, right then, as Trell was debating what to do, that he found him.

Kal Yu'ri was at the very back of the throng, separate from them even. He stood in the entrance of the wide alley directly across from the underworks' double doors, side by side with a man Trell didn't know. What was more, both men were in plain leather and furs, neither sporting the customary robes of Yu'ri's faith.

It didn't matter, though, Trell thought. In fact, he was so awash with relief at having found the man in a respectable time, so anxious to get to him as he started to push through the crowd, that he didn't notice the sudden tension around him once again. He was so busy pressing himself between bodies, trying to get to the High Priest, that he stumbled when the path opened suddenly for him, nearly falling down as he tripped into the sudden lack or resistance.

Looking around to see why the people had out of his way, Trell froze.

Though it was only for a moment, Raz i'Syul's golden eyes met his as the Monster passed. There was a fierceness there, instilling an absolute fear that lingered long after the atherian had moved along, making for the very alley Trell had been aiming for. The guard's mind, though, was for once torn away from his objective as he took the beast in.

No amount of his friends' descriptions would have adequately conveyed the Scourge of the South, and Trell couldn't help but think what fools those who chose to face him in the pit must be. Seven feet tall, the great mantle around his shoulders did little to hide the size and litheness of the man, and nothing at all to hide the steel claws of the intricate gauntlets he had on each hand. His wings were hidden in the furs, as was most of his tail, but Ahna, the famed great spear, was on one shoulder. An old leather bag hid her blades from view, and Trell was startled to find himself inexplicably saddened by the fact that he wasn't able to witness them in all their glory.

For a long moment the guard stood still, watching the atherian walk even as the crowd closed behind him. He didn't recall his mission at all, in fact, until Raz i'Syul was at the mouth of the alley along which Kal Yu'ri and his nameless companion waited.

Waking abruptly from his daze, Trell started to push forward, keeping an eye on the High Priest. He expected the two men to watch the atherian pass by in silence, or perhaps add their cheers to the crowd.

What he did not expect, though, was for the Monster to nod towards Yu'ri, and for Yu'ri's companion to nod back. Then as if that weren't surprise enough, after a moment the two men detached themselves from the wall and started following Raz i'Syul deeper into the city.

That had confused Trell beyond measure. What business could a High Priest of Laor—and whoever his companion was—have with the bloody champion of Azbar's great Arena?

As Trell finally broke through the crowd, reaching the freedom of the street just as the two men disappeared around a corner, his confusion shifted, though. The guard had been told of the trouble the Laorin were causing the city, trying to interrupt the economic upturn Azbar had seen since the reopening of the Arena. They'd been told to be on the watch for trouble and to report anything they found directly to Azzeki. It was this thought that morphed Trell's bewilderment. First it turned to doubt, then curiosity.

And then it became nothing less than full-blown suspicion.

Therefore, with the city's best interests in mind, Trell Hamus had chosen to follow the group, deciding that—if his hunch proved to be nothing of note—he could always make himself known and deliver his summons as scheduled.

And now, a half hour later, Trell was running for his life.

He hadn't waited to hear the full conversation. He'd heard enough as it was. Talo Brahnt, the Lifetaker, the betrayer of the Arena, had returned to Azbar. The master of the High Citadel far to the North had snuck back to skulk within the walls of their town, clearly looking to cause as much mayhem as he had in the stories Trell had heard from decades prior.

"And I would like to know if you would consider coming with us."

It was then that Trell had run, not waiting for the Monster's answer. It was then that he'd darted across the mouth of the alley. He had no doubt Talo Brahnt would use his cleverness—or maybe even his magic—to coax the champion of Azbar into turning traitor, just as the Lifetaker himself had. He had no doubt that the High Priest of Cyurgi' Di was determined to steal away the very foundation of the Arena, the heart of the Chairman's Tourney, and the heart of Azbar's people.

And he had no doubt that Quin Tern would want to know at once.

XXIX

"Wisdom may make you wise. Cleverness may make you clever. With just the wrong amount of each, though, both may make you a fool."

—Sigûrth proverb

Quin Tern sat behind the great desk that had once been his father's, his back to the glass doors leading out to the balcony overlooking the ravine. The fingers of one pudgy hand were pressed against his temple, the other rubbing the roughened wood of his chair's armrest as though it might coax out an answer to the problem before him.

"What do you want to do?"

Quin looked up. Azzeki stood as always. In the ten years the man had been a part of his retinue, Quin could barely remember the Percian ever sitting, in fact.

"Do?" he hissed in fury. "I want to burn every last fucking one of them to ash. I want to lock them up in their damn temple and set the whole fucking thing aflame! *That's* what I want to do!"

"Tempting." Azzeki chuckled darkly. "But ill-advised."

"And you don't think I know that, too? The Laorin have lost power in the last half century, but they still hold enough sway to destroy all we've built here if they set their mind to it. We're fortunate only the Lifetaker decided to show his face, for now. No. Kal Yu'ri will have to be left untouched. We may have need of him yet, regardless."

"To assist us with the mountain man?"

"*Fuck* the mountain man," Quin screamed, slamming a heavy fist down on the desk with such force it nearly toppled the inkwell in the corner. "He wants to hole himself up in the Woods? Hide himself away with his warriors and his slaves? Fine. For now I'm happy to leave him to it. Kassus has done the maths. Between Ystréd, Stullens, Drangstek, and Azbar, we could have our own army. Maybe forty thousand strong, if we conscript. Plenty large to keep Baoill at bay should he decide to peek his nose any further south."

"Then why do we need the Priest?" Azzeki asked, frowning. "The faith is already attempting to undermine what you've done here. You know I'm not happy to say it, but if the lizard leaves now, it would be chaos. The dungeons aren't near full enough to offer the fighters we need, the gladiators are out of favor, and with the freeze on us there isn't a soul in the city who would be willing to go out and hunt game for entertainment. The Monster needs to stay. Give me leave to handle Yu'ri. Cut the head off the snake, as you Northerners say."

"The problem," Quin said in exasperation, "is that Yu'ri is not the head."

Azzeki's eyes narrowed. "Your Lifetaker?" he asked.

Quin nodded. "Before I met you or Arro, I didn't think it would have been possible to show me a man more dangerous than Talo Brahnt. I saw him fight a dozen times before I was ten. I had to sneak into the Arena, because my father had forbidden me from witnessing the bouts, but I wouldn't have missed them for the world."

"That was almost forty years ago. I doubt he would even see me coming."

Tern shook his head. "With age does not necessarily come weakness, especially among the Laorin. He might be slower, might not have the strength he once did, but he has other talents that could pose problematic. Not to mention, if Arro is with him, even you won't offer much of a challenge to a pair like that."

"You give too much credit to your enemies, Quin."

"It's *you* who doesn't give them *enough*," Quin said sharply.

Azzeki didn't say anything to that.

"We let the Laorin live," Quin continued. "Whatever happens, Brahnt will have his hands full with the new Kayle anyway. If that resolves, though, Yu'ri might be valuable leverage against the faith, should it come to that."

"So you propose we do nothing," Azzeki said angrily. "Even as they shake the foundations of all you've fought for here."

"Oh, we do something," Quin said quietly. "But not to the Laorin. If Raz i'Syul wishes to change our contract without telling me, then I think it's time I do the same. We offered him kindness, gave him everything he wanted, and yet still he thinks he can leave. No. If compromise and diplomacy don't work, then we resort to other means."

At that, Azzeki smiled. It was a wicked thing, full of cruel pleasure and anticipation.

"Tell me what I need to do," he said.

XXX

"There are times, in my old age, that I look back and realize what a fool I have been. Even in my later years, when I thought myself as wise as I was ever going to be, there were things I could not see. Talo is at the center of many of those moments, instances where I did not see the toll his choices placed upon him. Now, in retrospect, I find myself thinking of those times often when I feel loneliest, wondering if I could have alleviated some of that weight if only I had paused more often and put myself in his place."

—private journal of Carro al'Dor

"He's not coming, Talo."

Talo looked around. Carro was a few paces ahead, his eyes set firmly forward, the stiffness in his posture barely shifting to accommodate the roll of the horse's gait beneath him.

A blind man would have been able to tell that something was irritating the Priest.

"I wasn't thinking of him," Talo lied, looking back over his shoulder again. "I was just considering what a sad waste this has all been."

In truth, of course, his mind had wandered back to Raz i'Syul Arro, but he couldn't tell Carro that. Carro wouldn't understand, after all. He couldn't understand, couldn't fathom what had come over Talo that would incite such a ludicrous act as proposing that the atherian join them on their way home. Carro was worried about the trip already, worried about Talo's leg, worried about the winter storms, worried about the dangers of the Arocklen that waited for them a week or so's good ride northward. Carro had no space left to worry about how, as Talo watched the last glimpses of Azbar's dark walls finally fade between the snowy trees, he was feeling old memories return with a bitterness they'd never had before.

The last time I walked away, I said you'd be fine, he thought, still watching the last place the city had vanished between the snowy pines. *I told Syrah you'd be fine. I didn't even give it a second thought.*

Talo felt a hand touch his knee, and he turned to see that Carro had slowed his mount to drop even with him. Their steel staffs, lying lengthwise across their laps, knocked and dinged together as the horses matched pace.

"I'm sorry," the man said sadly. "I know it's hard. It wasn't easy on me either, but we had to make a choice. We'll come back, though. When this business with the Kayle is done and over with, we'll return, and this time we'll bring enough help with us to make the voices of reason heard in truth."

Talo nodded, but said nothing. Ordinarily he hated lying to Carro, but for once the deceit didn't bother him. Maybe it was because it wasn't altogether a lie. The Arena still stood, a wretched stain on Talo's conscience. He hated that it continued to tower above the city they were leaving behind, a cancer of marble and mortar growing stronger on the blood and death it was fed daily. He'd set out from Cyurgi' Di all of six weeks prior, and hadn't dreamt he would be returning so soon, much less with so little accomplished. Yes, the continued thriving of the Arena would haunt him all the way back to the High Citadel, and every night until the opportunity came again to do something about it.

But it wouldn't haunt him as much as the conjured image of Raz i'Syul Arro, younger and leaner, standing within the fires and flashing blades that had left him orphaned and alone.

Fires and blades that Talo, in all his wisdom, had left him to without a second thought.

The only silver lining Talo could see in all that was happening was that he was leaving neither the man nor the Arena completely unaddressed. They would keep each other's company, in a sense, the pit giving Raz meaningful purpose, while Raz himself kept the pit in check and in control. Talo understood why the man hadn't come. It had taken him aback at first, yes, but thinking on it, Talo supposed he shouldn't have been all that surprised. If Arro had been the sort to run from a fight, he would never have become the man the citizens of Azbar cheered for and pinned their hopes on. He had *wanted* to come—he'd said as much, after all—but he'd articulated just as clearly that there was a difference between desire and need.

Arro had set things in motion in Azbar, and now he had to see them through to the end. He had lifted the terror of living within the shadow of the Arena from the citizens' shoulders, and now had to bear that weight.

Talo thought abruptly of the broken statue of the Lifetaker, nothing but a marble pedestal and cast-iron feet sawed off at the ankles. He remembered his conflicting emotions at the sight of it, wishing to see it in its entirety while simultaneously feeling ashamed it ever stood in the first place.

Will they cast one of him? he thought, feeling the saddle beneath him shift as the horse shook snow from its eyes and mane. *Will Raz i'Syul Arro, the Monster of Karth, the Scourge of the South, stand among the other greats in the Hall of Heroes?*

He thought it likely, one day.

Talo looked up from the road. He couldn't see them through the canopy, all thick branches and wet, clinging snow, but he knew the peaks of the Saragrias were somewhere there in the far, far distance. He hadn't heard from Syrah except for her hastily scribbled letter regarding Gûlraht Baoill and pleading for his and Carro's rapid return. He'd been disappointed that she hadn't written more, but again felt like he shouldn't have been surprised. It wasn't likely the bird he'd sent after meeting Arro had ever reached the High Citadel. If the rumors were true, the storms that had mercifully spared the lower parts of the North had not done the same to the ranges and the Arocklen. Talo's letter was likely scattered to the wind somewhere, or caught, wet and useless, lost among the Woods.

A pity, he thought, smiling sadly just in time for a rare ray of true sunlight to break through the clouds, shining down between the branches upon him and Carro. *You would have liked him, Syrah. And I know he would have liked you, too.*

XXXI

"It is not in the nature of man to hold true to his word. Honesty is a function of society, a construct of civilized culture. In truth, it is often in one's best interests to lie, to deceive. It is often the easiest path, the one with fewest immediate obstacles, the simplest way to get to what one desires. It is the reason the good fall victim to evil, why the pure of heart are preyed upon by those willing to exploit their kindness. But it is also dangerous, for with betrayal… one breeds vengeance."

—*Commonalities of Ancient & Modern Society*, author unknown

The crunch of snow on the stairs outside woke Raz before the pale light of dawn took the opportunity to. It had only been a day since Talo Brahnt had taken his leave northward, but already Raz found himself sleeping restlessly again. For a time, for the weeks he'd know the Laorin were out there, fighting the same fight, he'd felt something like safety. For a time he'd felt as though there was someone to watch his back.

Now, though, there was no one, and it made him sleep so lightly, even the shifting of snow outside was enough to wake him.

His bedroll still lay lengthwise on the floor parallel to the door some four feet away, as did the gladius, drawn and bare across the stone. Some habits would never die, and Raz had spent too many years sleeping in questionable places not to know the value of a blade that didn't need to be drawn from its sheath.

Picking the sword up gently, Raz eased himself to his feet. The furs he slept under slid off his wings and bare back, falling into a rumpled pile on the ground. To his right by the last smoldering glow of the previous night's fire, Arrun and Lueski slept on, close together on their own mats.

Raz took a few good whiffs of the air and smelled nothing strange. Only the woody scent of the hearth, as well as the lingering remnants of beef and oatcakes that had been the evening's dinner. Still, the Koyts had very few visitors in their time since returning to Azbar—most people wanting to keep their heads low and not fraternize more than was prudent with a pair of former fugitives—and Raz had never had a caller this early in the morning.

He listened hard. He thought of assassins, perhaps a whole contingent of the city guard, or even a gang of mercenaries who had grouped up, willing to risk the Chairman's judgment for a split of the ten thousand crowns still on Raz's head. He was so involved in calculating how best to address each possible scenario, in fact, that he jump violently when whoever was outside merely pounded on the door, nearly causing him to take his own arm off with his blade.

"Arro!" the familiar voice of Alyssa Rhen called through the wood. "Open up! Lifegiver's fat arse, I'm freezing out here!"

Cursing himself, Raz stepped forward and pulled the door wide. Sure enough, the Doctore stood alone on the stoop of the house, dressed in so many layers of white and brown furs Raz thought he wouldn't have recognized her had she not spoken up. He opened his mouth to say something smart about the time, but lost his words when he realized that the woman was standing in nothing short of knee-high snow.

"Sun have mercy!" he managed to croak out, not looking away from the door as the Doctore stepped inside. "What the hell is this?"

"The freeze," someone grumbled sleepily.

Arrun was up, peering groggily around the wall by the door to look outside. Behind him, Lueski, too, was moving, sitting up and rubbing her eyes with small fists.

"*This*?" Raz demanded, waving his free hand at the clear path the Doctore had cut up through the white to get to the door. "*This* is your freeze?"

"Yup," Arrun said with a resigned nod. "We're lucky it held out this long. Now shut the door. You're letting the cold in."

Raz realized he was indeed, feeling a wafting chill spill around his ankles like some invisible river of icy water. Shivering, he closed the door, shaking his head at what he'd seen. Once again he had to laugh at the ludicrous concept that he had, at one time, considered waiting out the winter in the woods.

"Wouldn't have made it a day," he mumbled to himself, turning away to sheathe the gladius on his belt, hanging by the door.

"What was that?" Rhen asked him, busy peeling herself out of her furs.

"Nothing," Raz said quickly, eyeing her. "Now why don't you tell us what's so important you had to wake us this early?"

"Tern is throwing a special event," the Doctore said, finally shedding the heavy undercoat she'd had on beneath all her layers. "If you think this is bad, consider how early my servants had to wake *me* up so I could come fetch you."

"A special event?" Raz asked suspiciously. "What is your Chairman up to now? His tournament is filling every seat and then some. From what I hear, you could start charging people standing outside the Arena trying to make out what's happening in the pit."

"I asked him the same thing, but he gave me some speech about 'monotony feeds stagnation.' You and I both know the man has his finger on every pulse in the city that might lead him to greater profit. So long as he's still using you as his primary source of entertainment, I'm fine with it."

"Your concern is noted," Raz said dryly.

Rhen waved the comment away. "You and I both know you're Tern's pride and joy. Even in this storm there were a dozen wagons come through the city's gate this morning, some to fight and some to watch. The only thing you could do to make yourself more endearing in Tern's eyes would be to literally shit gold, which at this point wouldn't surprise me, given your arsenal of apparent talents."

Raz blinked at that, surprised.

"Testy this morning, are we?" he said with a wry smile. "Since when are you so crass?"

"Since your being in my city means getting dragged out of bed before I've even really gotten to sleep," Rhen snapped, unamused. "Now would you get your gear? The earlier you deal with whatever farce Tern has cooked up, the earlier my day ends."

Raz chuckled again. Now that she was no longer hidden between all her coats and furs, the woman did seem distinctly disheveled. Her normally sleek hair was rumpled and untamed, which did not do much to flatter the ugly scar along her face, and her green eyes, usually so clear and alert, looked tired and red. She stiffened at his laugh, clearly in no mood, and Raz held his hands up in a sign of peace.

"All right, all right," he said, unable to hide a smile as he backed up towards the stairs. "I'll get my things. I admit I'm curious to see what new way Tern has found to toe the line."

"I suppose I'll get breakfast going, then," Arrun said with a shrug as his sister came dawdling up behind him. She looked upset, clutching at the cloth doll Kal Yu'ri had brought for her, her favorite—and only, really—toy.

"I thought you didn't have to deal with the bad men today," she said quietly to Raz, eyes on the floor, fingering the rope hair of the doll. "I though you were staying here…"

Raz glanced uncomfortably at Alyssa, who shrugged and gave him a "*What in every god's name are you looking at me for?*" look.

"I'm sorry, Lueski," he said gently, easing himself down on one knee. "Sometimes, though, I'm going to have to go like this. There are going to be days where there are more bad men than others, and they need my help to deal with them. Do you understand?"

When Lueski didn't say anything, he reached out to grip her chin carefully, pushing it up so that she was looking at him.

"It's alright," he told her with a smile. "It just means I'll have stories when I get home tonight. You like stories during dinner, right?"

At that, Lueski gave a halfhearted smile, then nodded.

"Good," Raz said, letting go of her and getting to his feet. "Now behave for Arrun while I'm gone. Maybe you two can go play in the snow?"

He paused and looked around at her brother.

"Is that safe?" he asked in a hissed whisper. Arrun rolled his eyes.

Raz took that as a yes.

"Arro," Alyssa said crossly.

Raz ignored her, looking back down at Lueski.

"Can I get a smile?"

This time Lueski's smile was more genuine.

"Good girl." Raz patted her on the head fondly, then headed upstairs.

Ten minutes later found him heading back down, weighed down with full gear, Ahna thrown over his shoulder as usual. Rhen was pacing impatiently by the door, already back in her heavy layers, and huffed aloud when he pulled his mantle from its peg in the wall and threw it around his shoulders.

"I can go without it if you want me to freeze to death," he told her with narrowed eyes, finally getting a little irritated. "Speaking of, how do you propose we get to the Arena? I hope you're not expecting me to walk through all that."

"And let you lose your legs?" the Doctore asked with a snort, striding for the door and pulling it open. "Tern would have me throttled. It's bad enough you fight without boots as is."

Then she whistled out into the morning, the shrill sound dampened to Raz's ears by the buffering snow.

At once the clopping of horse hooves picked up, iron shoe on stone, and a moment later a large black carriage rolled into view. It was pulled by a single burly stud, coat thick with gray winter hairs, impatiently hoofing the ground as a man seated on top of the carriage pulled the animal to a stop before the Koyts' home.

"Street sweepers are up all night clearing the roads during the storms," Rhen explained, pulling her hood over her head and the furs tighter around her neck. "Not an easy job, but they're well loved for it."

"I can see why," Raz said with a nod. Then he waved a hand through the doorway and gave a mock bow. "After you."

The Doctore raised a brow at the sarcasm, but stepped past him, careful not to slip as she took the stairs. After she did, Raz looked back. Arrun was busy getting his and his sister's breakfast ready, but Lueski was standing there in the draft, blue eyes wide as she watched him go.

"I'll be back with the best stories you've ever heard," he promised her with a wink.

Then he shut the door and followed the Doctore carefully down the steps, through the high snow, and into the carriage.

"Lueski, apples in your porridge?"

Lueski didn't answer. She didn't even look up from her place seated by the door.

She didn't feel much like talking.

"Lueski?"

Again she didn't say anything. Instead she kept toying with Marta, fingering the doll's hair unenthusiastically, more just to have something to do than for any real reason. She'd named the doll after her and Arrun's mother. When she'd done so, Arrun had laughed and said it was a good idea, and that one day he'd name a sword after their father.

That had made Lueski smile.

Raz gets to keep his sister, she'd thought. *And we get to keep Mama and Papa.*

Right now, though, she felt she'd rather have Raz back than the doll or some stupid sword.

Arrun's footsteps approached. When he reached her, she felt her brother pause, then crouch down at her side.

"Lueski? What's wrong?"

Lueski didn't look around at him. After a moment, though, she spoke up.

"I don't like it when he goes."

Arrun sighed. Lueski felt him shift, and a hand touched her head, stroking her black hair soothingly.

"I know, I know, but we've been through this. Raz has to leave so that we can stay. He'll come back, though. You know that. At the end of the day he always comes back."

"But what happens if he doesn't?"

Lueski felt Arrun tense beside her at her question, and finally she looked around. Her blue eyes met the identical set in her brother's face, and she was ashamed of the tears that hung upon them, bitterly fought.

"What happens on the day he doesn't come back?" she asked shakily, squeezing her doll to her chest. "What happens when the bad men win, and Raz doesn't come home? What happens if he… if he…?"

But she couldn't bring herself to say it, and the tears ran in truth. She looked away from Arrun then, back down at the ground, and held Marta even tighter as he sighed. She knew what he was thinking. *Not again*, or maybe, *When will this end?* She knew that she asked these questions often, with more and more frequency as the weeks went by, but she couldn't help it. She tried to be brave whenever Raz left. She'd even managed it at first, thinking the man untouchable, a titan among lowly mortals. As time had passed, though, she'd grown more and more afraid. As Raz came home with nicks and cuts and bruises, she'd grown to realize just how mortal he was, too. His injuries were always small, and healed in a matter of days if not overnight, but the blood was real. The blood was his.

And it had ripped the brave face from her and made Lueski realize that there might be a day when Raz *wouldn't* come home.

"Come here," Arrun said gently. She felt his arms slip behind her back and beneath her legs, and he lifted her up carefully, shifting himself to sit cross-legged against the wall. He held her there, cradling her in his lap, letting her rest her head against his chest as she cried.

"You have to believe in him, sis," he murmured to her as he rocked her gently. "You have to trust him. He'll come back. He'll come back every day, because he knows he has to. Do you think he'd let you down? Let either of us down?"

Lueski hesitated, then gave her head a little shake.

"Good," Arrun said, and Lueski thought she heard a smile in his voice. "Then that means you know he'll be alright. Every day I want you to think of that. I want you to think about how Raz has to be all right, because he has you. He has to be alright, because he can't let you down."

At that, Lueski smiled a little. Still holding tight to Marta, she looked up at her brother.

"He's gonna wallop the bad men, and he's gonna come home," she said, feeling more confident in the words.

Arrun nodded.

"He has to. He would never let us down."

Then he looked up, because someone was knocking at the door.

XXXII

"Goading Raz is much like kicking a sleeping sandcat: never a good idea, unless you're looking for a quick way out of this world."

—Allihmad Jerr, master smith

"So are you going to tell me what this is all about?"

Alyssa Rhen looked around at Raz. He was watching her intently, trying to gauge what she was about. He could feel the spines of his ears brushing the carriage ceiling as they rode and the gentle sway of the seats beneath him with the natural shift of the horse that pulled them. It wasn't an unpleasant feeling. Just as he had been when he'd stolen north out of Miropa in a smuggler's cart, Raz was reminded of years long behind him, part of a life he sometimes wondered if he'd ever really lived.

"If I knew, I would have told you at the house," the Doctore said. "Tern hasn't said any more to me than what you've heard."

Raz frowned, then looked away from the woman, out the carriage door window. The narrow glass panels were frosted over and half-covered in clinging snow, but what he could make out of the city passing by was almost enough to distract him from his curiosity at these unexpected summonings. While the roads appeared to have indeed been swept clean at regular intervals throughout the night, the rest of Azbar seemed vastly neglected such care. *Everything* was white. The buildings and roofs and chimneys, the alleys and side streets, the trees and vinework clinging to stone walls. What few people he was able to make out briefly were so swaddled in leathers and furs he could hardly distinguish man from woman, boy from girl. Barely anything moved out there in the winter world, the only shift in Raz's viewing being the constant whirl of the blizzard around them as it continued to storm down, cold and unrelenting.

So this is the freeze.

Raz pondered how anyone could survive in a place like this. The wonders of the woods, the magnificence of the greenery and life that had so entranced him on first arrival, were now all but swallowed up in the storm's onslaught. Suddenly Raz dreaded reaching the Arena.

Let's hope they clear the pit, at least....

"I'm worried."

Rhen's words were abrupt and tense, and as Raz turned back to her he saw that any residual resentment at being dragged out of bed into the snow was gone. The stern, calculating face of Alyssa Rhen was back in truth now, and she looked pensive.

"What about?" he asked her as they bumped over some uneven stone in the road.

"Exactly what we're discussing: the fact that I wasn't told," Rhen said slowly, a faraway look in her eyes as she thought. "Tern pulled me in so many times to advise while he and Azzeki were designing his 'Chairman's Tourney' that I might as well have had my own room in the town hall. He wanted to know about numbers, times, strategies, what training our gladiators had, what I thought you were capable of and what I thought might be your weaknesses. I think I spoke more with the man in those weeks than I have his entire life put together, despite how close his father and I were."

She frowned too, now, and looked out her own window.

"This time, though," she continued, "I hear nothing. I'm not told anything, and I can tell you whatever is going on wasn't part of any plan I've heard of…"

"You said you thought everything would be fine," Raz said gruffly. "You told me you thought I didn't have anything to worry about."

"And I don't *think* you do," Rhen insisted. "Still, though… You don't think it's odd?"

"Honestly? Not really, when you consider it. I would have been more surprised if Tern *didn't* throw us for a loop every now and again. He likes the gold I make him well enough, but I don't think he was ever happy with the fact that I made the terms of our arrangement. This is probably just his way of letting me know the ground I'm standing on isn't as steady as I might think."

"Maybe…" the Doctore said, sounding unconvinced. She let the subject drop, though, and the rest of the ride was spent in silence.

Ten minutes later the carriage turned the corner onto the wide road encircling the Arena, and Raz heard the driver shout "Whoa!" and the beat of the horse's hooves start to slow. The doors to the underworks came into view, and the carriage finally rolled to a halt.

As soon as he knew they were truly stopped, Raz pushed the door open and ducked out into the storm, careful to watch his step. The road and walkways all around the Arena had been cleared, it seemed, but more than an inch of snow had already built back up since the last sweeping. Turning, Raz held out a hand, ready to help the Doctore ease herself down the narrow carriage step rails.

The woman, though, took one look at the steely claws and scoffed. Then, holding the doorjamb with one hand, she dropped to the road lightly, unperturbed by the snow.

"Leave it to a Southerner to be afraid of a little winter storm," she laughed, striding past Raz as he let his hand fall.

Watching her make for the doors with narrowed eyes, Raz only paused to pull Ahna from where she'd been lying at his feet on the carriage floor before following.

Glancing back to make sure he was behind her, Rhen grabbed the iron rings that served as handles and pulled the doors open. At once warmth spilled out from within the underworks, washing over them both and causing Raz to shiver involuntarily at the agreeable settling of the heat on his skin. Other things came, too, though. The familiar scents of the Arena grabbed at Raz's snout at once, not all of them pleasant. He could taste old blood and oil on the air, mixing with that bitter bite of death that only clung to a place that had seen too many corpses come and go.

What hit Raz hardest, though, was the noise.

On opening day, the underworks had been bustling with dozens of men and women. Some were the Arena gladiators, prepping themselves for their exhibition matches to keep the crowds entertained during intermissions. Most, though, had been the bounty hunters, those come far and wide, each and every one preparing their weapons and gear, or else eyeing Raz behind his wall of guards as they waited for their shot at his head. Since that day, Raz had done his best to put a dent in their numbers, killing many and chasing off more as they realized they didn't have a prayer at taking him on.

The group that awaited them now, though, made Raz realize, with infinite finality, what little he'd managed to do.

There were *hundreds* of fighters packed in the underworks. Despite the early hour of the morning, it seemed that Tern had roused every remaining combatant left within the city walls. None of them was bleary-eyed, though. None of them seemed confused at what was going on. Instead they seemed agitated, the flood of voices buzzing with excitement and energy. As Raz and the Doctore stepped through the door, many turned to see who the latest arrivals were, and the barrage of voices reached new heights, shouting and hollering.

"What the…?" the Doctore hissed, stopped dead and looking around at the great group.

The response pretty much summed up Raz's feelings succinctly.

"Doctore."

Raz and Rhen both looked around. On either side of the doors, a dozen of the city guard stood at the ready. One was approaching them quickly.

"Officer Erute," the Doctore said in greeting as Raz, too, saw the gold stripe on the man's shoulder. "What's the meaning of all this? What's going on?"

"I'm only allowed to say so much, ma'am, and right now I'm to escort you to your quarters." The man seemed agitated, and he glanced nervously at the line of bounty hunters that stood not ten paces from them. Holding an arm out, he indicated the way, straight through the group. "If you please."

Rhen hesitated, looking at the guardsmen, then at the fighters, before finally turning to Raz. She didn't say anything, but her concerns—and question—were obvious.

Raz shrugged. "Doesn't seem like we have much of a choice," he said casually. He rested one hand on the head of the war ax at his waist, though, and twisted Ahna's handle pointedly.

Ready for a fight, he hoped to say.

Rhen seemed to get the message

"Lead the way," she told Erute.

The officer nodded, then signaled his men to form up. At once the guard positioned themselves in parallel lines on either side of Raz and the Doctore and, at a second signal from their commander, marched forward. Erute himself, though, stayed close to the pair of them.

"I've been told to instruct you that you are to stay in your quarters until it's time for the Monster to fight," he said quietly, his eyes scanning the clusters of shouting combatants on either side of them. "You're not to leave without express permission of the Chairman."

"What?" Rhen demanded, infuriated. "*Why*?"

"I don't know. I just know that Chairman Tern is holding some sort of special event to keep interest in the Arena high as the freeze begins."

"What kind of special event?" Raz asked. He, too, was watching the men and women on either side of them, eyeing swords and spears and all manner of other weaponry held slack in open promise at the sides of their wielders as they stared him down.

Erute jumped at Raz's voice.

"Don't know," he said. "Didn't ask."

"You have a guess, though," Raz prodded. "For example: maybe you can at least tell me why every one of my hopeful killers is here, now, and why they suddenly all look much more optimistic in their chances of claiming their winnings today."

The officer hesitated, coming to a halt as they reached the door to the Doctore's quarters. In rehearsed motions the men of the guard shifted to create a wall two deep between the bounty hunters and their charges.

"Rumor is that Tern is changing the rules just for the day," Erute told Raz and the Doctore quietly, dropping his voice as he reached out to pull open the door. "They"—he threw a thumb over his shoulder—"are all here because they think they're going to be given an even playing field to fight on."

Raz and the Doctore looked at each other.

"Well, there goes your theory on Tern's valuing me," Raz joked with as much of a chuckle as he could muster.

All Rhen responded with was a scowl, which Raz felt much like returning. The truth was that, for the first time in a long, long time, Raz felt a prick of fear touch along the back of his neck. Something was wrong. *Something* was off. Quin Tern was a bastard, but he was a clever bastard with a keen mind and wicked sense of self-fulfillment. Was there perhaps an angle to the games that Raz hadn't considered? Was there an approach that would make his death worth it in the Chairman's eyes? The tournaments had been carefully designed to always be in Raz's favor, if only slightly. The advantages he was granted, the weapons he might be allowed—depending on how the tourney finalists chose to face him—were calculated to give the crowd as good a show as possible while never putting their "Monster" in any situation he couldn't handle. Raz was the attraction, after all. Even the Doctore said so. Raz was the singular reason the Arena didn't have enough seats to accommodate all who wished to see the games.

So what had happened that suddenly made Tern feel gambling Raz's life was worth the risk?

"Arro."

Raz blinked and looked down at Rhen. She had stepped into her quarters, and was watching him to see if he followed. After a moment he did so, ducking under the low overhang on the door. Erute watched him through.

"If you require the latrine, or need anything at all, just knock. Otherwise, you will be fetched when it's time."

Time for WHAT? Raz wanted to shout, but the man had already shut the door with a bang.

"Sun and Moon and all Her Stars," he grumbled in annoyance as he turned to face the room. It was exactly as it was every other time he'd visited. Someone had already lit a hearty fire in the hearth in the back wall, and the flames cast shadows across the dirt walls and ceiling from the desk, chairs, and accoutrements scattered about the quarters.

"What?" the Doctore asked, eyebrows pinching together.

"Nothing," Raz said automatically. "Southern curses. Seemed appropriate."

"I'll say," the woman mumbled, obviously no more pleased with the situation than Raz was. "What the *hell* is he thinking?"

Raz, though, didn't respond. A realization had dawned on him abruptly. The names of his deities had brought up thoughts of other gods, and the leap hadn't been hard to make from there.

"The Laorin," he hissed, more to himself than anything. "Son of a—No. Not possible. There's no way he knows…"

"The Laorin?" Rhen asked, perplexed. "What do a bunch of old religious zealots have to do with Tern?"

Raz eyed her then, judging her in truth. He respected the woman. He even thought he liked her somewhat, if he allowed himself to consider it honestly.

I liked Mychal, too, though…

After a moment the Doctore raised an eyebrow. "Are you blind to our predicament, or just stupid? I've told you before, and I'll say it again: you die, and everything you've done dies with you. I have no interest in allowing the Arena to revert to the old way of supplying entertainment, so you might as well stop being hardheaded and just tell me what's going on."

When Raz still didn't say anything, she sighed.

"Look," she said, seating herself in the hard chair behind her desk, "I'm in here *with you.* I'm not out there"—she waved a hand at the room door—"screaming for your head or cheering you on as you take someone else's. Whatever you have to say doesn't have to leave this room."

"That, or the minute we're free you'll run to Tern," Raz growled.

The Doctore's face turned sour.

"You've been in Azbar for nearly two months now," she spat, pointing a finger at him. "Nearly two months. In all that time, in all those days, if you haven't figured out that's not something I would *ever* do, then there's nothing I can say that would convince you otherwise."

For a brief time they glared at each other in silence. Then Raz decided she was right.

"A few weeks back I was approached by two Priests," he told her, moving forward to seat himself in the chair across from her, leaning Ahna against the wall beside him. "One was master of the local chapter, the other of some temple up north. *Very* long story made *very* short, they asked for my help in closing down the Arena again."

The Doctore hissed at that, but said nothing more, obviously expecting him to continue. Raz obliged.

"I wasn't keen on the idea at first," he said, leaning back in the chair and crossing his arms. "At all. I've had my… uh… run-ins with their kind before, and let's just say it left me with a bad taste. But they convinced me to hear them out. In the end, their arguments were compelling."

"So you agreed?" Rhen asked. "You said you would help them?"

"Of a sorts," Raz said with a shrug, looking down at the desk as he spoke. "One of them, Yu'ri, wasn't too happy with my way of doing things, but Brahnt did a job of—"

Raz stopped, though, as the woman gave a sharp intake of breath, and looked up. He hadn't thought it possible for Alyssa Rhen to feel much more than sternness, anger, and mild amusement, so the myriad of emotions darting across her face took him completely aback. Shock, sadness, pain, even grief. All these and more registered one after the other, beating out the composure she so usually held and was clearly struggling to recover. One hand came up to cover her mouth, the most indicatively feminine gesture he'd ever witnessed from her.

"What?" he asked, suddenly concerned. "What's wrong?"

Rhen opened her mouth to speak, but nothing came out. She closed it, then tried again, with similar results. The third time, though, she managed to get out a few sparse words.

"Brahnt," she breathed. "T-Talo Brahnt?"

Raz blinked, surprised. "You know him?"

Rhen seemed partially frozen, staring at him. Then she lowered her hand slowly, took a breath, and nodded.

"This… this temple," she said in broken words. "You're talking about… about the High Citadel, aren't you?"

Raz thought about it. "… I think so," he said after a moment. "They might have said something like that. And Seeurgee, or Seeyurgee—"

"Cyurgi' Di," she finished for him. "That's it."

They sat in silence for a time, Raz waiting for an explanation, while Rhen seemed so caught up in old memories that words were failing her again.

"Rhen," Raz said finally, tiring of the wait. "What is it? What's got you so scared all of a sudden?"

Rhen jumped, then looked at him, bewildered, as though she'd only just noticed him.

When she spoke, though, it was with her normal, authoritative voice.

"If Tern found out you've been speaking with Talo Brahnt, that's not good."

"So I've heard," Raz grumbled crossly. "Brahnt wouldn't shut up about it someti—"

"No, you don't understand," the Doctore hissed. "Tern *hates* Talo. He hates the Laorin as a whole, but Talo holds a special place for him. He was responsible—"

"For shutting down the Arenas in the first place—yeah, I know," Raz said, thinking that he might as well get his interruptions in, too, where he could.

"It's more than that," Rhen insisted, and Raz was surprised to hear something like desperation in her voice. "Talo isn't some Priest who made it his life's work to preach the ending of the pit fights. Arro… Talo *was* a gladiator. Before you, he was the best. Nothing like him had ever been seen. There was a time when he was the one chasing the Laorin out of the Arena—sometimes out of town—whenever they came around trying to make people see reason about the fights. The crowd gave him a name for it, one that spoke to his brutality in the pit and his hatred of the faith. They called him—"

"Lifetaker."

It hit Raz, then. All the pieces fell into place. He remembered his first night in Azbar, climbing up the Arena's stairs into the Hall of Heroes. He'd never gone back, as he'd planned to, but he remembered vividly most of the statues he'd paused to peruse. The Queen of Arrows. The Ax Maiden. Retribution.

Lifetaker.

Raz remembered the oddity, the hollow iron-cast feet on a pile of skulls. He remembered the empty space where a plaque should have hung, denoting name and title, and the worn letters carved over time in the surface of the marble pedestal. He'd run a claw through them, intrigued by the mystery of the thing, curious as to the history.

And he hadn't given it so much as a thought since.

"He's a traitor," Raz said in realization. "To Tern, he's a traitor."

Rhen nodded furiously in agreement. "Talo was the man's favorite when he was a boy. He was the reason Tern loved the games so much."

"So when he left, Tern felt betrayed…" Raz finished for her. "No wonder Brahnt was so insistent on secrecy."

"Is it possible someone gave you away? Maybe one of the temple residents, in the hopes of gaining favor with the city council?"

"It's always possible," Raz mumbled thoughtfully. "Doubtful, though. I don't think anyone other than Brahnt, al'Dor, and Yu'ri knew we were in contact."

"Who's al'Dor?" Rhen asked with narrowed eyes.

Raz shook his head. "Another Priest come from the Citadel, but I wouldn't bother being too suspicious of him. I only met him two or three times, but I got the feeling he and Brahnt were more than riding companions, if you catch my drift."

Rhen looked surprised at that.

"Well that would explain a lot. When he was fighting, Talo had women of all kinds throwing themselves at him on a weekly basis. I always thought he turned them down because had some secret wife tucked away somewhere, hidden where no one could use her against him in the pit."

"Oh, is that how you know him, then?" Raz couldn't help himself smiling despite the predicament. "Were you one of his scorned women? Did he let you down easy?"

"I know Talo Brahnt because the Lifetaker is the one who gave me this scar."

Raz felt as though the whole room had gone silent. For a moment even the crackle of the flames and the rumbling of the men and women on the other side of the door were quieted. He took in Alyssa Rhen's face pointedly, marking the details of the ugly lines that marred her otherwise attractive features, pulling down the edge of her right eye and twisting up the corner of her mouth.

"That was the fight that ended it for Talo," the Doctore continued, not waiting for Raz to pose a question. "For both of us, actually. We'd never been close, always in our own circles, but the crowd had demanded the match, and so we gave it to them. I'm told Talo was reluctant to agree, but I leapt on the chance, thinking it the perfect opportunity to prove myself once and for all. To my credit, I gave it everything I had, and I wasn't the only one left bleeding. Still, I knew the instant we started our engagements that I was going to lose. Talo was just too strong, too fast. The only reason I lasted as long as I did was because he was hesitant. I thought it was because he saw me as nothing more than a woman, and it infuriated me, making me fight even harder. Looking back, though, I see his hesitation was more due to the Lifetaker's unraveling than anything else. Talo must have had his doubts for some time, to leave like he did. I was just the push that sent him over the edge."

There was another moment of silence. Raz was processing all of this in a rush, coming to terms with every puzzle piece that was falling into place.

"He has more history with this place than he ever let on..." he said quietly. "He should have told me..."

"If he didn't, it's because he was protecting you," Rhen said. "The Lifetaker died that day, and the man Talo Brahnt was always meant to be was finally allowed his birth. The next time I saw him was years later, and the Priest's robes fit him well. Over the course of a decade he spearheaded the shutting down of Azbar's Arena, and every other Arena in the North shortly after. In the same way people used to be drawn to his presence in the pit, so were they drawn to him as he preached. No one else could have done what he did."

"He should have just burned the place to the ground and been done with it," Raz growled.

"Azbar would have only rebuilt."

Raz nodded in resigned agreement. "Talo Brahnt," he said slowly, speaking to no one in particular. "What kind of trouble have you dragged me into?"

XXXIII

"All are capable of evil. It often seems, in fact, that it is in the very nature of man to be evil. Greed, envy, lust… We blame all wars, inevitably, on some outside causation, some external factor. Religion, resources, revenge. The truth, however, is more base: war comes from within. War comes from man himself. Man, and his infinite capability to do evil."

—Xaviun Fuerd, High Priest of Cyurgi' Di, c. 550 v.S.

"I think we've found ourselves a new favorite," Azzeki had to shout over the cheering crowd.

Quin nodded in agreement, but didn't say anything. He was too enthralled in the mayhem that was ensuing below them, too enraptured in his own creation.

The melees weren't his idea, in truth, but the suggestion was an old one, and he couldn't remember who had come up with it initially, weeks ago when the Monster had first shown up on their doorstep. It had been toyed with, then discarded, because it seemed a total waste of resources. In a duel or skirmish, the Arena only ever lost a few fighters at a time. In an all-out melee, though, the toll was much greater. While not all the defeated ended up dead, some ended up close, and the remainder were often too maimed to be of any use to the pit. Quin had decided, placing profit above desire, that such battles weren't worth the cost.

Today, though, he'd resurrected the thought, and was seriously reconsidering his prior decision.

Quin intended this day to be a one to shame all days within the Arena's walls. He didn't just want the men and women of the crowd to remember their experience, this time. He wanted them to *feel* it, wanted them to carry word of it home, beyond the borders of Azbar's woods, and all throughout the North.

Today was the day Quin Tern, Chairman of the council of the great city of Azbar, brought the terror of the Monster to heel.

And to start: the melees.

On opening day of the tourney, the Arena lists held over five hundred names. Raz i'Syul had frightened off a huge portion of that number with the actions of his first fight—as he had intended, Quin had no doubt. The lizard had probably expected the names would continue to dwindle until no one was left to face him, but Quin had seen to it that that plot failed miserably. By promising a building pot as time continued and the Monster remained undefeated, he had created an irresistible pull to the Arena. Today, with the coming of the freeze's first true storm, was the first day less than a score of new volunteers had slunk through the city gates to add their names to the lists.

It made for a large pot to draw from, and suddenly the council's fears of having no one left to fight had seemed much less significant.

The melees consisted of eight names each, drawn at random. The Doctore had not been asked to consult, nor had any special consideration been given to who faced who, and the results were spectacular. Of the four battles they'd already seen that morning, only one had been at all balanced, and it had been by far the most uneventful of the lot. The others, like that which they were witnessing now, were tilted so unfairly in one direction or the other that each brawl was almost as fun as watching Raz i'Syul fight.

"Zeko won't last much longer if he keeps this up," Azzeki said disapprovingly, still watching the pit.

"He'll last long enough to end it," Quin disagreed.

Ajana Zeko, the Percian they spoke of, was a massive specimen, nearly as broad as the mountain men who'd descended out of their cliffs to throw their names in for the pot, and half a head taller. He wore little more than furs around his waist and over his shoulders, along with a steel round helm crowned with a long, thin spike over a chain-mail neck guard. In his thick arms he wielded a massive two-handed warhammer, which he was flailing about to devastating effect. Two of the other seven were already still at his feet, one with her head caved in and the other with his hands resting where he'd clawed at crushed ribs that must have ripped through lung and heart alike. The other five were in chaos, half-concerned with steering clear of the dark-skinned behemoth while also attempting to smartly engage each other during the tumult.

It was utter chaos, and Quin couldn't take his eyes off it.

Nor, it seemed, could the crowd. Their combined voices ebbed and spiked as the battle ensued, reaching heights they usually only achieved on a four-day when the Monster himself was in the pit. As Zeko barreled around the ring, swinging his hammer with the same efficiency he might have had a battering ram, the stadium fawned over him, cheering him on in a bloodthirsty chorus. When one of his blows took a helmeted head so completely clean off its shoulders and sent it inadvertently flying into the crowd, the only piercing wails to be heard were the jealous cries of those *not* flecked in the dead man's blood.

Quin smiled. He had wanted to give the spectators an experience, today. He'd wanted to give them something almost tangible in its appeal, something sublime in its violence.

And he knew he was well on his way to succeeding.

"My Lord."

It took a moment for Quin to register the greeting, and another to realize that the voice didn't belong to Azzeki. Finally pulling his gaze away from the maelstrom of muscle and heavy steel that was Zeko below him, Quin looked around to find Kerret Terovel—one of Azzeki's most trusted soldiers, and the eldest son of a councilman—hovering behind his right shoulder. The man was out of uniform today, clothed in plain, uncolored layers that would have made it impossible to distinguish him in a crowd.

Which was the point, because the package he held in his hands was the most important part of Quin's plans for the day.

Quin felt his face fall at the sight of it, though.

"Already?" he asked, disappointed. "I'd hoped it would have taken the morning, at least."

Kerret shook his head, holding the package out for Azzeki as the Captain-Commander stepped forward to take it.

"Barely lasted two hours, My Lord," he said with a shrug. "Wasn't much to him in the end."

"I suppose so," Quin muttered in annoyance, following the parcel as Azzeki brought it forward. It was a box, he knew, but the pine lining of the thing itself was all hidden by a heavy burgundy cloth that had been wrapped around it for safekeeping. As Azzeki set it down on the wide arm of his chair, Quin itched to reach out and peel away the layers to see the wood itself, maybe even crack it open and peek at what lay inside.

He refrained, though, knowing the moment would be worth the wait.

There was upheaval of noise from the crowd, and Quin looked around in time to see Ajana Zeko pin his last competitor, a narrow spearwoman with the tanned skin of the Imperium, to the slanted wall of the pit with both hands. His hammer had been discarded—though whether this was out of necessity or in desire to provide the greatest show possible, Quin didn't know—but Zeko had hardly need of it. At first Quin thought the Percian would snap the woman's neck and be done with it, but to his great delight the man did no such thing. Instead he merely held her there, squeezing slowly, choking the life out of her one second at a time. The stands were suddenly quiet, the spectators falling silent as they watched, so that the rasping wheezes of the dying woman were just discernible, echoing off the walls of the stadium. For almost a full minute she kicked, her fingers scrabbling at Zeko's wrists, trying in vain to pull the man's hands free of her throat. It wasn't long before her face went pale, then blue, then purple, and shortly after her fighting began to lessen. First her motions became sluggish and lazy, her kicks grew slow and her grasps at the Percian's arms broad and pointless. Then her larger motions stopped altogether, and only the jump of her legs and the twitch of slack arms remained.

Finally, she stilled altogether, and Zeko let the woman's corpse slide to the snowy pit floor with a dull thump.

Quin should have known to expect the explosion of cheering by now. He had borne witness to a dozen of the Monster's fights, after all. Still, the roar took him by surprise, pitching with the keening shriek of excitement usually reserved only for the atherian.

A new crowd favorite indeed, Quin thought with a smile, watching Ajana Zeko turn slowly in place, both fists held in the air in triumph, basking in the glory of the crowd's approval. Then Quin's eyes shifted to the box at his arm, hidden beneath the red cloth that hung over it like the veil of a grieving woman, and he smiled.

He smiled , because he had so, *so* much more to share before the day was done.

XXXIV

"Of all the evils I have witnessed in my life, there are a few that cling to my dreams like angry spirits, insisting on haunting my very thoughts. That day, as the crowd rose above me and the chill of snow and wind bit into my flesh and bone, is perhaps the greatest of those nightmares."

—the Monster of Karth

Raz and the Doctore had been sitting in silence for some time when the clunk of the handle and the grind of hinges told them someone was opening the door. They'd been in Rhen's offices for hours by then, and had long since exhausted all theories they had about what might be going on out in the world and the Arena above. The only visitors they'd been allowed were an attendant who'd brought them each meals at midday, and another later to replenish the wood supply so they could keep the fire fed and the chambers warm.

Raz had been rapidly approaching his last nerve by the time the door opened this third time. He had told himself he would give the Chairman his mystery, grant him some patience. It wasn't as though he had any other choice with two dozen guards outside the room and another several hundred swords looking for any excuse to claim his head just beyond them. Still, Raz had to do *something*, and pretending he was giving Quin Tern some leeway was a heck of a lot easier than admitting there was virtually nothing they could do.

"Master Arro, I've been instructed to tell you to prepare yourself."

Raz looked around. Officer Erute was in the arch of the door, peering in at them. Raz had a retort on the tip of his tongue prepared, but decided to stow it.

There is a time for bravado, he told himself instead, standing up to face the man. *This is not it.*

"Can I at least prep outside?" he asked, reaching up to tap knuckles against the ceiling's wooden crossbeams for emphasis. "I could use the space."

The officer paused, then nodded. Raz heard Rhen stand up behind him as he pulled Ahna from her place on the wall, joining him as he made for the door.

"Have you heard anything more?" she asked Erute quietly as they passed. "Anything else you can tell us?"

The officer said nothing. Instead he instructed his men to stay put, then indicated a space between them and led the way.

The underworks were almost empty compared to what they had

looked like that morning. A few stragglers—maybe a dozen in all—were still huddled about the walls, most groaning and nursing wounds, trying to get the strength together to get back on their feet. One or two of them, Raz realized as they passed still forms huddled in corners, would never stand again.

They weren't taken to the physicians? he wondered in amazement. *Why? Were they not deemed worth saving? Or maybe there have just been too many injured for the surgeons to keep pace with?*

"What's the Chairman been up to?" he asked once they were out of earshot of the other guards. "Where did everyone go?"

"Most were sent away this morning shortly after your arrival," Erute said, coming to a halt in the wide space at the bottom of the gangway. "Heralds arrived to draw names, and those not chosen were told to go home."

"Draw?" the Doctore asked him, obviously surprised. "How many? For what?"

The man shook his head. "I'm not at liberty to tell you," he said sternly before waving at the dirt floor around them. "I'll leave you to your preparations. My men and I are at your disposal should you need anything more."

With a final nod, he turned on his heel and walked away.

At once Raz began to loosen up, rolling his shoulders and flexing his arms as he stretched his wings out to their full extent. He hadn't put them to much use of late, given how much more vulnerable their thin membranes were to the frigid cold than the rest of him, but it never hurt to be prepared.

The Doctore, in the meantime, stared at him.

"What are you doing?" she demanded of him as he squatted and bounced, stretching out his hips and knees.

Raz looked at her blankly. "Getting ready?" he stated, unsure of what other answer she might expect. "I don't know what's waiting for me up there. Could be a hundred armed men. Maybe they'll just set the stands loose on me and give the purse to whoever is left with the biggest chunk of Monster at the end."

"You're going to fight?" the woman hissed, stepping in front of him. Even kneeling so that he sat nearly on his heels, they were practically eye to eye. "Without knowing what you're up against? Without a plan?"

"Wouldn't be the first time," he told her with a shrug, standing up. "The real world doesn't run on a schedule, Rhen. Your battles aren't picked from a list. If I survived the Mahsadën and all their horrors, I can survive whatever Tern is going to throw at me."

"But this wasn't part of the deal, Arro! This wasn't part of the contract you—!"

"No, it wasn't," Raz cut the woman off, reaching back to loosen his gladius in its scabbard. "And if Tern feels he'd like to renegotiate our terms without informing me first, I'll let him know in spectacular fashion how poor a decision that is. For the time being, though, you and I are stuck. So—if you don't mind—you should get out of the way. It would be poor form for the Arena Doctore to get herself killed during my warm-up exercises."

Rhen frowned, but stepped back, and the next ten minutes were spent with Raz moving the dviassegai about him in smooth, gentle circles, prepping his body for whatever was to come. His concentration was hard to come by, his focus broken by the sound of battle rolling down the ramp from the pit above them. Still, he did his best to block it all out, and by the time the sounds quieted he was feeling good, the tension of sitting all day having been worked from his body.

Above them the portcullis started to rise, and abruptly attendants were all about them, come dutifully running from whatever chores they'd been about. Over a dozen in all, a few stole glances at Raz as they passed, but most ignored him, which he didn't mind. He'd been around the Arena too long now for any of the place's workers to be truly mystified by him anymore. In a ragged line they filed up the ramp, ducking into the light of the afternoon outside as a herald's voice began to call out over the crowd.

"Winner of your eighth and final melee!" the voice roared above the noises of the stadium. "All stand and hail the mighty Helena, Shield Bearer of the Seven Cities!"

The cheers pitched in response. There was a *thump*, and the first body came rolling down the gangway.

"Not one among you can deny the spectacle you have observed today, citizens of Azbar! You have borne witness to eight trials, and seen eight titans emerge victorious from them."

Thump, and the second body came.

"Have you had enough? Have you basked in the glory of the Arena to your fill? Or do. You. Want. MORE?"

The roar of approval drowned out the sound of the third and fourth bodies hitting the dirt, but they rolled into view just the same. Beside him. Raz felt Rhen tense, watching the dead pile at their feet.

"We thought not! We have prepared for you the most savage battle any man has ever witnessed within these great walls! We have designed a crucible, a match of such proportions, none has ever seen the like!"

Thump, thump. Two more came tumbling down the hill. The Doctore was positively shaking now as Raz continued to listen.

"You know what is to come, my lords and ladies! You can feel it in your bones, can taste it in the air! You have need of a champion to lead you in this fight, to hold your colors in the battle that is to come. Call on him, citizens of Azbar. LET US HEAR HIS NAME!"

As the seventh body made trails in the dust on the way down the ramp, the chant began. At first it was muddled, offbeat and unsure. Quickly, though, it built, gaining rhythm and tone and volume with every second. Before long it seemed the word would shake loose the stones of the Arena itself.

"MONSTER! MONSTER! MONSTER! MONSTER!"

Raz looked to the looming shape of light that was the open gate to the pit above them. Then he looked down at the pile of corpses at his feet.

A melee. He had heard it, had made out that word. An all-out, no-holds-barred melee. Eight went in, and only one was left standing. It explained the wounded and the dead scattered about the underworks around them, some groaning as they clutched at injuries, others not likely to ever make a sound again.

And he thought he could curb Tern's thirst for violence…

The prick of fear returned.

"Doctore," Raz said quietly, not taking his eyes off the bloody mass of bodies before him. "I have a favor to ask."

Rhen didn't turn towards him.

"A-a favor?" she asked.

He could hear the shake in her voice.

Raz nodded once. "The Koyts. Get them out of the city. If something should happen, get them out and as far away from here as you can. They have the papers. It shouldn't be hard, at least not if you move fast."

"If I… if I move fast, yes…" Rhen said unsteadily.

Raz turned to look at her then. The Doctore's eyes were fixed, wide and empty, on the dead. Even as the attendants swarmed down from the pit, pairing up to grab limp wrists and ankles, she couldn't seem to look away.

The woman had been bred and baptized in the blood of the pit, but even to one such as she this level of needless slaughter seemed almost too much to bear witness to…

"Alyssa!" Raz snapped. "Listen to me!"

At that, Rhen jumped. Blinking, she looked around at him.

"The Koyts," he said again, hating the hint of desperation he heard in his own voice. "I owe them. They are *my* responsibility. If I fall, they have no one and nothing to look forward to except hoping Tern forgets they ever existed. Get. Them. Out."

For a long moment Rhen stared at him. He steeled himself to argue with her, to contend with whatever resolve she might have that he wasn't going to die today, that Tern placed too much value on his life.

Instead, though, she nodded. Only once, and only briefly.

But she nodded.

Raz felt something like relief mix with the torrent of all the other feelings he was experiencing. The fear was true now. Raz wasn't afraid to die. Hell, a few months ago he'd have shrugged the concept off without much concern. He lived a violent life, full of violent people with violent tendencies. Any day could have been his last, and he'd grown comfortable with the concept.

Now, though, there were things he wasn't ready to leave behind just yet…

"MONSTER! MONSTER! MONSTER! MONSTER!"

When the last of the fallen had been hauled away, Raz started up the ramp, holding the dviassegai tight by his side.

Let's see what the bastard's cooked up for us, then, Ahna.

XXXV

Raz blinked in the dim gray light of the stormy afternoon. The pit, he realized with some relief, had been cleared at least once that day, though the still-falling snow was claiming back the ground around him in rapid fashion. A thin layer of white hung weakly over the churned red and brown of spilled blood and wet earth, but it was nothing compared to the heavy slush that piled everywhere in the stands that had not needed to be swept clean. Across from him, standing on the other side of the ring, was a lone woman. On one arm Helena, the final victor, carried a wide buckler, her other hand wrapped around the hilt of a plain longsword, whose tip rested against the ground. A white bandage was wrapped around her forehead where someone had managed to get a strike in, and she looked exhausted, her heavy breathing misting in the air.

Raz didn't for a second allow himself to think this was the extent of his trial.

Instead, he looked up above the woman's head, into the Chairman's box. The herald stood front and center, a tall man in heavy robes of white and gold that reminded him a little of those Brahnt, Yu'ri, and al'Dor had sometimes worn. The man was waving about him for quiet, trying to control the ten thousand voices that had exploded into cheers the minute Raz had stepped under the grounding tips of the portcullis. He was alone, though.

Quin Tern was nowhere to be found.

The prick came yet again, and Raz felt the crest along the back of his neck flick instinctively, as though in warning. Though he knew it was pointless, he couldn't stop himself scanning the crowd around the box, looking for a rotund figure with long blond hair.

"Where are you, you fat fuck?" he grumbled to himself.

The herald, meanwhile, seemed to have finally gained some control over the noise.

"Your champion, citizens of Azbar!" he called out with infectious enthusiasm. "You called for him, and he has come to deliver on you the entertainment you so desire! The Monster of Karth is here to fight for you, my lords and ladies! The Scourge of the South is here to kill for YOU!"

The crowd roared in response. Giving up on his search for the Chairman, Raz turned his eyes back to the herald, figuring he might as well pay attention and see what it was he could glean about the mess he was in.

"But where are his foes, my friends? Where are the vile men and women come to take him from you? Is Helena, the Shield Bearer of the Seven Cities, to stand against the Monster alone? I think not! Citizens of

Azbar, allow me to reintroduce you to your day's other victors, the vicious fighters who will have to set aside all the rivalries of today's melees and work together now to take on your champion. From the West Isles I give you… SURY ATHEUS!"

Footsteps behind him made Raz step away from the gate and turn around. From the shade of the underworks, a narrow figure with tanned skin and long jet-black hair appeared. He had the thin, slanting eyes of the Islers, and the same wiry build. Despite his slimness, though, he walked with a confident bearing, hands resting on the slender handles of the long, narrow blades on either hip, strapped over thick leather armor padded with fur for warmth.

As Atheus walked carefully by, Raz heard other steps crunching on the gangway after him.

"From the port city of Acrosia," the herald continued. "PIRATE KING KEHNT!"

The next man was a Southerner in truth, but unlike any Raz had ever seen. He'd forgone the skins and furs in favor of layers on layers of colorful silks and shirts, all tucked beneath a leather tunic and wide, baggy pants of very odd fashion. He had a wide-brimmed hat dipped lazily to one side, and a curved saber he held by the sheath in one hand.

"From the great lands of Perce… AJANA ZEKO!"

Zeko was a black behemoth, lumbering from the darkness of the underworks, the two-handed warhammer clenched in one fist looking like it might have matched Ahna for weight. After him the herald called out four others, but Raz didn't bother listening for their names. A spearwoman, another shield bearer, a large mountain man with a two-handed claymore over one shoulder, and a mace-wielder with a long-handled morning star in one hand and a flail in the other.

It was all he needed to know, watching each step out onto the pit and move to ring him. Their names were irrelevant compared to their number.

Four. Four was a number he could face—a number he *had* faced—and win. He'd taken on more in the past, of course, but rarely by choice and never of a caliber of the men and women that surrounded him now. Four he could handle and put on a show. Four had been the maximum, as agreed on when Tern had made his Chairman's Tourney.

Eight was a completely different story.

Raz didn't give away the thought, though. He met the eyes of each of the fighters evenly as they appeared, but didn't turn to study each one like some trapped animal frantically looking for a weak link. No. Such desperation would be apparent, firing up his opponents, and as much as Raz's every instinct was yelling at him to run, he knew there was nowhere to go.

"But there is one final surprise for you today, patrons of our wondrous Arena! There is one more for me to introduce to you, one more who will brave the pit, putting himself in arm's reach of your Monster at his own great risk. Good people, I bid you join me in applause of him, as you know him well! Please welcome the last member of today's final event, gambling his life for your entertainment! I give you, from our own city... YOUR COUNCIL CHAIRMAN HIMSELF! QUIN ETURIUS TERN!"

At first, Raz was utterly convinced he had misheard, had not understood what the herald had said. He blamed it on the voice in his head that had practically been screaming in panic at the thought that yet another would be added to the list, bringing the total to nine. His mind had gone straight to Azzeki Koro, a promising duel on his own, or perhaps the Doctore herself, forced into the pit after him against her wishes.

So when he heard Tern's name, he didn't believe it until the man himself waddled into the light.

At once it became apparent that the Chairman had no intention whatsoever of actually fighting. Apart from the fact that Raz would have bet Ahna the man had hardly lifted a sword in his life, Tern hadn't changed out of the luxurious furs and jewels he always wore on fight days. In fact, two attendants were flanking him, each bent on on keeping the edges of his sleek silver mantle clear of the mud and snow. The only thing Tern himself was carrying was what seemed to be some sort of box wrapped in dark-red cloth.

Raz's gaze lingered only a moment on this oddity, though, before moving up to search the Chairman's face. Tern was grinning with almost boyish delight, raising his free hand to acknowledge the cheering of the stands at his appearance. If the man had some trick up his sleeve, some plan to get Raz through this all in one piece, he wasn't about to show it.

For now, Raz was on his own...

"Thank you!" Tern's voice boomed out, echoing upwards as it bounced off the walls of the stadium. "Thank you all! It has always been a dream of mine to stand here, in the same place where each member of the Hall of Heroes once stood, and ten thousand more between them whose names have sadly been lost to memory. Today, on this first true day of the freeze, it was my desire to offer you something special, something heartwarming the likes of which will supply you with stories aplenty through the winter. Today I offer you a chance to witness more than just a battle for glory and freedom. I offer you a chance to witness a fight for true survival, an opportunity to see what happens when the world's most dangerous animal is cornered and given no place to run!"

The fear tugging at Raz's mind was suddenly withdrawn and replaced by a rush of anger. *Animal?* he thought. It was one thing to make such comments as asides and remarks, but to insult him so openly, before thousands of witnesses, was a fool's mistake.

If Tern was looking to get a rise out of him, he was well on his way.

"Can you imagine it, friends, compatriots? Can you imagine a beast greater still that anything you have yet seen, more dangerous even than your beloved Monster of Karth? DO YOU WISH TO WITNESS THAT?"

The rolling screams of agreement were answer enough. Tern grinned even wider.

"Then your desire is my duty, and I shall pull the beast forth, drag it from the bowels of whatever hell it hides, and force it to rear its head."

At this, Quin paused to say something quiet to one of his attendants. Then he held out the cloth-covered box.

The boy—for he couldn't be more than fourteen or fifteen—abruptly looked exceedingly nervous, but took it dutifully, handing his corner of Tern's mantle off to the other servant. As the Chairman returned to his speech, the attendant started walking towards Raz, passing between Zeko and the spearwoman to get to him. Raz gave the boy his full attention, wary of a trick, and not the least bit bothered by the Chairman's continued windbaggery. What did bother him, though, was the fact that the fighters around him seemed to be shifting, giving up their advantage of surrounding him in favor of lining up directly between him and Quin Tern. By the time the boy had reached him, the eight of them had formed a sort of pack, Zeko at its head, watching Raz warily.

Suddenly, the box in the attendant's arms was more frightening than anything the Arena could have ever thrown at him.

"M-My Lord Chairman bids you take this, and his message," the attendant stuttered, swallowing nervously and not meeting Raz's eye. "He says, 'Maybe next time you'll remember to tell the Lifegiver not to stick his nose where it doesn't belong.'"

The boy held it out then, the thing quivering in his shaking hands.

Raz was frozen, all will struck down by Tern's words. He didn't want to know what was in that box. He had tasted madness before. It seemed a lifetime ago, though the years had been short and brutal. If whatever was hiding beneath the cloth and wood in the attendant's hands was truly something Tern thought might bring back some of that darkness, Raz wanted nothing less than to open the box, than to know its contents.

Few things were left to him, after all, that could pull him back to that place.

But time is a tricky bastard, and as much as Raz would have liked the moment to extend into infinity, allowing him the eternal bliss of not knowing, there was no such power invented by man or god. He tried, though. Raz found himself, as though guided by some unseen hand, stepping away from the boy and his box, keeping as much space between the two of them as he could. The attendant, in turn, looked back over his shoulder, unsure of what to do.

Raz saw Tern's grin widen even as he continued to address the crowds, and the man nodded before raising a hand in signal.

As the boy stepped forward, egged on by his master, there was a *clunk*. Behind him, feet from his back, Raz heard the whirl of loose chains, and the portcullis fell shut with a crash that shook snow loose from the wall around and above it.

It didn't stop him from backing up, though, right up until he ran into the very wood itself.

And the boy kept coming.

Raz could hear the blood rushing through his ears, could feel his heart, feel it pounding in his chest so hard he feared the thing might tear itself free of his body. There was nothing he could do, nowhere to go. Ahna hung loose by his side, all but forgotten as Raz watched the attendant follow him hesitantly, the wrapped box still held before him like some unholy relic.

When he got within reach, and with nowhere else to go, Raz did the only thing that made sense in the moment.

He struck the box right out of the boy's hands.

Even if Raz had thought to, he would not have had the willpower to look away. As the covering cloth untangled itself from the wood, it was pulled away almost at once by the wind, carried off until it caught on one of the iron torch brackets hammered into the wall of the pit. It clung there, a red flapping streak against the gray of the stone.

The box itself, though, fell hard to the ground, bounced, broke open, and allowed the nightmare within to roll out onto the snow.

XXXVI

Arrun's face looked up at Raz from the ground, only it wasn't his face anymore. His features had been mangled, his flesh ripped and cut. The lids of his eyes had been removed, leaving behind staring orbs that never looked away. His ears had been sawed off, matching the gore of where his nose had been. His lips were sewn shut, the holes through which the twine snuck ragged and ripped as skin had stretched and protested.

And blood. There was blood everywhere.

It was this fact that punched though Raz's walls, a realization that wrapped like rope about his throat, making it hard to breathe. The invisible weight of it pulled him to his knees, Ahna falling from this numb hand.

Blood… blood only flowed when the heart was beating…

Winter was suddenly welcome, the wind and snow nothing more than a companion in its unrelenting fury. The cold flowed through Raz's arms like an icy stream. He couldn't look away even though he wanted to. He took in the boy's disfigured head for every bit it was worth, unable to see anything else. The world dissolved around him.

"And so, my dearest friends," Quin Tern's voice shouted from the other side of the veil, "prepare yourselves! Prepare yourselves to meet the creature tucked away for too long! Welcome the *true* Raz i'Syul Arro! Welcome him! Welcome the beast!"

But there was no beast, Raz thought, looking within himself. *There is only cold in this place, emptiness.*

There is nothing.

As though Arrun's staring blue eyes had drained him of his very existence, Raz felt no more. He forgot time and place and purpose. He forgot name and body and soul. There was nothing left to do, nothing left to *be*. He was devoid of meaning, sucked empty. Sucked empty by that horror, by that abomination still on the ground barely a pace away. Flecks of snow were already catching in Arrun's blond hair, thatched with blood.

Then the word came.

Tern.

At first it was only a spark. From the bleakness in which Raz found himself falling, a tiny flame rose, barely a flash in the dark. It grew, though, as the word clung to his mind like some rabid animal, latched on and unwilling to let go, shifting into a name.

Tern. Quin Tern.

The name fed the spark, the words like dry leaves over dying embers. For a moment there was only a building smolder, a realization of potential and existence.

Then, in one abrupt instant, fire engulfed Raz from the inside out.

For the first time in months, the animal returned.

Purpose came back in a rush. Awareness rocked through Raz like a cannonball, punching across the empty desperation Arrun's tortured grimace nearly drowned him in. The abyss ripped open, and Raz felt himself falling, plummeting down into the dark.

He didn't even try to slow his descent.

QUIN TERN!

Still on his knees, a snarl built up in Raz's chest, erupting into a screaming roar of defiance that silenced every sound from the spectators. The attendant who had brought him the box squealed and stumbled backward, tripping repeatedly as he sprinted back to his master. Lifting Ahna from the ground, Raz stood slowly, setting amber eyes back on the group before him.

The somberness of the Northern winter was gone from the day. No more were the stands around him accented in white and gray, highlighted by snow and stone. Instead, the world had fallen into shades of dark red and darker black, swallowing the details of the scene. There was nothing left to see, regardless, beyond what was directly in front of him. Even the eight men and women between him and his goal barely gave Raz pause, because behind them, still leering with obvious pleasure, Quin Tern was bathing in his success.

And all Raz knew was that he was going to peel the man's smile from his face with his bare hands.

The silence held its reign over the Arena for a long moment. No one spoke, no one cheered. Like the world itself had paused, holding its breath, ten thousand people watched Raz, waiting, wanting desperately to see what he would do.

When he finally moved, it was with such speed many would later swear the Monster of Karth became nothing more than a blur of black, red, and silver steel.

Zeko, at the head of the group, was the first to go down, and it happened so quickly the others barely had time to blink before the giant Percian was screaming. Raz hit him with the force of a bull, toppling him, while his free hand grabbed at the man's face, a clawed finger finding each of Zeko's eyes beneath the lip of his helm. The crowd barely had time to roar in thrilled amazement before steel buried into brain, and the man died.

It was the only easy kill Raz got, because then the rest were on him.

Raz ducked under the thrust of the spearwoman's blade, then somersaulted backwards off Zeko's body to avoid the simultaneous downward strikes of Pirate King Kehnt's saber and the mace wielder's morning star. Both weapons hit the dead man with echoed *thunks,* but caught nothing else.

Meanwhile, Ahna had begun her dance of death.

The dviassegai moved like a silver serpent about Raz, less graceful in his rage of insanity, but all the more deadly for it. She slashed left and right, up and down, striking with such vicious speed the men and women about him were hard-pressed to hang on to their blades as they blocked and deflected. They tried to press forward, tried to force him back, but Raz roared in defiance, the crest along the back of his neck flaring red, his wings whipping out from beneath the silver-and-black mantle to join the melee. As numerous as they were, the remaining champions could do nothing to get around him, nothing to position themselves to enclose him. Every time one tried, something knocked them back. It didn't matter if it was Ahna, a mailed fist, a clawed foot, rippling wings, or even a lithe, scaly tail. *Something* was always there to block them.

After a minute of chaotic combat, someone shouted, and the seven fell back to regroup. Most at that point would have scattered to get around Raz, but it seemed they'd all seen enough of his fights to know that would only make it easier for Raz to break up their defense. Instead they stayed close, a living wall between Raz and the Chairman, unwilling to give him the man he so desired.

Well beyond reason, Raz simply followed them, barreling into the group as a tempest might strike at the mountains.

They let Helena and the second shield bearer take the brunt of his rage, trusting the pair of them to play the defense and leave the rest up to the others. It was a good plan, and Raz's mindless assault cost him a deep slash across his abdomen and several nasty holes in his left thigh as the mace wielder's flail came out and around, crashing into the armor there and perforating the steel.

The wounds he granted them, though, cost the seven much more than they gained.

Barely feeling the metal points in his flesh, Raz twisted his hips away, pulling the embedded flail with him and dragging it from its owner's hand. At the same time, Raz grabbed the top of Helena's shield and—as the woman yelled in surprise—hauled it down to the ground with one hand, dragging the woman attached to it along for the ride. There was a *snap* as the arm the shield was strapped to broke, and Helena's shouts for assistance turned to shrieks of pain and fear. They were cut short when Raz's foot caught the bottom of her chin in a ferocious kick, snapping her neck back.

The corpse of Helena, Shield Bearer of the Seven Cities, flopped to the ground chest first, her head dangling by nothing more than flesh on her back, dead eyes staring into the sky.

There was no pause in the fighting, though. On the contrary, the six left standing pressed their advantage, seeking to attack in the moment Raz was finally open, leaving himself vulnerable as he went for the kill. Raz grunted as the spearwoman's blade bit into his side barely an inch below the old scar of a crossbow bolt that had punched through him not a few months before. The mace wielder acted fast, too, leaping up and swinging his morning star high for Raz's head. Instead of the killing blow he'd hoped for, though, he met Raz's outstretched hand, which caught him about the wrist and dragged him up and around, using the man's own momentum to roll him over Raz's back and slam him to the ground so hard it was possible to *hear* ribs break.

The man didn't have time to do more than gasp in shock and pain, though, before Raz reached down, ripped the flail still stuck in his thigh free, and brought the spiked metal ball down on the mace wielder's face.

Blood, gore, and bits of bone flew in every direction.

Raz tried to stand up then, but for once he was too slow. It had been a foolish move, leaving himself open to the five left alive, and even in the thrall of the all-consuming madness, Raz screamed in pain as what felt like white-hot iron was shoved into his back. A sudden weight seemed to collapse in on the left side of his chest, and Raz knew steel had nicked lung.

Reaching over his shoulder, he tried for a blind swipe at the offending attacker. His hand caught hair, and he had traction for a moment, but in the same instant whatever blade had taken him between the ribs was withdrawn, and his hold went slack. He whirled around to see the West Isler, Atheus, dancing back, a blade in each hand, his dark hair suddenly cropped short, leaving a handful in Raz's palm.

The pressure of his leaking lung pulled at Raz's chest, but it barely slowed him down. Taking a breath, he roared at the last of the champions, flecking the snow between them with blood that came up with the scream. Atheus, the shield bearer, the mountain man, and the spearwoman didn't flinch.

The Pirate King Kehnt, though, took a single step back, and Raz had his weak link.

Bolting forward, he dodged a spear thrust, sent the shield bearer tumbling with a heavy kick, and rolled under Atheus' horizontal strike. In a blink he was in the middle of them, the last place they would expect, and came up directly in front of Kehnt. The Pirate Kehnt shrieked, sounding unbefittingly womanish for his title, and struck blindly with his saber.

Raz caught the curved blade in a mailed hand, feeling the edge split through the thick leather that shielded his palm and bite into flesh. In the same instant, though, Ahna jutted forward. The dviassegai's twin blades took Kehnt through the chest and abdomen, spitting him like meat on a fork.

Without pausing, Raz roared and whipped Ahna around. Using the

Pirate King's corpse like the heavy end of some great grim hammer, he slammed her into the first person he found. Atheus went flying, tumbling away across the dirty snow.

Ahna, though, her grip slicked by the blood flowing from Raz's slashed palm, went with him.

There was a moment, a tiny instant where triumph flared in the eyes of the two left closest to him. The mountain man had leapt back at Raz's charge, but the unnamed spearwoman and shield bearer roared in victory. They pounced forward, one from either side, intent on meeting Raz's unprotected body with cutting steel.

What they met instead were the war ax and gladius, drawn with such speed many of the spectators could only claim the Monster of Karth had simply magicked them into his hands.

Blade met blade, pushing aside the shield bearer's sword so that the man stumbled past Raz, off-balance and taken by surprise. The ax, though, wooden haft gripped in Raz's wounded hand, slickened and slipped. The spear Raz had intended to parry didn't go wide enough, and the keen tip of the blade caught a lip in the armor of his shoulder, piercing the thick muscle of his arm.

The gladius, though, free of its own responsibility, was more accurate, and came around to take the spear's owner through the throat.

Raz left his blade there, thrust halfway to the hilt in the woman's neck as she fell, intent on other things. Tugging the spear from his arm with a grunt, he turned to meet the lumbering form of the mountain man, the claymore thrust forward like a lance, unstoppable behind the heavy rush of its wielder.

Unstoppable, that is, until Raz's thrown war ax took the big man between the eyes, ending his charge so abruptly he might have hit solid wall.

As the claymore and its owner fell to the earth, Raz turned to find the shield bearer struggling on all fours to get back on his feet, burdened by the weight of his armor and slipping in the bloody slush. He didn't even see Raz come up behind him.

Nor did he see the clawed foot come down on the back of his head, slamming him once more into the muck, crushing the fragile bones of his face and neck against the frozen earth.

The last one died almost as suddenly. Sury Atheus had just freed himself from the tangle that was Ahna and the still-speared Kehnt, pulling himself to his feet on the crossbeams of the portcullis behind him. He looked dazed, stumbling to and fro as he cast about for his swords, lost somewhere in the snow.

Twirling the borrowed spear in his good hand, Raz set it, aimed, and launched the thing like a javelin.

It took Atheus in the chest with the force of a ballista. The blade punched clean through his body, lodging itself in the wood of the gate behind him with a *thunk*. Atheus' limbs spasmed as it hit him, and he looked down in confusion at the five feet of shaft protruding from his furs, impaling him standing up. For a few seconds he wailed in terror and disbelief, his arms attempting to work through the shock, swiping at the thing, trying to get a grip. His fingers had just found the spear, though, when he died, and they dropped to his sides even as the man himself fell silent and slumped forward, still upright, like some grisly life-sized doll that had been nailed to the wall.

He was the last to stop moving, and the stillness of the pit, scattered now with bodies thrown about the bloodstained snow, matched the awed silence of the stadium around him.

Slowly, Raz staggered towards Atheus, distantly aware of the ten thousand eyes following his battered form. The heaviness in his chest was greater now, and he could hear the wheeze of air bubbling through the wound in his back with every breath. He limped as he moved, too, favoring the leg not lacerated by the flail. His left arm, skewered by the spear, ached like he was holding it in scalding water, and he held it close to his chest as he reached down for Ahna's haft. Putting a foot on Kehnt's chest, he ripped the dviassegai free of the man.

Then he turned to face the last figure standing with him in the pit.

Had he been in his right mind, Raz might have thought the smile on Quin Tern's face peculiar. The scattered corpses of the best he'd been able to offer lay about the Arena floor, and yet still the Chairman looked serene, long hair twisting about his face in the wind. His hands were in the deep sleeves of his robes, and he seemed not to have a care in the world. Even as Raz began advancing on him, Ahna in one hand, red wings and crest extended to their greatest extent. Even when Raz began to run, screaming his fury in the raging roar of his kind. Even when the attendants behind him abandoned him, running for their lives.

It was only when Raz took a step to leap, preparing to bring Ahna down on the man's head in payment for a murdered boy, that Tern moved at all. From within the sleeves of his robes he pulled something small, and held it aloft for Raz to see.

Between his fat fingers, Tern held the bloody form of a simple cloth doll.

XXXVII

The sight of the thing might as well have been some titanic hammer fallen from the sky, shocking Raz back into reality. He felt himself go limp mid-leap as the world rocked back into color and shape. Ahna fell, useless, from his grasp, and he tumbled to the ground at Tern's feet, barely managing to stumble to two knees and his good arm.

His golden eyes, though, never left the doll.

"Where is she?" he croaked, finding it hard to steal enough breath to speak. "WHERE IS SHE?"

Tern leered down at him in response, clearly pleased with himself. Not bothering to answer Raz, he looked up into the stands.

"My lords and ladies!" he bellowed, sweeping a hand around him at the strewn dead about the pit. "Behold! I promised a fight unlike anything you'd ever seen, and you had it! I promised a beast unlike any you'd ever imagined, and you found him! ARE YOU PLEASED, CITZENS OF AZBAR?"

The cheer that greeted him, for once, was not an immediate torrent of pounding applause and screams. Instead it was more like water flowing through a crumbling dam, more and more coming with every second the levees fell apart. As though the crowd needed to shake itself from whatever hypnosis the butchery of the last few minutes had dragged them into, the noise built up slowly. At first it was little more than a rumble, then a roll like approaching thunder.

Then it was an earth shattering, looming outcry unlike any Raz had ever heard within the Arena.

"WHERE IS SHE, TERN?" he screamed again, trying to be heard over the noise as he pushed himself into a half kneel and felt every inch of his battered body seize in protest at the motion. "WHAT HAVE YOU DONE WITH HER?"

Again the Chairman ignored him, basking once more in the glory of the crowd's praise. Clearly he knew he was untouchable. Until Raz found out what had happened to Lueski, the man might as well have been on the other side of the world to him.

"But I have done more even than I promised!" Tern continued as the tumult finally ebbed. "Yes! Much more! I have brought your champion, your god of war, to his knees! See him?" He swung a hand to point down at Raz. "See how he grovels! It was wanted. It was needed! Your Monster is made man, my friends! It may take time—years, even—but he will fall. If I have to go to the ends of the earth to find the slayer of Raz i'Syul Arro, I will do it for you. If he can be brought to his knees by a mere servant of the city, then it cannot be doubted that one day he. Will. FALL!"

The crowd whipped itself into a frenzy again, caught in the Chairman's bloodlust, entranced by the idea of fights even bloodier and grander than what they had just witnessed. None seemed to care that Arrun Koyt's head lay among the others, desecrated and tortured, sawed clear of its body even as the boy still lived. None seemed to care that it was a child's toy, bloody and foreboding, that had brought the Monster to his knees.

They only cared for more.

In that instant, Raz bore witness to the mistake he had made. He saw, in the faces of ten thousand people what he had offered everything for, been willing to give up his life for.

Nothing. Nothing worth ever saving.

Grief and shock ripped through him to mix with the pain of his wounds. He felt himself slipping, felt his conscience slide back down the hill towards the abyss. This time, though, he scrambled not to fall.

No, he told himself, the snow shifting around his hand as he clenched it into a fist. *No, there are some worth saving. There's at least one worth saving.*

With a pained groan Raz pushed himself agonizingly to his feet. Before him, Tern hesitated, looking around at him. The man's face still framed no concern, looking more annoyed than anything that Raz was being rebellious in this moment of triumph.

"Where is she, Tern?" Raz breathed, feeling searing heat along the wound in his back as he brought Ahna up with clear intent. "I'm not going to ask you again."

Tern frowned, studying Raz as though to deduce whether the threat was worth even considering. Then he raised a hand and gestured. There was a *clunk* of wood and the sounds of shifting chains, and with a grinding screech the portcullis began to lift. Raz turned in time to see Atheus' body being lifted off its feet. It climbed higher and higher until the spear couldn't bear the weight anymore, and dislodged itself from the wood.

As the West Isler fell to the ground, a score of figures appeared from the dim glow of the underworks, stepping out into the pit. Most of them were members of the city guard, pouring out to line the wall, blades drawn and clearly ready for a fight. One was Alyssa Rhen, looking shaken and distinctly not herself as she cast around at the bloody results of Quin Tern's finale.

And one was Azzeki Koro, a black shadow as always in his darkened leathers, his curved blade drawn and resting across Lueski Koyt's thin throat.

Raz's heart fell as he saw her. She still breathed, that much was obvious, but the girl clearly hadn't walked away from her captor's clutches unscathed. Her face was bruised and beaten, and her clothes were torn and disheveled. Her black hair, usually so straight and well cared for, was matted with drying blood and stuck to the wounds of her face.

But it was the stillness of her form, the quiet in her eyes, that disturbed Raz the most. Something had been taken from the child. Something had reached in and scarred the delicate pattern of her soul, leaving a silence in her body that was akin to living death. Raz was familiar with it, or at least some form of it.

Lueski had the same look about her he had witnessed for all too many years in the bearing of the Grandmother.

"Lueski?" he asked tentatively, taking a step towards the girl.

At once several of the guard on either side of her converged before him, partially blocking his path to her. He could still see her between them, though, and as he watched, Lueski seemed to shiver, shaken by the sound of her own name. She blinked and looked around at him, and the tears in her eyes flooded Raz with a mixed wash of relief and new grief.

"Raz," she whimpered. "Raz… They killed Arrun. They made him scream, and when he wouldn't stop they sewed his mouth shut. Then they killed him, Raz… They took a saw and they held him down and they… they…"

She blinked and reached up to wipe away her tears with the back of her sleeve. Then she looked back up at Raz with red eyes.

"Why would they do that, Raz?" she demanded of him, a child begging for an answer that made sense in the small world she knew. "Why would they kill him?"

"Because *Raz* didn't do what he was told," a voice cut in before Raz himself could respond.

Tern was walking around the ring nearby, picking his way through the carnage as the attendants stumbled behind him, doing their best to keep his long cloak off the ground. He seemed to be looking for something, eyes scanning the snow as he spoke.

"Arrun died because your oaf of a hero didn't do what he promised, little girl," Tern said. "He was killed because Raz didn't stick to our deal."

Raz shivered at the words, feeling the falling snow drifting around him as he listened.

"I'll bet anything he's made promises to you, too," the Chairman continued, coming to a halt over whatever it was he'd been searching for. "Did he give you his word, hmm? Did he swear he would look out for you? Look out for your brother?"

Stiff in Azzeki's grasp, Lueski hesitated.

Then she nodded slowly, and Tern smiled in wicked smugness. Toeing something loose from the snow, he kicked it over to the girl.

"And how did that work out for you, child?"

Lueski looked down at the thing as it bounced and settled at her feet. For a moment she seemed not to recognize it, staring at the object with watery eyes as though unsure of what it was. Then she made out of the face behind the snow and mud, filling in the missing pieces of the disfigured features.

As Arrun's dead eyes looked up into hers, blue meeting blue, Lueski opened her mouth and screamed.

She screamed and screamed, delirious in her horrified fear, trying to scramble away but barely moving as the Captain-Commander held her where she was. The sound echoed about the silent Arena. Though he didn't look up from the girl's face, Raz knew that ten thousand stares were fixed on them, avid in their attention. *This* was what Tern had wanted all along. *This* had been his grand plan for the day. He thought Raz had betrayed their contract, so he wanted to regain control in one fell swoop. With one act of unfathomable cruelty, witnessed by the packed stadium, the Chairman had brought Azbar back under his fearsome control.

And there wasn't a damn thing Raz could do about it.

"Lueski!" he shouted over the girl's pained screeches, ignoring the pressing guard and taking another step towards her. "Lueski! Child! Look at me! *Look at me*!"

The girl didn't so much as pause in her screaming. She fought Azzeki's grip even as her eyes remained fixed on her brother's head, completely ignorant of the blade at her throat.

"LUESKI!"

Raz roared her name, ignoring the pained weight in his chest. This time the girl heard him. Her shrieks stopped abruptly, but she still didn't manage to pull her eyes away from Arrun's.

"Lueski," Raz pleaded in quieter tones. "Lueski, please. Look away, child. Look at me."

Lueski's gaze didn't budge. For a moment she was still, her body quiet again, and Raz thought she had lost her mind to the darkness again.

Then she spoke, her words barely distinguishable, whispered to the winds.

"You promised."

Ice washed over Raz, cold as the snow that had long numbed his feet. He fought it off, though, desperate to keep the girl from falling away from him, from disappearing into a place she couldn't come back from.

"I know, Lueski," he said. "I know I did. I tried. I'm so sorry, I—"

"Kill them."

Raz stumbled on his words as Lueski cut him off. Though she still hadn't looked up, her face had suddenly hardened.

"What?" he asked her tentatively.

"I want you to kill them!" Lueski shrieked, her hands clenching into fists at her sides. "I want you to promise you'll kill them! I want you to promise and keep it, this time! PROMISE!"

Raz hesitated.

"Lueski…" he said quietly, shaking his head. "Lueski… I can't. I can't promise that. They'll hurt you if I try. They'll kill *you* if I try."

Lueski said nothing in return. For a time she just stood there, tense in Azzeki's grasp, wide eyes ever meeting her brother's. Then, all at once, she seemed to calm. The stiffness left her, and for a moment the little girl Raz had found in the woods returned in full. At last she looked away from Arrun, turning to Raz.

For a moment she just stared at him, taking him in, as though trying to fix him in her memory.

Then she smiled a sad sort of smile.

"I'll miss you."

And before anyone could so much as think to stop her, Lueski brought her hands up to the bare steel of Azzeki's blade, pressed the edge to her throat, and jerked it hard to one side.

XXXVIII

"*NO!*"

Raz's screeched roar ripped through the sudden hush of the stands. Blind to the guards in his way, he hurtled for Lueski, Ahna falling to the ground behind him. So shocked were the men around him that no one so much as moved to block his path. To a one they stared in horror at the little body tumbling from Azzeki's grasp, leaving a trail of red along the man's blade as she dropped.

Raz reached her so fast he caught her before her head hit the ground. Scooping her into his arms, he lifted her to his chest.

"No! No, no, no, no!"

Blood ran free from the great gash in the side of her neck and trickled in lines from the corners of her mouth. She coughed, spraying his chest and face, hacking as her body tried to breathe. In desperation Raz grabbed the hem of his mantle and ripped a clump free with his teeth, moving to press it against the wound.

Small hands stopped him.

He looked back up at Lueski's face. Even though they watered and bulged as her body fought to keep itself alive, there was a conviction in the girl's eyes, a certainty in the act. Even as blood bubbled on her lips, spilling in staggered spurts from her neck as her heart pumped harder in an attempt to keep beating, her hands urged Raz not to stem the flow.

"Lueski," Raz begged. "Lueski, *please…*"

All he got was the tiniest shake of her head, almost imperceptible in the writhing of a dying body. Instead her hands shifted on his, trying to tug free the cloth clenched in his fist. Eventually, he let it go.

Then he took her hands in his, and held them to his chest.

Lueski smiled. For a few seconds, through the spasms in her small body she gazed up at him, content and free.

Then she was gone.

Raz felt the throes leave her, felt the thrashing tightness subside. She sagged against him, head tucked up against the crook of his arm, and lay still. Pulling the girl tight against him, both her hands still held to his chest, Raz threw his head back and screamed at the sky.

The pain in that sound seemed to bring the world back to life. All about him men moved, gripped abruptly by a realization just as it struck Raz too. A singular, absolute thought that ripped through him, bringing fire and new life to his limbs.

No chains hold your Monster now.

He had just enough to time to lower Lueski's still form to the ground, settling her gently in the snow by what was left of her brother, when Tern's panicked order came.

"KILL HIM!"

But the world was black and red again, and Raz was gone even before Azzeki had time to bring his blade around.

As if the guards around him were statues, Raz slipped between and below their outstretched swords and hands with ease. He had but one purpose left to him now. One objective to which he intended to apply heart, mind, and soul.

Tern.

Nothing and no one could stand in his way. The two that happened to get close fell screaming, one clutching at the lacerations down his face, the other at the gashes across his abdomen. The knife at Raz's hip was forgotten, his other weapons scattered about the pit, but the steel tips of his claws were plenty enough to get him where he wanted to be.

And when he reached Tern, they were enough to take the man about the throat.

Tern's squeal of fear was choked away as the fat man found himself suddenly free of the ground. With terrifying strength fed from the burning hate that melted away pain and injury, Raz lifted the Chairman completely off his feet, both hands around his neck. For a few seconds he held him there, content to watch the man kick and struggle to get out garbled words, pudgy fingers working at the steel of Raz's gauntlets. Behind him, Raz knew the guard had frozen in their places, suddenly unsure of what to do.

Then he smiled up at Tern, a wicked, hungry smile he hoped matched the man's best leers, and began to squeeze.

"Arro! *Wait!*"

While color didn't return to the world, the black and red that made up Tern's struggling form certainly flickered. Through the rush of blood and hate Raz heard booted feet crunching against the snow, and he turned to snarl over his shoulder at whoever was fool enough to approach him.

He paused, though, when what little conscious part of his mind he had left recognized the Doctore.

The woman was walking around him cautiously, hands up and empty, not wanting to startle him. There was fear in her eyes, true, but more so there was concern. She moved around to be within easy view, coming to stand a little to the side and behind Tern's writhing feet.

"Arro," she hissed. "*Raz!* Listen to me! *Listen!*"

Raz ignored her, turning back to watch Tern's face darken, thick tongue sticking out as he mouthed at the air in desperation.

"Raz! Please! If he dies, you die. You won't get out of the city. If you don't get yourself killed here, the guard will close the gates and hunt you down."

"I've survived worse," Raz heard himself sneer.

"Not in the freeze, you haven't. *Think*! Do you believe Lueski wanted you to die? Do you believe she wanted you to throw away your life, too?"

"She wanted me to promise. She wanted to me to kill—!"

"'Them all,'" Rhen finished. "Yes, I heard. We all did. But you can't believe she wanted you dead, too!"

Raz didn't say anything to that, and the Doctore pressed her advantage.

"Killing Tern isn't killing them all, Raz. If you want to hold to that promise, then you need to live. And to live, you need to *let him down*."

Raz hesitated, but didn't relent.

"You die here, you've killed one bad man, but there are more out there. You survive, and you might live to kill a thousand more."

A memory flashed across Raz's thoughts. An image of Lueski smiling up at him, arms wrapped around his hips, greeting him after he'd finally come home.

Did you win? she'd asked him. *Did you beat the bad men? Did you? Did you? There are more out there.*

Raz felt some small parts of his mind slide back into place, and a little color returned. Tern's face was purple, and he looked about ready to pass out. Raz paused.

Then he let go of the fat man's throat, dropping him unceremoniously to the ground at his feet.

"You." Raz pointed a steel claw at one of the Chairman's attendants, ignoring the hacking and gasping form below him. "My sword and ax. *Now*!"

The boy jumped to like he'd been stuck with a hot poker.

"Get up," Raz growled, reaching down to grab Tern by the hair. "UP!"

The man staggered, half lifted, to his feet. Raz winced at the motion, feeling the ache of his wounds and the weight of the punctured lung return to him as consciousness started to win over the animal again.

"Anyone so much as twitches," Raz roared to the surrounding guardsmen, resting the claws of his free hand on Tern's bruised throat, "and your Chairman goes the same way as the girl! Let us pass, and he can go free once we're out of the city!"

"N-Nobody move!" Tern gasped, finding his voice at last. "Nobody-Nobody move! Do as he says!"

The guard did as ordered, lowering their blades and watching fearfully as Raz pushed Tern forward, limping on his bad leg again. Together the pair made their way through the men, Tern with his hands up, the Doctore following close behind.

The attendant met them near the center of the pit, where Ahna waited, half-covered in snow. Taking the war ax and gladius one after the other, Raz sheathed them on his hip and over his shoulder respectively. This done, he bent down and lifted the dviassegai from the ground, never letting go of Tern's long hair, and doing his best not to show the toll it took on him to pick up the weapon.

"Horses," Raz growled over his shoulder to Rhen. "Three of them."

If the Doctore nodded, he didn't see, but the next moment she was off running, slipping below the portcullis and down the gangway.

Pressing Ahna's twin tips into Tern's back, Raz pushed the man forward, moving to follow.

For the first time, someone stepped forward to block their path.

Azzeki Koro stood between them and the pit gate, reddened blade bare to the gray of the afternoon at his side. His dark eyes met Raz's evenly, testing, seeking, almost as though he were searching for the extent of Raz's weaknesses, searching for what kink in the Monster's armor to take advantage of.

"Tell your man to move, Chairman, or by every Southern, Northern, and unknown god alike I will spit you where you stand," Raz hissed into Tern's ear.

"Azzeki, *move*!" the Chairman squealed at once, eyes bulging. "Are you trying to get me killed? Get out of the way!"

For a few seconds the Captain-Commander didn't budge, still searching Raz's face.

Then he stepped aside.

Raz shoved Tern forward, pressing him stumbling past the Percian and the last of the guard. As they reached the portcullis, though, he stopped. A small form lay at the gate's feet, peaceful in death, looking like she might have simply been sleeping beneath the blanket of snow that was already starting to cover her.

Pulling Tern around, Raz kicked the knees out from beneath the fat man and bent him over Lueski's body.

"Pick her up," he growled.

"Wha—?" Tern spluttered, panicking. "No! I-I don't—"

"PICK HER UP!"

The Chairman jumped as Raz screamed in his ear, then scrambled to lift the girl into his arms. Struggling to his feet again, the man was huffing and puffing by the time he stood.

"Now tell your man to get her brother," Raz ordered.

Tern hesitated, then looked around at Azzeki and nodded. The Captain-Commander grimaced in distaste, but sheathed his blade and moved to grab Arrun's head from the ground. Stepping forward, he dropped it in the crook of Lueski's hips, bent up against Tern's chest.

"Now *walk*," Raz said, prodding the Chairman down the gangway.

This time he moved without pause.

They tottered down the ramp, Raz limping with his hand in Tern's hair while the Chairman struggled under the added weight of the Koyts. When they reached the bottom, what few fighters were left in the underworks looked around curiously, eyes widening as they watched the pair pass.

Raz ignored them all, heading straight for the entrance.

The doors were open for them, the streets outside almost devoid of traffic for once. Around the bend of the wall, though, Raz could hear the pounding of thousands of feet as the stadium emptied, the spectators intent on seeing out the day's events until the very end.

Feeling panic start to settle in again, Raz looked around in desperation for a place to hide.

"You can't get away," Tern said in a falsely calm voice. "Let me go now, and I'll make sure you get out of the city alive."

"Shut up," Raz growled.Making up his mind, he started pushing Tern towards the alley across from the underworks' doors.

"It's the only option you have," Tern insisted, stumbling forward. "You think they'll let you out of the gates in one-*AAH*!"

Losing patience, Raz had shoved Ahna's tips, hard, into the Chairman's back. Blood welled through the cuts in the man's rich cloak.

"They'll open the gates because you'll tell them to, Chairman," Raz hissed. "If you don't, well… You and I have both been lucky to make it this far. I hope you've realized by now I'm not overly bothered with dying if it means taking you with me."

Tern was quiet after that.

Clop, clop, clop.

Raz's ears twitched up at the sound just as they made the edge of the alley. Looking left, opposite where the muted thunder of footsteps was approaching from, he saw dark shapes loom out of the snow.

Doctore, atop a thick gray stud, with another, darker horse in tow.

"I thought I said three horses," Raz said suspiciously, eyeing the woman as she dismounted beside him in a rush.

"Two is all I could manage," she said, her breath steaming in the air. "It won't make a difference anyway."

"But what are you going to—?"

"If you thought I was going to come with you, you're wrong," she said with a shake of her head. "Someone has to stay and clean up this mess. People will panic. The council will need help."

"The council can go and—!" Raz began in a raspy yell, but Rhen cut him off again.

"What?" she demanded. "Can go fuck themselves? Kill themselves? I don't disagree after today, but without them the city falls to pieces, at least for now. I told you, Arro, there are more bad men out there. But there are more ways to deal with them than a knife in the throat, too."

Raz watched her with narrowed eyes. Then he shrugged, looking at the horses.

"Can you take Lueski and Arrun for a minute?" he asked her quietly.

Rhen's face fell, and she nodded sadly.

"Hand them over," Raz ordered Tern. "Then get up."

The Chairman did as he was told, allowing the Doctore to take Lueski and her brother's head from his arms, then moved to the closest of the two horses as Raz guided him by the hair.

Getting the Chairman into the saddle was an ordeal that required no small effort from Raz, and left him pained and aching once more, wheezing in the cold. Taking the reins before Tern thought of making a run for it, he led the horse to stand beside the other, then hauled himself up onto the back of the gray stud.

"Can you ride?" the Doctore asked hesitantly, glancing at his clawed feet.

Raz nodded. "My family had horses, growing up," he said, resting Ahna across his lap and reaching down to grab the end of his cloak again. "I learned with the best. Now give the children back to Tern."

As Rhen passed Lueski and Arrun up carefully to the Chairman, Raz ripped long strips of thick fur from the mantle with his teeth, bending down to wrap them around his bare feet. They might already be numb, but hopefully this way he would avoid losing them to the cold.

This done, he looked down at the Doctore again.

"Rhen… You're sure you don't want to come?"

The woman nodded. "I'm sure," she said with a smile that tugged at the scar on her face. "And call me Alyssa."

"Alyssa," Raz said with a nod. "If I come back, Raz will do as well."

He paused.

"Thank you," he said after a moment. "For everything."

"And the same to you," Alyssa replied. "Now *go*. They're coming!"

Sure enough, the crowd had reached them, billowing out of the snow from beyond the curve of the Arena.

Wheeling his horse around into the alley, Raz looked at Tern.

"If you drop them, your head hits the ground next. Is that clear?"

The Chairman blanched, then nodded. Satisfied, Raz kicked his horse into a gallop. Together the pair made their way west, heading for the closest city gate, iron shoes thundering across the cobblestone of the alley.

XXXIX

Night had long fallen by the time Raz pulled them to a halt, not nearly as far from the city as he would have liked. Other travelers and their carts had left paired divots in the west road, but still the snow choked the way, the storm making it impossible to move at more than a plodding trot once they'd made the forest paths. With his hood up, Raz had been able to press them forward an hour or two more than men would have dared, his keen eyes working better with what limited light the setting Sun had offered behind its shield of clouds.

Now, though, it was becoming too dangerous for even him, in the snow.

"This way," he said, turning his horse into the darkness of the trees to their left, leading Tern's behind him.

The Chairman had barely said a word once he'd ordered the guards to open the west gate and let them through, so intent was he on making sure Lueski's body and Arrun's head didn't fall from his grasp as they rode. Raz had expected him to complain, expected him to demand release, but the man had been surprisingly quiet.

It was as though being outside the walls of his city had suddenly made Tern realize that there really was no one left to help him now.

Beneath the trees was easier going, with much of the snow caught in the canopy above. Raz was able to pick their way through the pines with some effort, his way only lit by scattered beams of dim light that made it through the branches. For another hour he walked them, twisting the horses hopelessly this way and that, though he was careful to judge the position of the Moon above so he would know which way they'd come.

He had his doubts Tern knew enough of the world to do the same.

"Here," he said at last, coming to the edge of a hill beneath the jutting lip of a great rock outcropping.

The snow was all but clear beneath the boulders, and he eased himself down from his saddle, still careful to keep ahold of the reins of Tern's horse, and onto the forest floor. He grit his teeth against the shock of pain that ripped through him as his body moved in ways it hadn't for several hours, pulling at wounds he was starting to worry weren't about to heal on their own.

"Give the children to me," he said, resting Ahna against the trunk of a nearby tree and reaching up with one hand. "Then get down."

"Are we making camp?" Tern asked, speaking for the first time in several hours as he slowly eased the Koyts into the crook of Raz's good arm.

Raz didn't respond.

Once Tern had slid his weight down the horse's side and onto his feet, Raz drew his gladius from over his shoulder and pointed to a spot beneath the rocks.

"There. Move."

Tern did as he was told, hands up and head bowed as he hurried over, clearly not upset about getting out of the snow. Raz could feel the cold get to him now that they had stopped. Riding hard had kept him tense and warm, and if he didn't keep moving he knew the winter night was going to be the end of him.

Still… he would take the time for this.

Thrusting the gladius into the ground by his fur-wrapped feet, he pulled his knife from his belt and tossed it to Tern. The Chairman eyed it suspiciously.

"And what," he asked in a wavering voice, "am I supposed to do with that? If you think I'm going to fight you—"

"What I think you're going to do," Raz growled, "is dig."

Tern blinked. Then he looked at the knife, then at the body and head in Raz's arms, then back at the knife. Finally, with a sigh that said he had given up all hope, he lifted the blade in his gloved hands and started at the earth.

It was long, hard work. The ground was cold and solid, and even the looser soil beneath the frozen top layer was marbled with rocks and roots. It was a time before Tern made much of a dent in the space below the outcropping, the knife thunking and pinging dully through the night, any echo swallowed by the thickness of the trees. For half an hour he toiled before saying a word.

"This is your fault, you know."

Raz blinked, jerking into a full wakefulness. He was almost happy Tern had said something, because the chill had definitely started to make him sluggish. The statement, though, brought on a rush of fury that chased away all fatigue from his body.

"What did you say?" he demanded in a hiss.

"This. Is," Tern said again, punching every word in with a stab of the knife. "Your. Fault."

"And how do you figure that, *Chairman*?" Raz asked sarcastically, shifting to get his body moving again.

"We had a deal," Tern told him simply. "We made a contract. I even had the paperwork drafted, fulfilling every irritating condition you required. The Koyts had their freedom, had their debts cleared. The Arena stopped drafting from the dungeon and prisons. I sent the birds, built the demand, gave you your chance to fight your demons on even ground."

"You did," Raz said with a nod. "You did do all that."

"Then *why*," Tern huffed, a note of annoyance building in his voice as he continued to hack at the earth, "did you have *to fuck it all up*?"

"I didn't."

Tern stopped at that, looking around. He frowned.

"You did. You changed the deal. If you'd left with the Laorin, it would have—"

"I wasn't going to."

There was a second of icy silence.

"What?" Tern hissed, staring up from his hole in the ground.

"I wasn't leaving," Raz said. "Whoever your informant is didn't give you all the facts. I was *asked* to leave, yes. Brahnt and his friends and I had been speaking for weeks, trying to figure out how to drag your fat ass out of the false throne you'd built for yourself. When they got called away, they asked me to go."

"And you said what? 'No, thank you'?"

"Essentially."

For a time Tern only stared at him. Then he started to laugh.

"What's the joke?" Raz asked in a deadly whisper, pulling his gladius from the ground.

"You!" Tern chuckled, returning to his work. "To the world you're the great beast, this mythical Monster of Karth! Even the North sees that now! But you're not, are you? You're given a chance to leave, to get out of my city, and you *don't take it*? You had to know the Arena would claim you eventually! You had to know one day you would die there, if you didn't leave!"

He stopped only long enough to look over his shoulder.

"You're no Monster. You're a fool."

Then he looked back around and started at the earth again.

Raz watched him for a time more, feeling the anger burning inside him, feeling it bubble and churn. He remembered the jeering glee of the crowd, the delighted screams of thrill and joy as he murdered for them, butchered for them.

Those people he had saved from the pit. Those people he'd snatched from the greedy mouth of Quin Tern.

Raz felt the anger die, replaced by sadness.

"You're probably right," he said.

Tern didn't say anything.

The hole was just wide and deep enough for a small body to fit, tucked up against itself. As Raz stepped over it to judge, he nodded.

"Get out."

Tern hauled himself up at once, puffing and sweaty. He'd been at it for over an hour, which Raz mused silently was probably more hard labor than the man had ever done in his life.

"Now take off your cloak."

At that, Tern stiffened.

"W-What?" he demanded. "No. You can't—!"

"You can take off your cloak now, Tern, while you are willing and able to do so, or I can cut it from your corpse in about five seconds. I'm not fussy on which option you choose really, but the second one would warm me up more."

"But I'll *freeze*!" Tern yelled, taking a step back and clutching at his furs in the dark. "What am I supposed to do without it?"

Raz shrugged. "Have it your way, then," he said, stepping forward and raising the gladius in one hand.

"WAIT!" Tern said, throwing his hands up.

Raz stopped, but kept the blade raised poignantly. Muttering curses to himself, Tern undid the fastenings to his heavy mantle and pulled it off his shoulders. It fell in a thick pile to the forest floor.

"Now what?" Tern asked through gritted teeth, clutching at his arms as the winter night bit immediately through the thinner cottons and wools of the decorative shirts he had on beneath.

"Now," Raz said."… I let you go."

Tern looked surprised.

"G-Go?" he asked, almost hopefully. "What do you mean?"

"I mean you can go," Raz told him. "I said I would do it, so I am. And if you think I didn't notice you sticking the knife in the back of your pants, think again. Keep it. It might come in useful."

The Chairman stared at him, shivering, obviously suspecting some trap. When Raz said nothing more, though, he started for the horses.

"Ah," Raz interrupted, bringing the gladius up to block the man's path. "No. I don't think so."

"You're not going to give me a *horse*?" Tern spat in disbelief. "You can't be serious!"

He quailed under the cold look Raz gave him then.

"Be grateful I'm giving you even this small chance, Chairman," Raz growled. "You took more from me than even you realize. You ripped and tore and destroyed something I thought I'd never have again. I'm only giving you this chance because I think the freeze will find you before any of the search parties Azbar has undoubtedly sent out by now do. A blade to the heart is too quick for you, but I'm not going to dishonor the Koyts by torturing you to death beside their grave."

He moved the gladius, pointing it north. "The road is that way. If you start now and run to keep warm, you might make it before you lose your feet to the cold. Maybe they'll find you then, maybe not. All I know is this: if I still hear you by the time I'm done bidding farewell to these children, I'll drag you far enough away to ensure their spirits can't hear your screams."

"Bastard," Tern gasped, stumbling and tripping as he backed away. "*Bastard!*"

Then he was gone, running off through the dark trees faster than Raz would have thought the fat man was capable of.

For a minute Raz listened to him go. After a time, though, the snow and woods swallowed all sounds, and Raz was on his own.

Alone. Again.

Turning away from the trees, Raz kicked Tern's discarded cloak closer to the outcropping, then moved to follow. Bending to seat himself on the cold ground—hissing in pain as he did—he set the Koyts down gently beside him. Picking the cloak up, he cut several feet of the extra material from its end with the gladius, then another foot's worth as a separate piece. Setting the sword aside, he reached out, gently lifted Arrun's head into his lap, and began wrapping it in the smaller of the fur strips.

Lueski was next. Raz's fingers shook as he felt the stiffness in her tiny form, the rigidity of death, as he wrapped her up.

When he was done, Raz got to his feet and pulled what was left of the cloak over his own shoulders, welcoming the extra warmth. Bending down, he lifted the girl, hidden away in the swaddling cloths, carefully into his arms. Carrying her into the grave, he set her upon the cold, churned earth tenderly. Arrun's head he tucked in the crook of her lap.

For a long time Raz stood over the pair of them, looking down through the dark at their bundled outlines. He didn't think of anything in particular so much as he fought to find and hold on to the feelings and emotions he'd discovered again with the two of them, things he'd thought lost a long time ago.

He didn't want to forget, this time. He refused to forget.

When he'd had his moment, Raz moved to the loose pile of dirt that hovered over the hole. Grunting as he got to his knees, he shoved it to spill over and cover the bodies, hiding them from view forever. Once he'd patted the mound down, flattening it until the grave was little more than a faint lump in the earth, he got to his feet again. This time he looked to the sky.

Though he couldn't see Her Stars, he knew they were there, somewhere, eternal witnesses overhead.

Take care of them, he begged of the Arros, thinking of his mother and father. Then, bringing up the image of his little sister, he spoke to her privately.

You'll like her, Ahna. I know you'll be friends.

With that Raz turned, found the dviassegai and gladius in the dark, and made for the horses.

Once he'd wheezed and tugged his way into the gray stud's saddle, reaching down to wrap the reins of the other around its pommel, he pulled Ahna up to set her back across his lap. Thumbing the white wood of her haft, he kicked the animals into a trot through the Moon-lit trees.

"'The northbound road for Ystréd,'" he quoted under his breath, shifting the horses to head back for the road. "What do you think, sis? What are our chances of catching up before *we* freeze to death?"

Chuckling bleakly to himself, Raz allowed his hunched form, shivering in cold and pain, to be swallowed by the night.

XXXX

"To wage the game of war with success, one must garner and gain hold of all advantages. Most chief among them: surprise. There is an old saying in the Seven Cities, which we all know have had their fair share of blood and battle over the centuries. They say, 'Defeat comes when you least expect it,' which I find admirably sage. Even the greatest of warriors cannot see behind them, after all."

—*The Art of Sword & Shield*, by Kelo ev'Ret

Syrah ran as she had never run before. Her white robes whipped about her, her sandled feet smacking the stones of the hall loudly, echoing ahead. She took the twists and turns at full speed, not bothering to excuse herself as she dodged around other residents of the Citadel out enjoying a morning walk or heading to breakfast. She ignored their exclamations of surprise and curses.

Jofrey was down in the furnaces. He'd told her as much last night, saying that Kallet Brern had wanted his opinion on a crack in one of the forges first thing in the morning. The heating systems of Cyurgi' Di were an engineering miracle, rekindled and maintained by the Laorin since the great fortress had been first rediscovered by the faith. They required a lot of work, though, and a crack in the mechanisms could be nasty business if it meant shutting one of the forges down for repairs.

The letter in Syrah's hand, however, held far graver news.

Syrah turned a corner, pounding the slanting ground of the ramp leading downward into the mountain. For a time it twisted and turned, one solid incline going back and forth through the stone. Eventually, though, the ramp ended, and roughhewn stairs, their middle slick and well worn by a thousand years of booted and sandaled feet coming to and fro from the forges, descended steeply into a tunnel lit only by candlelight.

Grasping the old iron chain strung along one side of the stairs, Syrah took them as fast as she could.

Old man couldn't have found a worse place to hole himself up, Syrah thought bitterly as she moved. *Typical. First Talo, now Jofrey. When you need them most, they're always on the other side of the damn world.*

The steps seemed to go on forever, down and down and down into the earth. In truth they *were* rather long but—as is so common when one is pressed for time—Syrah's mind decided to drag them out eternally.

By the time she reached the bottom, the woman was half-convinced her news would arrive too late to do anything about.

The glow that greeted her at their base was semi-blinding to her sensitive eyes after the relative dimness of the tunnels. As she hurried forward into the room, Syrah had to block the blaze of the nearest forge with one hand while her vision adjusted. Despite this, even as her eyes watered in the light and heat, she looked around, trying to find Jofrey.

The furnace room, while awe-inspiring in its own way, was possibly Syrah's least favorite place in the Citadel. Her old classroom, where she'd spent hours every day in her youth, bored to the point of screaming with Reyn and two dozen other acolytes, was a close second, but the uncomfortable warmth and unbearable brightness did the furnaces in for her. Three great forges took up the colossal cavern, massive oblong things jutting upwards from the floor towards the curved ceiling high above. A plethora of copper piping spined outward from each one, some feeding water into the boiler that formed the top half of each forge, some pushing warm, humid air upward into the halls and rooms above, and some using the provided vacuum to drag fresh air in from outside.

Once, when she'd first come to the Citadel, Syrah and a number of her new friends had snuck down into the furnaces on the dare of an older acolyte. They'd run screaming back up the stairs, yelling about the lost heads of three wicked monsters with glowing eyes and shining golden hair.

It was estimated that—when the Cyurgi' Di had been a fortress of war, before written memory—over a hundred men had been needed to keep the furnaces going. Coal had to be mined and hauled from great shafts in the back of the room that had since been sealed by the Laorin, and the forges had to be maintained and carefully overseen.

Now, kept and conditioned regularly by magic, the furnaces needed only a half-dozen Priests and Priestesses per forge.

It was one such woman, dressed in the simple cotton shirt and pants of the trade, that Syrah ran into first.

"Jofrey al'Sen?" she asked, breathless after her run down the stair. "Is he here? Have you seen him?"

The Priestess blinked in surprise, then nodded, pointing towards the backmost forge at the far end of the room. Peering through the haze, Syrah saw the white robes of someone *not* planning to spend all day in the heat.

Suffering the blazes, Syrah made a line straight for him.

"I think you're right, Kallet," Jofrey was saying as she reached them. "I don't think we'll have much of a choice. The residence halls will have to go without heat for a few days."

He was speaking to Brern, also in simple cloth clothes, who nodded.

"I'll talk to Petrük," the forge master responded. "I'm sure she'll enjoy informing everyone of their forthcoming misery, then playing the hero when she finds volunteers to keep the halls at least temperate overnight. I'm not looking forward to—Oy! Hello, Syrah!"

Brern smiled at her, the motion crinkling his tanned, leathery face as he lifted a hand in welcome. Beside him, Jofrey turned at once to meet her. Surprise and concern etched the lines of his sweating face. He knew her well enough now to know that, if she was suffering the discomfort of coming to him down here, something was definitely wrong.

"Syrah?" he asked. "What's going on? What's happened?"

In response, Syrah held up the letter in her hand.

"It's a report," she told him through heavy breaths as he took the parchment and unrolled it. "Ystréd sent scouts into the Woods as soon as they heard about the Kayle, trying to figure out where he might strike from."

Jofrey was scanning the letter quickly, but Brern's face fell.

"How many casualties?" he asked sadly.

"None."

It was Jofrey who answered. There was a pause as he finished, then passed the letter on to the furnace master.

"The scouts pushed north along the west border of the Arocklen, all the way to the lip of the Saragrias," he summarized as the younger Priest began to read. "They encountered no resistance, but picked up the army's trail heading east, keeping to the bottom of the ranges."

"East?" Brern asked, perplexed, finishing the letter himself and looking up. "Along the mountains? But what does that mean?"

Jofrey frowned, the worry in his face deepening in the flicker of the forge before them.

"It means that Petrük was right, even though I doubt *she* thought it at the time," he mumbled.

"Right?" Brern asked, confused. "Right about what? Explain. If Baoill is heading for Ystréd, why is he going east?"

"Because he's not making for Ystréd anymore, if he ever was," Syrah explained without taking her eyes off Jofrey, watching him think. "There's something he wants more."

"But what could he want more than another Northern town?" Brern sputtered, clearly frustrated with his own lack of understanding.

"Cyurgi' Di," Jofrey said into the furnace fire. "Gûlraht Baoill is coming here."

EPILOGUE

"It is among the gods' great pleasures to ensure that a man dies in the same way he lived."

—Sigûrth proverb

It was Alyssa who found him.

That she came across the man was pure happenstance, perhaps even the cruel humor of some deity or another. Whatever the reason, she almost missed him among the other lumps of the forest floor, thinking him just another log or misshapen boulder beneath the snow.

When the lump shifted, though, her horse had nearly flung her off in fright.

"H-here," he said, hopeful voice broken by the cold. "H-here. P-please! Here!"

She saw an arm extend towards her then, and she recognized the man for who he was. The fat hand, still bearing its heavy gold and silver rings, was familiar to her, shaking so violently as it stretched in hopeful desperation towards her horse.

Shaking so violently it seemed the thick fingers, every one black and dead from the frost, might fall right off.

For a long time Alyssa looked down at the man from atop her mount. Her breath misted the air through the dark cloth wrapped around the bottom half of her face, vanishing even as the animal shifted nervously beneath her. She searched the curve of his body beneath the snow until she found his eyes, wide and bloodshot as they bulged with relief that someone had finally found him.

Those blue eyes that she had witnessed so often staring with insatiable desire down into the pit.

Alyssa's gaze traveled over his face. The loose, baggy skin of his cheeks wasn't as far gone as his hands, but his nose and ears were beyond saving. She had no doubt, taking in the rest of the figure's quivering bulk, now slowly shaking loose the snow that had piled over him in the night, that other parts of him were done for as well.

Maybe even those pieces of a man one could hardly call himself a *man* without…

"A-Alyssa?"

Alyssa shifted her gaze to meet his eyes once more. Green met blue, and for a brief moment the woman saw a different face than the blackened one below her, ravaged by the winter night and still-falling snow. For a moment she saw older, kinder features, lined and aged by laughter and smiles.

Then the face of the father was gone, and only what was left of the son's remained.

"W-What are you d-doing?" the man asked slowly.

There was a sudden fear in his voice that had not been there before, an abrupt hesitation replacing the hope and relief. As she sat there atop her horse, looking down upon his shivering form as the icy morning wind cut through the trees to blow her black hair about her face, Alyssa made her decision.

Wheeling her mount around, she heeled it into a trot back towards the road and the rest of the search party, through the silent pines, in the direction she'd come.

"A-Alyssa?" the man called out in hopeless desperation from behind her. "A-Alyssa! Wait! P-Please! Wait! *Wait!* WAAAAAIT!"

Pushing the horse into a gallop, Alyssa Rhen left the man and his screams to the cold.

Note From the Author

[aka: The Plight of the Writer]

As this chapter in Raz's story comes to a close, I cannot accurately portray exactly how much your support and enjoyment of this book means to me, as there are no words grand enough to paint the picture. *The Wings of War* is a labor of love, a commitment to the creation of a story that will entertain, enthrall, and inspire, as so many other tales have done for me before. Your appreciation and enjoyment of my writing is a massive portion of the rewards of being an author.

It is with this note that I move on to a more personal plea, a cry for assistance from all of you who got to the end of the book and were even just a little bit sad it didn't continue on:

Please, *please,* consider rating and reviewing *The Warring Son* on one or two major bookselling or book group sites.

Even better, *please* consider supporting me directly on Patreon, and get early access to chapters and books, art, cool stuff, and much more. Find me at:
patreon.com/bryceoconnor

Many people don't know that there are thousands of books published every day, most of those in the USA alone. Over the course of a year, a quarter of a million authors will vie for a small place in the massive world of print and publishing. We fight to get even the tiniest traction, fight to climb upward one inch at a time towards the bright light of bestsellers, publishing contracts, and busy book signings.

Thing is, we need all the help we can get.

Your positive input into that world, whether it's a review, a follow on social media, or financially supporting your favorite authors, makes the climb just a little bit easier. Rating and reviewing books you enjoy and following a writer's journey gives your favorite authors a boost upward.

With that all out of the way, thank you again so much for picking up *The Warring Son.* If you'd like to give me feedback directly, have a question about Raz and his adventures, or just want to chat, drop me a message any time on Facebook, or on my website.

It has been a pleasure entertaining you, and I vigorously hope you continue to follow *The Wings of War* series to see what becomes of Raz i'Syul Arro.

Bryce O'Connor

Made in the USA
Lexington, KY
21 November 2019

57371591R00081